India's Northeast
A Celebration of Cultures

India's Northeast
A Celebration of Cultures

Editors

Dr. Joy Thomas SVD

Dr. George Keduolhou Angami

2019

India's Northeast: A Celebration of Cultures— published by the Rev. Dr. Ashish Amos of the Indian Society for Promoting Christian Knowledge (ISPCK), Post Box 1585, Kashmere Gate, Delhi-110006.

ISBN: 978-93-88945-00-4

Cover Design Credit: Md. Tabrej, Director, BBA, St. Joseph's College (Autonomous), Jakhama, Nagaland.

Laser typeset by

ISPCK, Post Box 1585, 1654, Madarsa Road, Kashmere Gate, Delhi-110006
• *Tel:* 23866323

e-mail: ashish@ispck.org.in • ella@ispck.org.in
website: www.ispck.org.in

Contents

Editorial

National Seminar with the theme, "India's Northeast: A Celebration of (Indigenous) Cultures: A Phenomenological Approach" was held at St. Joseph's College, Jakhama in Nagaland from 23-25 November 2018, sponsored by UGC, ICPR and ICSSR. Twenty five resource persons from all over India were invited to present papers, and about 250 participants including staff members of the college, research scholars, post-graduate students from the college and Nagaland University and invited persons participated in the three day deliberations. We are happy to present all the deliberation in this book under the shortened name: India's Northeast: A Celebration of Cultures.

Key Concept of the National Seminar

India's Northeast consists of Arunachal Pradesh, Assam, Manipur, Meghalaya, Mizoram, Nagaland, Sikkim and Tripura. It has a unique landscape, cultural traits and shares international borders with several East and Southeast Asian countries. According to the Anthropological Survey of India there are 300 distinct tribes speaking over 400 dialects. The Northeast has 9.1 million indigenous people who have evolved their lives in concord with nature, thus creating a culture that has served them for centuries. Northeast India, known for its diversity on all fronts, is encountering numerous challenges and is exploring ways to harness the best of the region for its development. This region has an immense treasure of resources and yet is grappling with predicament of 'identity and ethnicity'.

Northeast Indian culture and society are going through a period of accelerated change. Nowhere is this more evident than in the education system. For much of the twentieth century the primary schools were operated in a society that was largely homogenous mainly in the form of dormitories where the level of change was gradual in response to the needs of the eight fledgling States. The advent of Globalisation, Communication Technology and the road-air connectivity has resulted an upturn in the economy, character, nature and quality of life in the Northeast. The growth in material prosperity, the questioning of traditional values and the influx and outflow of people has introduced a wider complexity.

A celebration of culture must come to grip with how things appear to us. Studies (philosophical, scientific, or otherwise) of the culture(s) are, indeed, heavily invested in careful examination of how our surroundings, others, things within our surroundings, mental episodes themselves, and countless other things make themselves present to us, affording themselves in experiences that we undergo, singly and collectively, and that we frequently ascribe to ourselves in the first person in the context of a clan/tribe/community. Far from dispensing with experiences understood in this way, the study of the culture is crucially dependent upon meticulous descriptions of those experiences as they are experienced, from that first-person but from a collective perspective. To take this step for granted is to egregiously neglect phenomena that are essential to the life, and to presume to forgo consideration of them is debilitating for the study of indignity. This conference was an attempt to show case the cultures of India's northeast as a phenomenon that has proved remarkably recalcitrant to reductionist approaches that purport to explain away such phenomena.

In contemporary usage, 'phenomenology' sometimes denotes the specific movement in the history of philosophy initiated by many twentieth century philosophers. In this conference we use 'phenomenology' to designate the sort of examination of human existence that takes the first-personal character of experience to be fundamental but in the context of a community/clan/tribe.

Phenomenology is the study of experiences, including their contents and structures, as they are experienced in the first person. Though the first-personal character of an experience may be implicit or pre-reflective, it is explicit where the subject of experience is able to attribute the contents or structures of the experience to itself by invoking the grammar of the first person. The relevant contents and structures, so experienced, can be considered both immanent and transcendental. Insofar as phenomenology focuses on the immanent character of the contents of experience, it considers mental phenomena with the aim of clarifying their make-up precisely as mental states and experiences. By focusing on the transcendent character of experiences, phenomenology examines mental phenomena insofar as they are world-disclosing or world-constituting. Phenomenology, as we understand it, is thus not restricted to an analysis of phenomena immanent to consciousness. On the contrary, how things appear to us is part of phenomenology's very subject matter and, hence, such themes as objectivity, world, and inter-subjectivity lie within its scope.

Inauguration of the Seminar

During the inaugural ceremony, the honourable governor of Nagaland, His Excellency **P. B. Acharya** spoke on his concern for the development of the state and challenged the universities to produce graduates of quality for service. He also stressed the need for graduates who can contribute to the society and not merely aim to amass wealth like some of the richest persons in India. He encouraged those present to learn not only English but the mother tongue to become people who strengthen the state and the country. And the bishop of Kohima, **Most Rev. James Thoppil** said that the present scenario in Northeast India is characterized by a need for peace, harmony, integration and development. He underlined that there are conflicts and divisions due to cultural and emotional differences. He called for a dispassionate and objective study and interpretation of religious traditions which will bring about better understanding of peace and harmony and aid progress and development. He highlighted the biblical understanding of peace, which along with other religious traditions can provide the right perspective for peace-efforts. And in the keynote address **Prof. Prasenjit Biswas** elaborated the cultural differences and the need to learn one's own culture together with that of others. He addressed the vast diversity of cultures and languages.

Technical Sessions

Sri Dipok Kumar Barthakur, the Vice-Chairman, Office of the State Innovation and Transformation Aayog (SITA), Assam spoke on the topic, "Tribal Challenges in the Northeast". He shared that personally he feels the negative connotation associated with the words like "Challenges", "problems", "issues", "barriers", etc. make it harder for us to look beyond. We get into a vicious cycle of negativity instead of taking small positive steps. What is an issue could be an opportunity. It's how we look — a glass as half full or half empty!

In his presentation he paid greater attention on the Northeast of India, especially the seven sisters that have been historically categorized and perceived as one homogenous region. In spite of having been an independent country for 71 years, the Indian policy makers have failed to take cognisance of the uneven distribution of assets, unequal political emancipation, unequal economic development, paucity of educational reach out among the various groups, inter and intra tribes and states that exist in the region. A more coherent and tailored mode of policy framework, better governance and parallel development in civic bodies and institutions to hold together our socio-cultural frameworks will allow us to shape a society and a region that we want and not parachuted from elsewhere.

Sri Lipokmar Tzudir, the former director of NEZCC, in his presentation entitled, "Traditions to Modernity: A Case Study of Nagaland" highlighted some of the factors that led to a transition from traditional to modernity and the challenges that it brought along. His paper had four segments: the first dealt with the advent of Christianity in Naga Hills and its impact on culture, second the impact of Colonialism and third the outbreak of modernity and its social impasse. In this paper, he pointed out that the sudden transition from traditional to modernity hits the core of the value system of the tribal societies.

Fr. Peter Haokip presented his paper on the "Cultural Tradition, Renewal and Modernity". He highlighted the issue of how most of the indigenous cultures in Northeast India are considered endangered cultures. He also focused on the challenges every indigenous culture faces in regard to its own tradition, its renewal and its transition to modernity. He also said that with the disappearance of one language one culture also disappears.

Prof. Sivasish Biswas presented his Paper on 'Indeterminacy and Shifting Power Equations in the Northeast'. He shared his understanding and lived experiences from the vantage point of an 'outsider-insider', a term describing himself as an outsider accepted in the Northeast, who has noted amazing shifts of power between different identities and their fluidity subject to change of space. Further, the crux of his findings was the presence of a third space of hybridity carefully kept under wraps but undeniably true. Prof. Biswas shared these 'untold stories' anticipating a chutnified India.

Prof. V.C. Thomas dealt with the topic, "Unity with Northeast through Cultural Understanding: A Phenomenological Overview" in three parts: First he discussed the general phenomenological principles involved in cultural understanding-the principle of (life) world, the concept of horizon and the theory of inter-subjectivity in life. Secondly he dealt with the Northeast culture from an anthropological and sociological point of view. He also expressed his desire to apply the principles of phenomenological principles to the context of Northeast culture as he feels that culture is not an isolated thing but falls within the parameters of general phenomenological principles that deal with culture in general. And in the third part, he made an attempt to show that within the unity of India, every state has its uniqueness and individuality. The uniqueness of the Northeast, he said, is the expression of its distinctiveness. He also opined that Northeast is not totally cut off from the rest of India; whatever happens in other parts of India are happening in the Northeast. In the southern states of India, including

Pondicherry, many students from the Northeast are pursuing their education. He concluded by saying that the differences are minimal and accidental, what matters most is the unity and oneness of India.

Dr. K. Jose began his paper on "Pluri-cultural Identities…" saying that we, as a nation, accommodate various people and culture, each with its own specificities, which we need to accept, accommodate and cherish. We cannot forget that under the overarching 'Indian-ness' resulting from cultural convergence, there always have been varying degrees of linguistic, ethnic, geographical, religious and cultural variations over historical periods of time. Therefore, we need to move on not merely forgetting the past, but rooted in the life-enhancing thoughts and ideas of the past and envisioning a new and more creative future for us and for the posterity. He concluded by saying that celebrating pluri-cultural identities is not only imperative but it is essential to the existence of peoples and communities in the larger framework of our nation and indeed of the world.

Shri. Paramananda Rajbongshi's paper was entitled, "Tribal Languages of Assam and Assam Sahitya Sabha. He said that Kamrupee language started getting patronage from the tribal kings since the 5th Century. Through intellectual and academic cooperation from the Aryan scholars the language became significantly developed and earned mass popularity and circulation. Through royal support from Kachari kings, Dimasa language of Assam also developed. But Bodo language which developed in organised manner in the middle period of the 20th Century has been recognised by the Central government. Through the efforts of Christian missionaries, after Assam went under British rule, Kamrupee language was redesigned. Thus, the modern Assamese language came into being. The first Assamese news-magazine, 'Arunodoi' was published by Christian missionaries from Sivasagar in 1846. Although the priority of Assam Sahitya Sabha is development of Assamese language, it also works for eight other languages which include Bodo, Rabha, Deuri, Mising, Karbi, Dimasa, Tiwa and Garo. It also works for the development of other languages like Tea Community, Koch-Rajbongshi, Sonowal-Kachari, and others.

The topic "Ethno-Cultural Identity and Boundaries Maintenance in Northeast India" was presented by **Dr. Kaba Daniel**. He said that Northeast India comprises of eight states of which Manipur, Tripura and Assam have been planned and made during the times of Ahoms. This is proved by the district of Sibsagar, Lakhimpur, Darrang, Nowgong and Kamrup. They existed as independent feudal states from the middle ages almost down to their annexation by the British in the 19th century. However, the four other states with their indigenous inhabitants were labelled as scheduled tribes and carved out of British Assam after partition in 1947. India is comfortably accommodating them under the label of different ethnic related terms such as ethno-regions, ethno-religions, ethno-cultures and ethno-languages. The paper attempted to study some of the most relevant phenomena of ethno-cultural identity and boundary maintenance in Northeast India for a general understanding.

Dr. Babu Joseph looked at the metamorphosis and the transformation in the cultures of Northeast from a phenomenological point of view. The word 'culture' encompasses religion, food, clothes, languages, marriage, music and beliefs of right and wrong. Hence, to understand one's culture, there is a need to delve deeply into a variety of human activities which is termed as the collective experience. This paper is an analysis of the cultural metamorphosis of both Naga tribes and Khasi tribe of Meghalaya which have undergone a significant cultural transformation, assimilation and adoption into a modern and liberal society.

Dr. C. V. Babu made a presentation on "Phenomenology and the culture of Movement" and sought to address how phenomenology as culture is different from phenomenology of culture. The former views phenomenology in its existential dimension of culture in general as a movement of lived essences, the forms of culture, while the latter tries to describe the genesis and existential structure of the forms of a particular culture. He also highlighted the phenomenology and Northeast (Indigenous) culture and the accelerated change in the Northeast as a result of globalization, communication and transportation, road-air connectivity, values and essences.

Dr. E. Thangasamy and **Dr. C. Periasamy** presented, "Influence of Culture on Business in Northeast India: A Marketing Perspective of Nagaland". Emphasising on the rich folk songs and folk dances of the Nagas, they pointed out the prospects of culture on business opportunities of the Nagas. Nagaland as an eco-friendly state, rich in its culture, abundance in flora and fauna, with enough man-power and progress in education, it can open rich avenues and employment opportunities. They also focused on Nagaland being next to Sikkim as a chemical free state in agriculture. They recommended vocational training centres for promoting and marketing the rich culture.

Dr. H. S. Palep in his paper, "Tribal Medicine in Northeast India: Its Practices and Potential" pointed out that the healthcare systems of tribes have evolved by following natural laws as that affect the universe and people. The three prime factors that control universe are air, sun and moon and the three prime factors in people are *vata, pitta* and *kapha*. The imbalance of these factors leads to illness. The different systems of world medicines to cure diseases have their origin in the tribal wisdom. The main contribution of tribal wisdom lies in the identification of non-poisonous plants and their power to cure the diseases. This information is gathered from their elders and local practitioners. He concluded his paper presentation with a remark that a sustainable health care of tribal population in Northeast India would be possible only by providing intellectual property rights and empowering men and women who have acumen to tribal medicine.

Dr. Laltluangliana Khiangte's paper was entitled, "India's Northeast Culture: Mizo Tlawmngaihna". It is a term used for the Mizo code of morals and conduct, a highly prized virtue and a wonderful philosophy of life. When translated into English, it stands for 'altruism' and 'chivalry' but the translation is inadequate. Putting it contextually, a person who possesses Tlawmngaihna must be obedient and respectful to elders, courteous in dealing with the weak and the lowly, generous and hospitable to the poor and needy, etc.

Speaking on the topic, "Representation of cultural Other: Reflection on Saidian Perspectives", **Dr. M. P. Terrance Samuel** critically analysed the observation made by Edward Said on 'Orientalism'. He explained how the unequal relationship between the West and the Orient established cultural imperialism through the textual exercise of the Orientals with its supporting institutions. Orientalism represented the people of the Orient in a way as the other of the occident. He makes made an attempt to understand the cultural representation of the weak other by a dominant self in general based on Saidian perspectives on Orientalism.

Dr. S Lourdunathan's paper was entitled, "Tribal and Subaltern Culture: Phenomenological Rendering of the Tribal Consciousness". It explicated the tribe based community consciousness and the internal colonialism taking place with the tribal people. He also stated that the non-tribal worldviews on the tribal consciousness attempt to engage the tribal life/world through their geo-political and cultural perspective and practices. In specific sense, the tribal world is transcendental phenomenological and phenomenologically hermeneutical.

The paper entitled, "Vocation of Religion in a Conflictual World: A Philosophical Narrative of Distancing without Belonging" was presented by **Prof. Sebastian Velassey**. He offered his view that the phenomenological analysis of religious experience demands a new understanding of subjectivity. The paper points out that the idea of God may come from an inner dynamism of man's own nature. Therefore, if we are capable of comprehending the meaning of this enfoldment between the creator and the creation, we may be able to progress towards a non-conflictual world where we focus not on differences but similarities or the common insight of love and acceptance that every religion shares.

Dr. Archana Singh in her paper titled, "Invisibles Lives: De-Notified Tribes of Uttar Pradesh", highlighted the dominant section of people subjugating the de-notified tribes. One such marginalised tribe is the Kabutari Nat community residing in Bundelkhand region who still suffers from social stigma since long time. They are deprived of the many policies and schemes that are introduced in the country due to non-recognition of their tribe. They are also treated as outcast within the state, which directly degrade their social status and their tribal identity. The most vulnerable section of the people are the women, who suffer from social evils such as prostitution.

Dr. Tapan Kumar De presented, "A Phenomenological Study on the Adivasi Culture in West Bengal". He began his presentation with a descriptive study of culture. He said that in today's digital world, where culture has been materialised everything will be dominated and operated by the criterion of economic development. In such a situation, the Adivasis remain firm and uphold their culture. They follow their tradition from birth to death. Songs, dances, literature and artistic skills are the four pillars of their culture. He further explained the different types of songs and dances performed during different occasions. They have rich folk literature, which is one of the important cultural heritages they follow. He also articulated the Artistic skills the people possessed and concluded by stating that the culture of the Adivasi is both static and dynamic.

"Indigenous Culture of the Zeliangrong Nagas through Orality", was presented by Mr. **James H.K.** He discussed the oral traditions of the Zeliangrong Nagas and pointed out the importance of orality which is relevant even in the practical life of the tribals in terms of administration, education, indigenous religion called 'Zouzangmei' or Heraka, understanding of medicine, celebrations, historical records, time of harvest, etc. He argued that it is through orality that wisdom of the past is passed on to the future generation so that continuity would be sustained.

Mr. Mhonthung Yanthan and Mr. Libemo Kithan asked, "How and why did Naga Morung culture lose its relevance today?" while they presented the paper entitled, "Re-looking the Naga Morung Culture: A Stronghold of Tradition." The Nagas were renowned for their rich culture, having their own distinct traditions and cultural ethos. The Naga Morung institution played a vital role in socio-religious, education and cultural activities of the Naga society. The Morung also played a vital role in preparing the younger generations in the village council. It was the club, the public school, the military training centre, the hostel for boys and meeting place for village elders. It was also a well-known centre for social-religious and political activities. However, it is sad to see that in our present generation, many of the Naga essential and rich cultural ethics are rapidly diminishing. The good qualities and the standards of our culture are often spoken but the meaning and the significance behind these features are never addressed as a result their importance are vanishing. This paper attempted to bring the past Naga Morung tradition into present context and restore stories of the rich Naga Morung traditions.

The paper entitled, "Tel- Khukhu, A Festvial of Felicity: A Case Study with Special reference to Viswema Village" was presented by **Asst. Prof. Kelengol Neikha and Mr. Vizapo Kikhi**. Tel Khukhu is a festival that falls on the 13th of Chiinyi (July) and it is dedicated and celebrated only by girls below 15 years. One of the conditions to celebrate this feast is to shave their hair. It is also a time of giving and sharing of food with one another. This is the only festival dedicated to girls. For the celebration, young girls prepare themselves by collecting flowers in advance to decorate the Chokrwii (Eaves) at the entrance of the house. The flowers are put on the eaves and roof opening and roof including the Kika (a 'V' shaped wooden board). During the preparation, the men folk cut trees and collect Olo (Carpenter worms). Womenfolk grind millet and catch Kona (edible snails) for the fest. The cooked food is served mostly in Banana leaf or Peepal leaf. The leaves are rolled in the shape of cone and pinned with small bamboo sticks. This festival is celebrated mainly to felicitate love, peace and joy in the community.

Valedictory Function

The three days National Seminar at St. Joseph's College (Autonomous) at Jakhama, concluded with sharing of insightful thoughts by Fr. Dr. C. P. Anto (Principal, MSW, Dimapur and Director of Peace Channel, Nagaland), the Valedictory speaker of the National Seminar. The speaker opened his talk by quoting "People without the knowledge of their past history, origin, culture are like a tree without its roots". He spoke on the culture from Micro level to macro level, and how cultures from Nagaland and the Northeast can be put together to form a global culture, and to check the possibilities of thinking from sub-cultures to culture and to the global culture. He shared his reminiscence of old men carrying a bamboo basket on their back while going to the field which reflects the culture of hard work. Honesty, sincerity, openness, hard work and belongingness are the beauty of the tribal culture.

He pointed out that Northeast India is a land of diversity, a land of festival and cultures. He asserted that diversity is one of the most important aspects of tribal community of Northeast India and enunciated that diversity is an asset. He also questioned whether the culture of sincerity, hard work, commitment and honesty is limited only to a particular clan, tribe or community? He opined that there is a need to extend such good practices to other tribes and communities as well. He highlighted that countries like Denmark and Finland have a culture of questioning (inquisitiveness) and training, which make them unique in the whole world. He regretted that such culture is non-existent in the Northeast region. He asserted that questioning culture brings justice, stops exploitation and protects the needy people. He also mentioned that the evolution of a new culture of women empowerment in decision making bodies at various levels is essential for building the tribe, community or Nation. He cited as an example, the Rwanda Nation, which has more than 50% women participation in the parliament.

Apart from other pertinent areas, the speaker focused on creating a new culture of peace. He suggested that division and disharmony can be rectified by transcending from the sectarian mentality, moving from authoritarian to participatory learning, control of information to absolute transparency, competition to cooperation, misunderstanding to mutual understanding, tolerance to solidarity, exploitation to respect of human rights and dignity, controlled resources to sustainable development, education to education of peace culture. He encouraged the participants to initiate and adapt the new culture of peace.

This National Conference in actuality not only brought together the diverse experiences across Northeast but also indigenous experiences from other parts of the country too, by demonstrating how work in phenomenology may lead to significant progress on problems central to tribal conflicts, identity, ethnicity, family community and development. The case studies have deliberated upon how an analytical philosophy can shed light on phenomenological concerns vexed with real issues of identity, otherness and development. The scholarly presentations demonstrated that these different approaches do not stand in opposition to each other, but are mutually illuminating.

Editors
Dr. Joy Thomas SVD
Dr. George Keduolhou Angami

Bishop's Message

Becoming Agents of Peace and National Integration

I am very happy that St. Joseph's Autonomous College, Jakhama is organizing this National Seminar with the theme, "India's Northeast: A Celebration of Cultures, a Phenomenological Approach." As mentioned in the Key Concept, "India's Northeast consists of Arunachal Pradesh, Assam, Manipur, Meghalaya, Mizoram, Nagaland, Sikkim and Tripura. Northeast has a unique landscape and cultural traits. It is said that there are 300 distinct tribes speaking over 400 dialects in the Northeast, consisting of 9.1 million indigenous people who have evolved their lives in concord with nature, thus creating a culture that has served them for centuries. Northeast India, known for its diversity on all fronts, is encountering numerous challenges and is exploring ways to harness the best of the region for its development.

The present scenario in Northeast India is characterized by a need for peace, harmony, integration and development. On the one hand, there are conflicts and divisions due to cultural and emotional differences. At times peoples are hostile to one another. Political, social, economic, ethnic, ideological and religious factors divide them. Some feel that they are marginalized, isolated and exploited by others to achieve their selfish goals and cultural superiority. Some would say that there is a tendency to impose a mono-culturalism, which means the process of supporting, advocating or allowing the expression of the culture of a single group, under the belief that the cultural practices of one group is superior to those of others. These divisions have generated tension and fear either real or perceived, robbing the communities of peace and harmony, the much needed condition for systematic progress and development.

On the other hand, there are noticeable signs of a deep longing for peace and harmony, fellowship and co-operation, development and progress. One notices that there are many who are willing to sacrifice everything, to achieve these goals. Efforts at mediating peace at all levels are encouraging signs. Even in the midst of hostilities there are shining examples of individuals and groups who risk even their own lives to bring help to the opposite camps. They witness to the fact that we are first and foremost human beings and children of God and differences at other levels are only secondary. In fact the ideological pride of India has been that it is not a land of one culture but multi-cultures. Pluralism and multiculturalism is what India represents. The very idea of having a super culture dominating others is inimical to the idea of an inclusive India. It is, in fact, self defeating as it will be against the very fundamental idea of "unity in diversity", the corner-stone of 'National Integration'.

I believe that a dispassionate and objective study and interpretation of religious traditions can bring about better understanding of peace and harmony and aid progress and development. I would like to highlight the biblical understanding of peace, which along with other religious traditions can provide the right perspective for peace-efforts. Jesus is OUR PEACE (Eph 2:14). His coming was heralded as the coming of the "Prince of Peace" (Isa 9:5-6). His birth heralded the message of peace (Lk 2:14) and his death was an act of 'reconciling humanity' with God, who is the source of life (2 Cor 5:15, 19). Though he was innocent, he allowed himself to be a victim of the worst form of oppression, i.e. human selfishness-sin (2 Cor 5:21). After his victory over sin, he offered 'peace' as his parting gift to his disciples (Jn 20:19) which he had promised (Jn 14:27). He inaugurated a new humanity, and a new kind of belongingness, beyond all barriers and distinctions

(Gal 3:28; Col 3:11; Eph 2:14). He also entrusted the 'reconciling' mission to his disciples (2 Cor 5:19-20), promising a 'blessing' to all peace-makers (Mt 5:9). Christians as followers of Christ cannot but be peace-makers.

Therefore, I hope this National Seminar will engage in various interactions within innumerable changing contexts to help resolve the contradictions and tensions in the society, and to transform the signs of hope into reality, to experience Shalom (wholeness) with its full implications. Let there be a hundred flowers. Let each one of them, bloom, flourish, nourish, and nurture. Let every single flower shine in all its glory. Let there be 'diversity in unity'.

I conclude my message wishing you three days of fruitful interaction engendering new meanings that can bring together the diverse experiences across Northeast by demonstrating how work in phenomenology may lead to significant progress on problems central to tribal (indigenous) conflicts, identity, ethnicity, family, community, progress and development.

Most Rev. Dr. James Thoppil,
Bishop of Kohima

~~~~~God bless you all~~~~~

Foreword

Northeast and its Touching
Facets of Culture and Tradition

Looking back through the corridor of time to the distant past in the Northeast one can easily see the phenomenological changes that has taken place in culture and tradition in Northeast. And I feel assured that as St. Joseph's college, autonomous, is making an all-out effort to get the best scholars and experts in culture and tradition to analyse, and synthesize the structures of historical data through a seminar on "India's Northeast: A Celebration of Cultures, a Phenomenological Approach." What will emerge will be deeply enlightening and revealing for the participants and for the paper presenters. Northeast holds its own wealth of knowledge and is rich in culture and traditions. Down through the centuries Northeast has developed on its own way. In fact, she is considered as an enigma, wrapped in a riddle, hidden in a mystery. This seminar could be an occasion when the galaxy of experts and scholars join together with a scholarly mind for research and endeavour to reveal the mystery of ages, the result could easily be a phenomenological epoch making event.

We are living in an era of globalization, privatization and liberalization and we see, in our daily life its impact and effect leading into monoculture and challenging the richness. Diversity and uniqueness of Northeast, in this context this seminar, becomes a timely intervention to protect and preserve the cultural heritage of Northeast.

Northeast has experienced troubled and tormented togetherness for centuries and this phenomenon, this lived experience, need to be studied, analysed, understood and accepted in today's existential situation as it can integrate human culture and behaviour pattern which is the real need of our time. And only a student of the past can be a prophet of future. As late president Kennedy, speaking to the Harvard university students said, "In these times of turbulence and change it is true more than ever knowledge is power". And here in this seminar we are going to deal with knowledge that are our lived experience touching the core of our behaviour pattern and our life itself. And this aspect makes it all the more relevant and meaningful to participate in this seminar actively and learn lessons from the lived experience of the past that can touch the core of our heart.

I wish all the participants, animators and resource persons all the best, and sincerely hope that this seminar will have a lasting impact and effect in the Northeast and will touch the rhythm of our daily life.

Rev. Dr. Sebastian Ousepparanpil,
Principal, SJAC,
Jakhama,
Nagaland

Keynote Address

Northeast India: A Celebration of Cultures in Conceptual Terms

Prof. Prasenjit Biswas

The plurlicultural and nononesided existence of religious, ethnic and linguistic diversities in Northeast India open up a possibility of experiencing a variety of 'inner worlds' through an ethics of relational, recognitional and shared intersubjective modes of understanding the Other. A cultural celebration is necessarily a celebration of otherness of the Other without much about a repetitive and a collaborative reconstrual of one's own inner worlds. This is simultaneously qualified and an open ended manner of self-understanding, self-realization and a negation of dichotomies that arise of cognitive given inside/outside distinction. The situation could be best described in terms of what theorists of decolonization termed as 'epistemic disobedience', which is de-linking constitution of knowledge by nexus of colonial/modern power from what is constituted by 'free decisions' of 'free agents'.[1] Rediscovery of such an inner world is what 'celebration' of diversity in the context of Northeast India would mean. The inner worlds weaved around the percipient agency of inherently relational terms of epistemic stance towards the world by shared intentionality of the collectively knowing selves gives rise to 'emergent forms of life' produced out of complex encounters of 'a dialectic of reciprocity, relationality, interdependence and de-linking'. Understanding the nature of this relational ontology in the context of India's Northeast is the task before this paper.

The Inner Worlds of Tribes

Tribes are not a monolithic constructs, they are an evolving form of heterogeneity and specificity in cultural, ethnographical and even in political terms of 'strategic essentialism'.[2]All these continually evolved aspects of inner worlds are deeply interrelated that establishes the link between constitutive relationality between these aspects that opens itself up to a percipient other. This is how auto-ethnographic picturing of this inner world finds its expression in a variety of decolonized and autonomous representation by oneself as well as by another, by a conscious choice of boundary crossing. A good example of this innerworldy boundary crossing could be given here from Buddhist Monpas cutting the body of their dead members into hundred pieces and throwing it into the river *Tawanchu* in Tawang district. The ritual crosses the boundary between ethnic and religious practices and goes beyond the 'incarcerated consciousness' of the self and the other in a ritual of celebration of dependent body parts and their survival in more complex 'incarnated' material substratum. Similar is the Mao Naga story of origin in which three brothers Tiger, Spirit and Man compete for inheriting mother's land, in which Man wins the contest by hitting the target with a bow and an arrow. This is a kind of an anthropocentric episteme which fulfils the need for human being's superiority in race over others such as animals and spirits. But such a contest is far from conclusive in other cases. In Idu-Mishmi case, members of the tribe believe that they originated from the enchanting place called *Apesha* where death ritual called *Reh* was performed for the first time with the song that stated, as per their belief,

> "Oh, the boatman, please take the boat and cross the river
>
> The soul starts the journey to the other side of the river."[3]

The death ritual and the presence of goddess Apeh Milli bringing good harvest from Apesha is another way of combining death and harvest as sources of sustainability in travelling to the other side of the river, a cross over that nurtures sustainability in this earth. Similarly in the folk tales centering Loktak, Ibudhou Pakhangba (the Supreme Snake God) incarnating as the wooden boat (locally known as hee) shows a celebration of an ecosystem that nurtures homes on the lake called Phum. Fear and gratitude together marks making of the *Phum* and *Hee*.[4] Creating a holistic ecosystem of belief and practices by way of combining crucial elements of the lifeworld have been the mainstay of philosophical conceptualization by a variety of communities in Northeast India. Mamang Dai's statement that 'we have long journeys in our blood' or 'we descend from solitude and miracles' conceptualize a certain kind of whispering sounds of words spoken by unknown spirits in one's voice has a shamanic symbolism. She recounts it beautifully in her 'songs of rhapsodists',

> In the end we all have *remembrance*. The sword *rattles* and the dancers *sing* in chorus. (…) it is a language that never ceases, and they sing *because hills are old*, older than all sin and desolation and man's *fascination* with blood.[5]

Can remembrance recount the old and the past in a never ending language? Seemingly music fills the temporal gap between where it all begins and where it all ends. This is a rendering of the ordinary in a different tonality, in a different form of body swaying and silencing that are part of an experiential transition to a desired world that makes entry into one's life-world. It's much more than merely a product of an anthropological machine, but it is a shared, believed and participated form of life that organizes itself around its inner symbols and performs its meanings in multiple ways that need to be celebrated.

There is an inimitable singularity in a collaborative reconstrual of one's own inner world through a variety of performances that simultaneously produces a biography, an individuality and a specificity of a tribe, ethnic group or a community. This reconstrual involves a certain amount of embodiment of other spirits, other elements. Use of buffalo heads, floral designs, dancing bodies and many such aesthetic signifiers create an ambience of an inner world that could be accessed from outside, yet it cannot reach out to elements like 'soul figures', beads of snakes and woodpecker, or the heart of the insect. This inability to reach out to its cultural otherness makes us celebrate them as they give them to us in the mode that they decide autonomously. Celebration of such specific symbolism and its attendant schemes of interpretation are embedded in figurative descriptions and tropes of belief working together in an encoded fashion.

Arnold Berleant[6] states that the idea of nature is how it affects, which refuses to be constraint by discreet boundaries. Suzi Gablik[7] discussed the case of tribal imagination in this manner: if something is natural, then it is beautiful. In India, even a thorn, or worm, even an earthquake is sacred, because something is happening whether the earth is maintaining itself, correcting itself, balancing itself. The case is homologous in India's Northeast. Rather it is more complicated in the sense that natural phenomena and natural objects are attributed human faculties and vice versa, which is a trans-human perspective.[8] Both the ontological and the artifactual are part of these trans-human understanding of human-nature relationship. Such a manifested in cults and rituals. For example, the cult of recalling the ancestors prevalent among the Nagas, Mizos and Khasis assumed a complex symbolic form. Ancestors are called back through ritualized natural object such as, bamboo poles, collection of stones and bones and by specific water rituals. The complexity of such ritual forms in symbolic practices arises out of construction of 'natural will'.[9]

Linguistic embeddedness of participation of nature-as-subject in the constitution of the life-world is another feature of tribal subjectivity. In the narrative constitution of the life-world as a Thou (in the second person form), wisdom stands out as an irreducible quality of that life-world. Narrative, in the first person mode gives rise to the 'hard problem' of making intentional acts of any constitutive subjectivity converge with the horizon of meaning already formed within the life-world.

One example may be drawn from the context of Ethnophilosophy. Ethno-philosophically speaking, these concepts are connected and instantiated only in a worldly way: 'where the world is not construed as a surrounding space, but as the multiple tracing out of the singularity of existence as a tribe'. In the multiplicity of ethnic and tribal plurality in certain parts of the world, a tribe is only a fragment of access, it comes only when the commodities, digits and the formulas of modern world is absent. In other world, tribes present themselves more than a gift of intellect and wisdom, as a surplus of knowing, that lies in its phenomenology of world making. One example of such phenomenology is Apatani concept of *Kojum Koja*, the lost civilization that is represented in the body of the hills above Subansiri valley, literally the rib of the hills. It is not merely the memory of loss due to deluge, but it is precisely the location of the civilization on the hills. As descendants of Kojum Kuja, the present Apatanis stand against the god of deluge called Biri-Bote. The hill and the river enter into a binary contestation in the narrative refiguration of the self that is never present in the present. This comes quite close to Hmong notion of *saib loojmem*, or 'sighting the veins of the mountains'. There is a kind of geomancy involved in Apatani and Hmong imagination of the earth. Khasis, in a similar manner speak of *Law Kyntang* (sacred forest) as a sacred part of nature, which is a figuration of the self in the depth of nature. In Zeliangrong and Tangkhul tribes, the main pillar (*sana yumbi*) of the house there are human carving, supposedly prepared to signify ancestral descent.

The indignity of indistinction between tribal world and the techno-scientific 'modern' world is anticipated in the presence of the tribe that comes in the absence of all the sense-making artefacts of 'our' world. To put it differently, the act of signification is not a catch in the unlimited networks of meaning, as an act of giving meaning begins from the secret of the symbols that act as the 'condition of possibility' of wisdom. This Ethno-philosophically empathic statement of wisdom through symbols as condition of its possibility manifests the singularity of the tribe without manifestation. It is an ambivalent expression of the multiple worlds that remain unmanifested in wisdom, while it expresses itself as a secret, a secret of wisdom, a condition of possibility for an interlacing and interfacing between language and praxis, between thought and action. The tribal self-arises from this ambivalence of symbols that communicates and shares a secret that remains unmanifest as a singular entity, while its multiplicity of senses do not make any sense unless the tribal self-interlaces itself in the very act of sharing.

Cultural Logic of Festivity

The winter Bihu known as Bhogali Bihu, as opposed to Rongali Bihu of the beginning of the sowing season in summer is marked by several rituals pregnant with very deep faith and meaning. Post-harvest, one needs to reclaim the land and seed and clean up the ecosystem, when water is in short supply. Burning the house of hay in the middle of the field clears up the left over hay after rice crops are collected by the community. The burnt ashes replenish the field with its nutrients. Anthropologically this is an exercise of biocultural rights over land that sustains an agrarian economy in rural Assam.

Young people erecting *Meji* and *bhelaghar* as makeshift huts for the purpose of feasting and then burning it next morning signify a collective bonhomie. One could also see the symbolic continuance of the practice of erstwhile youth dormitory as it prevailed across Northeast, where young people were trained physical and mental exercises and cultural norms and values. Bhogali Bihu celebrated in different names and differently evolved rituals among tribes like Mishing, Deuri, Moran, Bodo, Rabha, in all, some 36 plain and hill tribes assume a colourful form of feasting, dancing, singing and rejoicing coinciding with progress of winter season. Interesting recreational and competitive fights involving animals, birds and their eggs, water sports are organized across Assam to replenish the community after days of hard work in the field. People belonging to various professions too get involved in agrarian rites that reconnect them to their roots.

What is significant at this point is not just a celebration of a traditional ritual, but exercise of biocultural rights in the context of Assam and the entire Northeast. The Kuki-Chin festival of Chavang Kut also brings in a parallel ritual of invocation of ancestors and burning of weeds from the field near the store holes of grains come close to agricultural practices of the hills. Chapchar Kut among the Mizos as post-harvest festival has a significant bamboo dance where men will only sit and tap the bamboo, while women will perform the dance also reminds the matrilineal past of the Mizos, where women were the main cultivators and protectors of the harvest. Among the Southern Angamis of Nagaland, Phousnyi or Sekrenyi festival translated as sanctification or purification festival comes pretty close to Makarsankranti in its style and spirit. Sekrenyi involves ritual observance of *Mi-KI* fire after cleaning the sources of water, absolutely necessary for the next harvesting season. Among the Eastern Nagas like Lothas celebrate post-harvest festival called *Tokhu Emomg* marking a ritual collection of foodgrains and edibles in their traditional baskets, which is redistributed by the community priest.

The winter-festivals celebrated across Northeastern ethnic groups involve a preparation of the next harvesting season. A kind of reobjectification of the rice and maize seeds happen in a variety of ways. In case of Assam, sowing Boro rice is an effective way of making use of early summer flood carrying sediments and also preserving a good harvest. The cycle of harvesting is regenerated through burning the field, ritually symbolized in Uruka and Meji burning. In case of Angami Nagas, for preparation of Zhuto, spouted rice grains along with the hulls is fermented into mash and mixed with bamboo shoot and preserved in a wooden vessel. This preparation during winter allows the rural community to save seeds to be harvested during rainy seasons. Be it winter harvest or preparation for the next season of harvest, the whole process involves rituals meant for preparation of the next farming season.

The entire preparation and processing is guided by a biocultural need and such need is preserved in ritual practices. Such ritual practices have its positive and negative meanings. When rice is turned into feast, it is rice beer that is ritually used to signify both success and future sustenance. The variety of rice beers used during winter festivals involve a long chain of grain collection onward to fermentation and observance of strict cultural norms and taboos in ensuring a tasty and healthy drink. Angami and Chakesanga genna (meaning Taboo) guides the community toward certain do's and don't's that are practically useful in making rice beer.

The large number of rice beer of various kinds across Northeast also marks the possibility of a material basis for rituals of rejuvenation. Rejuvenation of both ancestral and other spirits living across hills, rivers and fields occupy the ritual imagination of naming them, possessing them and celebrating their release in the form of healing and successful harvest. The interrelationship between enhancing values of harvest in rituals and production of rice beer is an anthropological delight that fascinated many observers. The traditional *Laupani* during the currently held loom festival or hornbill speaks volume about continued significance of an agricultural life-world despite the turbulence in social world.

On the negative side of it, certainly, there is a perpetuation of witchcraft and superstition in certain parts of Northeast. Repeated witch hunting in Assam, Tripura, Meghalaya and other parts shows a kind of failure of state promises and a failure to comprehend rapid technological changes that suddenly dislodges the agrarian land relations and cultural practices. The disruption and displacement affect a variety of significant ritual practices, art, image-making and craftsmanship. As some philosophers have argued, this also marks a recession of the sacred and the rise of the so called secular life that abandons quintessential aspects of customary and traditional practices.

In case of Assam, internal displacement of minorities and smaller ethnic groups like Tiwa and laung along with Bengali Muslims, sandals and Bodos created a situation of lack of inter-cultural empathy and ambience. One of the major reasons for decline in traditional faith is a kind of extreme inward looking affirmation of culture that is not able to catch up with new challenges coming from new technologies and symbols. The traditional artefacts and their symbolic significance within folk culture and narrative are often given a go by in the upsurge of religious identities that pushes out cultural symbols. One interesting case is a gradual conversion of imageless cults such as Sankari culture, or Doyni-Polo into some iconic Hindu features that internally changes the rules of a culture. Such changes leave their debilitating mark on rituals and festivals like Bihu. Although everyone agrees about its Bihu's great unifying role in Assam's assimilative culture, yet there are signs of depletion that affects its cultural reproduction. The unifying role is both literal and metaphorical as cultural and religious difference are levelled by Bihu by its culinary, musical, ritual and social commonalities that is shared between Hindus, Christians, Muslims and others. This can play a significant role in catalysing public knowledge of each other that feeds back into each other's responses to each other's culture expanding the domains of cultural logic in a democratic manner.

Selves in Transition

The terrains of migrations find its descriptive, symbolic and existential representation within the self-definition or within the core notion of self in many of tribes and communities. For example among the Kuki-Chin group of tribes, narratives of a common origin somewhere in Southwest China called Chhinlung/Khul and similarly among the Naga groups, a shared common origin called Makhel etc. give rise to an oral narrative of migration through various places in the entire Mekong-Sino-Myanmar terrain. What is more interesting is the dialogical and interactive motifs within these tribes in the form of water-spirit, rock-spirit and hill-spirit that enter into existentially lived self's reflection on its own life. Such spirits assume a variety of forms and functions such as kinship relations, transformations into insects, animals and birds. Spirits act as potential and efficient causes behind natural disasters or gifts and boons that are received from Gods and Goddesses. There is an implicit ordering of all that one experiences in terms of spirit functions and its relationship with higher order beings. One may surmise that concrete objects such as rocks and mountains are situated as spirits that live in the neighbourhood and are contained within a sacred boundary within which the tribal self can define itself. Only on the occasion of death, such a self-travels across the threshold and goes onto land of dead that lies beyond the bounds of the immediate sacred boundaries drawn by concrete hills and rocks. A boundary of the sacred and its beyond often signifies the inside and the outside that determines the subject position of the communitarian ethno-tribal self.

These boundaries are conceptualised by tribes in terms of belief about past, present and future. Time and boundary lead to abstractions and interpretative surpluses such as memory tales, limits of finite and infinite beings, ritual means of propitiation of these beings, metaphors and images of the supernatural, sickness and healing processes of the mortals etc. These interpretative surpluses open up specific conceptual tokens to a hermeneutic interface with other concepts and beliefs drawn up from other tribes and communities. For example, in a fascinating story of lived experience, there is a competition between sister rivers (who are river goddesses in Khasi tale), namely, KaUmtong, KaTorasa, KaPasbira, KaJani and KaDwara to reach the plains of Sylhet. As all of them take short cuts they lose their way in the hard rocks. Contrastingly the river Umiam quietly flows down the serpentine hills to reach the plains. The flow of the river is construed as river spirit that gets its representation in competition between rivers with a rider that one who does not take a short cut reaches the destination. River stories and river spirits are absent among those tribes who did not migrate following the course of river. For example, in the Kuki-Chin group of tribes, it is the water creatures such as crabs and insects that assume an anthropomorphic function in determining fate of humans, but there are no significant tales of rivers connected with thick and thin of life. It is rather an issue of survival that arises from such river based animals. It needs to be further explored whether two different kinds of narratives based on two different terrains of migration can find some parallels and comparisons.

On the core concept of self, for example, in the Kuki-Chin context, the concept of Tlawmngaihna/Tomngaina and the concept of Rngiew in the Khasi context that defines the presence of the self/ person could be compared in their fine-grained shades of meaning. Any such comparison cannot just be a semantic exercise, but it needs to be correlated to the whole course of migration. How a string of concepts that are available within a specific worldview give rise to a coherent meaning token and how each of these concepts remain connected with some pre-history of migration can provide a better understanding and perspective on conception of self. For example, Khasi concept of Nongshonoh as the keeper of U Thlen, Palaung (Myanmar and Northern Thailand) concept of snake spirit called I-ran-ti and a place where such snake spirit lives called *Kok-ya* has a close connection.[10] In the course of migration, Palaungs and Khasis are supposed to have close ties in terms of cultural memory and concepts from one worldview got its repercussions in another. It got altered, transformed and fine-tuned by taking off from each other's specific moorings. Similarly, in the Kuki-Chin group of peoples, the *Ciimnuai* genealogy of belonging to a common ancestral tree with tribes such as Miao, Lolo, Moso, Yao, Tung and Lai in Northern Thailand and Southwest China produce an intensional notion of self, a self that derives itself from its relation with other brethren tribes with whom they are separated in the course of migration. An example of this arises in Tlwamngaihna/Tomngaina or the Mizo notion of personhood that finds its close reverberation in Zothang/ Zokang of Lai-Zo and *Tlang* of Zo seemingly travelled from Kham region of Southwest China to move down to Yesago of Northwest Myanmar to Zo-Tlang of Chin state of Myanmar. Seemingly, Tlang as a locale with its institution of Kuki-Chin group of people assumes the form of Kham-tung-mi, literally, "people on the hill slope" as well as a form of "soul" in the animal or in any other natural object that later gets transformed into human form of kinship relations and associated norms and codes of behaviour to find itself emerging into *Tlawmngaihna*, as in present Lushei hills. Contrasting people with Zo line of descent further hone the concept as La-Pao as in Kuki culture. Similarly the commonality between Zo and Karen worldviews can be noted in Pa-O and Sgaw Karen belief in *yawa*, the creator who is dispersed in forest, river, field and land and the ancestral female spirit known as *Naka cheng*. The interconnections between tlang, Tlwamngaihna and nakacheng and their mutual transformations deserve exploration into many a hidden contours.

In contrast to Mon-Khmer and Tibeto-Burman tales of origin, ambivalence of origin among the Abo and Tani group of tribes opens up a new dimension of self-conception. Tani conception of Doyni-Polo as the creator involves the Sun goddess and the moon god and their union to give birth to all the living creatures of the world. Further, Tani group's ceremonies such as *Myoko* and *Murung* perform elaborate rituals to regenerate the souls. It is said among the Tani groups, "Miyu Saliang La Gyunyang Santa Tiggo Santa Lingi Du" (man is born with the ceremonies for spirit and therefore we cannot have a prosperous life without these spirits). In a sense, the connection between place of origin and spirit worship is transformational, the former transforming into the latter. In case of such a transformation, there is a creative appropriation of the idea of origin in symbolic forms. Tai speaking people such as Hmongs, normally settled in lower valleys intimate and indicate the emergent social formations in upper hills of Northwest Laos. This marks a transition from Hmong to successor societies such as Tai Nua to Khmu communities and their settlement. Karen ritual of au brae in Mae M'Lau as an animated landscape of spirits comprising of land of the dead (pblukau) as well as domesticated wild that are invisible located at Doi Inthanon in Northern Thailand. In their agreement with Hmongs that gave rise to the ritual called 'eating the head of the rice' and 'conserving old bamboo groves' that essentially meant continuation with rai munwian system of swidden farming. Below the area of swidden farming is the taboo area called *doo ta* area. Similarly, Tani ambivalence towards water-spirits and a greater attachment to hill and celestial spirits mark an aversion towards riverine routes, routes which are occupied with more ancestral or other communities such as Akas, Khampas, Padamyongs and/or Tibetans and Bhutiyas. Indeed water-spirits in Tani tradition assume the form of *wiyu* or evil spirit. Territorially water-spirits come from trans-border of Southern Tibet, marking a kind of descent into lower depths and finally they are supposed to reside in the nether world. This is a non-hierarchical horizontal construction of self that purges out alien spaces and spirits from the inner core of self-definition.

Successor Societies

Such lived experiences of shared cultural concepts throw up a history of migration that has been captured fundamentally in two distinct frameworks: one by James C. Scott's model of non-state spaces inhabited by stateless peoples who lived beyond the frontiers of organised state in upland Southeast Asia and lived a migratory nomadic life (Scott, 2009). The other framework by Richard A. O'Connor speaks of "ethnic succession" in relation to agro-cultural complexes involving subordination of lowland ecology by a succession to complex agro-cultural systems on the upland leading to a "closure" for later migrants[11]. These two frameworks throw up logical and paradigmatic models to understand empirical details and systematise these details by going beyond local knowledge of the subjects. One of the major debates in such systematisation is the constitution of the State as a relationship between subjects and power, between agents and structure. James C. Scott provides an account of "liminal zones" that are neither inside nor outside the State that reduces the authority and the functional control of the State. Such zones are elevated uplands that pose physical barrier to the entity called State. This physical barrier served those communities that wanted to flee or resist the State and in the process these communities avoided governance under the State and choose to live in a stateless condition. Examples of migrating communities from Upper Mekong to lower Mekong delta, Northern Thai and Burmese communities including major communities like Mon, Khmer, Han and numerous nomadic tribes such as Chin, Lisu, Karen, Akha, Hmong, Kayah to name just a few, whom Scott labelled as Zomiyas. Zomiyas are, in Scott's (2009: ix-x) inimitable words:

> *Zomia* is a new name for virtually all the lands at altitudes above roughly three hundred meters all the way from the Central Highlands of Vietnam to Northeastern India and traversing five Southeast Asian nations (Vietnam, Cambodia, Laos, Thailand, and Burma) and four provinces of China… It is an expanse of 2.5 million square kilometres containing about one hundred million peoples… at the periphery of nine states…virtually everything about these people's livelihoods, social organization, ideologies, and… even their largely oral cultures, can be read as strategic positionings designed to

> keep the state at arm's length... to avoid incorporation into states and to
> prevent states from springing up among them.

The Zomiyas remained illegible as they escaped the abstract categorisation by the State and remained elusive to the processes of settlement and subjection within the territorial jurisdiction of the State. As legibility implies a viewer whose vision is synoptic and who can see from outside, the Zomiyas not only remained outside the pale of institutionalised land tenure, legally appointed chieftainship and such other forms of systematised constructions of identity. Indeed the illegibility of the Zomiyas prevented the State from coming into being. Zomiyas could follow a parallel path of livelihood and belief system that does not require an arbitrator or an authority over and above their social organisations.

These illegible Zomiyas of Scott turns out to be singular and specific agro-cultural complexes marked by a set of agrarian and cultural practices such as home-garden or wet-rice cultivation in O'Connor's understanding. Wet rice cultivators left the lowland delta and inhabited the highlands as successors to sedentary agriculturalists. The highlanders carried the practice of wet rice cultivation by shifting from flood management to flow management. This transition is explained by O'Connor[12] in the following way,

> Now let us map peoples and contrast, say, 700 A.D. and 1700 A.D. In the early era Pyu, Mon, Khmer, and Cham rule the mainland, while to their north are Burmese, Tai, and Vietnamese. Ten centuries later the northerners dominate everywhere. In irrigable niches the southerners are gone (Pyu) or in decline (Cham), and their remaining strength is in the unirrigable lower deltas where Mon and Khmer floodfarmers live in states under northern overlords. Juxtaposing these two eras reveals an epochal change. The date, pace, and completeness of the change vary but not the larger fact of a succession.

The larger fact of succession from lowland to highland in the form of a disjunction between cultivating practices and practices of rule or state acts as the source of "social contrast" between lowland settlers and highland successors. If Scott's Zomiyas are the highland successors who always moved away from the state and lived in the periphery of centralised states, then Zomiyas also are the successors of settled agro-cultural complexes from the lowland. This contrast of state and non-state spaces in terms of highland and lowland gives rise to interesting cultural contrasts as well. Lowland communities practice a kind of collective burial of the dead in their fields, who ensure land right and collective belief in such spirits, while highlanders have no such ownership attachment to their land and community spirits become lineal spirits. Transformation of community spirits into lineal spirits also marks a kind of transformation from patrilineage of community spirits to matriliny of lineal spirits, a contrasting transformation that marks the story of migration to highland. Matriliny goes with highland as successor community could see itself as a lineage not from the pastoral lowland but from the mountainous upland that held them on its laps and contours. Mountains connecting the world above are conceived as maternal nature, while the plain land below is conceived as paternal. Lineages and its imaginative domains formed around mountains imagined themselves to be freed from patrilineal regulations and tended to remain more matri-local and matrilineal in its pristine connection with sky and the world beyond. This matrilineal tendency in-built around settlement in mountainous terrains and spaces separated by deep gorges and steep hills often converged in water-heads and watersheds. The Brahmaputra river system in the Northwest of Southeast Asia, the Irrawady on the North and many other rivers act as common meeting grounds between hilly terrains and adjacent plains.

In Lieu of a Conclusion

There is a reciprocal and alternating convergence and divergence between physical and cultural spaces with the basic elements of self-conception. Initial organisation of a dwelling space brings out the underside of tribal imagination: presence of an alter subjectivity to whom experience could be related in the mode of conscious self-relation. The idea of Kojum Koja and saibloojmem is a form of everyday cognition that gives rise to a various levels of conscious understanding of how the self cognizes itself. Such a cognition is relational that arises through specific representations. Another form of representation is construction of conceptual artefacts that it is not only that the reflective consciousness of the world is modified by the pre-reflective in the form of a transformation of pre-reflective into reflective, but it also produces a "phenomenological datum" within any expressive, metaphorical, rhetorical and literary rendering of the experiential. In the phenomenology of the tribal world, any rendering of the experiential takes the form of geomancy or some kind of spiritual explanation of the phenomenon.

Such a construction of self-combining the lived space and the phenomenological datum from the lived space along with a variety of conceptual artefacts draws up its resources from beyond, which is the larger terrain of Southeast Asia. The Project aims to explore certain close connection between tribes of Northeast India and Southeast Asia. Apart from the tribes, there are Major cultural inter-relatedness between Shan people and Ahoms, Meitei people and other Tibeto-Burman groups of people.

As far as Naga tribes are concerned, they have their close kins with Mao, Kham and Akha people of Southwestern China. There are significant linguistic and cultural similarities that can be understood on a closer examination. Kuki-Chin group of people has significant and shareable cultural similarities with Hmong, Miao, Kham, Lai, Tai Lue communities. Indeed there are cross-cutting beliefs, folk motifs and shared stories of origin in space and time that opens up possibilities of wider comparison. For example, Hmong origination from the hills and their settlement to the plains point to a reverse migration that happened in search of water, which is similar to Naga migration in search of sources of water for swidden cultivation.

This comparison would open up various core notions of self as it is available in the worldviews of various communities and tribes. An important constituent of these worldviews is the religious beliefs and practices that throw up a number of ideological categories. For example, among Tai Lue community of Southwest China, there are conception of self that sink deeper below the surface level praxis, adjusting to a subterranean world of secret alliances and multiple meanings. Tai

Lue community adjusts itself to dry plains, to the spirits of shrubs and groves and flower valleys that are invoked in festivals such as *Wat Phrathat Sob Van* performed to bless the community. Similarly in the context of Northeast India putting down roots in a deeper substratum of personal and social networks will lead us to intricate ways of world-making that various tribes engage in.

The account brings into play religious belief and rites of passage from one territory to other in a larger function of 'grain producing community' that keeps copying itself, from plains to hills and from hills to plains in relation to fields, water, mountains and spiritual well-being.[13] Taking this as a point that undergirds much of Southeast and South Asian formation of successor communities and their boundaries within the landscape, one needs to inquire how nation-spaces with its logic of territorialisation actually subverts the sense of belonging of those who own a fuzzy history of migration of their life-worlds. Such a subversion is more metaphysical and ideological, as it consists in a project of appropriation of these nascent communitarian forms of life into a legitimised narrative of national identity with its force of unification. Depending on the level of tolerance of plurality and difference, various nation-states attempt to draft a variety of policies of recognition and assimilation of these essentially minority-ised fuzzy ethnic identities. Scott and van Schendel's description of these identities as North-western "borderland" identities of Southeast Asia[14] Graham Chapman's description of these identities as 'resource owning and resource sharing deterritorialized identities'[15] are more liberal than that of 'singularities' of nation-state. Singularities that create a binary opposition between native vs. settlers, indigenous vs. non-indigenous actually subvert both the common space of belonging as well as the idea of 'indigenous citizenship'. The conflict is patently reflected in territorial claims beyond one's lived spaces that result into certain singularities. The question is, why such claims are made? Do such claims create a conflict between ethnically defined citizenship and civic citizenship? How borderland identities deal with these questions of adaptations, struggles and cross-border alliances is a major question.

Such adaptations give rise to altered conceptual schemes and frames of interpretation of one's own culture in its proximity and distance from other cultures. It also creates a nexus of lifeworlds in the context of Northeast India. Decoding such a nexus in terms of multiple shared roots and routes is still a cultural project, which is like a work in progress. More reflections on such possible sharing of meanings and ideas of life in its variety of manifestations and in its existential quest for authenticity unravels dialogic subjectivities that clamour for recognition and difference.

Endnotes

[1] Associate Professor, Philosophy, North Eastern Hill University, Shillong.

[2] Walter D. Mignolo, "Epistemic Disobedience and the Decolonial Option: A Manifesto" in file:///C:/Users/Acer/Downloads/Dialnet-EpistemicDisobedience AndTheDecolonialOption-3979075.pdf, accessed on 30th October, 2018. Mognolo argued for a free world conceived by decoloniality of being in which many worlds can fit. My argument is that such plural worlds are part and parcel of decolonized inner worlds of tribal and indigenous communities.

[3] Elisabeth Eide, "Strategic Essentialism and Ethnification: Hand in Glove?" in *Nordicom Review* 31 (2010) 2, 63-78.

[4] Rashmirekha Sarma, Disappearing Dialect: the Idu-Mishmi Language of Arunachal Pradesh (India) available in file:///C:/Users/Acer/Downloads/06-The%20Idu-Mishmi%20Language.pdf, accessed on 30.10.2018.

[5] Asem Manimala, from her personal communication related to the project entitled, Litoral Community in Loktak Lake: precarity and everyday life.

[6] Mamang Dai, *The Legends of Pensam* (New Delhi: Penguin India, 2006), 55.

[7] Arnold Berleant, "Human Being and Natural World," in *Ethics and the Environment*, ed. Richard E. Hart (Lanham:University Press of America,1992), 25-28.

[8] Suzi Gablik, *Living the Magical Life: An Oracular Adventure* (Grand Rapids: Phanes Press, 2002), 45.

[9] Stories of 'speaking frog', transformation of human to hornbill, soul leaving or entering the body that presents an impossibility of mind or body or self-attaining Nature in terms of presentation of ideas.

[10] Emile Durkheim *The Rules of Sociological Method*, edited by George E.G. Catlin, Translated by Sarah A. Solovay & John H. Mueller (New York: The Free Press of Glenco, 1964), 41-2.

[11] My Colleague and co-researcher Basil Pohlong have found this out through our field research among Palaungs of Northern Thailand.

[12] Richard A. O'Connor, "Agricultural Change and Ethnic Succession in Southeast Asian States: A Case for Regional Anthropology", *The Journal of Asian Studies*, Vol. 54, No. 4, 1995, 968-996.

[13] Ibid., 970.

[14] James C. Scott, *The Art of Not Being Governed: An Anarchist History of Upland Southeast Asia* (New Haven:Yale University Press, 2009), 9-10, 23.

[15] Van Schendel, Willem, "Geographies of Knowing, Geographies of Ignorance: Jumping Scale in Southeast Asia" in Paul H Krastoska, Raben Remco and Nordholt Schulta Henk (eds.) *Locating Southeast Asia: Geographies of Space and Politics of Knowledge* (Singapore: Singapore university Press, 2005), 275.

[16] Graham Chapman, *The Geopolitics of South Asia: From early Empires to the Nuclear Age* (London: Ashgate, 2009).

Tribal Challenges in the Northeast

Sri Dipok Kr. Barthakur

I would now like to give today's topic, "Tribal Challenges" a positive twist – I personally feel that the negative connotation associated with words like "Challenges", "problems", "issues", "barriers", etc. make it harder for us to look beyond. We get into a vicious cycle of negativity instead of taking small positive steps. What is an issue, could be an opportunity? It's how we look – a glass is half full or half empty!

The Northeast of India, especially the seven sisters, has been historically categorised and perceived as one homogenous region. However, in conventional terms of tribes, language, customs etc. we are perhaps one of the most diverse groups of people to inhabit in one small land mass. As per census there are around 200 Tribal Groups that exists in Northeast India. About 220 languages and dialects in multiple language families are spoken here. Arunachal Pradesh consists of around 25 tribes. Nagaland has around more than 16 major tribes and so on and so forth. Within Assam we have the Brahmaputra Valley, the Barak Valley and the hill districts broadly. Even though there is a majority dominance of various indigenous tribes in the hill districts and Bodoland Territorial Areas of Assam, we have significant population of Deoris in Upper Assam, Mishings in Majuli, of Tiwa and Rabha tribes near Nagaon/Morigaon. Even in and around Guwahati we have pockets of Bodo dominated areas from time immemorial. And who can forget the Koch Rajbongshis to whom we owe the Kamakhya Temple as it stands today and whose areas spill into the Coochbehar region of West Bengal.

What exactly do we mean by tribes - The tribe can be seen as a social formation in two ways: first as part of evolution of societies in a historical context; second, as a coherent community on the basis of kinship ties which enables it to be a socio-cultural and economic group. So the way we define a tribe to me is a narrow construct.

So for me to divide Assam into tribal and non-tribal is not how I would like to see my state or even this region. Despite our differences we are bound by geography, history and our future destiny together. Hence, what I speak today resonates not only for tribes of Assam but of the Northeast and the entire region.

Whilst most of Northeast India had historically remained isolated and have thus preserved our religion, customs and traditions from millennia, the journey towards assimilation and integration have started from pre-independence itself. At the dawn of independence safeguards, were incorporated into the Constitution.

However, 71 years after Independence, our policy makers have still failed to take cognizance of the uneven distribution of assets amongst us, unequal political emancipation, economic development and educational reach amongst various groups inter and intra tribes, and states. Our tribes and communities are not only numerous, but we also vary in our habitat, level of development, modes of livelihood, exposure to the wider world, traditional values, customs, beliefs, etc. There are communities living in inaccessible hilly areas, having minimal contact with the world. There are tribes in the plains who obviously have a large degree of interdependence, access and intermingling with the rest of the country.

However, a one size fits all approach has been the approach in most of our policies. Particularly, the approach oversimplifies the complex problem of tribal development by making it a purely economic one.

But what we are facing today is more nuanced and includes, apart from economic development, a demand on preservation of ethnic identity, ecology, language, culture, style of living, indigenous practices, etc.

Thus, development, because of the diverse situations, has to be very area specific even within a state, I believe. Again how do we define "development" – it is not simply imposition of others way of life or will on our communities. If we look at the impact of economic development and increasing urbanisation in our region, there is almost a pattern. Because of the exposure to the wider economy, polity and society, the urban or semi-urban communities have retained very little of our indigenous economic and political practices and cultural institutions in its purest forms. Barring some socio-cultural practices and physical features, we are indistinguishable in our lifestyle and pattern of consumption from others. Inflow of money and capital have made these societies of ours transactional. Division of labour on the basis of skill and education has taken place. But barring a few, we have also seen traditional communities being pushed out of their homeland and facing impoverishment economically as the traditional means of livelihood and way of life has been taken away from these groups.

Tribes living in the hills, with some minor exceptions, have only recently been exposed to the mainstream economic system to some extent. A headlong rush into embracing development and progress without safeguards has seen us lose our balance as a society. The impact on our lives have already been enormous – from the cultural to political. Our Society cannot be modernized only in consumption and luxury, and not in production. Thus a word of caution here again as attempts to extend the mainstream economy to these communities in a hurry is likely to be counter-productive of development, besides setting in motion more social unrest. The mainstream economy is a money economy with private ownership and individualism at its heart. The tribal communities, on the other hand, are communities focused on community holdings, barter systems and follow largely self- sustaining models of economy. Money is therefore, till recently not equated with status symbol, measure of values or even mode of transactions in most instances. Collective endeavour is a strongly developed feature in much of our societies. These also give us a sense of identity, of belonging of roots. But now the disparity between income and aspiration has led to many moral, social and political problems. The birth of many violent movements can be traced to these threats that face us as a tribal societies and our values. Drugs, Alcoholism, erosion of family values can also be traced to rampant urbanisation and superficial development. It is hence societies like ours are expressing our angst and our worries of developmental transformation and its impacts.

Development is a double edged sword for us. Take for example infrastructure: as geographical areas, we are grossly deficient in infrastructural facilities. Our roads and connectivity is poor. We are land locked. But when roads and railway lines are constructed linking the isolated areas, more people come from outside, not only as tourists, but for economic gains. There is land grabbing; our land gets alienated. Migration is a burning issue in Assam and in most parts of the Northeast. We feel threatened; we feel vulnerable and we feel we are losing our way of life. There is even a threat of us becoming a minority. The fear of losing our ethnic identity is no longer then a probability but looms large on the horizon.

Again our per capita income is one of the lowest in India. This is a contradiction in itself as the Northeast and particularly Assam has been a source of raw materials such as coal, oil, forests and tea since during the British raj. There was a mass extraction of these resources which were then exported to other parts of the country for processing. Thus this region however did not benefit from this process. And till many decade, post-independence this has been our fate. It is still in our region that much of the Nation's mineral, forest and water resources are located and national economic development demands utilization of these resources. So should we not extend the national developmental measures to our tribal societies? The answer is not simple. Our areas constitute a very important chunk of the national economy. In this backdrop, some social scientists have put forward the theory that the concept of a tribe is an anachronism in the present-day world, as smaller, isolated, self –contained, cohesive communities have either ceased to be thus or have become part of one other greater civilization or political boundaries of the world. However, the pace and intensity of utilization of resources must be in a manner which produces the least adverse effects on our tribal societies.

What should be emphasized in the development strategy for our areas is to ensure the impact of the transformation is cushioned and as much priority is given to the preservation of socio-culture ethos of our societies. Our societies should also be primed to inherently defend what is good in our societies, without losing confidence in who we are and that we are different. We don't need to be defensive of who we are and what we represent as communities, as tribes.

Economic development for us as tribal societies, must be achieved while minimizing the adverse effects on future resource availability and ecology and without jeopardizing, ethnic identity. But as I said in the beginning the glass is half full - our region has performed reasonably well in comparison to all India average situations in respect of human development indicators and is now being propelled to centre stage of national economic growth. Various terms have been coined – Astha Lakshmi, Northeast-Gateway to ASEAN, Act East from Northeast, etc. I hope a more coherent and tailor made policy framework, better governance and a parallel development in civic bodies and institutions to hold together our socio-cultural framework, will allow us to shape a society and a region that we want and not parachuted from elsewhere.

Traditions to Modernity:
A Case Study of Nagaland

Sri. Lipokmar Tzudir

I t is a natural phenomenon that every culture or society witnesses changes that are beyond human control, and which often shake the core of their ethical foundations. Similarly, the Naga culture which had its foundations in the dictates of traditional norms is encountering such dilemma as a consequence of a sudden rush of modernity ushered in through various aspects. As Furer (1977:673) observes, "Nagas...have been subjected to many alien influences aiming at a transformation of their life-style." Furthermore, Giddens states that:

> In traditional societies, individual actions do not have to be analysed and thought about so much, because choices are already prescribed by the traditions and customs whereas in post-traditional societies we have to work out the roles for ourselves. What to do? How to act? Who to be? Become the focal question for everyone. The prominence of these questions of identity in modern society is both a consequence and a cause of changes at the institutional level (Giddens 1991:70 cited in Gaunlett 2002:91).

This paper aims to highlight some factors that led to a transition from traditional to modernity and the challenges that it brought along. My intention here is not to discount the importance of modernity, but to highlight the consequences of disregarding the traditional values in quest for modernity.

The intend of this paper is therefore to draw awareness among scholars and policy makers alike, to help showcase the realities of this kind of changes that are occurring in traditional societies, hoping that it will shed light on the urgency to act promptly.

In the first segment, I will discuss about the advent of Christianity in the Naga Hills and its impact on their culture. In the second segment, I will talk about the effects brought about by the impact of colonialism. In the third segment, I will discuss the outbreak of modernity, and in the last segment, I will highlight the effects of the transition to modernity that resulted in a social impasse.

Animism to Christianity

The arrival of American missionaries in 1872 at Molungkimong village (An Ao village under Mokokchung district of Nagaland) marked the advent of Christianity in the Naga hills, and subsequent setting up of a new Christian village at Molungyimsen in 1876, marks the expansion of Christianity and birth of modern Education, which is to be considered a hallmark in the history of the Nagas, and befittingly, Molungyimsen village is today recognised as the 'Naga Educational Heritage Village' (Naga Student Federation 2006) and 'Pilgrimage village'. The Ao Nagas prior to the arrival of Christianity were known for their quest of head-hunting and it was in fact a marvellous achievement for the American missionaries to be able to penetrate their territory, and even being able to contain it later on.

The missionaries translated the Bible and Christian literatures and hymns to the local dialect for usage in worship which led to a tremendous development and advancement of the dialects beyond their inhabited territories. The extraordinary pace in which Christianity spread amongst the Aos and later to all parts of the Naga Hills was significantly due to the appeal of the gospel present in the Christian hymns as Mills predicted:

> A point of small importance now, but which may have greater significance later, is the Ao love of hymn-singing and the importance he attaches to it. The services in the little village churches consist largely of hymns and an Ao usually speaks of going to church as going to sing (Mills: 1926:418).

The Nagas known for their love of singing were quickly attracted to this new form of songs which did play a factor in alluring the non-believers towards Christianity. For the missionaries, the gospel was their main intent, yet the moral etiquettes in their own interpretations were inevitable, and therefore, besides the positive contributions that came about, there were other implications as well, and Mills observes that:

> Of the mistakes made by the mission, the gravest, in my opinion, and the one most fraught with danger for the future is their policy of strenuously imposing an alien western culture on the converts…I think I am right in saying that no member of the mission has ever studied Ao customs deeply, but nearly all have been eager to uproot what they neither understand nor sympathize with, and to substitute for it a superficial civilization (Mills 1926:420).

As he clearly puts it, the missionaries neglected the cultural uniqueness of the natives, and its importance on their daily lives, and concentrated entirely on converting them according to the doctrine of their theology. The transition from animism to Christianity was volatile, rather than steady, and seen as important from a sociological point of view, yet it came at a cost of their *yimsu* (custom), and this in a bigger light resulted in the discard of their age old traditions that have bound and defined them as a community. Alemchiba explains that:

> From the moment of their conversion to the Christian faith, people were no longer allowed to participate in dances or to sing traditional songs, and we have news of episodes of excommunication when this order was disobeyed. This fact had a most detrimental effect on the maintenance and the flourishing of oral literature (Alemchiba 1992:164).

A prevailing attitude of their approach, and later by the new converts was that they branded the old practices and beliefs as taboo and overlooked the quality of the moral codes and literary content in their songs, folklores and folk tales that later contributed towards a decline in grasping its importance by the generation that followed.

For instance, the *sungkong* (log drum) is an example of one element of the culture which is at the verge of extinction. According to an old Ao belief, *sungkong* was considered a Deity of blessing and guardian of the village that was anointed by a god named *Ayongpang Tsungrem* (god of the river bank). *Sungkong* was used to communicate messages in times of emergency and festivities and in true sense, for over many generations it safeguarded the Ao from many harm's way. There were different beat patterns such as to communicate fire emergencies, for danger of wild beasts, for events of enemy attacks, for new moon and full moon. These drum beats were coded messages and could be understood by members of the village. The rituals involved in carving the log drum and the importance they bestowed upon it thereafter became irrelevant to the teachings of the new faith, and they thus started detaching themselves from it. Conversion to Christianity marks the decrease of the *sungkong* activities. Less did the Ao realise that they were disposing 'one of their most striking specimens of handiwork' as described by Mills (1926:76); and in a musical point of view, an enormous collection of rhythmic beat patterns vanished along with the loss of *sungkong*.

Similarly, traditional attires were discouraged as the process of its creation involved rituals of the old faith, songs of evolution became contrary to the new belief that God is the supreme creator of Heaven and Earth, songs of adulations for warriors was interpreted as idol worship which was contrary to the new teaching that professed that God alone deserved all glory and honour.

Today, majority of the Nagas profess Christianity as their religion. The activities of the Church are planned in such a way that it would cater to all age groups such as, Sunday school for children, youth fellowship, and adult fellowship and so on and so forth. In any of these group meetings, half of the time is spend in singing their devotional songs and hymns, which clearly highlights the important role that songs play in their worship life. In every religion, music plays a vital role; and so have hymns and popular Christian songs been an integral part of the Naga Christian worship life. They congregate in not less than 1000 on any Sunday service and all the members singing in parts is truly an experience beyond description. All the songs in their hymnal are staff notated, although majority cannot read the notes, but ever since the advent of Christianity, hymns have been a regular ingredient in their church services and so they can almost sing it by memory.

On thinking critically on this new trend brought about by modernity, there is a negative factor emerging and that is, they often carelessly claim these songs and hymns, for instance as 'traditional Ao or Angami or Sumi Christian songs', which is inaccurate. I am not criticising their belief nor the importance that the Christian songs play in their modern belief system but these songs that they often refer to as 'traditional Naga Christian songs' are actually either Welsh, German or American, which are merely translated to the local vernacular. It needs to be emphasised here, that song texts, no matter how proficiently translated do not realistically transmit the experience from one community to another and so the foreign songs and hymns, although playing an important role in their life; does not necessarily express their cultural identity or their thought process.

From one point of view, the transition from animism to Christianity brought about modern education, better hygiene, modern values and so forth. However, from another point of view, the unsympathetic approach towards the natives' customs and traditions by the early Christians contributed towards endangering their heritages that are vital for their identity and obstructed the development of their arts.

Colonial Impact: Naga Nationalism and its Impact on the Culture

The Naga society as a whole went through several phases of transitions since the mid-19th century and one among them is the impact resulting out of the British annexation of the Naga territory and later by India that led to the rise of the Naga National Movement. The British annexed the Ao territory in 1889 after overcoming several decades of resistance from the Angami Nagas in the South (Mills 1926:4). The Naga tribes prior to the British invasion were living independently from any outside domain, the villages were self-sufficient and autonomously governed by their own set of customary laws and as such there was no need of interference in the usual business of their daily lives from outsiders.

The British government for the convenience of their administration subdivided the Naga tribes under the administrations of British – Burma government and British – Indian government, and this radical move awakened the political consciousness of the Nagas that led to the formation of the Naga club to address the Naga political interests. After several failed attempts of peaceful negotiations, the Naga National movement gained momentum towards the eve of the Indian Independence and declared Nagaland Independent on the 14th of August 1947, a day before India's declaration of independence. The Indian union eventually did not honour the declaration of the Nagas which culminated from then on to decades of warfare between the two.

Naga Nationalism was a clarion call for every Naga man and tribe to rise up in defence of their birth right to be their own masters and not fall subject to a foreign power which was met with such overwhelming responses from every corner of the Naga Hills. Sovereignty, for the Nagas therefore became the utmost importance of that time. Men from every village took up arms to oppose the foreign military advance resulting in huge loss of lives and properties and the outcome of it was total chaos.

Many young Nagas who received modern education were among those who took up leadership in the national movement; and on the other hand, had several others who were involved in the civil services since the British rule and later with the Indian government and were therefore one of the most vulnerable to scrutiny and suspicion by the Military as well as their comrades. The military was always suspicious of the villager's activities and kept vigil of their movements and gatherings thus making it difficult and even impossible for the villagers to go to their fields.

My parents who were born in the 1930s experienced the trauma of living in such fear under the military rule. My mother recollects how one day they had to hide in the ceilings when the army came ransacking their home of being informed that one of her brothers has joined the National movement and helplessly watched her father get beaten by the army in their kitchen. She sadly laments the agony of living each day worrying for her brother's fate who never returned back. My father who during this time was studying in a school in Assam talks about how he often felt rejected as an outsider by the residents in the state of Assam and upon return to his homeland on holidays, lived with the fear of being branded an Indian sympathiser.

The Naga socio-cultural life was thus pushed to a dark corner of fear and uncertainty as a consequence of the colonial impact. The Nagas who were known for their love of festivities and merry making was therefore psychologically reduced to mere beings. The village streets that once reverberated with laughter, music and singing was replaced by gunfire and silence. *Morung*, which served as their learning institution and gathering place, was now wearing a deserted look as assembling in groups was prohibited. Many schools were burned down during this time as the revolutionists disapproved the curricula introduced by the Indian Educational system. Festivals became superficial and not really a celebration of life.

The Naga tribes speaks highly variant dialects, and so had to resort to a common medium of communication, and in that, English emerged as the official language. The consequence of English emerging as the official language was that, the tribal dialects took a back seat and similarly the traditional songs because of the language barrier lost its valour as it became incommunicative in the multi- dialect scenario.

Socialist philosophy and black spiritual songs like *We Shall Overcome* and *Till We Meet Again* took more prominence in the National movement which although served its purpose in inspiring the nationalists, however, did not really support their culture and unique ethnicity that they were fighting to protect. In a broader aspect, the attributes of patriotism and moral relevance present in their traditional songs were not taken advantage of, and this also contributed to disintegration of the national movement leaving a big impact for the present generation to turn around.

Outburst of Modernity

In March of this year (1961), a new state – Nagaland – was added to the Indian map... By and large the problem of the tribes is that of a people at a transitional stage whose relative backwardness exposes them to economic exploitation and who therefore require special protection (Gokhale, 1961).

The declaration of the statehood was received with mixed reactions. The proponents of statehood at that time felt that it was the nearest possible way to bring development to the people who had been deprived of it for decades, whilst others opposed and declared it as against the wishes of the people who have fought and laid their lives in quest of Naga Independence. Mike Wooldridge of British Broadcasting Corporation (BBC) reporting about the unfortunate continuity of violence in Nagaland writes:

> Few of the world's simmering civil wars have lasted as long as the conflict in Nagaland, in Northeastern India. It's a small but beautiful land of around a million and a half people. For the best part of fifty years, since Naga political leaders declared Nagaland to be independent, saying that as tribal people they had always ruled themselves, there's been an on/off war between militant groups and the Indian security forces (Wooldridge, 1997).

India did not promptly deliver its promises of developments which is one of the reasons that frustrated the Nagas who over a long period of time have been yearning for modern amenities. The disparity in allocating economic privileges in comparison to other states was apparent. This step-motherly attitude of treatment at that juncture of transition by the Indian government should be understood as one of the main reasons that led to the offspring of an extremist approach towards Naga Sovereignty leading to renewed tensions among Naga Nationalist factions and the Indian government. And this in turn delayed the prospects of development in the newly declared state.

I grew up in the early eighties and can clearly remember that only government offices had telephone connections during those days. Television was a rare luxury and only the rich could afford to buy it from outside Nagaland. I counted myself fortunate to know a rich family in town who owned a black and white television and would treat myself to a TV program at least once a week, but often returned home disappointed because of power interruptions. Walking 3kms to school every day with friends was so much fun and never knew that kids in other parts of the country were riding buses or even driving their own cars to school. My father used to encourage me and my brothers to read newspapers and so did we, but it was at least three days after publications that we got the newspapers as it came all the way from Calcutta (now Kolkata). Listening to friends about their fortune of seeing trains and aeroplanes in India felt like they have returned from heaven. It was only later in the late eighties that I came to a realisation of how much we have been deprived of, and how unfair it was.

By the late eighties, telephone connections were easily available and so did television become affordable and with that came the western satellite cable networks. In contrast to a prior single channel afforded by the Indian state owned network they were now enjoying access to various networks: BBC, Cable News Network (CNN), Music Television (MTV) or Home Box Office (HBO) and many others which provided a glimpse of the outside world. The glamour of the western world that they saw on television came rushing like a storm and captivated the imagination of the youth that resulted in a trend of lifestyle change that later brought about adverse effects.

The Naga society, particularly among the youth were breaking out of traditional inclinations and attempting to redefine their self-identity in tune to the west's lifestyle. Heavy metal bands of the 1980s, such as led zeppelin, Aerosmith, Black Sabbath and Iron Maiden became household names. The youths idolised these rock bands and musicians as heroes and started to imitate their music as well as their lifestyles. Local rock bands emerged from all corners and concerts were a regular event.

Owing to modern media, in the case of the Nagas, the transition from traditional to modernity took place rapidly within a span of a decade that caught the society off-guard and the inevitable question of "What to do? How to act? Who to be?" became eminent. A society so unfamiliar to the challenges faced by the western world was therefore encountered with the same and got immersed in an unprecedented dilemma.

As discussed earlier, this was a generation that have long been oppressed and deprived of a free will to express and develop their potentials as consequences to years of violence, uncertainty and backwardness. It was like a volcano waiting to erupt, and in the moment of their weakness, erupted beyond control pushing them to a post-traditional dilemma.

A Social Impasse

The Naga culture with no written history of its origin but one that relied merely on its oral traditions arrived to a point of social impasse shadowed by a grave risk of losing its cultural worth owing to discontinuity of their customs in desire for modernity. This social impasse was an outcome of new issues that were cropping out within the society as Munslow and Brown (1999:207) note how the 20th century was witnessing breakdowns of civil societies as an outcome of "internal economic, social, cultural and political imbroglio and armed conflicts escalating further complexes".

Furthermore, as Burroughs and Rindfleisch (2002) observe, there are adverse effects to the society as a whole when individuals engage in a lavish lifestyle. Individual materialistic mind-set contributes to an overall economic disparity within a society which further escalates to an alienation of the under-privileged majority, resulting to social dropouts and as such, their society which was once a culturally and economically homogeneous one was witnessing an unwarranted division of economic and social classes due to an individualistic mindset and urge for material benefits at any cost and in regard to these perpetrators or the elites in the Naga society, and as Wongtong observes:

> By virtue of their position, they do in fact play to a certain extend the role
> of distorting the overall social order, and in addition they are associated
> with a poor and inadequate knowledge of the state of affairs as a whole,
> if not with compliance without choice (Wongtong 1992:193).

The political front was submerged in full scale corruptions coupled by dealing with armed conflicts between the Nationalists and the Indian army. The bureaucrats were far from being professionally trained or educated in the fields of their service and so were many teachers in schools. The church took a pro-active role in addressing the social issues but their approach was aimed more towards condemnation of the evil rather than a psychological rehabilitation.

Outside forces and factors may have contributed to its origin but it was a case of oblivious negligence in dealing with the issues at hand. In other words, it was an institutional failure to notice the rapidity of modification that was occurring in and to a society who were psychologically not ready for such abrupt change.

Not surprisingly the attitude of the youths toward society became a total contrast to the traditional norms of respect and moral decency and got submerged in the hopes and pleasure Rock music was offering. In the year 1995, when I was still a freshman in college, I attended a peace concert at Mokokchung town, and in that concert one of the leading bands in Nagaland played a cover song of Pink Floyd – *Another Brick in the Wall*. At that time, I enjoyed the music and thought it was quite appropriate. But in retrospection, if we study the content of the text, it was contrary to the theme and motive of the concert. And the lyrics explains the attitude of the youth of those days of which I was part of:

Another Brick in the Wall by **Pink Floyd**

We don't need no education

We don't need no thought control

No dark sarcasm in the classroom

Teachers leave them kids alone

Hey! Teachers! Leave them kids alone!

All in all it's just another brick in the wall.

All in all you're just another brick in the wall.

Wrong, Do it again!

If you don't eat yer meat, you can't have any pudding.

How can you have any pudding if you don't eat yer meat?

You! Yes, you behind the bike sheds, stand still laddy!

The transition to modernity was a long cherished fulfilment, but it shook the core of their moral base and as consequence, their once most valued traditions that have been changing hands through series of generations are confined to a very few in the villages and may encounter certain lapses in due time if some drastic measures are not taken. As Merriam wrote:

> No matter where we look, change is constant in human experience; although rates of change are differential from one culture to another and from one aspect to another within a given culture, no culture escapes the dynamics of change overnight; the threads of continuity run through every culture, and thus change must always be considered against a background of stability (Merriam 1964: 303).

In the case of the Nagas, the transition to Christianity started from the south of the Ao territory in 1870s and slowly moved towards the midland, and until the 1940s many villages in the Ongpangkong range clung to the old practice and it was in these villages that the practice endured as it was till the 1940s, and therefore the people born around 1940s are considered in light of Merriam's opinion as the 'thread'.

Every indigenous community can be considered as a repository of a distinctive body of knowledge, which have evolved over a long period of time. Knowledge accumulated through generations and stored in myths, legends, tales, proverbs, songs, dances, beliefs, rituals, ceremonies, arts and crafts and handed down from generation to generation have determined and enriched the course of the human race. In cases similar to the Nagas; the policy makers and scholars need to step in and ensure that there are amenities available so as to extract the information before the 'thread' encounters memory lapse or even worse.

References

Alemchiba, Ao. 'The Art of the Nagas,' in *The Nagas*, Somaré, Grata and Vigorelli, Leonardo (Eds.). Galleria Lorenzelli: Bergamo,1992.

Burroughs, James E. and Rindfleisch, Aric. "Materialism and Well-Being: A Conflicting Values Perspective," in *Journal of Consumer Research*, Vol.29, 348-370, 2002.

Fulbrook, Mar. *Historical Theory*. London: Routledge, 2002.

Furer, Christopher Van-Haimendorf. "The Changing Position of Tribal Population in India" in *Bulletin of the School of Oriental Studies*. University of London: London, 1977.

Gaunlett, David. *Media, Gender and Identity: An Introduction*. London: Routledge, 2002.

Gokhale, B. G. "Nagaland – The sixteenth state" in *Asian survey*, Vol.1, 36-40, 1961.

Harwood, Frances. "Myth, Memory, and the Oral Tradition: Cicero in the Trobriands" in *American Anthropologist*, New Series, Vol.78, No.4 (December), 783-796, 1976.

Jacobs, Julian. *The Nagas*, London: Thames and Hudson, 1989.

Merriam, Alan. *The Anthropology of Music*, Illinois:North-western University press, 1964.

Mills, James P. *The Ao Nagas*, London: MacMillan and Co, 1926.

Munslow and Brown. "Complex Political Emergencies", *Third world quarterly* Vol.20, pp.207-222, 1999.

Naga Student Federation. Minutes of 'Naga Students Federation,' *4th General Assembly*, 6 September, Matikhru village, 2006.

National Information Centre. No date. *The Constitution (Thirteenth Amendment) Act 1962* [Online]: http://indiacode.nic.in/coiweb/fullact1.asp?tfnm=13, accessed: 30 July 2008.

Snyder, Bob. *Music and Memory: An Introduction*. Cambridge: The MIT Press, 2000.

Somaré, Grata and Vigorelli, Leonardo. 'The Twentieth Century,' The Nagas, Somare`, Grata and Vigorelli, Leonardo (EDS.) Bergamo: Galleria Lorenzelli, 1992.

Temsula, Ao. *The Ao-Naga Oral Tradition*, Baroda: Bhasha Publication, 1999.

Vansina, Jan. *Oral Tradition as History*. London: James Currey Ltd, 1985.

Wongtong, Toshi. 'Outline of a Culture in Transformation.' *The Nagas*, Somaré, Grata and Vigorelli, Leonardo (Eds.) Galleria Lorenzelli: Bergamo, 1992.

Wooldridge, Mike. *The Forgotten War in Nagaland*, 1997.

http://news.bbc.co.uk/1/hi/programmes/from_our_own_correspondent/32885. stm, accessed: 22 June 2008

Cultural Tradition, Renewal and Modernity: A Challenge to all Cultures

Fr. Peter Haokip

It is refreshing in the first place to participate in a seminar that celebrates the multiplicity of indigenous cultures in Northeast India. Too many seminars have been organized on the conflicts of tribes of the region. It is the responsibility of all lovers of cultures that these cultures not only exist but also thrive and prosper. Most of the indigenous cultures of the region are endangered. The disappearance one of these means the disappearance of a civilization, and a loss of a civilization will make our region and the world the poorer for it. It is often difficult to enumerate the exact number of tribes in the region because of the "twin processes of fusion and fission. In the past some smaller communities came together and claimed a common identity. Thus today, most communities of the Mizo group are clubbed together. On the other hand some communities, like the *Puomai* of Manipur, have claimed and have secured a distinct identity. The twin phenomenon is reflected in the reports of the Census of India and the official lists of Scheduled tribes in the different states. Hence no list is accurate and complete, and no list reflects the actual ground reality."[1] Credit for the existence of the multiplicity of tribes in the region may be due to the so-called "protectionist policy" of Nehru-Elwin.[2] They were accused of trying to keep the tribals as 'museum specimens' for anthropologists.

Pandit Nehru's famous Panchsheel[3] (five principles) towards tribals might have contributed to the survival of many tribes. It may also be pointed out the Naga people's movement for self-determination from the very beginning of India's independence might have inspired other tribes to survive and fight for their rights. My paper will dwell on the challenge every indigenous culture faces in regard to its own cultural tradition, its renewal and its transition to modernity. On the one hand, the world is fast becoming a global village and the onslaught of globalization is threatening to swallow up many cultures especially the weaker indigenous cultures. However, on the other hand too, there is an awakening and a battle of survivor for these weaker cultures. The challenge for all cultures, especially for the weaker cultures, in this situation is, first of all, to be aware of their cultural traditions, to renew them and modernize them so that they will not only survive but also thrive. My paper will attempt to indicate ways of doing it. The role social scientists can play in this regard is to enable the weaker cultures to achieve this.

Culture, Cultural Tradition and Identity

To understand one's cultural tradition, one should first understand what culture means. It has become difficult not to describe the most commonplace details of everyday life without using the word 'culture.'[4] Etymologically, the noun is from the French *culture* or directly from Latin *cultura* which means growing, cultivation and the verb is from the obsolete French *culturer* or from the Medieval Latin *culturare*, both based on Latin *colere* "tend' or 'cultivate.' From it the idea of the cultivation of the mind, faculties or manners has risen.[5] *The New Shorter Oxford English Dictionary's* description of culture is still a simpler way of looking at a culture. Culture means the "the distinctive customs, achievements, products, outlook, etc., of a society or group;" or "the way of life of a society or group."[6]

One of the most frequently quoted definitions of culture is that of Clifford Geertz who said "Man is an animal suspended in webs of significance he himself has spun. I take culture to be those webs."[7] A simpler definition of culture may be: "A sum total of ideas, images, myths, language, laws, values and institutions that express a given society's analysis of itself and of the world as it knows it."[8] It means then that culture is the 'webs of significance' spun by human beings, or the distinctive ideas, images, myths, language, laws, values that give identity to a given society. These distinctive features of an indigenous people should not be forgotten because these distinctive features of a tribal community are not borrowed ideas of of some people but they became characteristic of their lives through their lived-experience. Verrier Elwin has rightly pointed out that the tribals "had discovered the secrets of living under hard conditions that the rest of us needed..."[9] In many cultural celebrations today, the slogan, 'our culture is our identity' is displayed prominently. One of the keenest cynosures of the aspirations of the people of the Northeast from mainland India is the Magsaysay award winner B. G. Verghese. In his highly appreciated book, *India's Northeast Resurgent: Ethnicity, Insurgency, Governance, Development*[10] says: "the various movements in the Northeast have all to do with identity." It is a powerful statement in full accord with the sentiments of the people of the region. However, celebrations of cultural festivals which is very popular among the different tribes are the simplest vehicles of identity. Hence we shall try to show the cultural identity of tribes through the celebration of festivals. As we celebrate our cultural festivals, we must show the elements of the festival that signify our identity.

Festivals: Signatures of Identity

The main festival of the Kukis is *Hun*. It is a spring time festival which used to last about a week. At the heart of this festival is the renewal of *Indoi* which is the heart and soul of Kuki traditional religion.[11] It is translated as "house-god,"[12] or "house-magic", "a bundle of charms."[13] The components of *Indoi* are taken from the flora and fauna of the Kuki world.[14] The items also represent household animals or other household things. Each of them also has great significance.[15] These items represent of the best of their kind. The father of family prays to God for himself and his family asking God to bless them as he has blessed the best of nature and the household things.[16] It is a festival that mainly signifies the religious identity of the tribe and renews human relationship with the divine as well it relationship with nature.

Kut Festival: Signifies Religious and Social Identity

The next important festival of the Kuki-Chin-Mizo groups is the festival of Kut. In Manipur, it officially now falls on 1 November. Originally it has no date. The full name of the festival is Chang Kut which means the bending of paddy plant heavy with grains about to ripen. It also was called *Chavang* (autumn) Kut because it takes place during the season of Autumn. It is essentially a thanksgiving celebration to the Almighty God (*Pathen*) for the gift of a new crop which is visible as the harvest is imminent. The substance of the festival is the ritual of *changlhakou* (literally calling upon the spirit of paddy) signifying a prayer for the abundance of paddy (the staple food of the people). The rest that follow these two initial rituals like traditional games and sports, food and drink, etc., are only accidentals to the festival. The perennial values embedded in this festival are the spirit of gratitude to God the giver of all good gifts. It also shows the deep religiosity of the tribe.

Diplomatic Feast: Gives Religious and Social Identity

Among the Nagas, there is what is known a **Diplomatic feast**. It is a rare feast because it is held among feuding or warring villages to sheathe the sword and maintain friendly relations.[17] The Mao Nagas call this festival *Aso koto* which means a covenant of solidarity meal."[18] The perennial value of such a festival would be that though as human beings people into conflict against each other, they are also people who are willing to forgive and forget the wrongs done to them. It is religiously important and socially too. As the saying goes "to err is human, but to forgive is divine." Thus the festival gives the religious identity of the tribe as well as the social identity. Forgetting a festival like this can also mean forgetting its value.

Festivals of Merit: Social Identity

Festivals of merit are quite common to many tribes. For the Kukis the main festivals of merit are. *Sa-ai* and *Chang-ai*. Tarun Goswami calls *Sa-ai* as the *Hunter's Ritual*, and Chang –Ai as the *Ritual of victory over*

Paddy.[19] According to Goswami, the word *ai* means subjugation.[20] I must confess that the exact meaning of the word is unclear. It is an old Kuki word, not much in use these days. Goswami's interpretation may have some significance in the sense that *ai* signifies the personalization of the success, making it one's very own, as if were.[21] William Shaw mentions a third festival ritual called *Chon* which is "the mostly highly prized feast of the lot and can only be performed by those who have done the *Sa-Ai* three times. The significance *Sa-ai* is honour to the man for his skills in hunting as well as thanksgiving and prayer for his continued success in hunting.

The festival of *Chang-Ai*[22] belongs to women. In traditional Kuki society, cultivation of the field was largely left to the responsibility of the women folk.[23] William Shaw is right in saying that "this is a feast to the entire village and is the only known ceremony in which a Thadou/Kuki woman plays the leading part."[24] Goswami's assertion that, "amidst the Kukis the housewife is considered to be the owner of the paddy"[25] too is correct. The significance of the ritual is first of all to thank God for the gift of abundance of paddy to the family and to pray for its continued abundance. It is also to honour the mother of the family whose main role it is to cultivate and keep the family sufficient food. This honour of the woman of the family is not only for this life but also in the life after. Such a woman who has celebrated this ritual is not troubled by *Khulsamnu*[26] at the gate of the *Mithikho*. When such a woman dies she is also accorded the privilege of *langa kilap* (her body placed on a palanquin is carried back and forth in the court yard of the house nine times before burial). The social function of these rituals of merit is by the performance of these rituals which are expensive, the person has to feed the whole village for two to three days, he or she becomes like everybody else. The ritual is against hoarding of wealth and fostering egalitarianism in the tribe.

Among the Naga tribes too, the rituals of the feast of merit is widely celebrated. The Mao Nagas, in fact, celebrate several feasts of merit and those who have celebrated these festivals wear special shawls of social distinction. [27] The social function of this ritual is the same in all the tribes. These lavished celebrations by the well-to-do make them like all others. The rituals of these festivals inculcate the value of egalitarianism imbedded in the culture of tribals. Its philosophy holds that wealth is not for hoarding but for sharing.

Myths of Origin: Identity Signatures

The myth of the origin of the *Kuki-Chin-Mizo* tribes says that they came out of a cave in the earth, *khula pen*. This unites them and gives them identity. The hardships they had to overcome before they reached their present homeland are something comparable to what the Israelites went through the desert before they reach their Promised Land.[28]

The myth of origin of the Naga tribes which says originally they migrated from somewhere in the Far East and came to a place called *Makhel* in present day Manipur (Senapati District), and from here they were dispersed in different directions to their present homes is also something that unites all the Naga tribes.[29] For the *Khasi* tribe of Meghalaya, the myth of their origin is believed to be from *U Hynniew Trep U Hynniew Skum* (Seven Huts and Seven Nests) which God created and put in these beautiful hills which is called by the name "*Ka Ri Lum Khasi*."[30] A golden bridge grew on the top *U Lum Sohpetbneng* (The Navel of the Peak of Heaven) and became a ladder of communication between man and God. Thus, *Tip-Briew Tip-Blei* (knowing man and knowing God became the heart of Khasi religion and spirituality.[31] These examples of tribal myths are examples of identity giving and enhancing myths which control the lives and goals of tribal communities even today.

I have illustrated the signatures of identity through celebrations of some festivals and myths of origin. The same can be shown with ideas, values, institutions, values, etc., that are characteristic of a tribe or community. What is important is to make sure that the values enshrined in these traditions are made clear. Only can we say that our culture is our identity.

Cultural Tradition and Renewal

Culture is thus, 'webs of significance spun' by human beings, or ideas, laws, values, institutions, etc., characteristic of a human society. Hence culture is a human creation, and after they have become characteristic of a society they are handed down from one generation to the next and they become traditions (from the Latin word *tradere*, to hand over). In the process of being handed down, they also undergo changes as human beings too change. The changes that have taken place in human societies, is not just because it is fashionable to change, but because it is part of renewal of our lives and also a response to the progress human beings have made as regard the human sciences. The question is how should this change take place? Should it be left to chances or should be done in a planned way? Our humble proposal is that cultural changes should not be left to external forces like the powerful market forces of the multinational companies of today. The right people to guide us through a panned change are the social scientists. Accelerated changes have taken place among the indigenous cultures of the Northeast. Let us hope it is not too late to make a well-planned change.

Verrier Elwin, the renowned anthropologist, appointed by Nehru as adviser on tribals affairs in 1953, especially as regards the Northeastern Frontier Agency (NEFA), now Arunachal Pradesh, had advocated that tribals should change with what he called 'a tribal touch' or 'tribal bias' which he explains in details thus:

> A 'tribal touch' or 'tribal bias' means that we must look, if we can, at things through the tribal eyes and from the tribal point of view. We must find out what means most to them. We must see that they do in fact get a square meal; we must save them from the exploiters who still invade their villages, and ensure that in the future they will be in a position to administer and develop their own areas.

A tribal bias means that we recognize and honour their way of doing things, not because it is old or picturesque but because it is theirs, and they have as much right to their own culture and religion as anyone else in India. It means that we must talk their language, and not only the language that is expressed in words but the deeper language of the heart. It means that we will not make the tribes ashamed of their past or force a sudden break with it, but that we will help them to build upon it and grow by a natural process of evolution. It does not mean a policy of mere preservation; it implies a constant development and change, a change that in time will bring unbelievable enrichment, as there is ever closer integration in the main stream of India life and culture.[32]

I think, these thoughts of Elwin make it clear that he was a man who knew the tribals well[33] and spoke the language of their heart too. He was also echoing the principles of his mentor, Jawaharlal Nehru, especially the first principle: "Tribal people should develop along the lines of their own genius, and the imposition of alien values should be avoided." This is how human beings and societies should change themselves, not through external forces but from within their own cultural milieu. One can hardly disagree with this basic principle. The task ahead is not easy, as Elwin himself confessed: "how to give the tribes the good things of our life without destroying the good things of theirs, ... To reconcile these two aims, to develop, yet not to destroy, is not easy but I believe it can be done."[34]

What Elwin was advocating in the early or mid-fifties is what we are trying to do for tribal Christians today in terms of inculturation or contextualization. They should be Christians without giving up their tribal cultural heritage. They have received a foreign version of Christianity. Now they should make a tribal version of Christianity. The same principle can be applied to any other activity. For example, education is a process of which starts with what the students know and builds upon what they have.[35]

It is probably beyond the scope of one seminar and much less of one paper to spell out the way indigenous cultures should bring about changes to their cultural traditions. But one thing is clear that change should not be a complete disjunction with tradition, much less superimposition of an alien culture giving a parallel system that will never meet but an internal interface that would bring about a transformation that would enhance indigenous culture and life. The same holds true for the relationship between indigenous culture and modernity.

Indigenous Culture and Modernity

We have spoken about our cultural identity that defines us as a people and the way we should change while keeping the perennial values of our culture. The goal to the change is to reach the pearly gates of modernity. Modernity is usually associated with the use of the latest techniques, machines, ideas as compared to the previous stage which has become outdated. This idea of modernity is the technological sense of modernity. But we should also speak about modernity in human terms – to be the best human person we can be. As technological sciences have developed tremendously so have the human sciences. We have better understanding about the human person, the qualities and the capabilities he/she can develop. We also have a fuller understanding of human equality, the equality between men and women. As many of the indigenous tribes or most of them, are Christians, they are inheritors of the laws of Christ. Our customary or traditional laws must also be transformed by life-enhancing values of the Gospel of Jesus Christ.

In a study of 14 tribes[36] by the *Northeastern Indian Social Research Centre* (NESRC) referred to above says that "many tribal communities are re-asserting their identity through their customary law..." and they are falling back on "customary law as the defining character of their uniqueness and distinctive lifestyle. However, the domain of customary law is a contested terrain. On one side, most tribes consider their customary law intrinsic to their identity and regard it as the epitome of their culture. On the other, while going back to it many of them give it a fundamental interpretation, especially on the gender issue and re-interpret it from the male perspective alone. Thus despite its relevance and continuing hold on society, customary laws are challenged by women groups and others. They desire to bring about changes in customary law in order to make them gender just."[37]

This is the crux of the problem. Unless we can bring about a gender just society, we cannot claim to reach modernity by our capacity to avail ourselves of the latest modern machines and tools. We must also be a society practices the best results of the progress in human sciences. According to the findings of the study mentioned "gender discrimination in education is almost non-existent as regards primary education, but in higher education, some tribes need to improve upon it.[38] There is a demand for change in inheritance rights. In the two matrilineal tribes of Meghalaya, men are demanding the right of inheritance. But in the other 12 twelve tribes, women are the ones asking for inheritance rights.[39] We often attribute the changes in our traditional laws to our conversion to Christianity. But in a book, *Essays on Christianity in Northeast India*, Frederick S. Downs says that social changes brought about by Christianity to the tribals in Northeast India were almost minimal. He says: "the basic social customs related to marriage, family relationships, inheritance, decision-making procedures and the management of the village and its lands were accepted and continued to function within the Christian community."[40] Another area of worry in the customary law of many tribes is the denial of maintenance to women in the case of divorce. Much needs to be done also as regards the political rights of women.[41] Some of the recommendations of the study are: Men should share in the household chores. Women should have a better access for higher education. Women should be encouraged for employment in service sector. They should also be encouraged to be entrepreneurs. Changes in laws of inheritance in favour of women should also be done.[42]

There are many customary laws in favour of women in most tribes too, but some of them have been misinterpreted and practised not in accordance with the spirit of the customary law. In the Kuki customary law, all the male relations of one's mother's clan are addressed '*pu*' (usually translated as uncle but it has a much deeper and respectful sense than uncle and this is to give honour to one's mother. The practice of the so-called bride-price was also originally meant to honour women. For example, for the Haokip clan, the bride-price was ten (10) *mithuns*. *Mithun* was the most precious domestic animal and it was a way of saying that a daughter is ten times as precious a *mithun*.

It was never meant to be practised literally. In fact, the full term is *man le mol* (a *merism*, two words used to describe one reality. *Man* by itself means price and *mol* has no meaning in itself. The combination of the two gives the idea that the so-called bride-price is not to be understood as the price of a commodity. Some tribes, in the name simplification put the bride price higher for a beautiful girl and less for a less beautiful one making them like commodities. This is not the spirit of the custom.

Though the customary laws of many tribes discriminate against women, the customary laws of tribals as regards their relation to each other, to nature and the land are something that can be described as modern. Tribal culture in broadly described as that which includes "extraordinary values of solidarity with nature, egalitarianism, a non-competitive collaboration with one another, and a filial (not mercantile) relationship with the land"[43]. Modernity in terms of technical capability can reduce the world to smithereens in seconds, but if it decides to survive, the most modern way, tribal culture as described above "offers a valuable alternative to the rampant individualism, unchecked greed, aggressive competiveness and a growing alienation from nature which is leading the post-modern world to nuclear and ecological disaster."[44] In this tribal communities have to be faithful to their culture. This is the reason why the recent Earth Summit in Rio (20-22 June 2012)[45] opted for sustainable development and green economy. The indigenous way of managing their natural resources is exactly what the Rio summit has opted for.[46]

I think, the indigenous communities of Northeast are quite smart in catching up with modernity especially in the use and possession of the latest technological advancement can offer. In this age of science and technology, they should also strive to be scientists, engineers, mechanics and technocrats. To learn to use what other scientists and technocrats have produced is the easier path; to learn to be a technocrat is the more challenging one. Technological advancement is not reserved for any community. It can be done by anyone who is willing to take up the challenge. Another downside of the craze for the latest of things is that in the process of trying to avail themselves of the latest things, they have probably thrown overboard some of their hallowed traditional cultural values. They seem to be too preoccupied with measuring their worth in terms of per capita income. They should also learn to measure their status in terms of their worth as human beings and persons. In this respect, indigenous communities should fall back to their hallowed traditional values of 'extraordinary solidarity with nature and 'their filial relationship with the land' (not mercantile. No modernity will be against it. Their social value of egalitarianism and of non-competitive collaboration will make every civilization more life enhancing. While they have to improve upon some of their customary laws to make them gender just, they have to be faithful to be more human and to be fully human is to be closer to the divine.

Endnotes

[1] Cf. Melville Pereira, *Gender Implications of Tribal Customary Law* (Guwahati: Northeastern Social Research Centre, 2015), 3. There are other examples. The grouping into one *Zeliangrong*of *Zemei*, *Liangmei* and *Rongmei*is questioned by some who argue for the distinct identity of its components.

[2] Cf. Gurudas Das, ed., *Research Priorities in Northeast India with Special Reference to Arunachal Pradesh* (New Delhi: Regency Publications, 2001),4.

[3] https://www.indiantribalheritage.org/?p=17554, Jawaharlal Nehru's "five principles" for the policy to be pursued vis-a-vis the tribals (Posted on 24/03/2015 by website administrator): (1) Tribal people should develop along the lines of their own genius, and the imposition of alien values should be avoided; (2) Tribal rights in land and forest should be respected;(3) Teams of tribals should be trained in the work of administration and development;(4) Tribal areas should not be over administered or overwhelmed with a multiplicity of schemes;(5) Results should be judged not by statistics or the amount of money spent, but by the human character that is evolved.

[4] Fred Inglis, *Culture* (Cambridge: Polity Press, 2004), 1.

[5] Cf. Judy Pearsall, ed., *The New Oxford Dictionary of English* (Oxford: Clarendon Press, 1998), 447.

[6] Lesley Brown, ed., *The New shorter Oxford English Dictionary Vol. I* (Oxford: Clarendon Press, 1993), 568.

[7] Clifford Geertz, *Interpretation of Cultures* (London: Fontana, 1993), 5.

[8] John Kilgallen, "The Christian Bible and culture, " *StudiaMissionalia* 44 (1995) 45

[9] Verrier Elwin, *The Tribal World of Verrier Elwin: An Autobiography* (New Delhi: Oxford University Press, 1964), 290.

[10] B. G. Verghese, *India's Northeast Resurgent: Ethnicity, Insurgency, Governance, Development* (Delhi: Konark Publishers, 1996), 285.

[11] For a detail treatment of the same, see Hemkhochon Chongloi, *Indoi: A Study of the Primal Kuki Religious Symbolism in the Hermeneutical Framework of Mircea Eliade* (Delhi: ISPCK, 2008) 183-192; see also Peter Haokip, "A Philosophy of Myths and Rituals: A Tribal Perspective," 9-10.

[12] W. Shaw, *Notes on the ThadouKukis* (Kohima: Published on behalf of the Govt. of Assam, 1929) 73, n. 1. Shaw says that it has a very close parallel in the *siapaioh* of the Kenyahs in Borneo (Hose and McDougall, *Pagan Tribes of Borneo*, II, 124). So far as he (Shaw) knows it is typical of the Kuki culture as distinct from the Naga. The most detailed study on this so far is that of Hemkhochon Chongloi, *Indoi: A Study of Primal Kuki Religious Symbolism in the Hermeneutical Framework of Mircea Eliade* (Delhi: ISPCK, 2008) referred to above.

[13] W. Shaw, *Notes*, 153 (Appendix G).

[14] Cf. W. Shaw, Notes, 153; P. Haokip, *Kuki Culture*, 44 (with a diagram of Indoi); see also H. Chongloi, Indoi, 192-204. William Shaw gives two pictures of Indoi and says that the items of Indoi for Singson clans differ (See Shaw, Notes, 152). However, there is hardly any Kuki practicing this Indoi ritual anymore and hence it is difficult to verify. But it is possible that variations do take place in the items used for the *Indoi*.

[15] W. Shaw, *Notes*, 153 (Appendix G); see also H. Chongloi, *Indoi*, 192-203.

[16] Cf. P. Haokip, "Eco-Theology and Spirituality: A Perspective of the Kuki Tribe," *Oriens Journal for Contextual Theology* III (2012) 77-89, esp. 83-86.

[17] Cf. Lotsüro, *The Nagas*, 18; see also A. Yonuo, *The Rising Nagas: A Historical and Political Study* (Delhi: Vivek Publishing House, 1974), 33.

[18] L. Neli, Christianity and Experiences of the Nagas (Unpublished B.Th Thesis (Pune: Janana Deepa Vidyapeeth, 1984), 3.

[19] Tarun Goswami, *Kuki Life and Lore* (Haflong: North Cachar Hills District Council, 1985) 115-172; see also Shaw, Notes, 74-76.

[20] Goswami, *Kuki Life*, 157.

[21] In the myth of Thimzin, universal darkness and flood, everything, even dead trees grew again. Even bones dead animals became alive again, but skulls of animals over which *sa-ai* ritual had been performed did not become alive again. Hence, it has some sense of subjugation.

[22] Cf. Goswami, *Kuki Life*, 157-176; see also Haokip, *Kuki Culture*, 37-38.

[23] Men do help in the initial clearing of the forest, planting and harvesting, but they have to see to other needs of the family like earning some cash, making the house and household tools, etc.

[24] Shaw, *Notes*, 74.

[25] Goswami, *Kuki Life*, 157.

[26] *Khulsamnu* is the name given to the woman who guards the gate of the Mithikho (village of the dead, Kuki heavenly abode) to check who can go in there or who cannot go in there.

[27] Angeline Lutsüro, *The Nagas: A Missionary Challenge* (Shillong: Vendrame Institute Publications, 2000),16-17.

[28] William Shaw, *Notes on ThadouKukis* (Kohima: Government of Assam, 1929) 24-32; see also Peter Haokip, *Kuki Culture and the Christian Message: Theologizing in the Context of Kuki Culture* (Unpublished M.Th thesis) (Pune: Jnana Deepa Vidyapeeth, 1979), 3-7.

[29] Angeline Lotsüro, *The Nagas: A Missionary Challenge* (Shillong: Vendrame Institute Publications, 2000), 6-9.

[30] H. O. Mawrie, *U Khasi bad la ka Niam* (Shillong: Ri Khasi Press, 1973), 48.

[31] Adlyn Mary Khyllep, *Spirituality of Ka Niam Tip-Briew Tip-Blei: Religion of Knowing Man and Knowing God of the Khasis* (Unpublished M. Th. Thesis) (Roma: PontificiaUniversitasUrbaniana, 1994).

[32] Elwin, *The Tribal World*, 245.

[33] Of his 64 years of life, he spent about twenty two years with the tribals of Central India and 11 years with the tribals of Northeast India.

[34] Verrier, *The Tribal World*, 303.

[35] Peter Haokip, "Building up the Local Church," in Thomas Manjaly, Peter Haokip, and James Thoppil, eds., *Towards Building Up the Local Church: Priestly Ministry for the 21st Century* (Shillong: Oriens Publications, 2004), 269.

[36] The tribes studied were: Khampti, Nyishi (Nishang, Nissi) (from Arunachal), Karbi, Bodo (from Assam, Puomai, Zou (from Manipur), Jaintia, Lyngngam (from Meghalaya), Mara (also known as Lakher) , Mizo (from Mizoram), Konyak, Sumi (from Nagaland), Halam, Riang (Reang (from Tripura) (Melville Pereira, *Gender Implications of Tribal customary Law* (Guwahati: Northeastern Social Research Centre, Guwahati, 2015), 3-4.

[37] Pereira, *Gender Implications*, 1.

[38] Pereira, *Gender implications*, 19.

[39] Pereira, *Gender Implications*, 20.

[40] Frederick S. Downs, "Christianity and Social Change in Northeast India," in Frederick Downs, *Essays in Christianity in Northeast India*, edited by Milton S. Sangma and David R. Syiemlieh (New Delhi: Indus Publishing Company, 1994), 189. Frederick S. Downs is the son of a medical missionary in the Garo Hills. He was born and brought up in Tura and is a renowned historian of the Church, especially of Northeast India. He is a member of Church History Association of India (CHAI) and authored the fifth volume of the church History of India series: *Christianity in Northeast India.*

[41] Pereira, *Gender Implications*, 20-21.

[42] Pereira, *Gender Implication*, 21-22.

[43] Cf. George M. Soares-Prabhu, "Tribal Values in India," *Jeevadhara* xxiv/140 (March 1994), 84.

[44] Soares-Prabhu, Tribal Values, 84.

[45] Cf. Pushpam Kumar, "A Promising Pathway: Rio + 30, Green Economy and India," *Down to earth: Science and Environment Fortnightly* (1-15 August 2012), 52.

[46] Peter Haokip, "Indigenous Resource Management for Sustainable Development," in Gautam Kumar Bera and K. Jose, *India's Traditional Wisdom and Indigenous Resource Management* (New Delhi: Abhijeet Publications in collaboration with *Sanskriti–* NEICER, Guwahati, 2014), 94-109.

Indeterminacy and Shifting Power Equations in the Northeast

Prof. Sivasish Biswas

The Northeast, celebrated as the anthropologist's paradise, has been 'gazed' at and 'structured' by researchers. It has become the hot-bed of politics, secessionism, insurgency, violence… Discrimination and otherization by the powers that be across decades, high-handed suppression, violation of human rights and fomenting of trouble from both outside and inside the border has not helped. This paper would attempt to look afresh at the Northeast as a multi-layered text where the most certain aspect is uncertainty: in day to day life and human relations, and the use of power tactics within communities as also vis-à-vis the 'Big Bad Outsider', the shadow-boxing with the 'other' from the context of the Northeast while remaining in a fluid relationship of Northeast-based-living-together. The existence of antagonism and acrimony has effectively camouflaged interesting bonding both between the outsider and insider, as also between insider and insider. Bonding and formation of Northeast identity again generates exclusion. The opposite forces counter each other like the centrifugal and centripetal forces that keep the world in place, and justify Derrida's consciousness of deconstruction. Being suspended in a liminal zone like the mythical Trishanku, this paper would 're'-present the indeterminacy and shifting power equations in the Northeast from my take of being neither an insider nor an outsider.

I'll try to re-present the Northeast in a way I have understood and experienced the Northeast, from my vantage point of an outsider-insider. I landed in the Northeast in search of job opportunity- and started teaching from 1987. That time was the hey-day of the ULFA Movement, preceded by the Bongal-khedao Movement, and my status of a 'Bahiragato' was very sensitive. An outsider is usually the target of suspect, rejection and often, abuse in the Northeast. But my position of a teacher and involvement with students have put me in a vantage point of being highly respected, and being accepted as almost an insider to their charmed circle. Hence I've coined this term 'outsider-insider'. My openness to diverse cultures and cultural practices, anytarian food preferences, religious beliefs and practice of such has, I guess, attracted them into accepting me. Contact with such different cultures have caused a sea-change in my bones. But yes- it is a very hybrid identity that I possess, a hybridization of cultures, and I guess I traverse the in-between liminal zone suspended like our mythical Trishanku.

When I am asked by my friends as to why I've stuck to the Northeast for 30-odd years, I answer: the most certain aspect that I like here is its uncertainty. Every moment there is something new. Every moment there is a change. Hence, with uncertainty as the certainty of my point of departure, let me try to represent the Northeast and its subtle power equations as they constantly shift and gel and shift again.

The Northeast as we know today is a geographical space connected with the Mainland by a chicken's neck between Siliguri and Alipurduar, and surrounded by Bhutan, China, Myanmar and Bangladesh. The name Northeast is a misnomer, a geographical pointer, a non-name rather than a name clubbing together the disparate identities of 7 sister-States of Assam, Arunachal Pradesh, Meghalaya, Nagaland, Mizoram, Manipur and Tripura. And now a distant cousin brother Sikkim is illogically attached to the Northeast. The 7-Sisters, apart from being predominantly Mongoloid, have numerous differences and political, cultural, religious, linguistic oppositions. It is wrong to club them under a blanket identity of the Northeast. They have migrated from China via Thailand or Myanmar or Tibet at various ages of history and have made it to what today is their home. Some tribes have retained more of their ethnicity than others. Some tribes have got hybridized and assimilated. Diversity has created different power equations between the tribes and made the Northeast a shifting tapestry of identity and tradition and culture.

The British incursions started into the tribal areas of the Northeast around 1850s. The Nagas and Mizos (then called Lushais) were known to be very dangerous head-hunters. Initially the British tried to keep these 'savage' people away. They had to take a special pass to enter into the non-tribal areas for the village markets, where they would buy salt and sugar, kerosene and cotton threads. By denigrating them as 'savages' who need to be excluded from the mainstream non-tribals, the British sowed the seeds of difference in a different way in the Northeast (not the Hindu-Muslim card), and latter violence and insurgency was conceived from an injured identity issue. Today the shifting power-equations demand non-tribals to apply for and procure an ILP (Inner Line Permit) for a very brief visit into Nagaland, Mizoram, and Arunachal Pradesh, and new demands for ILP are cropping up every day.

Confrontations took place at various times. The kidnapping of Mary Winchester in 1871 and murdering of her father at Alexandrapore Tea Estate bordering Mizoram is one landmark instance to cite- and the British pride and honour had to be salvaged. They sent a three-pronged attack deep into the Lushai Hills (as Mizoram was called at that time) and the girl was recovered almost one year later.

Missionary activities began in earnest thereafter. The tribal religious practices soon gave way before the organized preaching of Christianity. And Christian missionaries capitalized on exactly where the presence of the other two major religions had failed: they welcomed these 'savage' tribes with open arms, and then controlled their life-style and 'civilized' them. Unlike the Hindus and Muslims both of who have restrictions in food intake, the Christians were different in taking everything and thus they became accepted in a very sensitive area. I'm using these two politically improper terms 'savage' and 'civilized' knowingly, for the tribes referred to are so transformed and Anglesized today that it must be appreciated. In fact the modern attitude and sophistication of most tribes of the Northeast makes me wonder at their still preferring the tribal identity. The brutal practice of head-hunting is eliminated, the excess energy is tamed by the opiate of an organized religion and its rituals. Church going is enforced with heavy-handedness, and absenteeism is fined. The missionaries gave the Northeast tribes a religion which was up to 1947 the Master's religion, the Roman script for their language, and a pride in their identity which was aligned to the White Master.

There was no impact of the Independence Movement in the Northeast against the British. Rather, the famous Battle of Kohima between the Japanese and British Indian forces had the local Nagas fight for the British against the Japanese who were aligned to Netaji Subhas Chandra Bose.

The Naga demand for secession from India in the post-1947 political scenario set the tone for the Mizo appraisal for independence in 1966, the ULFA Movement in 1979 and widespread anti-India feelings all over the Northeast. It was no better with the Government using the Armed Forces with unlimited power which translated into horrendous excesses and rapes and killings, and the AFSPA is still operative. An unfortunate by-product was an aversion towards Hindi, a language linked to the armed forces. The attempts at subversion through guerilla warfare generously supported by our friends across the borders encircling the Northeast, political movements like the Manipuri lady Irom Sharmila Chanu's marathon fasting over the years, are ultimately bringing up the issue of an injured identity, a feeling of non-belonging or alienation, a suspicion and rejection of the Mainland Indian, a ventilation of the above in a single word in all the Northeast States designated to describe the hated outsider: Bahiragato, Vai, Parokh, Dkhar, Mayang. Within the same linguistic community, too, there is otherization: the Bengali from Kolkata is referred to as 'Calcatian' in Silchar which echoes of an Alsatian. But with the change of space, equations change. The Northeasterner is 'Chinky' or 'Chinese' or 'Nepalese' in the megalopolises like Delhi and Mumbai. The Silcharite Bengali is however very much welcome at Kolkata, where there are exclusive Sylheti colonies like Sribhumi.

Let us experience this Northeast from a short story from Manipur: Thaballei by Lamabam Viramani:

> I see a frightening figure coming slowly towards me. Thaballei! Not a shred of cloth on her body, her breasts smeared red. Nail marks had left no part of her breasts untouched..................... "Look Tai'bi, this body which I guarded with great care, for you, isn't it beautiful?"...... "These imprints left by various hands – you hate it as you do leftover food, don't you?" (*Viramani* 29)

Temsula Ao vividly describes a scene in 'The Last Song' where a military contingent attacks a group of villagers who had gathered to celebrate the opening of a new Church they had built. As they go berserk among the villagers beating them up and firing at them, a blind handicapped girl with a divine voice keeps on singing louder and louder in defiance. She and her mother who tries to shield her are brutally raped and killed and the Church is set on fire.

> Libeni was now frantic. Calling out her daughter's name loudly, she began to search for her in the direction where she was last seen being dragged away by the leader. When she came upon the scene at last, what she saw turned her stomach: the young Captain was raping Apenyo while a few other soldiers were watching the act and seemed to be waiting for their turn. (Ao 28)

It is in this scenario of rejection as an outsider that I landed, and within that I discovered another identity which is sacrosanct almost all over the Northeast, but a little more so in the most dominant and aggressively identity conscious tribes like the Mizos and the Nagas: the teacher. It is the reverence for a teacher, and also the similarity of a teacher and a preacher from a pulpit which is a major acceptability criteria.

Some folk traditions or stories get recorded as cited from Temsula Ao. Others are just there and probably no one might write them down.

In Arunachal Pradesh, apart from Buddhism and Christianity, there exists an animist faith called Donyi Polo, or the cult of the Sun and the Moon. People who follow the Donyi Polo faith have the image of the sun and the moon painted on their gates. Similarly, among the Karbis of Assam, the traditional faith is Sansari. Pronounced hanghari, it translates into the Cult of Garhasthya. Belief in spirits, mediation through priests and some very interesting practices can be identified. There are tales of a 'tiger-man', a man or a spirit taking the shape of a tiger who metes out justice or takes revenge. A slaughtered cock indicates the future status of a marriage from the way it falls. Engagement suffices for a couple to live together and have a family, but in case they have a daughter they have to marry before the marriage of the daughter. People cling to identities, and also lose them as space changes. Many Karbis in Nowgong and Tezpur cannot speak Karbi; same with Hmars and Mizos in Diphu. New religious cults grow: like the 'Lokhimon' in Karbi Anglong.

Talking of Assam immediately brings up images of the famous folk dance 'Bihu'. It has become iconic of Assamese culture and stories and songs and every aspect of life. But the prestigious Brahmins of Assam who were brought on invitation by the Ahom kings from North India often don't subscribe to this dance. The hallmark Bihu dance celebrates fertility and harvest of the land, and by extension, it becomes a courtship dance. The boys play on drums, cymbals and 'shingas' or horns, while the girls gyrate in an enchanting and tantalizing manner with an ever-present smile of invitation playing on their lips to which the boys respond with their overtures of love through song. The banter continues and can culminate in love and marriage; if disallowed, marriage happens by elopement.

The tradition of marriage by elopement happens all across the Northeast cutting across all racial/tribal, linguistic or religious identities. The presence of the Mainland Indian attitude/s makes the Northeasterners reticent to express such practices even though their very identity and culture is based on such. But the lilting Bihu songs are embedded with the motif of love and the lovers' bid to get married! In Mizoram, courtship is a long-drawn game. The girls would be weaving and making nicotine water in the evenings when it is time for her to receive male suitors. Usually the old people/parents leave the house free in the evening and sit and chat in the village centre. But before the selection is made, usually, the interested boy feels shy or afraid to go and face the girl alone. He musters his friends and they all go in a group. The girl has to be equally civil to all and she offers them 'zu' i.e. rice beer, now frowned upon by the Christian fathers, tobacco to smoke, and nicotine water. They sit around the fire as the girl keeps on doing her work – weaving, etc. but the whole drama is a pretext to the grand finale when the choosing or acceptance takes place. If the girl comes to know and approves of the boy, or may be love has blossomed on a different branch and the girl inclines towards a different boy, she would offer them 'thinpui' or tea, but unlike other days, all cups except one would contain cold tea, and the one special cup would have hot tea! She would offer that hot tea to the 'tlangval' or unmarried boy of her choice and the decision is passed on and understood and accepted without a complain and no questions asked. In choosing and granting her favours, the Mizo 'nula' or maiden is totally free. And her Prince today would be slowly and proudly sipping the hot tea while the other hapless bachelors gulp down their cold tea and leave, to find better reception at a different parlour...

Among my students I have students from different communities of the Northeast who eloped and married. One such made me her adopted father- and I gave her away in marriage: probably, the only non-Mizo to be so honoured as 'Palal'! Amongst the Mizos, the eloped lovers remain in hiding for three days and then send a friend to inform the parents about their hideout. Usually the parents and guardians from both sides come and fume in anger, which is their cut-out duty as per tradition, then they accept them back home and the marriage dates are announced. The wedding cards mention very importantly- whether the marriage is to be held inside the Church or outside on the porch: because now with the fusion of tradition and Christianity, in cases like elopement or pre-marital pregnancy, the marriage cannot be held within the Church. Further, the bride is disallowed the prestige of wearing a white bridal gown- a symbol of purity; so she usually wears a very attractive pink or blue or red!

Amongst Mizos, Nagas and the Arunachalee tribes there is a bride-price to be paid. Mizo women lament their price is the price of two buffaloes. The missionaries quantified the price of two 'mithuns' at 420 rupees and it remains. In pre-Christian times, the status, beauty and achievements of a girl used to attract higher price or more 'mithuns'. Christianity erased this ethnic practice as slaughtering these animals resembles the Hindu sacrifices.

A little attention needs to be given to a unique tribal custom among the Mizos regarding divorce and compensation for not marrying after an unmarried girl becomes pregnant: 'Ka ma chhe' or 'I divorce you' is the dreaded sentence Mizo women grow up fearing. And 'sawm man' or 'compensation' of just 40 rupees allows a man to go Scot free if he doesn't want to marry his pregnant girlfriend or even take care of the child.

A totally unique practice called 'Tlawmngaihna' gives a stamp of identity on the Mizo: not translateable, it means the epitome of exemplary conduct which is voluntarily rendered. Helping others in need is one aspect of such Tlawmngaihna. If there is a death in a family, the entire society comes down to help. The YMA or Young Mizo Association takes care of the mourning practices, the MHIP or Women's organization takes care of food for the family and tea for the visitors and mourners, and the burial is simplified to avoid financial pressure on the less privileged and entirely conducted by the YMA. During my stay I found the YMA helping in the Hindu cremations as well.

Among Arunachalees and Nagas, not very overtly today of course, polygamy is practiced. B.K. Bhattacharya's *Yaruingam* (1960) tells us the story of Ngathingkhui proposing to Sharengla to be his second wife. Probably the record is claimed by a Mizo with around 39 wives: Ziona Chana of Baktawang village in Mizoram!

Image: 'The world's biggest family: The man with 39 wives, 94 children and 33 grandchildren'

These details of their lives are not represented in literature. I got to know these by living with them. However, the 'Big Bad Outsider Syndrome' and resultant otherization would be the most important attitude of any Northeast people. But, there are exceptions to the outsider, and possibly by my status of a teacher I am accepted. It is my reading that the cultures and traditions of the peoples of the Northeast are so different from those in Mainland India that there is a feeling of otherization. The otherized Northeasterner is now otherizing the Mainlander in their own territory or home turf. The power equations shift as the geographical space shifts from Delhi to Kohima. It starts with the Mongoloid features- often referred to as Chinkies, Nepalese or Chinese. The Northeast peoples, when they venture out to the Mainland, feel marginalized and thus insecure in the Mainland. Their food habits are frowned upon as aberrant- many peoples in the Northeast eat whatever moves- hence they are abused and targeted as uncultured. I tell my holy friends that cow's milk contains the sin of being snatched away from the hungry calf; there are live organisms in curd; the silk we boast of comes out of silkworm larvae boiled to death. Let us accept these as different food preferences / practices. Linguistic difference is a big factor. Hindi is not spoken or understood widely. Ironically, the very devout and exclusivist Christian Mizos unknowingly are chanting Sanskrit Saraswati Vandana as part of their Hindi training after 800 posts of Hindi teachers was given to Mizoram! Being identified with the outsider who carries a baggage of no good- 'he will cheat us', 'molest our women', and 'show his cultural superiority', Hindi is always unpopular and terms like 'Vai Sipai' (Jacob 99) or soldiers of the Big Bad Outsider are used by Malsawmi Jacob in *Zorami*. Interestingly, 'Sahib' though a Hindi word, stands for the European Master. And English language in Mizoram is the respected language of power and awe: 'Sap tawng'! Again, Hindi is very welcome in Arunachal Pradesh due to their threat perception from China and hegemony of Assam.

I have therefore three takes on the shifting power equations:

1. The obvious oppositional attitude which would be the Big Bad Outsider Syndrome! Stereo-typing ultimately does not represent the truth. All outsiders are not like the young Captain from Temsula Ao's *'The Last Song'*. All Northeasterners too do not subscribe to this attitude, but are wary of the outsider.

2. My position as a teacher which has made me accepted. Thus I know about various practices which are carefully kept under wraps from the outsiders as the untold story.

3. Inspite of the Big Bad Outsider Syndrome, acceptance and hybridization: both miscegenation and cultural, is a living presence and for that I must share 3 experiences:

a. Travelling by Sumo from Aizawl to Silchar, I had a Mizo girl Mapuii and her daughter Venii next to me. There was a Muslim labourer, easily identifiable by appearance at the far off seat, who was often turning his attention towards me talking to Mapuii. At Bhaga Bazar on the plains of Assam near Silchar, Mapuii went to a roadside 'rice hotel', and returned clad in a black burqha! When asked, she giggled that she was going to her in-laws' at Hailakandi. Instantly I understood that the Muslim guy must be her husband. She said that her name was Ameena now. Among other things, I asked her whether the rice and fish fare at Hailakandi suits her. She giggled! What about the staple Mizo diet of 'vawksa-rice chaw'(ie.

pork rice meal)? She denied vehemently: it is considered as dirty and strictly off-menu in Hailakandi...but she would make up once back to Aizawl. 'What about Abdul?'- was my next question. She replied: 'Abdul doesn't touch pork at Hailakandi ; but at Aizawl, Joseph loves vawksa!' She would catch a few stray dogs for free and bring back too.

b. One of my friend's daughter in Aizawl had fallen in love with a Hindu boy from Dehradun. They married as per Hindu customs. They had a son, too. Because of severe resistance, they stayed away from Mizoram. But once they visited the girl's family. There was a Christian marriage after due conversion of the 'Vai' or outsider non-Mizo son-in-law. They returned back and the girl donned the sari again and the red vermillion returned on her forehead. They relocated to New York and sent air tickets for parents on both sides to visit them. In a multicultural foreign country like the States, who was the outsider and which culture prevailed? My own cousin sister, married to an American in California, goes to Church at Christmas and attends the Bengali Durga Puja in October...and no questions asked. With the space of 'home' or roots shifting beyond borders, identities and power equations change.

c. I met a Naga lady on a train to Dimapur. She had a little angel of a daughter, and a middle aged Muslim husband. Failing to remain politely aloof, I asked her regarding her preferring a Bengali Muslim to a Naga guy. She said that she had had differences with her Naga husband; so she walked out. And this Bengali Muslim, also referred to as 'Mia' in the Northeast, takes care of her business, doesn't drink, and she is having a secure family life.

Hybrids are not well accepted in the Northeast. But as numbers grow, a new identity asserts its presence. In Nagaland's Dimapur, the inter-marriages between Naga girls to Bengali Muslim men or 'Mias', have given rise to the 'Nagamia' syndrome. They typically straddle the shadow line, and their identities shift: in Nagaland, their parentage is traced to the Naga mother; outside Nagaland, to the non-Naga father. And now Nagamia poetry is coming up!

In attempting to wind up, the Northeast has been misunderstood, mismanaged and constructed as a zone of distrust with a sense of marginalization and otherization. If these jargons invoke colonialism, now reverse colonialism is on. Also, an in-between hybrid space has emerged. The very identity Northeast attempts to stereotype. I would prefer that the so-called non-name 'Northeast' is erased and the differences and diversity recognized and honoured. The Vaishnavite Manipuri and Assamese are not Mizos or Nagas or Khasis; the Mizos and the Nagas, inspite of having similarities are different. Interestingly, while the Mizos fight shy of referring to their head-hunting past, the Nagas celebrate and show-case it. One has to visit the Hornbill festival site or model village to experience it. I am sure that acceptance, hybridization and assimilation are going to continue being natural processes. A Bengali Air India Commander lives happily with his Mizo wife in Kolkata. The Bengali-Mizo duo, Doctors Banerjee and Banerjee accepted each other while doing autopsy on a human cadaver at a Medical College in West Bengal. We can find them at Kolkata and Barddhaman, and on flights to Aizawl.

Other winds of change are blowing. Education is one releasing-factor: releasing people from narrow cliches of identity. V.S.Naipaul, Salman Rushdie, Amitav Ghosh, Amartya Sen...the list is endless. We can add Priyanka Chopra, too. Health requirements are next. No one checks out the identity of a surgeon when there is imminent danger of losing a dear one! A bottle of blood by an 'other' is very much welcome too!..and the blood is not of a different colour or content really. As borders are opening up, borders are also becoming shadow lines under globalization. Economic needs pushed forward by the information explosion, acceptance of Hindi serials like "Saas bhi kabhi Bahu thi" so much so that they are translated in Mizo and viewed twice, Saraswati Vandana is acceptable because it ensures a job of Hindi teacher, Abdul considers pork 'haraam' at Hailakandi but enjoys it as Joseph when Mapuii serves him 'vawksa' lovingly, very much like the doctors Banerjee & Banerjee, and a few thousand examples remain 'untold stories' which anticipate a hybrid, multicultural 'chutnification' (Rushdie 643).

References

Ao, Temsula. 'The Last Song' in *These Hills Called Home: Stories From A War Zone*. New Delhi,: Penguin Books, 2006.

Bhattacharya, B.K. *Yaruingam*. Guwahati: Christian Literature Centre, 1984.

Jacob, Malsawmi. *Zorami*. Bangalore: Primalogue Publishing Media Pvt. Ltd, 2015.

Rushdie, Salman. *Midnight's Children*. London: Vintage Books, 2006.

'The world's biggest family: The man with 39 wives, 94 children and 33 grand-children' from Mail Online News, By DAILY MAIL REPORTER CREATED: 17:04 GMT, 19 February 2011. https://www.dailymail.co.uk/news/article-1358654/The-worlds-biggest-family-Ziona-Chan-39-wives-94-children-33-grandchildren.htmlAccessed on Wednesday, Dec 12th 2018 6AM.

Viramani, Lamabam. 'Thaballei' in *The Heart of the Matter*. Northeast Writers' Forum, Katha, New Delhi, 2004.

Towards Unity with Northeast through Cultural Understanding: A Phenomenological Overview

Prof. V. C. Thomas

This paper has three parts. First I discuss the general phenomenological principles involved in what is called cultural understanding. The principles I use are from both Husserl and Heidegger. Some of those principles are the notion of the (life) world, the concept of horizon, the theory of inter-subjectivity and the like. In the second part I wish to dwell upon the Northeast from an anthropological and/ or sociological point of view. One limitation that I have here is that Northeast culture is not a part of my lived experience although I do have a number of friends from the Northeast and I visited Northeast Hill University (NEHU) at Shillong and Assam Central University at Silchar several times for different academic activities. I wish to apply the phenomenological principles elucidated here to the context of Northeastern culture and say that that culture is not an isolated one rather it falls within the parameters of general phenomenological principles dealing with culture in general. In the third part I try to show that within the unity of India, every state has its peculiarity and individuality and whatever uniqueness that Northeast exhibits is an expression of its distinctiveness.

From the scholastic philosophical point of view what an individual is incommunicable, "individuum est ineffable." If the individual is ineffable, from the perspective of scholasticism, then intercultural understanding is problematic. However, from a phenomenological perspective, surely, an intercultural understanding is possible. But to elucidate this point, both (Edmund) Husserl and (Martin) Heidegger speak of the (life) world, meaning, horizon and the like. There are, indeed, differences in their elucidation of all these concepts. In the final analysis, Heidegger speaks of the interest world, the world in which I am engrossed. Why am I interested and engrossed in the world? It because the world is relevant to me. Husserl's standpoint of the world begins from the notion of horizon. It may be noted that in as much as Heidegger is not speaking just not about the world but about the world relevant to me, Husserl is examining not just the world but the life-world. The world, or to be precise, the life-world, is the horizon of all meanings. Husserl's treatment of life-world is the logical culmination of his investigation into the notion of the world which began around 1900 when he was working on his book *Logical Investigations*. In the course of his exploration of the world, he began to lay emphasis on the notion of the world as it is given to us in our immediate experience. What we immediately experience are the things around us, they are not isolated phenomena. Every material thing, manifesting itself in our experience, reveals a horizon which is spatially and temporally extended. The world is the horizon of all our experiences, horizon of all our attitudes. Things experienced manifest themselves in a certain horizon. The fundamental contention of horizon is that the known leads us to the unknown. What is now unknown will reveal itself, disclose itself or manifest itself as something known and recognized, provided we put in a little effort to discover it, to uncover it, to ascertain it. We start our pilgrimage to the unknown from what is already known for what is already known leads us to the unknown. Let me give one or two examples.

For centuries together scientists and philosophers believed that atom is the final point of matter beyond which no further division is possible of atom. In the language of phenomenology, it would mean to say that atom does not have any further horizons. But towards the end of 19th century, scientists declared that atom is composed of some finer elements like electron, neutron and proton. And, authorities of science recognized the value of the contributions of Dr J. J. Thompson and awarded him the Nobel Prize in 1897. In the language of phenomenology, it means that atom revealed its horizons in relation to electron, neutron and proton. Thereafter, for a long time scientists thought that it was the end of the story. However, a few years later, another group of scientists discovered sub-atomic particles like quarks and that would mean further revelation of horizons. Then another group of scientists found out that there are six different kinds of quarks, and thus new and novel horizons revealed themselves. The recent Large Hadron Collider experiments revealed more and more horizons of atom. In fact, Sartre's notion of trans-phenomenality of phenomenon refers precisely to this horizon aspect. Instead of looking into such high sounding and complicated examples, let us look at a very ordinary and simple example. I stand at the entrance of this college. I see its façade. Although I see only the façade of it now, basing myself on the façade and knowing well that this is a college, I wish to explore what the façade indicates. When I begin to move about, I see the class rooms, the teachers' rooms, the office of the principal, the labs, the library, the play grounds, the canteen, the hostels, the residential quarters, and the like. All these facilities constitute the horizons of the façade. Having arrived at the entrance of the college and after seeing the façade, I put in a little more effort to discover what the façade constitutes and what it constitutes is its horizons. While seeing the façade, its horizons are as such unknown. They reveal themselves to me when I make some efforts to discover or unearth them. And, Husserl's contention in this context is this: everything is given along with its horizon, nothing is given devoid of its horizon, and the world is the horizon of everything experienced and experience-able. The world from the Husserlian stand point is not a physical, material and concrete entity. The world cannot be perceived unless things are experienced. In other words the world cannot be experienced the way I experience different things. Rather, in and through the experience of things, the world is perceived. It means that the world cannot be an object of our everyday ordinary experience. I perceive or grasp the world as the horizon of things that I experience. In the experience of individual things, the world as horizon is co-present for the world is co-perceived as the horizon of things that I experience. This contention enables Husserl to say that the world (and for that matter the horizon) is pre-given, i.e. it is always and already given. It means that unless and until the world already exists as object of perception, it cannot be given or cannot exist. And, from that perspective, as Heidegger puts it, the world is a priori as well.

I wish to make a slight diversion here as I wish to speak of Wittgenstein's notion of language games in the context of intercultural understanding. From the perspective of language games, cultural or intercultural understanding is like a language game. The intricacies of a game can be understood only by participants who are actively involved in it. Similarly, a culture can be understood well only by those for whom it is a lived experience; only by those for whom that particular culture is a life-world. Life-world is an intuitive world. It is a pre-scientific world. It is a world of my immediate experience. Science makes abstractions and generalizations. Abstractions distances oneself from experiences. The experienced world is subjective. It is subjective, not in the sense mind dependent but in the sense of meaningful to me. It is the everyday world. It is the world in which I play and work, in which I study and sleep. It is the world in which I ordinarily live and spend my time. It is the world in which I pray and seek the forgiveness of the Almighty for my sins. It is the world which is far, far away from the mathmatico-logico-objectivist world Descartes, Newton and Galileo. What I am speaking here is of my world, the life-world.

The most serious contention of Husserl here is that everything is given along with its horizon; nothing is given devoid of its horizon. Horizon constitutes the world. This being the case, the world cannot be perceived the way I experience things. I have sense perception of things around me. The world, being the meaning of these sense perceptions, can be grasped, only intellectually and conceptually. In and through the experience of these things, I encounter or perceive the world. It means that the world is co-perceived as the horizon of things that I experience. It means that the word, as horizon, is pre-given it is always already given. Unless and until the world is already given, things cannot be grasped but only perceived by sense organs. But sense organs cannot experience the world; they can only experience things. For, the world as horizon is the meaning of things perceived.

The life-world has an inter-subjective character. Technically speaking, whatever I have said so far is what is called the sphere of "owness". This sphere of owness is not a domain in opposition to the other. The other is not an antinomy to me, rather the other is my fulfilment. The other is complimentary to me from the point of phenomenology in general. This is all the more so in the context of family, friendship and intimate circles. On account of the complimentary character of the other, I mirror the other and the other mirrors in me. I see my reflection in the other. The other is not alien to me; the other is not a stranger to me, but rather the other is the one with whom I have intimate relationships, I have cherished friendship with the other. The other is my brother and protector. The question raised by Cain to Yahweh (Gen 4:9), "Am I my brother's keeper?" is answered affirmatively and positively by Husserl. These principles that I have elucidated here is also applicable to the Northeast as well. We do notice intimate relationships and friendships everywhere. True, there are conflicts and discords in different places. But they are all being reduced and minimized to a great extent now. They are nothing compared to the world wars and other major conflicts that the world had faced in the recent past. The world is moving slowly, gradually towards that idealized vision of the world of Husserl and other great minds. From this perspective, Sartre's phenomenology of the other cannot find much place in our scheme of things. It may be noted that Sartre could not practice his social philosophy even in his personal dealings and in his public life. I specially refer to his lifelong friendship with Simone de Beauvoir which was based on mutual friendship and intimate relationship. He also had very close personal friendship with Bertrand Russell with whom he worked closely for international peace. It appears to me Sartre rejected his existential philosophical position regarding the treatment of the other when he gave an interview to the press when former Pakistani Prime Minister, Mr. Zulficar Ali Bhutto, was hanged by the then Pakistani government. My point is this. The Husserlian phenomenological position regarding the notion of the other has a universal validity and comprehensive legitimacy.

Let me instantiate my position with respect to Northeast tribe. In fact, the word tribe was used for the first time in the history of the human race in the Bible (vide the Book of Genesis, Ch. 49, 16 and 23.). Jacob, before his death, was giving his last blessings to his 12 children, starting from the eldest to the youngest. The word tribe was used by him in that salvific context, not as a descriptive or a prescriptive terminology but as redemptive expression. Even in this redemptive context, the terminology has a reference blood relation and acquaintances. But contemporary use, the term tribe has a lot of differences although there are some similarities. The term tribe, as we understand it today, is a name imposed upon the indigenous people, i.e. the most early and original natives or settlers of a particular place, by the outsiders who came into the midst of natives as social works, missionaries, political and social activists and government administrators from the beginning of the British colonial era or even earlier. This means that the term tribe was closely linked to administrative, social and political considerations. It has also be pointed out by some anthropologists and ethnographers that the term tribe was used in the sense the expression barbarian, meaning one who does not speak our language. The Romans who spoke Latin used the term barbarian for the first time to characterize the Gauls (mostly the present day French people) who spoke ancient variants of French. The term therefore means people who do not belong to our civilization, i.e. uncivilized and uncultured. This means people who came from outside claimed superiority, high quality life styles and exclusiveness. Once the outsiders positioned themselves at a high pedestal, they started looking for criteria to distinguish indigenous people from their own assumed superior position. Some such criteria were the geographical isolation of the indigenous people, the kind of technology used by the indigenous people in their everyday life especially in agriculture, the general backwardness of the natives, their language, their religious practices, etc. Unfortunately, these criteria were neither clearly formulated, nor systematically applied. Therefore, strikingly different sets of people were jointly called tribals. In fact some early ethnographers identified caste and tribe, they used both these expressions synonymously exhibiting shamelessly their ignorance about caste and tribe.

Some British anthropologists pointed out at one time that tribals lived in complete isolation from the rest of population and without any interaction or relation with others. They also showed that at one time tribes were a stage of the society that lacked positive traits of modern society; i.e. tribals were considered simple people who lived in a back word society and they were fundamentally illiterate. However, now the tribal society is no more considered to be so. Now it is shown that there is a close interaction between larger Indian, nay, Hindu society and the tribals.

A little while ago I happen to say that the so called infiltrators used several terminologies to characterize the tribals such as indigenous people (i.e. original settlers), aboriginals (i.e. inhabiting in the land from very early times), *vanavasi* (i.e. forest dwellers) and many other such terminologies based on the different physical features, language, religion, customs, social organizations, the place where they live, and the like. Unfortunately none of the terminologies fully or truly describe them. The primary characteristic of all such terminologies were marginalization, i.e. telling such people that you are not in the main stream. This means that telling them indirectly that "you are an excluded people", "we are keeping you out", and "you are prohibited from entering into our group". It means that all these terminologies had a subtle sense repugnance, a faint taste of hatred, a cunning touch of aversion. All the terminologies were used in the sense of barbaric, savage, primitive and uncivilized. They were all to a great extent derogatory expressions, used to tell the local people that they were unrefined, uncultured, uncouth and uncivilized people. The irony is this: they all came from outsiders who came from somewhere who did not even shake their little finger to learn or study the local people, their customs or habits. Yet they claimed to be the masters, superiors, overlords. No alien master is going to accept the contention that his culture, civilization, ideology, societal life style are poorer than that of the natives. Without realizing any of these negative implications and harmful ramifications of those expressions, the tragedy was that the indigenous people in the course of time appropriated and internalized the meaning and contention of such terminologies and began to believe that the outsiders were superior to them in every possible respect. What the foreigners wished for and wanted to have, they, the local people, gave them freely in silver plates. In other words, the outsiders exploited the innocence, goodness and virtues of the local people. That was the end of our progress, our development, nay we ourselves.

Let me give a few examples to show ancient India's superiority by way of our scientific achievement. It was Aryabhatta, the great astronomer and mathematician, who first discovered the value of zero, also discovered the formula for the circumference of the circle. There was error in his discovery. His erroneous formula was corrected by Madhvacharya of Sangram village Irinjalakuda, Trissur in AD1500. He was a great mathematician especially of spherical geometry. (Please note this Madhvachrya is different from Madhvachrya of Dwata philosophy.) The Department of Mathematics at Kyoto University in Japan studied the mathematical achievements of Madvacherya in depth and sent a team to visit his ancestral home in Trissur. Only then even the neighbouring villagers came to know about the greatness of Madhvacharya. However, the westerns found out the formula only in 1800. But today ask a school going child as to who found out the value of $2\pi r$, the child will immediately answer it saying that the Europeans. What a shame!

Again, who discovered the chronometers (clock)? The truth is like this. Matheo Reechi, an Italian Jesuit missionary, was on his way to China in the early 16th Century. When he reached Goa, the capital of the then Portuguese India, he, for the first time in his life saw a clock and got enamoured by it for it was an instrument that could measure time. He got a clock. The clock had some mechanical problems. And, he took it with him to China. He handed it over to another Jesuit missionary who was returning to Europe, with a request to rectify the mechanical error and the error was rectified in the course of time. Now the question is who invented the clock? People will answer it saying that the westerns. What a pity! The westerners were not willing to accept the value and worth of Indian culture and Indian discoveries because of their ignorance about India and on account of their arrogance that they were superiors to everybody.

One more example and with it we stop this section. I knew Dr. Raju, who was a scientists at Indian National Science Academy (INSA) in New Delhi. His grandfather, a professor of Sanskrit at Sagar University in Madhya Pradesh, migrated to M. P. from Kerala due to his teaching profession at Sagar University. From his grandfather, Dr. Raju came to know that it was the Kerala Brahmins who discovered first that the sun was the centre of the universe and the earth was moving around the sun. This is the famous heliocentric theory. To know the truth about it, Dr. Raju visited Northern Kerala several times and got a large number of palm leave manuscripts (*Thaliola grandham*) from several Brahmin *Illams* and Nair ancestral homes (*Tharavadu*). He was convinced of the theory and was busy with further studies on it. But, today how is it that heliocentric theory stands in the name of Copernicus, a European monk? Dr. Raju has his answer. Viscoid Gama came to Calicut, a town in northern Kerala, and happened to hear about this new theory and he also got the palm leaves manuscripts about it. On his return to Portugal, he gave the manuscripts to some monks in Lisbon who in turn deposited them in Vatican State Library. Copernicus, a regular visitor to that library and a good scholar in Sanskrit language and literature, got hold of it and got so attracted to the new theory, translated it from Sanskrit to Latin, and today Copernicus is the discoverer of heliocentric theory. How sad! When I met Dr. Raju a few years ago in an ICPR seminar, he was preparing to go to Vatican. But unfortunately, he was also suffering from cancer. I am not sure whether he went to Rome at all or not.

On one occasion, the great scholar Professor Kunjunni Raja told me that ancient Kerala is known for three contributions: contributions to spherical geometry, astronomy and Sanskrit grammar. Several things regarding Indian scientific inventions can be said like this. Unfortunately, this is the fate of tribal discoveries and inventions as well. Thus, we made ourselves impoverished, pauperized and deficient. We did not give any meaning or value to our scientific culture, discoveries or inventions and by making them available to the westerners, they became masters, scholars and scientists. Do we not accept even today unquestionably and unequivocally the statements of westerners about India? The Europeans considered themselves to be culture providers, religion providers, technology providers, customs and habit providers. India gave the world the Kama Sutra texts. Yet we, Indians, accepted the expression "missionary position" in the context of sexual relations as if it was a position taught to us by foreign missionaries who came from the west. In short they declared themselves superiors in every possible things. Unfortunately, in the course of time, Indians in general and tribals in particulars appropriated, interiorized, internalized and accepted, all those that the foreigners stood for. The foreigners were installed in high pedestals.

Thus we allowed ourselves to be slaves of various kinds, intellectual slavery, cultural slavery, religious slavery, technological slavery, administrative slavery and the like. And this slavery continued until our day of self- realization—a realization that I am my master. In political terms this is the meaning of what Bala Gangadhar Thilak taught us: Swaraj is my birth right. This is an existential awakening, or existential realization about which Kierkegaard spoke. The awareness that I am not the master of my own affairs instil a sense of anxiety which tears myself apart violently in all possible directions because of which I look around for my liberation and in the course of time it becomes a collective movement, i.e. our movement, and finally it becomes something like a tempest which swallowed the foreigners. In India we find the culmination of such a movement on 15th August 1947.

This was the past. In the third part of the paper, let us look into the present. I study the present Indian society from a sociological point of view and then compare it with the Northeast to arrive at my conclusions. What are some of the characteristics of contemporary Indian society? First of all what we notice is that in the course of last several years there is improvement of life conditions of people in terms of life expectancy and literary advancement. *India Today* weekly reported a few months ago that life expectancy in India in the 1960s was 50 years. But in the year 2000 it became 67 years and in 2015 it is 72 years. In the present era when sufficient food is available, when nutrition content of food has improved, and when medical facilities are very much available, life expectancy will go up further.

So is the case with education. Poor and pauperized parents are taught the need to send their children to school and children are motivated to go to school due different incentives. The enrolment of children in the school and college level has gone up very much. All of us, working at the higher levels of education, know very well that in the beginning of the academic year there is so much rush to our institutions for admission. Education is no more a prerogative of the rich and the affluent but rather the right of every one. This is what Right to Education (RTE) means. The central government brought forward appropriate constitutional amendments and administrative protocols for this purpose. It is indeed true to say that education of the masses is the torch bearer of the progress of the country. When educated, people realize that they are their own masters and on account of it they demand participation in the political process. People realize that their votes do count and they do have a value. Education epitomizes modernity. It enables people to set goals and make effort to achieve them.

The second is social Justice. This has emerged into the forefront today on account of the past neglect of a section of people by the predominant group. Social inequalities which prevailed in the

Indian society at large for centuries create a wide spectrum of social discriminations among people.

Let me give two or three examples of social discrimination from my own personal life. These are about or more than 60 year old stories. There was a man by name Chacko who was looking after my grandfather's agricultural land and paddy fields. He was from the *pulaya* community, considered to be low cast at that time. We children in the joint family could have been taught by our elders to address that elderly *person with some respectable name. But we were taught to address that man Chacko*-pulayan, i.e. adding his community name to his personal name. He could be called by his personal name, Chacko, only by the elders at home. Was calling him by name Chackopulayan to show him respect by children of the house hold or to instil a sense of superiority in the hearts and minds of the children over his caste or to make him aware that he is a person of low caste origin? One can argue on this endlessly. So is the case with one Raman *paravan*, one who climbs the coconut tree to cut coconuts. Although his name was Raman, we children called him Ramanparavan, adding his profession to his name. So is the case with Madhvanchokon, one who was supplying fish to the household. Because he belonged to the *Ezava* community, he was called locally by name *chokon*. The reason why I say all these is because at that point of time a large number of people were insensitive to caste discrimination. Nobody ever thought how such people felt about themselves when they are addressed by their caste name. Their feelings were immaterial to the others. Even such people, I feel, accepted it as their lot and fate. But things have changed for good now. People now recognize equality and fraternity.

Third, however, this levelling of caste and equalization of people are not magnanimously accepted or generously embraced by all. Some recent events like the Bharat Bandh called by the Scheduled Caste, Bhima-Koregaon incidents show that there is social tension and opposition to change. What such incidents show is that there is a group of people who are interested in social change and there is also another group who is for maintaining the status quo. The spread of social, political, cultural, and economic evolution sweeps away old habits, traditional religious beliefs and ancestral moral convictions, all of which contribute tension from those who are against such changes.

The fourth, contemporary society is defined by technical innovations, increasing human interconnections, globalization, etc. This also enhances increased life expectancy, literary and higher levels of education and gender equality. Technical advancement and innovations in the domain of two wheeler industries, I would say, give a lot of freedom, more than anything else, to our boys and girls who are studying in the colleges and universities. They need not wait and waste their precious time for buses and other means of transportation to reach their destinations. Accessibility to any national or international information improved vastly due to internet connectivity. Often, we find students more informed than teachers about many things because they are well versed in operating computers and other such electronic gadgets than their teachers.

The fifth is the spread of communication: radio, television, internet, cell phone of various kinds and innumerable brands increase accessibility to communication. In fact, communication business is the most profitable enterprise and is the most spread out mode of employment in India to day. The communication and allied business of Tata, Wipro, Infosys, etc. have advanced the career opportunities of tens of thousands of our young people.

Why do I say all these? My point is this. What happens in the rest of India happens in the Northeast as well. Northeast is not totally cut off from the rest of India. When the average life expectancy of India in general increases, the same also improves in the Northeast. When the enrolment of schools and colleges increases in the rest of India, it also proportionately improves in the Northeast's educational institutions. So is the case with technical innovations and communication facilities. In other words, Northeast is not totally separated from the rest of India, educationally, culturally, ethnographically or in communication-wise. Let me give an example from my experience in Pondicherry University. We have a very large number of students from the Northeast. If this is the case with an ordinary university deep down in the south, having enormous problems of transportation to reach there, then one can imagine the number of students joining good universities in the metropolis. If this is so, then what will be number of students joining local colleges and universities in the Northeast itself? Now there are central universities in all the Northeastern states and the most leading and the oldest being Northeastern Hill (NEHU) University at Shillong. Let me also add. United Nations Developmental Programme (UNDP) report on Human Research Development 2003 points out that the literary rate of Northeast is 66%, much more than national or all India average. And the female literacy is much more than the rest of India. Moreover, even in the case of GDP there is a lot of difference between the North –east and the rest of India. GDP in the Northeast in the years 2004—05 was 6% whereas the rest of India was only 4.4%.

Does it mean that everything in the Northeast is silver and gold? Not at all. The most serious difficulty in the Northeast is the geographical condition. Arunachal Pradesh, Meghalaya, Mizoram and Nagaland are almost entirely of hills of different size and various height. But Assam has 4/5plain. Manipur and Tripura have both plains and hills. As a whole, it can be remarked that hills account for about 70% of the Northeast. Because of this phenomenon of hills, accessibility is very poor. Because of this difficulty and strenuous geographical and terrain conditions, railway network is very deficient. Building bridges demand large sums of money. Another major difficulty is insurgency and intrusion. In Arunachal Pradesh we have intrusion from China. ULFA, ATTF, Bodo land agitation are often heard in the Northeast. Illegal infiltration from Bangladesh is another major issue.

However, having a problem is not unique to the Northeast. Every region of India has its unique problem. Let us consider Bangalore, the garden city of India, blessed with so many wonderful parks, beautiful climate. It has sobriquet like Silicon Valley of India. It is the city if enormous development and great growth. It is hub of IT industry. It consists of InfoTech city, Aero city. It is home for more than 1700 software companies. Bangalore is the home for eminent educational institutions like Indian Institution of Science (IIC), National Institute of Mental Health and Neuro-Sciences (NIMHANS) and several others. Many architectural marvels of B'lore city can be traced back to 19th century. Long ago during the height of Mogul emperors, it was written in the *Divane Ikkas* of the Red Fort in Delhi saying: "if there is a heaven here on the earth, it is this, it is this". In a similar vein, the Bangalorians can also proudly repeat the same now a days about their city.

Does it mean that Bangalore does not have any problem at all? In fact, I would even say that unless there are some problems, we may not understand the goodness present in that place. It suffers from drinking water shortage, garbage problem, chaotic traffic problems, inadequate infrastructure problems, very exorbitant rent because of which middle class and poor people cannot get settled there. And, there are very many problems too which are not listed here.

The question now is what is the point in talking about Bangalore in an essay devoted mainly to the issues concerning the Northeast? My point is to tell you that every place has its advantageous and disadvantageous, strong points and weak points, good and bad aspects. If this is the case with Bangalore, it is also the case with the Northeast as well.

We often hear about nature and nurture especially in the context of physiological psychology. Nature speaks of the basic inherent features, qualities or characteristics of the individual. But when nurture is spoken about, we are considering upbringing, education, environment and the like which influence or determine a person. All human beings do have both these characteristics. Nature cannot be changed, it is that with which we are born, it is natural to a person, it is rooted in our essence. All human beings, whether one is an Asian, European, African or an American, are determined by nature. The people of Northeast India has certain physiological features, arising from their nature that cannot be changed. All Indians have such features. For example the

Dravidians have in general dark skin whereas the Northeast Indians are fare and have certain facial characteristics. Baldy South- Indians are common, whereas baldy Northeast Indians are few and far between. In my opinion these differences are very minor, negligible and insignificant. What is important, significant and meaningful is that we are all Indians. Indian-ness is our essence, it is our nature; it is that which unites us. Being Indians is the bond that brings us together. That is what establishes our cultural togetherness. That is what gives meaning to our lives. That is our unity. That is our strength.

Celebrate Pluri-Cultural Identities and Envision a Desirable Future: Anthropological Perspectives

Dr. K. Jose SVD

O ften in our media - both print and visual, we come across debates on India as a civilization which is gasping for a statistical global power and we all believe it might overcome that predicament over a period of time, but how about the social, economic, spiritual and ecological health among other major parameters? It will not be so easy for us to rise up to this challenge, surely, because resisting social inequality and removing poverty has become a tall order today. We can surpass this predicament only with a prolonged concern for better governance taking cues from the past as well. But still it all depends on us to re-imagine and re-visit the best traditions of Indian cultures, juxtaposed in the matrix of best of modernity. This is a collective vision of reliving the mammoth history of our civilization, inclusive in nature where even the present day underprivileged are empowered to taste a semblance of hope.

Now, recent debates on world civilizations continuously remind us that our cultures are under pressure from modern and post-modern trends. In our journey onward we realize that the traditions are invaluable, but changes are inevitable too. The path to a better future may not always be through a throw-back to the ways of old. Therefore, there is urgency today for creative and critical thinking, to break new grounds, and take humanity forward. We come across a number of hurdles in embarking desirable changes in the society. Though traditionalists often tend to grow over-defensive and their sense of insecurity leads them to take rigid stands, the ever inviting need to integrate the old and the new is crucial. Fast changing India would do well in celebrating this magnificent civilization with innumerable identities and stupendous resources on many counts. In this timely task we, as individuals and more so as forward-looking communities, have a great role to play.

The willingness to contemplate a new way of being, drawing from various cultural assets, is the need of the time. We are aware of the tremendous forces at work, which will try to suppress our small yet decisive initiatives but we have no other option than to build upon the collective cultural assets which will equip us to build upon the synergy. This debate is also necessitated by an increasingly globalized socio-cultural, economic, and political scenario that has been impacting young people in their homes, in their religious beliefs, and in the realm of awareness of their cultural roots/community identities —often displacing them in the hazy shores of uncertainties. It is here one is reminded to be socially responsible, take ecology and technology into consideration, embrace life giving dimensions of culture, and move on being aware of even the aggressive and contentious issues, negotiating between real and imagined enemies. Today when we visualise a desirable and inclusive future for our country certainly we cannot but take into adequate consideration of the pluri-cultural identities which exist at various life situations and we shall do this taking a special reference to the vista of Anthropology as well.

Pluri-Cultural Identities in a Multi-cultural Nation

We, as a nation, accommodate various peoples and culture, each with its own beauty and agility. People of each category need room to live, grow, and flourish. Though all of us live in the larger geographical arena of India, we have also specificities to accept, accommodate, and cherish. We cannot forget that under the overarching 'Indian-ness' resulting from cultural convergence, there always have been varying degrees of linguistic, ethnic, geographical, religious, and cultural variations over historical periods of time. Therefore, we need to move on not merely forgetting the past, but rooted in the life-enhancing thoughts and ideas of the past and envisioning a new and more creative future for us and for the posterity. Otherwise, we may end up merely mourning our failures, and in that process we may miss out major possibilities of the future. No doubt, the secular and pluralistic fabric of the nation needs to be strengthened not by merely living in the glorious past but by engaging with creative ideas of positive change and inclusive progress for all.

India is one of the best known multi-cultural nations across the globe which has 1.21 billion populations (Census 2011). This is one of the best known multi-cultural and multi-lingual nations on our planet demonstrating a vibrant capacity for innovation, competition, and embracing success. True, we have also much diversity when we dwell on dissimilarities, while we cannot forget that these diversities themselves should become our vast resource on which we can build the edifice of this nation. It is also important for us to remember that diversities can often overwhelm us with some possible challenges. Yes, we need to face them and move on imbibing the wisdom of ages – social and cultural, political and economic, and religious too. These challenges should not put us out; but our tenacity to hold on to the greater possibility of doing creative tasks should enliven us to move forward cherishing the air, water, forest, and other elements in the nature as hospitality of our mother earth, and in response we need to engage in hard work and appreciate people of all walks of life for the betterment of a new society and the ever protecting magnanimity of God-head.

India is an immensely diverse country with many distinct pursuits, vastly disparate convictions, widely divergent customs, and a veritable feast of viewpoints. The issues of plurality and of choice are immensely relevant to the understanding and analysis of the idea of Indian identity (Sen, 2005). However, in India it is never a vision based on any particular religion or culture that should get the primary focus but our great civilizational ethos which is handed down from time immemorial. Certainly it is a pluralistic vision of India that will hold sway for any futuristic and desirable society. Strong and valiant voices should amalgamate salient philanthropy side by side with the vibrant local governments, empowering the pluri-cultural identities on real time basis (Parekh, 2010).

However, one may immediately ask as to how we shall celebrate the vast diversity of our civilization taking adequate cognizance also of the diversity that attempts to tear us apart. Can a dose of vigour and enthusiasm provide us the adequate steam for the forward leap of this gigantic nation with all its twists and turns? This is a vital concern for administrators and bureaucrats, academicians and social workers, and of course the commoner too. This is the context which has given me reflections on this very pertinent theme of this essay – Celebrating Pluri-Cultural Identities and Envisioning a Desirable Future for India: Anthropological Perspectives, and I choose to call it a challenge and an opportunity side by side. If at all we visualize a vital future which is for the larger benefit of a greater number, it has to be visualized today with futuristic possibilities. I certainly believe this new wave of interest in our age-old civilization should become a lively discourse, primarily because this opens up avenues for recapturing the intellectual and historical heritage of a nation. Secondly, it tickles our nostalgic collective memory and triggers our imagination for a more vibrant futuristic vision of a desirable society. As this Seminar focuses intends to focus on indigenous cultures we have a specific invitation to look at the Tribal Conglomerations in Perspective

The Tribal Conglomerations in Perspective

Our Motherland, India is home to large number of indigenous people whom we often call tribals. Though they are a vast population of about 10.2 crores (1.02 million), the second largest tribal fraternity in the world, they often live in relative deprivation and penury; most importantly they have been increasingly subjugated by state agencies, landlords, and money lenders, and even seemingly by development-oriented agencies. It is also observed empirically that that their traditional culture and religion have been undergoing sporadic changes. However, in some quarters we time and again observe tendencies which deliberately ignore the multi-ethnic, multi-cultural, multi-linguistic realities – by trumpeting "One nation, one culture, one religion," and "tribals are Hindus, adivasis are *vanvasis*" (=the indigenous are forest dwellers), and the like.

In order to live side by side with people of various religions and cultures we have to progressively learn soft skills to negotiate between various situations. In this sense, we can expect every encounter with a new cultural setting to expose us to frightening uncertainties, unprepared negotiations, unwanted conflicts, belittling destabilization, with special reference to land and resource. And of course, we cannot exclude a positive possibility of hybridity, new vistas and cross-fertilization, therefore, a new beginning too.

It is empirically observed that tribal communities take decisions based on their deep rooted ecological awareness. In fact, they have traditional wisdom which drives them to observe their own peculiar ways of doing things. In that sense, we can say that their decisions most often place a higher premium on long term sustainability based on extensive systems of ecological knowledge (Mander, 1992; Padel, 1998). These deep-seated and ecologically inspired practices are often faced with threats of competition as a basic principle of modern economic and social organization. Therefore, it is fitting for us to agree that when we count success stories merely in terms of the economic parameters, we make a big mistake. Anyone who understands the tribal communities in their various categories would undoubtedly observe that tribal ways of perceiving the development projects, their ways of involving in their execution, planning, division of labour, and monitoring all these are very different from other segments of people.

Cultures can Play Important Role in Building Trust and Understanding

Among other ordinarily understood vistas of life, "culture" more tenaciously refers to the inner refinement of human being – both of the head and the heart. Therefore, there is an ardent urgency to get not only the concepts clear from early stages of human formation, but the practical, lived experiences would also be called for. This should be imbibed in a graded manner, each according to his/her capability to incorporate together with a formal training at home, in school, in institutions of higher learning, and even thereafter. The challenge is to celebrate diversities and enhance identities. Since multi-lingualism and cultural pluralism are the essence of Indian society, we have no other option than learn to live in trust and fellowship in pluri-cultural situations. Anthropologists and social scientists of bygone years have done their part reasonably well; now it is for us to chart out a new destiny – challenging, but ever desirable. In this context one may ask what our original academic contributions in the present decade are. Or do we blindly hang on to Gurdon, Hutton, Mills, Elwin, etc., who were true stalwarts and pathfinders of their day?

We know cultures separate people more sharply than political boundaries. But we need to discover the uniting elements in each of the individual cultures, more importantly than what divides and separates us. Then we enrich each other even while holding on to our individual identities. In Northeast India, while we analyse growth and movements of people during the past 25 years, we see that two contradictory forces have been simultaneously at work: broadly we may name them as *life-enhancing forces* and *negative or destructive forces*. The life-enhancing forces are the democratic institutions, ecological concerns, and cultural awakening. Of course, all these did not take place at a single stroke. They became a true force through the consistent efforts of people who dared to dream big; they were built painstakingly as a large edifice by the valiant men and women who decisively upheld pluri-cultural identities as a collective wisdom of ages. The negative and destructive forces are: insurgency, terrorism, and corruption. These are deadliest poisons which eat into the very fabric of community cohesion and fraternal solidarity. Here we have only two vital options to uphold. One - while we interact with cultures other than our own, we may feel overwhelmed by the variety and heterogeneity. This scenario may compel us to make ourselves cultural fundamentalists. Or, we may learn to appreciate diversity and profit from the pluralism that confronts us.

What option shall we appropriate? The choice is essentially decisive. Yet, it is certainly ours.

Today increasingly a new awareness need to be constructed and fostered among the people of different religions, cultures, and ideologies that everyone is ultimately children of one and only God, therefore, related to one another as members of one human family. Tribal and non-tribal fraternities have many things to learn from each other. For example, tribal communities may teach their neighbours that they are proven sustainable resource managers for generations. The invitation to contribute towards the common welfare, realization of the common vision – fullness of life, loving service, and human rights and value-added life - will become a reality when larger numbers of people work with determination and imagination for a much more liveable world. And certainly, no country can grow into a robust civilization without persons who are not concertedly building minds and hearts both for professional acumen and above all with a veritable search for upholding values and ethics. This will inspire changes and make a positive difference in the entire gamut of the country.

The Need for Daring Responses

We know cultures separate people more sharply than political boundaries. But we need to discover the uniting elements in each of the individual cultures, more importantly than what divide and separate us. Then we enrich each other even while holding on to our individual identities. In Northeast India, while we analyse growth and movements of people during the past several years, we see that two contradictory forces have been simultaneously at work: broadly we may name them as *life-enhancing forces* and *negative or destructive forces.* It is important for a diligent citizen of our ethno-space to consistently promote life-enhancing forces so as to weaken and eliminate the negative and destructive forces.

In this context we cannot overemphasize the fact that we must watch out on pessimism which are lurking in any ordinary minds. When one is confronted with challenging situations, there is a very strong possibility of embracing pessimistic attitude, thinking that nothing can be done, or, what good can come out of my small initiatives, and why should I try when there is a very big possibility of meeting with failure. Yes, overcoming the seemingly larger challenges is not seen as something usual and ordinary. And why should they be so? Celebrating the communities' strengths is definitely recognizing the possibility of living and working together in spite of differences. These are times when we may need to partake in the shared vision, build up synergy, and chart out often the unusual and rough paths planning for the future, accepting emerging inclusive religious ideologies, engaging in consistent hard work, and above all, believing in miracles.

Our society is fast changing. So do value systems. It is important for us to adapt ourselves and become relevant. We cannot completely throw away the vital lessons which we learned in the childhood. Our dear ancestors have taught us many things. Anyway we need to prepare ourselves to face the future building upon the positive energy is all that is important…In fact we need to plan well in advance for the changes we want to embrace, that will be directed course of action, and not a sporadic change which we are least prepared to face.

When one is confronted with challenging situations, there is a very strong possibility of embracing pessimistic attitude, thinking that nothing can be done, or, what good can come out of my small initiatives, and why should I try when there is a very big possibility of meeting with failure. Yes, overcoming the seemingly larger challenges is not seen as something usual and ordinary. And why should they be so? Celebrating the communities' strengths is definitely recognizing the possibility of living and working together in spite of differences. The process of development should decisively continue for this we need to engage in consistent hard work, at various spheres.

Learning from Tradition and Wisdom of Ages

There is a churning of traditionalisation and modernisation at work side by side. Certainly this process is to be seen in the light of a reckless rejection of tradition *vis-a-vis* an overenthusiastic leaning towards anything modern. However, what may be praiseworthy is a contemplated and selective retention of the core values of the primordial cultures while rejecting what is not life enhancing for today and for a long time to come. A vehement entry of monetized economy has been a hallmark of the communities in transition, added to this Christianity as a religion became a formidable force, proliferation of transport and communication, far reaching welfare programmes initiated by scores of agencies and so forth have created push and pull factors in the tribal fraternities and thereby they were forced to evaluate and rethink their original customs, traditions and value systems.

India can boast of ever expanding diversity – cultural, religious, ethnic, linguistic, and political. We might wonder how we have survived as a nation with such heterogeneous elements. The answer lies in this very heterogeneity and diversity. Time and again it has been proved that any coercive method of homogenization under the popular banner of "national integration" or "assimilation of cultures" has given rise to agitation and revolt. Our existence and survival have not been in accordance with the "one nation-state" theory but has been engraved in diversity and multiplicity. However, recent events based on a narrow culture-based interpretation of nationalism, lack of clarity on the organizations' and even government's stand on intolerance amid growing fundamentalism, and increasing politicization of education have been identified among the key challenges facing India today.

This is the time we need to realize the rightful role of social science research. Social science research has to be revamped for a better and effective understanding of our nation and formulation of policies because it is very important to know the traditional social environment to chart out our destiny, sailing through smooth transition. Learning from the major concerns of society and suggesting measures for their amelioration are only possible when rigorous social science research is put in place. Today we come to know that in the institutions of higher learning, theories which are taught often do not amply explain the social realities. That is the time we are invited yet again to fall back to our enduring wisdom of the ages that gently remind us to learn from traditions while creatively open ourselves to the possibilities of a brighter future.

When we look back to the various programmes of the government, it becomes amply clear that so far social scientists have been largely ignored in evolving policies and social management. It is of great concern with far reaching consequences. Why, because political parties which have majority in the state or at the centre may take decisions which are based merely on the party interests while neglecting the larger impact it will create for the welfare of the people at large. So today we need society/local specific social science research to find out reasons for widening of inequality and lack of tolerance towards various ideologies though they all have something positive to contribute towards the welfare of the people at large. Today one is more than aware that strategy for planned development is possible only through broad based and shared vision, foresight, and data-based research.

Scenario from Northeast India

Every geographical area has its own specificities. Land and resources of a particular territory hasve to be gauged by the people who live and work in every individual segment of the territory – community property, customary laws – sustainability, Indigenous methods of resource utilization – indigenous knowledge systems, modernization of traditions – IT should be used to enhance progress without compromising on traditional knowledge and values. Development and sustainability should be planned with active participation of people. That calls for broad based planning, decision making, policy formation, execution and evaluation at every level, for e.g. village, civil circles, district, and the entire Northeast as a whole.

Northeast India is India's least known and often least understood regions. It still evokes the colonialist image of 'exotic' and the 'primal' partly because of the hangover from colonial writers who were political agents and administrators with anthropologist garb. Today many of the tribal communities are searching for their roots as evidenced by the passionate movement to build-up language identity of Kok-Barak in

Tripura, Sanamahi as element of religio-cultural unity among Meiteis (Manipur), Seng-Khasi and its deep rooted ethnic aspirations in Meghalaya, and *Donyi-Poloism* and its various socio-religious implications in Arunachal Pradesh. These searches for identity are important movements taking place in other States of Northeast India too. These are a few of the many simmering identity assertion movements which rightly need a space of debate and consideration in terms of community identity and empowerment. Here we cannot emphasize enough on the need for the indigenous scholars who have a great responsibility to unravel the actual scenario amidst the context of overarching modernization and globalization.

In any case, the land and the people of Northeast India should hold fast to the dictum of cultural pluralism with special reference to the tribal communities who really are part of the great national culture. Understanding this region of India can only be done in its bits and pieces. But it should somehow be done with great devotion and commitment. For this, we need to dispassionately learn the context both in times of calm and turbulence, listen to the heart beats of the people. As cultural integration and development aspirations are major points of departure for any forward-moving community in any geographical part of the world, a comprehensive understanding of this region with special reference to ethnic conflicts, insurgency, and poor governance buttressed with escalating corruption, and scores of disturbing trends need to be addressed. Let us not be content with a minimum awareness of this vast region of ours which has wonderful people who are often deprived of the much valued natural resources waiting to be harnessed for the benefit of people who are often poverty-stricken (Jose, 2012).

The tribal situation of the Northeastern region of India is different from those prevailing in other parts of the country due to its unique geo-political and historical background. As the area is surrounded by international boundaries, the tribal people have shared ethnic and cultural affinities with the tribesmen across the frontiers. As the British followed a policy of keeping the people separate and given difficult topography of the area, the whole of Northeast India is still not completely integrated with the rest of India. This failure has been amplified due to the development paradigm adopted by the government of India, which are not responsive to the needs and features of the tribal people and land. The values the tribals hold dear need to be understood, especially the indigenous knowledge systems which are not merely for the material progress of the people, but are collective endeavours to make life meaningful taking each one of the members as equals.

Response to Challenges Faced by Tribal Communities in Northeast India

While planning is done for a specific community, one has to take into account the indigenous ethos of the people considering the diversity and complexity within the local communities. This is to say that while program for resource development and its utilization is done, it should account for the socio-cultural mores of the people under consideration; otherwise, the best of the intentions may bring in very little or even adverse impact for a prolonged period of time. It is important to note that communities are far from homogenous and any program or scheme initiated in Northeast India should be tailored to meet the specific needs of the diverse peoples taking adequate care with regard to their present state of overall development perspectives in the region. Resource utilization among the people depends on the availability of the resource; yet new resources can often be introduced and adapted within the ecological and cultural parameters of the land and the people. This will call for endurance and innovative methods by the economic planners and the indigenous people.

Underdevelopment is a herculean challenge one needs to address most specially among the tribal areas of the country. There is no point in simply making hyped jargons such as "Make in India"; what is essential is that we seek to understand and analyse the dangers that lie ahead in the field of environmental degradation – massive mining, hazardous factories that grow day by day without creating any meaningful avenue for the ordinary tribal fraternity. Aspirations of youth need attention because there is an overwhelming under-performance in job placement. Every day escalating corruption is in the news – which skyrockets the number of *crorepatis* (millionaires) amassing national wealth into their personal assets/bank balances. The real concern is that of leadership that creates large social spaces for oneself and for one's close kith and kins. Do they understand the grim situation– one-fifth of the nation lives in semi-starvation? Are the basic issues affecting the country their prime concern, or are they more interested in watching if anyone indulges in eating beef or not, or if we stand while singing national anthem, should the *Bhagavad Gita* be declared the holy book of India, or if one is willing to say Bharat *Mata Ki Jai* (Long live, Mother India)?

For example, when Arunachal Pradesh made that long Journey from NEFA (1954) to Statehood (20 February 1987) it was not very clear that this land would take more time than expected to become "the land of the rising sun." Even today the challenges are many; however, possibilities and vision for a vibrant society are also open. One needs to heed to the emerging religious identities side by side with the development aspirations of the people: people have moved from the state of cattle to a state of cash, one crore to thousands of crores. The pristine oral traditions will have to be re-read under the new events and global trends. Outsiders-insiders syndrome might spark a border skirmish or two – demographic changes will challenge the internal cohesion and oneness of the people. We may need to understand that the money spent should enhance quality of human character. Growth pangs in the communities over a period of time should turn into a sense of well-being. Though it is important to become adequately aware of our history, it is more essential for us to envision our near future with planning our distant possibilities as well.

Years rolled by, generations have passed by, much leadership were formed, people celebrated community festivals with much gusto; and performed community dances as an item of identity marker a number of times. The ancestors made many valiant hunting expeditions, engaged in fish-cum-paddy cultivation in vast expanse of land in the case of many communities in Northeast India, many have cleared steep mountains to nurture *jhum* fields for everyday sustenance. Now what are the present day generation up to? We have a golden duty to take our society onward. Don't merely mourn the present tragic scenario or envy the glorious past. Remember: Those who work very hard are successful and prosperous because, we have abundance of land and plenty of natural resources to count on. Maybe we can pursue a bit of Ethno-Botany to sort out and document health enhancing herbs which our ancestors cherished and nourished in their days. We may recall the mystery elements in the sacred groves where our forefathers felt the Sacred and planted sacred cultural symbols in upholding the customary institutions. Our youth have the ability to cherish inter-cultural, community-centred living, and openness to face new challenges. We need to build upon both human resources and environmental strengths. Why not emphasize the aspect of celebrating the positive goodness of people, pluri-cultural identities which is our strength on various counts?

The Larger Picture of National Scenario vis-à-vis Regional Concerns

Today we are more than aware that there are a large number of people in India coming under the category of the 'young.' We need to be aware of their concerns, their values, aspirations, and challenges they face on a daily basis. Of course, they have a lot to say and do; but they also need guidance and accompaniment to undertake their arduous journey forward. Here, I am reminded of a TED Talk the main content of the talk was that "We decide what gets attention to, which in turn shapes our culture," How true it is in the case of the young people of the nation! Developing critical thinking is one of the most precious (often rare) aspects of education and we decisively have to promote it today among the youth. Human development, environmental up-gradation, improving the quality of life, and recognizing the aspirations of the younger generation are all major concerns in Northeast India.

If these have to take place we need to make better use of the resources – both human and material – available at our disposal. Then we cannot allow the funds for our multifaceted engagements to be drained off (e.g., in some cases even up to 90 per cent grant-in-aid from Central Government are under-utilized and siphoned off). We need to voice our concerns intelligently, certainly with more reasons and much less with emotion. We need to address issues of escalating un-employment, unattended refugee issues, and herculean land alienation. In some sense, protective discrimination keeps the tribal in the lower strata of Indian population. This is to say that in the name of 8.6 per cent of the population of the country huge chunk of resources are set apart – how much of it is put into optimum use! It is here we urgently need to create a synergy between stakeholders, NGOs, and Government.

We need to celebrate the luminaries of our day. Promoting the indigenous talents in various fields especially in leadership, research, indigenous medicines, technology and management, artists of various categories, socially committed media are some of the major ones one can immediately think of. Identifying enthusiastic visionaries with revolutionizing ideas, enhancing sense of mutual belonging, re-envisaging the social dimension of private property, a sense of equality, honesty, dignity of labour; love of parents for children; and respect of children for elders etc also cannot be forgotten by any means. Does modernization mean only proliferation of market economy? We praise the great work done by Verrier Elwin (1964/1988, 1999); but what are we up to: are we willing to apply our minds to analyse the currents and undercurrents that are at work in our society? Creative imagination and hard work, not merely passive dreams, will bring our aspirations to fruition. Finally, we shall promise to uphold a peaceful, pluralistic, egalitarian, moral, and nationalistic vision for our land or else we shall fail to see a vibrant future. We shall uphold the dictum of healthy competition while upholding the idea of globalization. We value our traditions but remain open to an adequate dose of creativity and modernity, spirit of co-existence rather than sectarian ideologies and fanaticism; inclusive growth and productive employment. If we do not join hands (force), we fail. Change in the world is more towards fast food culture: comfort and less hard work. This will not take us far.

Sanskriti: Northeastern Institute of Cultural Research at Guwahati is also an agent of change in a small measure. In the past 13 years we have created platform for hundreds of senior professors to interact with scholars both young and not-so-young, to engage in debates that are vital for the very existence of our nation as a united whole and Northeast India in particular. The books we have brought out based on annual national conferences, the select number of small yet valuable monographs, and annual newsletters may instil optimism and academic temper in scholars of today who have the enthusiasm to take arduous paths for charting out their destiny. Other works by *Sanskriti* group of institutes, and institutes of similar nature, universities, colleges, and various individual scholars too certainly contribute to the enhancement of pluri-cultural context of the nation. And scholars of various disciplines are aware that these and other initiatives should enhance the pluri-cultural fabric of our nation day by day.

Charting out Pathways for a Desirable Future

Often we hear that it is important to envision a desirable future. But it is not enough to think of a future which is desirable but working with utmost earnestness is also equally important. This is because; our tomorrows will be built on daring imaginations and passionate undertakings. Young people of today need to take responsibility for the plans we make for tomorrow. We need to be decisively aware that the fuel of enthusiasm that took us so far will be by far not sufficient to sail through the ever soaring competition in any conceivable arena of life and work. Therefore, we have no other option than to embrace the idea of more original researches, leading to better quality publications, and faster and greater dissemination of information that will ultimately matter.

Today globalization has been a tangible phenomenon wherein there is a consistent and rapid deterioration of ecological and social health. This has happened because of the mammoth structural changes in the urban areas without adequate strategies for the rest of the rural conglomeration. The future seems to be grim for large number of people who face the brunt of inequalities, displacement, and other forms of exploitation (Shrivastava & Kothari, 2012). Here we may be rightly reminded of McKinsey Research Foundation (2013) that studied companies across Asia and reiterated that those that globalized with a clear focus and purpose thrived well. For this, we need people with global perspectives, i.e., people with right motivation, clarity of thought, and performance; otherwise, we choose to embrace devastating failure rather than become pioneers and pathfinders of today for a more desirable future.

We cannot forget that we have the great duty of eliminating poverty of the masses which is intolerably high at about 40 per cent. Yet, the largest and unused heap of food stocks in the world is within India! It was estimated to be 62 million tons in 2001. Then, what about the enormous illiterate population of our country? In 21st century when we are passionately engaging with fast-paced supercomputers and nanotechnology, we are sadly reminded of the hungry millions who are deprived of daily meal for their sustenance. How do we respond to these anomalies amidst scientific advancement and craze for plenty? Undoubtedly, individualism and corruption eat into the very fabric of our social life. It is estimated that at least up to 16.6 per cent of the black money is generated through fraudulent means. Certainly, we need to recheck and bring in a qualitative change in character role and influence of people who are placed high in the social ladder. It is often true that people are angry at the levels of corruption, but anger is not enough to turn their miseries into alternative vision and constructive future. We need to focus more on broader national agenda to turn a challenge to an opportunity. Surely we need to preserve the steam long enough to churn out ideas for the more desired and vibrant India for ourselves and for the posterity (Varma, 2004).

Unless each of us commits oneself to embracing a peaceful, pluralistic, egalitarian, moral, and nationalistic vision we shall only fail to reap the fruits of a reasonably meaningful present and obviously a vibrant future. We should emphasize the need to promote humanitarian values in families, schools, and work places, rather than harp on the identity based on religions and castes and other categories. We certainly have to make a commitment to healthy competition and reconcile with the idea of globalization at every stage of our involvement, without which none of our dreams will soar high enough to make a difference. Perhaps, we need some valiant activists who will not sacrifice the wealth of intellectual pursuits side by side. Of course, both of these – activism and intellectual acumen – are in plenty while a desirable combination is often lacking to say the least.

Today we also need to see that the traditions are enlivened with adequate dose of modernity where the spirit of co-existence takes priority over the narrow sectarian ideologies and fanaticism. For this, we need to promote in a decisive way educational research in humanities and social sciences. Look at the contemporary research output in many of our universities and other established research institutions in the Northeast! They might have contributed their share in the yester years, but are they relevant and making any significant contribution of contemporary relevance today? India is passing through some very difficult times wherein we observe day to day elements of fanaticism being tacitly allowed to creep in and grow. These elements breed in sectarianism and venom of violence and discord day by day. Do we not come across invitations to debates on banning cow slaughter and other issues while never taking a deep look at the human rights violations of annihilating human beings in the name of religion and its sectarian ideologies, political affiliations, and other categories?

Finally it is important for us as a nation to celebrate the luminaries who made the seemingly impossible often possible. They also upheld social responsibility, net-working with other academic institutions of excellence, undertaking documentation of tribal welfare activities within the state and elsewhere. There are those who contributed to women empowerment which has positively impacted families and society as a whole. There are those who took keen interest in environment management of the community and protection of natural resources while adhering to contemporary knowledge of customary practices/laws. There are a few of them, a very few original researches, publications, and dissemination of information, upholding a progressive pluralistic vision of India, promoting vibrant local government who will seek people's proactive participation while working hand in hand with select NGOs who have proven record of trust. We shall nurture a creative imagination in the young to form them into visionary leaders. Those who work very hard will reap the fruits of success. It's time to break loose of pessimism and guard against short term political agendas that violate the social fabric. Let us trust in our ability to do more and commit ourselves to embracing a peaceful, pluralistic, egalitarian, moral, and nationalistic vision. We shall then truly celebrate not only our individual identities, but group and national identities for a more cohesive, prosperous tomorrow.

Our future will have to be built on time tested traditions. For example, customary laws should be re-imagined not merely for curiosity, not even for maintaining traditions, but identify their positive aspects for the contemporary society. This is to study the interface between traditions of old and contemporary adaptations which has taken place for the larger welfare of individual communities side by side with the intercommunity interactions. May be a comparative study of tribal identities in the context of various subtle movements taking place in many communities with special reference to their religious affiliations will require adequate Social Science Research. However, one keen observer of this phenomenon will not be so naïve to believe that it is a mere concern with the religion per se. It is certainly a greater concern with the identity of a community in question. So comparative study of ideals and values each of these religious movements stands for will be imperative to understand the churnings taking place among the communities as a whole. In sum, celebrating pluri-cultural identities is not only imperative but it is essential to the existence of peoples and communities in the larger framework of our nation and indeed of the world.

References

Elwin, V. *The tribal world of Verrier Elwin: An autobiography.* Delhi: Oxford India. (Original work published 1964), 1988.

_____*A philosophy for NEFA.* Itanagar: Directorate of Research, 1999.

Jose, K. *Understanding Northeast India: Contemporary Cultural Perspectives.* New Delhi: Omsons Publications. 2012.

Mander, J. *In the absence of the sacred: The failure of technology and the survival of the Indian nations.* San Francisco: Sierra Club Books, 1992.

McKinsey & Co. (Ed.). *Reimagining India: Unlocking the potential of Asia's next superpower.* New York: Simon and Schuster, 2013.

Padel, F. "Forest knowledge: Tribal people, their environment and the structure of power." In R. Grove, V. Damodaran, & S. Sangwan (Eds.), *Nature and the orient: The environmental history of South and Southeast Asia.* Delhi: Oxford University Press, 1998.

Parekh, B. "Re-imagining India. In Institute of Social Sciences" (Ed.), *Re-imagining India.* New Delhi: Orient BlackSwan, 2010.

Sen, A. *The argumentative Indian: Writings on Indian culture, history and identity.* London: Penguin Books India. 2005.

Shrivastava, A., & Kothari, A. *Churning the Earth: The making of global India.* New Delhi: Penguin Books. 2012.

Varma, P. K. *The new Indian middle class.* New Delhi: Harper Collins Publishers. 2014.

Tribal Languages of Assam
and Asam Sahita Sabha

Dr. Paramananda Rajbongshi

It was since 5th Century that the Kamrupee Language started getting great patronage from the tribal kings of the then Assam and intellectual, academic cooperation from Aryan scholars for which the language became tremendously developed by dint of which it earned mass popularity and circulation. At one time, people following more than one thousand different marginal languages and dialects had even accepted Kamrupee Language as the *lingua franca*. Especially, the kings of Kachari Kingdom in Assam had put forward commanding efforts to facilitate Kamrupee Language scholars to write down various episodes of the epics *The Ramayana* and *The Mahabharata*. The most profound example was Kachari king Mahamnikya's royal patronage to Madhav Kandali for translation of *The Ramayana* from Sanskrit which was the second of such effort in India. The practice of various forms of this ancient Kamrupee Language was observed in Upper Assam, Lower Assam, undivided Bengal including presently Bangladesh, Kalinga and other places. Significantly, at that very period, Dimasa language of Assam by dint of royal patronage from Kachari kings, also became developed with its own distinctive features. But the Bodo language which had developed in an organised manner in the middle period of the 20th century has earned the recognition of the Central government. Kokbarak language of Tripura and Bodo and Dimasa languages of Assam although share the same origin, only

Kokbarak and Bodo languages have become able to maintain their own pride. Despite possessing rich tradition and heritage as a full-fledged language, Dimasa language is still fighting for existence.

As the result of historic Yandabu Pact in 1826, Assam had gone under British rule and it paved the way for the Christian missionaries to Assam. A batch of elite, educated and reformist Christian missionaries attempted to redesign the existing Kamrupee Language in a new and refreshing form, and thus the modern Assamese language—what it is now today—came into being. In 1836, the British rulers introduced Bangla as the official language in Assam and it created serious concern among the masses in general and writers and students of Assam in particular. Therefore, in 1872, a group of Assamese students who were studying in Kolkata, formed a forum called 'Assam Socio-Literary Club' or in short ASL Club to fight to rescue the lost pride and glory of Assamese language. Anandaram Dhekial Phukan took the firm leadership of this movement and a few Christian missionaries also extended cooperation to this effort. Another organisation came up in Kolkata with the same objective and it was 'Asomiya Bhasa Unnati Sdhini Sabha' in 1888. In fact, this new forum was an extended form of the ASL Club, and the people associated with this forum also dedicated themselves fully for the cause of survival of Assamese language.

The process of growth and development of modern Assamese language found new and great boost from two remarkable and historic incidents. The first one was publication of first ever Assamese news-magazine '*Arunodoi*' by Christian missionaries from Sivasagar in 1846 and the second one was publication of first ever Assamese literary journal '*Jonaki*' from Kolkata in 1888 by Asomiya Bhasa Unnati Sadhini Sabha. Especially the literary journal '*Jonaki*' worked like a tremendous steering force of the beginning of 'Romantic Era' in modern Assamese literature. It was followed by publication of a couple of other Assamese literary journals, such as, '*Banhi*', '*Jayanti*', '*Ramdhenu*' and '*Avahan*' during the period of World War I and World War II. It may be mentioned here that much before the formation of Asam Sahitya Sabha, the first ever forum for development of modern Assamese language, literature and culture was formed in 1895 in Kohima under the initiative of Padmanath Gohain Barua. Interestingly, Gohain Barua was the first Assamese to pass matriculation from Nagaland, the then a district of Assam and now a prosperous state of India. Gohain Barua's efforts was the main inspiring force behind formation of Lakhimpur Sahitya Sabha in 1912 and Jorhat Sahitya Sabha in 1914. (These two are now heritage branches—*sakha*s—of Asam Sahitya Sabha.)

Despite there being such laudable efforts for the cause of modern Assamese language and literature, the necessity for a state-wide body was greatly felt by the cross-sections of Assamese people by and large. The idea of a common platform to work for the development of Assamese language, literature and culture was conceived by Ambikagiri Raychoudhury, a poet, writer and veteran Freedom Fighter. The idea was endorsed by Lakshminath Bezbaroa, considered as the 'Father of Modern Assamese Literature'. The efforts of a number of Assamese writers and organizations, mainly the Kolkata-based ASL Club and Asamiya Bhasa Unnati Sadhani Sabha, led to the formation of the Asam Sahitya Sabha on December 27, 1917, at the historical town of Sivasagar to fulfil the hopes and aspirations of the people of Assam irrespective of caste, creed and religion for better growth and development of modern Assamese language and literature.

Came 1901 and the people of Assam saw the first ever institution of higher education in Guwahati. It was Cotton College, formed by the British rulers in the name of the first Lt Governor of Assam, Sir John Henry Cotton. There is no denying the fact that Cotton College since its inception proved to be the centre of excellence not only in the then educational scenario of Assam but also in the literary-socio-cultural life of the greater Assamese nationality. In this very context, I may please be allowed to quote Prof. Sudemersen, the founder Principal of Cotton College, who said: "What Cottonians think today, Assam will think tomorrow".

Anyway, the basic thing is that it was Cotton College which offered the people of Assam and the Northeastern Region the most illustrious and prestigious platform for individual academic and intellectual uplift.

This was of great benefit for the new generation people of the region and also for the further growth and development of modern Assamese language and literature. In 1948, Guwahati University was established, and a few key office bearers of Assam Sahitya Sabha put forward all efforts behind it. The opening of Gauhati University gave birth to a number of colleges all over Assam and the region. Moreover, like Assam Sahitya Sabha, Guwahati University too became a platform for study and research of various indigenous languages of Assam. Assam Sahitya Sabha's one of the major agendas is to publish a number of books and also to open avenues for research on language-literature-culture of various ethno-linguistic communities of Assam. As of now eight indigenous languages of eight ethno-linguistic communities of Assam have earned government recognition and these are: Bodo, Rabha, Deuri, Missing, Karbi, Dimasa, Tiwa and Garo. It has already been mentioned that Bodo language has already earned recognition from Govt. of India as one of the modern Indian languages and since then this very language has been enjoying the status of associate state language in Assam.

It is significant to note that for protection, preservation and circulation of these eight languages, their own literary organisations have been formed in the line of Assam Sahitya Sabha. Of course, development of Assamese language is the first priority of Asam Sahitya Sabha, but even though the Sabha is also committed to work for these eight languages and also for some other indigenous languages of Assam, such as, Tea Community, Koch-Rajbongshi, Sonowal-Kachari and others. Assam Sahitya Sabha's moto is *"Chira Chenehi Mor Bhasa Janani..."* ('My Mother Language is My Ever Beloved'). In other sense, Sabha possesses respect and admiration for all mother languages.

Annual conventions of Assam Sahitya Sabha and all other Sahitya Sabhas of various languages of Assam are glaring examples of what a huge kind of enthusiasm is generated by those events. Lakh of common people are gathered in such annual sessions and it is hardly seen anywhere in the world. Assam Sahitya Sabha has already celebrated its centenary. This century-old organisation had extended cooperation to the Christian missionaries in their sincere efforts to spread and develop Assamese and English language in Kohima and Dimapur in Nagaland and also in other places of the Northeast, such as, Khashi Jayantia Hills (presently Meghalaya), NEFA (presently Arunachal Pradesh), and others. Assam Sahitya Sabha had never opposed to opening of English medium schools because one of the main objectives of Sabha is to enlighten underdeveloped communities with proper education. At present, most of the indigenous language Sahitya Sabhas have adopted Roman script and the Bodo Sahitya Sabha has adopted Devanagiri script.

In the Assam Sahitya Sabha annual session in 2015 held at Kaliabor in Nagaon district, Sabha's the then President Rong Bong Terang had said that Assamese language is the patron of all the tribal languages of the Northeastern Region.

Very recently, Assam's eight indigenous language Sahitya Sabhas, 28 student and youth organisations and other communities have joined hands with Assam Sahitya Sabha to raise voice for proper preparation of National Register of Citizens, to oppose Citizens' Act (Amendment) Bill and also to introduce flawless and completely acceptable State Language Policy, Education Policy and Employment Policy in Assam. If such goodwill and mutual trust among all the organisations remain intact, then even in this age of globalisation, a new nationalism will come into being for the sake of interest of the indigenous people of Assam.

Ethno-Cultural Identity and Boundaries Maintenance in Northeast India

Dr. Kaba Daniel

Northeast India is a frontier region in India sharing international borders with China, Burma, Bhutan and Bangladesh. The region provides a strategic link with West Bengal in India. Northeast India comprises of eight states: Arunachal Pradesh, Assam, Manipur, Meghalaya, Mizoram, Nagaland, Tripura and Sikkim. Of these, the three states of Manipur, Tripura and Assam were organized during the time of Ahoms and the districts of Sibsagar, Lakhimpur, Darrang, Nowgong and Kamrup reflect the existence of these independent feudal states from the Middle Ages down to their annexation by the British in the 19th century. The other four states of Arunachal Pradesh, Meghalaya, Mizoram and Nagaland with indigenous inhabitants were labeled as scheduled tribes. These states were curved out of British Assam after 1947 which invited ethnic issues, problems and challenges in the region. Even Assam is partly a legacy of the British rule as it reverberates with ethno-political unrest. Therefore, if India is comfortably accommodating the label of different ethnic related terms such as ethno-regional, ethno-religions, ethno-cultural, ethno languages, ethno-identity, ethno-race, ethno mosaic culture, ethno conflicts and ethnic boundaries issues, problems and challenges than the ethnic-cultural identity and boundary issues in Northeast region is no exception. The present ethnic and boundary issues and situation in Northeast region have become more complex in nature. This paper is an attempt to make a study on some of the most relevant phenomena of ethno-cultural identity and boundary maintenance in Northeast India. The author uses social scientific approach as well as phenomenological approach for the study.

Concept and Theoretical Understanding of the Study

The Greek work 'ethnos' is polysemantic in meaning. The term refers to 'people of the same race or nationality who share a distinctive culture.' When it is used in ethnographical or ethnological sense, it refers to people like the English, Japanese, Esmimos, Assamese, Nagas, Ashantis, Bushmen, Gonds, Oriyas, Lalungs and others. As such, communities with large or small population, primitive and modern alike may be addressed as ethnos (S. K, Acharya 1990:69, D.Saikia and D.N. Majumdar 1990:28). The Nagas in Nagaland or Manipuris (Meitie) in Manipur, with distinct identity and culture which are not present in any other group of people give good examples of ethnicity. The specific cultural attributes include spoken language, religion, folklore, folk customs, rites and ceremonies, standards of behaviour which include courtesy greetings, food, dress, habits, aesthetic ideals and artistic culture and different types of house constructions. No single cultural component, however, may be regarded as an indispensable ethno-differentiating attribute.

The scholars who work in Northeast India express that one of the absolutely necessary ethnic features is ethnic consciousness which means the realization by certain members of an ethnic group that they belong to a particular and distinct culture. It is in this context that ethnic consciousness produces an ethnonym, a name applied to a given ethnic group. Another component of ethnic consciousness is the belief in a common origin but often mystical. Such belief may also take the form of shared memory of past migrations [folk tradition of migrations among Garos, Khasis, Jaintias, Tiwas, various Naga tribes and others] in the Northeast India (*Ibid*).

Clifford Geertz, an American cultural anthropologist writes that ethno-cultural identity is attached with primordial. He says "By a

Primordial is meant one that stems from the 'givens' or, more precisely, as culture is inevitably involved in such matters, the assumed 'givens' of social existence: immediate contiguity and kin connection mainly, but beyond them the givenness that stems from being born into a particular religious community, speaking a particular language, or even a dialect of a language, and following particular social practices. These congruities of blood, speech, custom, and so on, are seen to have an ineffable, and at times an overpowering, coerciveness in and of themselves" (Clifford Geertz 1973:259). According to Clifford Geertz, the chief elements of ethnic community boundary markers include assumed blood ties, race, language, region, religion and customs (*ibid*, Clifford Geertz 1994: 29-34).

Pierre van den Berghe also shares that ethnicity or ethnic boundary always involves the cultural and genetic boundaries of a population bounded by the rule or practice of endogamy (Pierre van den Berghe 1994:97-98). As Berghe expresses "Culture is a merely proximate explanation of why people behave ethnocentrically and nepotically. As every ethnographer knows, when natives are asked why they behave a certain way, the answer: because it is the custom. The anthropologist then translates: because of his culture; the sociologist says: because he has been socialized into the norms of his society; and the psychologist counters: because of his learning experiences. All of them are right as far as they go, but none of them has explained why all human societies practice kin selection and are ethnocentric." (*Ibid*)

By boundary maintenance the author does not refer to physical boundary but ethnic boundary. Of course, sometimes physical boundary also do influence ethnic boundary. Thus, by 'ethnic boundary', we mean 'the social boundaries of a group that maintains its identity when its members interact with others, and this entails criteria for determining membership and ways of signalling membership and exclusion.' (Fredrick Barth (ed.) 1969:12) Ethnic boundaries are articulated in terms of man-made distinctions on the basis of language, religion, social organization, endogamy and exogamy, shifts and drifts by ethnic actors (Andreas Wimmer 2008:997). Unlike physical boundaries, **ethnic**

boundaries are not fixed (**Sun-Ki Chai** 2005:375) and they are fluid one. Ethnic dynamics are the outcome of the efforts on the part of ethnic actors to construct and maintain ethnic boundaries. Construction and maintenance of ethnic boundaries involve complex processes of contraction and expansion through exclusion and inclusion of a group of people within an ethnic community based on cultural markers and social interactions. The community leaders and organizations play very important roles in the politics of boundary making and maintenance. According to Bent D. Jorgenson, ethnic boundaries are best understood as cognitive or mental boundaries situated in the minds of people and the result of the collective efforts of construction and maintenance. It dichotomizes insiders from outsiders -'us' from 'them' (Accessed on 24 October, 2009). Ethnic boundaries are open to multiple individual perceptions and interpretations. Ethnic boundaries are social constructions and reconstructions mostly made in peace interaction.

Fredrik Barth, the Norwegian Social Anthropologist goes further into investigation and says: "First, we give primary emphasis to the fact that ethnic groups are categories of ascription and identification by the actors themselves, and thus have the characteristic of organizing interaction between people. We attempt to relate other characteristics of ethnic groups to this primary feature. Second, the essays all apply a generative viewpoint to the analysis: rather than working through a typology of forms of ethnic groups and relations, we attempt to explore the different processes that seem to be involved in generating and maintaining ethnic groups. Third, to observe these processes we shift the focus of investigation from internal constitution and history of separate groups to ethnic boundaries and boundary maintenance (Fredrik Barth 1969:12)." Barth's ideas that ethnic boundaries maintain ethnic communities is insufficient as primordialist scholars argue that it involves historical, economic, social and political circumstances. Further, Barth says that to actively construct ethnic boundary and maintain ethnic boundaries, mobilization and motivation factors are not enough. The communities' elites and organizations play important roles for the successful boundary maintenance.

Analysis of Northeast Indian Situations

The Existence of Cultural Plurality and Identity Crisis

T. Raatan study shows that the Northeast India region is situated between the two great traditions of the Indic Asia and the Mongoloid Asia. This geographical-cultural condition of 'in-between-ness' is a necessary factor for the crisis of identity. He pointed out that it was only since the British period that the entire region came to be consociated with India politically. Many leaders of the 'underground outfits' of the region may argue that political integration of the region to India was done without the consultation of the people of this region. The lack of cultural relatedness, especially of the 'tribal' culture, weakens the political merger, and the racial and cultural difference that came to play a crux role in defining the self-identity (T. Raatan 2006:11).

Raatan further pointed out that the Northeast peoples are politically Indian but are racially and culturally Mongoloid. The consciousness of these two attitudinal differences of identities is pulling the people and shaking political loyalty. The problem of acceptance on the part of Indic culture with its caste-ridden social system or Verna, and the problem of identification on the part of the Northeasterners because of the underlying cultural difference create identity problem. He also points out that when one talks about cultural plurality in India, since it shares little or no commonality in its traditional culture with the rest of India, the case of the 'tribal' people in Northeast India is especially acute (*Ibid*).

To address the identity crisis in this part of the region, one has to bear in mind the cultural plurality of the Northeast in general and the sharp difference between the people assimilated into Indic culture and the unassimilated 'tribal' people in particular. Out of constant interactions, cultures influenced each other and developed commonalities. The Indic-sanskritic culture of India is as a foreign culture assumed by indigenous ethnic communities wherein the live at home for many centuries for a large part of the regions. The assimilation of the people into the Indic culture became a defining question of the people of the region today (*Ibid:* 11-12). He also agrees with the view of Ananda Bhagabati who says that the distinctive 'geo-ethnic character' of the Northeast is helpful in clarifying the multicultural nature and the cultural differences between the people (*Ibid*).

Role of Colonial Rule in Ethnic Conflicts

The British ideology of encouraging ethnic, sub-ethnic, religious, and linguistic identities and communities made the Northeast regions go against the Indian nation in building a sovereign nation-state. They marched recklessly along the very path prescribed by the British Raj in 1862, when they laid down the law of social discriminate policy to isolate 'tribals'. However, there is no clear cut how long this fateful route will last; there is little doubt what awaits them at the end (*Ibid*:12). As an outcome, the continuing radical actions and violent demonstrations over the last five decades have turned India's Northeast into a life-threatening place. Large-scale introduction of narcotics and arms from neighbouring Myanmar (Burma) and China has added volume to this strategically crucial area a potential theatre of violent secessionist movements in the Northeast India.

Elites' Roles of Ethnic Communities and Boundary Maintenance

Fredrik Barth says, "First....boundaries persists despite a flow of personnel across them. In other words, categorical ethnic distinctions do not depend on an absence of mobility, contact and information. But do entail social processes of exclusion and incorporation where by discrete categories are maintained despite changing participation and membership in the course of individual life histories. Secondly, one finds that stable, persisting, and often vitally important social relations are maintained across such boundaries, and are frequently based precisely on the dichotomized ethnic statuses. In other words, ethnic distinctions do not depend on an absence of social interaction and acceptance, but are quite contrary to the very foundations on which embracing social systems are built. Interaction in such a social system does not lead to its liquidation through change and acculturation; cultural differences can persist despite inter-ethnic contact and interdependence" (Fredrik Barth 1969:10).

The highlighted statement of Barth shows that while maintaining ethnic boundaries communities' elites and social organizations play vital roles in social interaction. The big and small ethnic communities of the elites play important roles. For instance, Khasis, Jaintias and Garos in Meghalaya state; Meiteis, Nagas and Kukis in Manipur state, tribals and non-tribals of ethnic communities in Assam and Tripura; Arunachal Pradesh, Nagaland, Mizoram and Sikkim among the tribal ethnic communities; all these have related to ethnic issues, problems and challenges. They are often not asserted or re-asserted, contested and dismantled by each state ethnic communities' elites and social organizations.

Growth of Separatist Movement with Ethnic Militancy in Protection of Identity

The Northeastern region of India faces insurgencies or separatist movements from over 50 groups. Although each conflicts has its own roots and antecedents, the issues raised include language and ethnicity, tribal rivalry, migration, control over local resources, access to water, and widespread feeling of exploitation and alienation. The region has witnessed more violence in the last 50 years than any other part of the country. Raatan figured out that according to reliable estimates, fatalities caused by insurgency in the Northeast have gradually increased from about 400 in 1992 to four times that amount in 2002. Besides loss of human life, hundreds of thousands and more are internally displaced, forced to live in unhygienic and makeshift camps and, as a consequence, hundreds of them lose their lives due to disease and lack of basic life amenities (T. Raatan 2006:21).

Examining some of the facts and experiences related to ethnic issues, problems and challenges in this part of the region, Raatan pointed out that the state of Nagaland bears the scars of the region's long-drawn history of insurgency, which served as a precursor and a model for other constituent states of the region. The Naga tribes are fragmented by state and national boundaries. The principal Naga militant group today, the National Socialist Council of Nagalim (Isak-

Muivah), demands a united homeland, Nagalim and claims a territory six times the size of present-day Nagaland, including most of Manipur, as well as parts of Assam, Arunachal Pradesh, and Myanmar of their ancestral homeland. Late A. Z. Phizo, the founder of the Naga insurgency, opened the Myanmar front to the insurgency in the 1950s. Phizo's group gradually established links with Chinese and Pakistani leaderships as well. Tribalism and tribal fragmentations with the Naga insurgency that surfaced in the 1960s continue to plague the movement even today (*Ibid*). As a matter of fact, the Nagas protect their rights with the slogan that 'what Nagas are, what Nagas were.' Similarly the Mizos in the Mizo Hills under the leadership of Laldenga signed an accord with central government of India in 1986. Through dialogue, the accord effectively ended the insurgency and he emerged as the Chief Minister in the newly pacified state (*Ibid*).

Raatan recorded that Assamese nationalism was first articulated in 1979 as a protest against immigration from West Bengal and Bangladesh. The Indian government's effort to settle the problem, notably through the Assam Accord of 1985, proved unsuccessful. The United Liberation Front for Asom (ULFA), which demands secessions, referring the economic exploitation of Assam has been the most prominent insurgent group in recent years. It represents Assamese-speaking Hindu descendants of the Ahoms, but has also made preludes to other groups. While the ULFA has lost some of the credibility and influence, it continues to be a major source of violence and instability of this region (*Ibid*).

Within Assam, the Bodos are the largest plain tribals and their movement is a struggle for indigenous rights and tribal empowerment in a majority of non-tribal state. In 1987, they got mobilized to demand the creation of a separate state of 'Bodoland' based on the historical precedent of forming new states out of Assam. The Bodos have a pattern of ethnic cleansing that is missing from the ULFA, and India's response to their insurgency has been predominantly military (*Ibid: 22*).

Raatan study also showed that organised tribal insurgency in Tripura began with the emergence of erstwhile Tripura National Volunteer

(TNV) in 1978 and has been continuing since then with only one and half years' peaceful interregnum. Having signed a tripartite peace accord with the government of Tripura, the TNV insurgents laid down arms en masse in 1988. The state passed through a relatively peaceful period till May 1990 when the All Tripura Tribal Force (ATTF) was formed. In September 1991 the outlawed National Liberation Front of Tripura (NLFT) made its appearance. The ATTF group, widely believed to have been sponsored by political elements aligned with the then oppositions, carried on operations by selectively killing leaders and workers of Congress and Tripura Upajati Juba Samiti (TUJS), who were ruling the state then. The NLFT, on the other hand, continued their hit and run operational targeting unarmed civilians as well as security forces after a number of former TNV commanders who had availed themselves of all rehabilitation benefits, joined the outfit (*Ibid:23*). The reason behind Tripura's insurgency problem lies in the deep resentment among tribals over the demographic imbalance in the state. The majority status of non-tribals Bengalis as a result of influx of refugees from erstwhile East Pakistan (present Bangladesh) is perceived as a threat to identity, culture and tradition (*Ibid*). In Manipur state, there are more than 40 militant groups. Of these groups, some of them include United National Liberation Front (UNLF), Kanglei Yawol Kanna Lup (KYKL), Kuki Revolutionary Army (KRA), Kuki National Army (KNA), People's United Liberation Front (PULF), United People's Party of Kangleipak (UPPK), Kangleipak Communist Party (KCP).

Questions of Ethno-Cultural Identity of Each and Common Tragedy

The striking demographic feature of Northeast India is that the hills are predominantly inhabited by scheduled tribe ethnic communities while in the plains the dominant population belongs to other ethnic communities. Moreover, no significant scheduled caste population is found in the hills. The total population of this area according to census of India 1971 was 19,581,785 out of which 4346117 were members of scheduled tribes. The percentage of scheduled tribe population varies widely from state to state (D. Saikia and D.N. Majumder 1990:28).

As per census data from 1971 to 2011 about four percent of India's total population comes from the northeastern region. According to the census 2011, the total population of the region is about 45 million, of which Assam contributes the highest [68%] of the total population followed by Tripura [8 %] (accessed on 21/10/2018).

In preservation of ethno-cultural identity, Singh's work in 1982 shows that the ethnic movements in Northeast India has three essential factors- to assert the identity around certain social problems, to concretize the identity by forming an ethnic association and to claim for a separate administrative arrangement, so that the group concerned can preserve their cultural heritage, language, etc. The final step is to demand a separate administrative unit comprising the areas where the ethno-cultural group forms a majority (K.S. Singh 1990). Within the pan-Nagas, the Zeliangrong movement is another case (GangmumeiKabui 1982). The Kabuis, Liangmais, Rougmas and the Jemis who are closely akin to each other spread over three states, Assam, Manipur and Nagaland and have merged together to claim a separate homeland for themselves which appears to be an impossible mission. The same is the case with the Kuki movement trying to unite all the fragmentary Kuki groups into one strong ethno-cultural identity (*Ibid*).

Pandora Box: Ethno-Cultural Issues, Problems and Challenges

S. K. Chaube expressed that part of the ethnic complexity of the region must be traced in the ethno-cultural factors. Migration from different directions from the prehistoric period has completely confused the racial picture. Hinduism penetrated the organized states of the area long before the British advent but hardly cast its spell below their feudal hierarchy and its paraphernalia. This explains the presence of large number of half-Hindus. Islam never had political sway and the entire Muslim population is migratory. Political fragmentation on ethnic lines clearly dates from the British period (S. K. Chaube 1982:18). It is probably because of the complexity of the ethnic situation in the plains of Assam, theoretically expressed in the phrase 'cross cutting cleavages', that the region has weathered the 1972 reorganization of Northeast India (*Ibid*).

S. K. Chaube study showed that there is something in 'tribalism' which is out of tune with the modern political order. The first is based on kinship relations, the second on territorial loyalty. Political boundaries inevitably cut across the ethnic [or, for that matter], religious or linguistic boundaries, and create minority problems. Border adjustments of Assam with Bengal, Manipur and Tripura in the 19th century, not only created problems for the Assamese but caused numerous tribal groups (Garo, Khasis, Mizo and Naga). Separation of Burma (1937) and partition of British India gave international significance to their borders and restricted the mobility of the tribal people living on shifting cultivation and doing trade with neighbouring countries. Finally, the establishment of district boundaries affected most of the tribal groups and created multi-ethnic district. With the transformation of administrative districts into political entities, inter-district borders created political problems (*Ibid: 20*). In addition it may be pointed that it is sometimes political boundaries or physical boundaries that necessarily influence ethnic boundaries and boundaries maintenance.

Chaube also observed in his study that no less significant was the institutionalization of tribal authority traditionally based on customs. Rules for administration of justice and police vested the 'village Chiefs'- usually the chiefs of the dominant clans- with administrative, judicial and political powers under the overall control of the District Officers, thus combining lineage with territorial authority. Where there was no chief a 'headman' was created. As a matter of fact, paradoxically, the authoritarian structure was strengthened at the village level and, at the same time, a district orientation was to the political outlook of the hill men. The District Officer being virtually the supreme authority, all appeals from the verdicts of the village chiefs were sent to the officers. Naturally the recourse to such appeal was taken more frequently by the educated sections than the uneducated and the District Officer's decisions were not always liked by the Chiefs. An agitation to replace the system of executive appeal by the jurisdiction of the High Court was started by the Chiefs with the beginning of reform moves in the name of preservation of tribal autonomy (*Ibid:20-21*).

K. Kamkhenthang study showed that a case can be reflected here, the tribes of Manipur are often unacceptably classified either into (a) Naga and non-Naga or (b) Naga and Kuki or (c) Naga and Chin-Kuki-Mizo tribes. This is a general classification based on naming given by outsiders. The generic terms like Naga, Chin, Kuki were given by outsiders for their own easy reference. Aitchinson (1978:45) mentioned how the term Kuki came to be applied to the Chin-Kuki-Mizo constellation of tribes.

Kamkhenthang records the old Kukis towards Nagaism and says that there are a number of small tribes known anthropologically as old Kuki tribes. They are called Old Kukis because of the fact (a) they were found in Manipur earlier than the so-called Chin-Kui-Mizo tribes and (b) secondly they have more affinities to the late comers who are their cognate tribes than to the Naga tribes. Ethnic transformation of the old Kukis goes along the line of political loyalty of the tribes concerned. They are also motivated by the Naga movement or Naga politics. As such they are culturally Chin-Kuki, domestically Meitei by long settlement in the plain in the vicinity of the Meitei and politically Naga under the influence of the Naga politics. Kamkhenthang has cited R.C Ranjit and A. Bhagabati (1980) and states that small tribes like Anal, Moyon, Monsang were influenced by the Tangkhul to be Naga by inducting them to Naga movement. R. K. Das (1984:18) states that Tangkhul Nagas are taking the leading role in transforming the tribes into Naga ethni label by different agencies. Among the Marings, from the Pawis of Falam and Haka areas of the Chin State of Burma, are now Naga due to the activities of Tangkhul Baptist Association. They have evangelists and pastors working among the Mring, the cultural activities of All Manipur Naga Students' Association headed by Tangkhul Students' and various socio-cultural interactions. Among some of the tribes the opinion is divided as to join Kuki group or Naga group (K. Kamkhenthang 1990:297).

The past memories between two major ethnic communities of Nagas-Kukis in the 1990s and other ethnic related issues, perhaps led to the erection of monolith stones as a commemoration of 'Kuki Genocide' on 13th September, 2018 at Churachanpur District of Manipur. A week ahead of 13th September, they tried to erect three monolith stones but one of the monoliths broke into two pieces. The split took place right in the middle of the monolith. As per the oral tradition for the Nagas, it is believed to be a bad sign, an omen that in future problems may occur. How do the Kukis perceive it? The epitome memory stone reads, "COMMEMORATION OF BLACK SEPTEMBER (1992-2018), 25th Anniversary of Kuki Genocide by Tangkhul-Led NSCN (IM)". This day is celebrated as a day of honour and an achievement. It recalls the 25th Anniversary of Kuki Genocide by Tangkhul-Led NSCN (IM). The Monolith contains a list of all the victims. The monolith could turn into the graveyard of ethnic violent of the two ethnic communities in future. Moreover, just after few days, a mass rally was organized in the capital city of Delhi to redress their rights with a slogon "Lest we get" and "seeking justice to victims of Kuki Genocide". This is sowing seed for the future violence. The 1990s conflict was very unfortunate as both the two communities suffered and were equally victimized. The report from the United Naga Council (UNC) shows a collateral damage meted out to the Kukis and Nagas: The table below indicates the killed, injured and burnt houses during the Ethnic Conflict from 1992-1997 (Source: Report from UNC, Manipur 1992-1998).

Sl.No	Year	Killed		Injured		House Burnt	
		Kuki	Naga	Kuki	Naga	Kuki	Naga
1	1992	11	02	22	26	Nil	11
2	1993	261	60	68	72	2,144	1, 365
3	1994	95	67	49	28	262	425
4	1995	65	44	39	43	404	653
5	1996	32	21	18	15	61	127
6	1997	06	13	09	13	Nil	Nil
Total		470	207	205	197	2,870	2,582

In fact, the Kuki brethren must be sincerely grateful to the Nagas for their generosity in sheltering and accommodating them as peaceful co-existing ethnic communities for the past many years and till date. To substantiate what is being said, the historical evidence says:

"The standing Order of the President Manipur State Darbar issued by Captain Harvey. Part-I: Order No. 11 of 18th August, 1931, Read "The Kukis shall not be issued fire arms because of the savagery nature against the Nagas". Part II: Declared that "They shall be granted firearms on loan for protection against wild animals". Order no.9th September, 1933 declared that, "Kuki village having 20 household shall pay House Tax of Rs 6/- per annum. Standing Order of the President Manipur State Darbar issued by T. A. Sharp in his order reads "Kukis in the Naga Areas in Manipur are Aliens and Refugees". Standing Order of PMSD No. 2 of 23rd July, 1941 declared that: "The Kukis shall obtain prior permission from the Chief of Naga Village for settlement and pay House Tax to the Naga Chief". Note: The GOI agreed to the requisition of R. Suisa (an eminent Naga leader) to grant the Kukis relief fund or refugee fund under Memo P3/9/66 of Finance Ministry of Home Affairs GOI and payment made to the Kukis by the state Govt. of Manipur vide Memo No. 01/R/RFL.

1st Payment   : 22/4/1957

2nd payment   : 7/7/1959

3rd payment   : 28/2/1966

In spite of all the historical facts and figures that the above record, the Nagas in particular and other ethnic communities of Northeast India in general are accommodating them (Kukis) for peaceful co-existence. For instance, they (Kukis) are given accommodation in Manipur Naga four dominant districts of Senapati, Chandel, Ukhrul and Tamenglong in the Hills and Manipuris (*Meities*) in the valley; in Nagaland in the Medziphema areas, in Assam Half-Long and Nowgong areas, in Meghalaya in the Happy Valley areas, etc.

Who will Bell the Cat?

To conclude, no one is certain, how old the ethno-cultural identity and attachment is to one's community of this region. It is difficult to ascertain who are the original settlers and who are not, which needs to be addressed. The visible trend is that every ethnic community of this region is claiming, asserting and protecting its ethno-cultural identity and boundaries maintenance. It has become the present day contested issues, problems and challenges in Northeast India. The challenge before each ethnic group in Northeast India is 'To Bell the Cat'. The fiction concerns a group of mice who debate plans to negate the threat of a predatory cat. One of them proposes placing a bell around its neck, so that they are warned of its approach. The plan is acclaimed by the others, until one mouse asks who will volunteer to place the bell on the cat. All of them make excuses.

The tale is applied to teach the wisdom of evaluating a plan, not only how desirable the outcome would be but also how it can be carried out. It substantiates a moral lesson about the fundamental difference between ideas and their feasibility, and how this affects the value of a given plan. The tale gives rise to the idiom 'to bell the cat', which means to attempt, or agree to perform, an impossibly difficult task. Tracing the historical finding, it was basically the nickname given by the Scottish nobleman Archibald Douglas, 5th Earl of Angus.

In a similar manner, may I throw this common question to all of us here 'who will bell the Cat?' with regard to ethnic related issues, problems and challenges of Northeast India? My suggestion is, if the two communities fail peace negotiation and peaceful co-existence, who will do it for us? Why not we look for possibilities to construct bridges to live in peace for the brighter future instead of constructing walls and engulf ourselves with enmity in this 'global village' world. My sincere appeals to the intellectuals and academicians is to look forward, contribute peace, dismantle and deconstruct ethnic boundaries of social differences experienced in the region.

References

Acharya S. K. "Ethnic Processes in North-Eastern India" in B. Pakim (edit.) *Nationality, Ethnicity and Cultural Identity in Northeast India.* New Delhi: Omsons Publications, 1990.

Barth Fredrick. (ed.) *Ethnic groups and Boundaries: The Social organization of Cultural Differences,* Boston: Little Brown and Company, 1969.

Chaube, S.K. "Tribal Societies and the Problem of Nation-building" in K.S. Singh (Edit.) *Tribal Movement in India, Manohar*, New Delhi, 1982.

Chai, Sun-Ki. 'Predicting Ethnic Boundaries', *European Sociological Review*, Vol.21, No. 4, September 2005.

Geertz, Clifford. *The Interpretation of Cultures, Selected Essays*. New York: Basic Book, 1973.

_____. 'Primordial and Civic Ties' in John Hutchinson and Anthony D Smith (eds.) *Theories of Nationalism*. New York: Oxford University Press, 1994.

Jorgenson Bent D., 'Ethnic Boundaries and the Margins of Margin: in a Post-Colonial and Conflict Resolution Perspective, http://www.gmu.edu/programs/ icar/ pcs/jorgens html (accessed on 24 October, 2009).

Kabui, Gangmumei. "TheZeliangrong Movement: An Historical Study" in K.S. Singh (Edit.) *Tribal Movement in India, Manohar*, New Delhi, 1982.

Kamkhenthang K., "Identity Crisis among the Tribes of Manipur" in B. Pakim (edit.) *Nationality, Ethnicity and Cultural Identity In North-East India*. New Delhi: Omsons Publications, 1990.

Pierre van den Berghe, 'A Socio-Biological Perspective', in John Hutchinson and Anthony D Smith (eds.) in John Hutchinson and Anthony D Smith (eds.) *Theories of Nationalism*. New York: Oxford University Press, 1994.

Raatan ,T. *History, Religion and Culture of North East India*. Delhi: Isha Book, 2006.

Saikia, D. and D.N. Majumder. "Some Characteristics of Ethno-Cultural Identity in North-East India" in B. Pakim (edit.) *Nationality, Ethnicity and Cultural Identity In North-East India*, New Delhi: Omsons Publications, 1990.

Singh, K.S. *Tribal Movement in India, Manohar*, New Delhi, 1982.

Wimmer, Andreas. 'The Making and Unmaking of Ethnic Boundaries: A Multilevel Process Theory' in *American Journal of Sociology* Vol.113, No. 4 January 2008.

Northeastern Cultural Metamorphosis: A Phenomenological View

Dr. Babu Joseph Karakombil SVD

The discipline of phenomenology, as espoused by Edmund Husserl may be understood as the study of structures of experience, or consciousness. Literally, phenomenology is the study of "phenomena": appearances of things, or things as they appear in our experience, or the ways we experience things, thus the meanings things assume in our experience. Phenomenology studies conscious experience as experienced from the subjective point of view.

In recent philosophy of mind, the term "phenomenology" is often restricted to the characterization of sensory qualities of seeing, hearing, etc.: it is focused on sensations of various kinds. However, our experience is usually not limited to mere sensation; it much richer in content. Accordingly, in the phenomenological tradition, phenomenology is given a much wider range, addressing the meaning things have in our experience, notably, the significance of objects, events, tools, the flow of time, the self, and others, as these things arise and are experienced in our "life-world". In other words, the 'life-world' is the template from where we experience which includes sensation and the structure of our experience.

Our focus in this paper is to take a phenomenological view of the cultural metamorphosis in the context of Northeast which prides itself as a kaleidoscope of cultures that are at once steeped in tradition as well as soaked in modernity. A cursory look at the large number of Northeastern Tribal societies, their different languages, cuisines, dress patterns, social interactions, professions, economic activities, belief systems, traditions, social institutions will make us realize one thing prominently: it is a complex system attempting to retain their precious traditions on the one hand and the openness to embrace the emerging modernity on the other. It is the study of this complexity found in the intertwining of tradition and modernity that the Northeastern culture that makes this study fascinating and relevant.

Unfolding of Culture

How can we understand the phenomenon of culture? It is not a monolithic entity as often made out to be; in common parlance it is more often made out to be a single identifiable entity with its own distinctiveness and contrast with other similar cultures. That is why one finds mention of a Naga culture as distinct from a Khasi culture, or a Nishi culture or any other for that matter. While there is some merit in saying that each culture is identifiable and distinct from another, it must also be borne in mind that culture as an entity is constituted of several related aspects that are concurrently experienced in actual life. "Culture encompasses religion, food, what we wear, how we wear it, our language, marriage, music, what we believe is right or wrong, how we sit at the table, how we greet visitors, how we behave with loved ones, and a million other things." [1] It is then clear that the culture is not an isolated entity that can be viewed in an secluded manner but it is, to use a term from the fast food world, a 'combo' which includes many aspects of our life in society. To understand a culture, therefore, we need to delve deep into a variety of human activities done within a social milieu that collectively earn the term culture. In other words it is this collective experience of people belonging to a particular society that has earned the nomenclature – culture.

Religion – Foundational Aspect of a Culture

Religion, as one of the constitutive aspects of a culture, has a more foundational role to play. This is because of its critical role in creating and sustaining meaning system that guides people's lives. And this meaning system is transmitted to the succeeding generation of people of a particular society through a series of myths developed; and these myths are recounted and 'relived' in the ritual performances. In his book, 'The power of Myth'[2] Joseph Campell speaks of myths dealing with personhood and humankind. Just as parables and analogies are used in our human discourse because our words cannot exhaustively convey the truths so also myths are invoked in religious discourses to convey perennial values and meanings of human existence. Myths have therefore a central role to play in keeping the personhood of a certain society alive and therefore they are narrated in social gatherings in formal and informal manner.

Before the written word came into existence myths have orally been communicated either in prose or poetry form. As for instance, you have the myth of creation among the Khasis of Meghalaya which speaks about the 'origin' of Khasi people. The Khasi mythology traces the Tribe's original abode to 'Ki *Hynñiewtrep* ("The Seven Huts"). According to the Khasi mythology, "U Blei Trai Kynrad" (God, the Lord Master) had originally distributed the human race into 16 heavenly families (*Khadhynriew Trep*). And among these 16 families seven families are stuck on earth while the other nine are stuck in Heaven. According to the myth, a heavenly ladder kept on the sacred Lum Sohpetbneng Peak (found in the present-day Ri-Bhoi district) enabled people to go freely and frequently to heaven whenever they wanted. However this privilege was lost when one day they were tricked into cutting a divine tree which was situated at Lum Diengiei Peak (also in present-day Ri-Bhoi district). This act of chopping this divine tree was considered a grave error and that made the Khasi people to lose access to heaven for ever.

Although the Nagas have different stories about their origin, most of them point towards their origin from hill or rock. The Angamis, Semas, Rengmas and the Lothas Naga Tribes have the KHEZA-KHONOMA legend which speaks about a village named KENDMA, with a huge stone slab that had magical properties. People used to spread farm-produce over it for drying in morning used to get doubled in quantity by evening. The three sons of the old couple used to take turns to use it. One day there was a quarrel between the sons regarding whose turn it was. The couple fearing violence and murder, set the stone on fire, and it got cracked. The spirit contained within the stone escaped and the stone no longer had its magical powers. The sons thereafter left the village to bring the spirit back, but never came back and became the forefathers of the Angami, the Sema and the Lotha Tribes.

According to another legend, subscribed by the western Angamis, the first man evolved from a lake called 'THEMIAKELKUZIE' near Khonoma village. The Rengmas believe that until recently they and Lothas formed one tribe. The Aos and the Phoms trace their origin to the LUNGTEROK (Six Stones) on the Chongliemdi hill. There are similar 'creation' myths prevalent in other Tribes of Northeast, but I am not going to illustrate all that since that would require a full length paper in itself. And in the following sections of my paper I am limiting my phenomenological description of a few cultural facets of two communities in the otherwise vast and varied cultures of the Northeast, namely, that of the Khasis of Meghalaya and the Rongmei Tribe of Nagaland. They are taken into account in my paper for no special consideration but as mere representatives of two cultures at variance as well as those subjected to the process of metamorphosis.

Initiation Rituals

An important constituent aspect of religion is the initiation rituals where a new member is inducted into the community. Induction into the community is not ensured by mere birth in that community; it has to be formally done by a designated person of the community who would perform some established rituals that makes the new individual eligible to become a bonefide member. As for instance, among the Rongmei Tribe of the Nagas, there is the tradition, that when the baby completes five days, a ceremony called 'Penbam –Reimei is observed in the early morning of the fifth day. It is believed that the deity called penbam-pu-penbampui' may give arm to the child when they come to take the placenta that was hidden inside the house. As a precaution, they are propitiated so that no harm is done to the child. This is the first and obligatory ceremony in the life of an individual. This ritual is performed by a priest (Mhu) just at the outside wall where the placenta is disposed. The items used in the ceremony are a cock, a piece of ginger, a plantain leaf, and a plantain cup. The ceremony has got its methodical procedure.[3]

Among the Khasi Tribe, the naming rites (Ka Jer Ka Thoh) is quite significant. The naming rite is to be performed soon after the birth of a child, that too only in the morning. In preparing to perform the rite certain articles such as a winnowing tray (U prah) Sla Lakhar commonly known as 'Chandada' on which a small heap of powdered rice is placed, a gourd (U klong) powdered rice(purew) and liquor from fermented rice (Ka ladum). A model of a bow (Ka Tieh lawbei) and three arrows (Ka Nam Lawbei) are also to be included in case of naming a male child. Each arrow has certain meaning and significance.

Marriage Rituals

Another significant moment in a person's life is when he enters in to matrimony. It, in a sense, creates a 'break' in the hitherto status of a bachelor, as he assumes a new identity in the family as well as in society as a married man. A married man has multiple roles: one being a son to his parents, brother to his siblings, husband to his wife, father to his children. However, in order to effect this change over from a bachelor to a married man he has to go through certain rituals performed by a community designated person whose validity is collectively accepted and endorsed.

Among the Khasi Tribe, a marriage ceremony takes place at the residence of the bride and the couple exchange rings or betel nut bags. Both girls and the boys of the tribe are free to choose their own desired partners. The marriage is confirmed once the groom shifts into the bride's ancestral household. The Khasi tribes of Meghalaya have different customs and traditions that are unique in respect of wedding practices.

The wedding attire in traditional Khasi Tribal wedding is a unique representation of their culture in Meghalaya. As practiced, a portion of the bride's wedding attire as well as jewelry is given by the bridegroom. The bride dresses herself in traditional Khasi dress on her wedding day. She wears a dhara or Jainesm in Khasi language. Both these dresses are quite detailed and comprise of several pieces of clothing bringing out the shape of the woman's body. The Jainesm includes two pieces of contrasting clothes, which rest on each shoulder of the bride. As part of the ritual the bride also wears a crown on the wedding day which is either made from gold or from silver. The groom too wears a traditional outfit on his special day which is known as Jymphong. Jymphong is actually a long coat without any sleeves or collar, and it is fastened with the help of two straps attached in the front. Nowadays many grooms also use their Jymphong with sarongs, and some of them also wear turban.

Among the Rongmei Naga Tribe marriage is performed at the groom's house. This is called "Mailapmei" when the bride arrives at the groom's house; she is received by the mother and elder sisters of the groom. Then the couple is seated on Nouhmibam, the marriage bed. The groom will sit on the right and the bride on the left dangling their legs on the side. The left foot of the groom and the right foot of the bride are placed on the piece of iron hoe (laogai) kept on the right side of a banana leaf. The performance of this ritual involves the sacrifice of a cock to propitiate the ancestral deity seeking God's blessings. The legs of the sacrificed bird are minutely observed. If the right leg of the cock overlapped the left, it was considered a good omen. A priest or one elder of the village performs this rite by holding the cock in his hands. In this ceremony, the priest and elders of the village pray to God and seek blessings for newly wedded couple for their prosperous life.[4]

Burial Customs

Among the Khasis it is customary to keep the body for two-nights, for the convenience of relatives to arrive for the cremation ritual. While the body is in the house it is a common custom among the Khasis to give modest food for all who attend and shower their sympathy and togetherness with the bereaved family. Among the Pnars it is not a custom to serve food to friends and neighbours, rather neighbours would bring food and 'kwai' for the family members and others who have come for the last rites of the deceased. In Life and Death: Reciprocity and Solidarity

As respect to the departed soul and the bereaved family, neighbours would stop going to the fields and take turns to be with the family members day and night till the body is cremated. Men are assigned to prepare the 'Krong' which is like an open coffin for carrying the body to the cremation ground, while women busy themselves preparing the 'Kwai' and food etc.

After cremation, female relatives would collect some of the bones and a primary burial takes place. Depending on the convenience of the lineage and/or clan members, a secondary burial is done a year after or later, when the remains would be deposited in the clan ossuary. Such an occasion is usually accompanied by more elaborate feasting for the lineage members and villagers. Both family and lineage members bear the expenses of such feasting; each family contributes animals for the feast as well as other food materials. It is a practice among the people in west Khasi hills that on the secondary burial of the father's mother 'Ka Meikha', her sons, sons' children and their clan members should bring at least one pig for the occasion. Respect for father is shown by the respect meted to his mother while alive and on her death the numbers of pigs brought by the son's children 'Khun-kha' speaks of the 'Mei-Kha' worthiness.[5]

Although funeral practices vary somewhat from one Naga Tribe to another there are also many similarities among them. The deceased is usually buried in a ceremony arranged by male relatives along a village path or in front of his house. The body of a male is buried with a live chicken, a fire stick and one or two spears in a coffin which is covered with a white cloth. A *gadozi* seed is placed between the teeth of the deceased, symbolic offering made to a devil in the afterlife.

A female's burial is slightly different; her body is buried with beads, a reaping hook and a young chicken and the gadzoso seed in a coffin that is covered with flat stones. On the stones are kept the contents of her carrying basket, rice seeds, millet, other grains, rice beer and drinking cups. The coffin is covered with dirt and with personal items belonging to the dead placed on the grave. The souls of righteous are expected to join the sky god Ukenpenofu. The souls of the evil people pass through seven existence below the earth. Life with the sky god is considered as similar as but better than life on earth. In order to enter this paradise one has to undergo the *zhatho genna* and refrain from eating unclean meat afterwards. Along with that the deceased has to wrestle with the devil on the narrow bridge that leads to sky god's domain. Failure to defeat him leads to the soul wandering between heaven and earth as a spirit that can cause harm. The bridge episode is found among all Naga tribes.[6]

Belief in Immortality of the Soul

The Rongmei people believe in the existence of life after death. It means the souls of the dead go to two places: one in Tingkao Kai, i.e., heaven and the other in Taruairam (land of the dead). The souls of those who lived a righteous life go to Tingkao Kai (heaven) and that of those who lived unrighteous life go to Taruairam where dreadful king called Taruai Gwangh or Joungangpu supervises them. It is also believed that the good souls are reborn into this world.

The Khasis also believe in the immortality of the soul; it means the soul survives the physical death of a person. In fact, they believe that, after the death of a person his soul goes to its heavenly home and waits for God on the threshold. The Khasis call it *'ka dwar U Blei'* which means the doorway of God. When the Khasis say a departed soul will experience eternal peace and rest with God, they metaphorically mean that his departed soul goes and enjoys *chewing betel nut with God {bam kwai ha iing u Blei)*. The supreme joy in Khasi eschatological thought is to chew *betel-nut* uninterruptedly in God's House. This idea follows from the day to day custom in Khasi society that eating *betel-nut* at leisure time means the time of complete relaxation. Hence, the metaphor *"Bam kwai ha iing U Blei" (eating betel-nut in the House of God)* means complete eternal rest in heaven with God. This idea implies that the Khasis believe in the immortality of human soul. It is precisely for this reason that the Khasi people pay respect to the souls of their departed relatives or parents.[7]

We have described the various cultural facets of two Tribes in the Northeast India in order to show how they have maintained these traditions that carry certain meaning for individuals and as well as for their Tribal community. These meanings are commonly shared and they are reinforced through their constant reenactment in the rituals described above. The traditional rituals and their meanings have been undergoing overt and covert transformation in their meeting with the Christian religion and western culture. This process of meeting with another culture and the transformation that occurs is a common phenomenon and this is often described by anthropologists as acculturation.

The Process of Acculturation

These communities of the Northeast have been undergoing change and transformation as a result of their contact with the western culture and Christian religion. The western culture came to influence these two cultures because of the arrival and impact of the European and American missionaries who introduced Christian faith among these two Tribes. These two influencing factors have brought in cultural assimilation and consequently transformation among these Tribes. Sociologists, anthropologists and archaeologists together have described this process of cultural change through cultural contact as 'acculturation'. The concept of acculturation has been defined as "... those phenomena which result when groups of individuals having different cultures come into continuous first hand contact ..."[8]

This process of acculturation is perceptible in the life of both Khasis and Ronhmei Naga Tribes majority of who have accepted Christianity. It is to be noted here that these Tribes have not left their traditional customs and values completely; rather they have assimilated the values and rituals of Christianity and have formed a new syncretic culture which is the contemporary culture of these Tribes. In this process what is significant is that the new syncretic culture is not a total break from the past but a continuum; new additions have been made giving rise to a rainbow culture based on a new meaning system. As a matter of fact, both the Khasis and the Nagas maintained their Tribal identity and membership even after converting to Christianity and the missionaries never saw the need to alter that,[9] although their world views have undergone noticeable transformation.

Formation of New Value Structures and Reinforcement of the Existing Ones

With the encounter with Christianity, the Naga as well as the Khasi Tribes have been exposed to new individual and social values while some of their existing values were reinforced. As for example, with the advent of Christian faith among these Tribes the practice of 'youth dormitories' for structuring the Tribal societies as well as the practice of erecting megalithic structures and rituals focused on them have declined. In its place modern schools, churches have become the locale for new social structuring. While the school became the focal point for the Tribal youth to train themselves to be inducted into the society as productive members, the rituals are now church centered. The cross became the 'neo-megalithic' structure and rituals around it on different occasions as per the Christian faith and practices. This process is often termed as assimilation of values of another culture to the existing cultures. [10]

In this process of assimilation of cultural values the old framework of understanding is often invoked to accommodate the new ones. As for example, the Khasis believe in a supreme God (*U Blei*), and this concept of God could easily fit into the Christian understanding of God who is almighty and creator of all. In this case the transition of the notion of God from the old to the new was relatively easy, and probably it did not invite much of resistance. Similarly the belief in the immortality of soul as taught in Christianity found an easy entry into the belief system of both the Khasis and Rongmei Nagas as it already existed. But in some other instances the same could not be said, as the Christian missionaries considered them 'pagan' and therefore demanded their dismantling and adopt totally new Christian ways. To cite an example, the initial interpretation of all Naga practices by Baptist missionaries, such as healing and dance, were seen as pagan, and therefore were to be rejected. Early Naga Christians, in turn setting high standards for Church membership, adopted this strict interpretation including suppression of dance and music.[11]

Structural Transformation of Tribal Beliefs

Cultural assimilation also gives rise to structural transformation of the Tribal beliefs which means that the earlier beliefs have now been metamorphosed into a new. New dimensions have been adduced with a view to Christianize them. As for instance, the Nagas who already had healing practices which mainly focused on the physical aspects have now been introduced into the Christian practice of healing that encompasses not only the physical but also the spiritual aspects. In other words, the existing belief system of the Naga Tribe was expanded to include the physical as well as the spiritual thus giving rise to a new belief system among the Naga Christians.[12]

This structural transformation is more pronounced in what is known as cultural 'adoption.' That is to say, when people of one culture encounter another, they opt out of their own culture and adopt the new one and make it their own. In this process there is a radical break from the past, and the new culture becomes normative. The Khasis and Nagas in certain cultural aspects have completely renounced their earlier traditions and world view, and opted for the Christian world view and associated categories and values.[13] This metamorphosis has not, in my opinion, weakened these communities; on the contrary it has given them a new identity and vigour to be progressive.

The short analysis of the cultural metamorphosis of both Naga and Khasi Tribes has clearly shown that the process of transformation is a continuous one; it keeps evolving in course of time. In this dynamics there are several streams of thoughts, beliefs, customs and rituals crisscrossing, sometimes giving a renewed vigour to the already existing ones, other times introducing totally new ones in place of the old thereby creating a new narrative and world views. Individuals and communities are active agents in this process of metamorphosis, and the contemporary life of both the Nagas and Khasis is a sterling example of this.

Culture being a social construct, it forms the foundation of a community's identity. And the attempt to decipher at least some aspects of the culture of both the Khasis and Nagas has brought to the fore their enormous capability for cultural assimilation, adoption and transformation into a modern and liberal society.

Endnotes

[1] Cristina De Rossi as told to Live Science, *Live Science Culture,* July 2017.

[2] Joseph Campell, "The Power of Myth", www.goodreads.com.

[3] Kamei Budha Kabui, "Historical Traditions, Religious Beliefs and Practices of the Rongmei Tribe," Unpublished Thesis, Manipur University, 2008.

[4] Rajat Kanti Das, *Manipur Tribal Scene,* Delhi, 1985,40 as cited in *The Customs of Marriage and Divorce,* 102 chapter iv.

[5] Valentina Pakyntein, "In Life and Death: Reciprocity and Solidarity" in *Khasi-Pnar society, Women's World,* Ottawa, July 06, 2011.

[6] Facts and Details, Nagas: Their History, Life and Customs, Facts and Details. com/South–East Asia/Myanmar/Sub 5.

[7] Gurdon on the Khasis, Chp 2, p. 40 Shodgnaga. Inflibnet.ac.in.

[8] Robert Redfield, Ralph Linton and Melville. J. Herskovits, "Memorandum for the Study of Acculturation", American Anthropologist, Vol. 38, 1936, 149-152.

[9] Ben den Ouden, Their Christianity, conversion, cultural change and indigenization among Khasi, Sora and Naga of India, Rijkuniversiteit, Groningen: Study program: Masters in Religion, culture Institution, 16.

[10] Ibid., 25.

[11] Ibid., 26.

[12] Ibid., 27.

[13] Ibid., 28

Phenomenology
and the Culture of Movement

Dr. C. V. Babu

Phenomenology as culture is different from phenomenology of culture as the former views phenomenology in its existential dimension of culture in general as a movement of lived essences, the forms of culture, while the latter tires to describe the genesis and existential structure of the forms of a particular culture. In the former case, the essences are varying forms of culture as lived experiences that are inexhaustible as an unending movement in the life-world in its beginningless and endless history as the world itself is mysterious and paradoxical. Phenomenology as culture is to be understood primarily from the perspective of phenomenology as a movement through the subtle changes of essences as the idealities of direct accessing of what we are as involving in the life-world in communication with the world. They being the essences of unique mode of existence they are also essences of behavior, the very forms of culture. It is the phenomenological methodology of reduction that makes the phenomenology as culture possible as detaching oneself from the naïve attitudes of objectivity which culminated to its maximum in scientific enterprise as the mode of interaction with the world. Phenomenology attempts to establish, on the other hand, a primitive contact with the world beyond the everyday naïve attitude of objectivity and its modern manifestation in scientific explorations as the unified domain of singularity of subject and object. Phenomenology as a cultural approach in the sense of withdrawing from the notion of absolute objectivity can be related to tribal culture, that its attitude towards nature though inherits the naïve attitude of objectivity is not contaminated by approach towards nature as dead objectivity as science managed to develop.

In this sense phenomenological life-world is related to the tribal life-world with reference to its view towards nature in addition to the sense that it is yet to be largely contaminated by scientific practice of experimental verification, mathematical structuring by hyper calculations and large scale technological intervention. Tribal culture with its purity of life in the nature uncontaminated by scientific objectification might be more suitable to understand phenomenological culture with reference to its attitude towards nature in integrity with human primitive relations to it. In this case, phenomenology can be considered as a new trend or style of approach to nature to regain its pure presence as the basis of a cultural movement.

Phenomenology, in this sense, attempts to view world as not objective detached from the subject as passively waiting for the latter to be intervened and even to be exploited according to her whims and fancies but as life-world as existing in its unification with the subject and modulating itself according to the inheritance, attitudes and activities of the subjects with reference to the manifold dimensions of the relations among subjects themselves and the manifold dimensions of relations of objects themselves in their totality of interrelations between them and reacting itself without waiting for the objective intervention by the subjects but prompting the subjects to see the essences or relations as varying and to evaluate them by means of reconstituting them in view of the outcomes.

The other sense of phenomenology as culture is also related to tribal culture since it thrives to undergo radical changes questioning traditional values viewing phenomenological essences as experiences of what we are that are never constant but undergo even radical changes as a never ending process even without knowing where it is heading to. This process is not losing the primitive contact with nature but revealing nature as mysterious and paradoxical and realizing that it is in view of the lived outcomes of the cultural forms they are to be evaluated and re-constituted.

Though science speaks of different states of matter from gross state to more subtle states such as solid, liquid, gas, plasma, etc., though in objective sense, in case of human existence it stops within the domain of gross objectivity as where the brain stops or where heart failures and subtle states of consciousness is still a puzzle for scientific experiments as neither to locate it objectively nor to access what one subjectively and directly experience as the end of the applicability of the notion of experimental or scientific objectivity. Husserl's phenomenology simply assures that consciousness is not where we experiment with it but it is there where we experience. We are looking for it in certain neuron networks in brain but it is actually there in the network of relations in the life-world and it is neither subject nor object but the singularity of both. In this sense, science deals with blind subject and blank object. It posits the question: does experience really stop where brain stop or heart stuck with if it is not approached from a naïve objective attitude? Husserl's method of transcendental reduction gives certain insights to these issues as transcendental consciousness beyond the notion of gross objective existence as it exists in the pure phenomenological world. Transcendental consciousness need not be necessarily a brainy thing though not postulating as an absolute mental substance in a Cartesian manner but may transcend the thing of brain and to approach it as not transcending it is to make it a subject of objective search with the naïve attitude regarding its existence but only to miss it due to the inherent contradiction of something subjective objectively. According to Husserl, it is the subject itself but of the object as a unified singularity of consciousness with the world given to it as it is given to itself. In this sense, it might even get emptied once its all essential relations are lived up being a project in the world. The network of relations in the life-world are the essences that are lived as meanings constituting the cultural forms of interaction with the nature and the other and, indeed, even to oneself. Phenomenological world is the place of life-world beyond the objective space-time of both naïve attitude as well as scientific approach.

This paper is an examination of Mearlea-Ponty's view of Husserl's phenomenology based on his study ranging from Husserl's *Logical Investigations*, and *Formal and Transcendental Logic* to *Cartesian Meditations* and *The Krisis of European Sciences*. Merleau-Ponty begins mentioning the perplexed situation of phenomenological school in the seventies even after fifty years of its origin right in the beginning of 20th century. Many of these confusions were the results of certain contradiction seemingly appeared in Husserl's standpoints. In the beginning Husserl viewed phenomenology as the direct description of experience without its psychological origin and causal explanation but later he spoke of "genetic phenomenology" (Husserl 1977, 120) and even constructive phenomenology in the unpublished 6th Cartesian Meditation[1] and it seemed to be in contradiction to the earlier standpoint. According to him, Husserl's notion of 'Lebenswelt' which he, towards the end of his life, identified as the central theme of phenomenology in his Krisis is the reappearance of the same contradiction. For Merleau-Ponty, it shows that phenomenology in the beginning was a movement as a style of thinking before it became a system of philosophy: "*Phenomenology can be practiced and identified as a manner or style of thinking, that it existed as a movement before arriving at complete awareness of itself as a philosophy*" (Merleau-Ponty, 1962, viii). According to him, it made phenomenology remain as a problem to be solved and a hope to be realized. In this paper, it is argued that phenomenology as Husserl engaged in was always a movement and in this sense it is the culture of movement rather than a fashion or trend of mere thinking just in its beginning. The culture of phenomenology as a movement also gives an insight that even every culture is a movement though phenomenology of a particular culture may vary from that of the other in describing the genesis and existential structure of their separate forms of essences. It is argued in this paper that phenomenology as Husserl initiated and developed was always a movement and it speaks of the culture of unique mode of existence through and through the historicity of life-world without an end and prior knowing where it is moving exampling itself from various phase of psychological, causal, eidetic, transcendental, genetic, constitutive, etc. Husserl himself moved from the psychological origin of universal content of mathematical concepts to experiential contents of phenomenological objects and from logical essences of linguistic concepts to existential essences of life-world. In this process it rests on itself postulating its own grounds of constituted reason to communicate with the world. It is clear when Merleau-Ponty writes, "It must therefore put to itself the question which it puts to all branches of knowledge, and so duplicate itself infinitely, being, as Husserl says, a dialogue or infinite meditation, and, in so far as it remains faithful to its intention, never knowing where it is going" (1962, viii). Though Husserl in the beginning called for a movement which seemed to be a movement back to the original objects themselves, essences themselves, transcendental consciousness itself, it was also a movement forward of placing the phenomenological objects into concrete facticity, ideal essences into experiential existence and transcendental consciousness in the life-world. Life-world is the unified horizon of subject and object with their relationships in between them with reference to the interrelations among the subjects themselves and objects themselves in the form of one's own experiences with oneself as well as with others intersected by similarities and contrasts as the base of rationality forming new meanings and changing them with the culture of living through the historicity. In this sense, even the later steps of genetic or constitutive phenomenology in the introduction of his concept of life-world is a movement. It shows that phenomenology is always a movement that it signifies the culture of movement and culture as movement.

Husserl as born and lived in one of the most scientifically advanced nations in Europe especially the second half of his life in the first half of the 20th century in which the scientific advancement began to take its quicker and wider influence must have felt some alienation of human soul from the purity of nature through modern culture structured by scientific discoveries and technological intervention and he, consequently, attempted to regain the purity of primitive forms of life. One of the major reason as the very basis of science for this alienation is the strong belief in the hardcore objectivity of the world under the misconception that it is the scientific and unchallengeable right approach to inert matter. According to Husserl, it inherits the same naïve attitude of objectivity and culminated into scientific establishment of research and invention and continued even if some scientists themselves came to challenge it by the celebrated double slit experiment putting forward the notion of contradiction as the basis at the micro level of universe. Philosophically the division begins explicitly from the very times of Descartes, the very beginning of modern western philosophy, as the hardcore distinction between mind and body. The common man's naïve attitude got culminated into rational philosophical mind boggling mind-body problem and into unproblematic scientific objectification leading to aggressive technological intrusion and cultural isolation from the nature. It became the basis of scientific thinking, experimental verifications and mathematical calculations and technological intervention maddening the hostility towards nature alienating it from its primitive presence to human kind into the level of it being uninhabitable due to the gradual consequences of alarming level of pollution, global warming, sea level arousal, etc. It was Husserl's attempt to bridge the gap which seemed to be unbridgeable by that time. Husserl's phenomenological movement made a call to go back to the original objects themselves aiming at a new life-culture of evaluating lived experiences and re-constituting livable essences of life-world. Husserl's phenomenological endeavor attempted to the utmost level to get rid of the naïve notion of objectivity bracketing all that are believed to be existing objectively even to its extreme position of bracketing the whole world relentlessly by means of phenomenological methodology of reduction.

Husserl invented different levels of reductions in order to access the original objects as the very experiential entities beyond the dichotomical distinction. It is the very fact that Husserl arrived at as the truth that there is the impossibility of reduction in an ultimate level of transcendental reduction as resisted by temporality is the same that gave rise to the notion that there is a move in Husserl which is contradictory to the initial one. According to Merleau-Ponty, Husserl's phenomenology is the study of essences: the essence of perception, the essence of consciousness, which, at the same time puts back essences into facticity and existence. On the one hand, phenomenology is a transcendental philosophy that puts all the naïve attitudes including that is within scientific assertions about the world in abeyance and, on the other hand, it tries to re-achieve a direct and primitive contact with the world. Phenomenology is the attempt to reawaken the basic experience of the world of which science is the second order expression. Husserl's description of consciousness as essentially intuitive and intentional gives the process of re-achieving the world as the primitive unification of subject and object. Phenomenology as the description of immediate experiences as the unified dimension of life-world describes objects of consciousness in its double spheres of the unreflected and the reflected. Phenomenology is the description of the relations in the horizon the life-world of reflected experiences in the background of unreflected experiences. Phenomenology is an attempt to dismantle the veil of naïve beliefs and scientific assertions and common prejudices and everyday perceptual blindness to the world in order to expose it as it is unreflectively experienced and reflectively sensed as the lived world with the essences of the relationships existing in the life-world as a dimension of transcendental consciousness with the intentional structure of streaming logos in the phenomenological world in its existential temporality.

Absolute Beginning

Phenomenology has got a beginning, indeed, the subject itself as the very source of experience though it does not stop there and even does not return to it as an absolute subject. Returning to objects themselves as objects of consciousness is neither to return to consciousness itself nor to fall upon the objects of the naïve attitude as existing objectively but to the unified singularity of subject and object in its experiential dimension. To identify the source of experience is not an idealistic return to consciousness and description of consciousness is not analytical reflection and unravelling of life-world is not scientific explanation of objective natural phenomenon.

Merleau-Ponty writes: "Descartes and particularly Kant *detached* the subject, or consciousness, by showing that I could not possibly apprehend anything as existing unless I first experienced myself as existing in the act of apprehending it" (1987, 57). Descartes and Kant detached consciousness or subject as existing first as the condition for the act of apprehending the world. They established consciousness as the absolute certainty of existence as such and the condition of there being anything else at all including the body and the act of relating as the basis of relatedness in the world. Unless I experience myself as existing in the act of apprehending, anything could not be apprehended. It is the condition of there being experience and the act of relating as the basis of relatedness.

Merleau-Ponty says that as the act of relating is nothing if divorced from the relations in the world, in Kant, the unity of consciousness is achieved simultaneously with that of the world. In Descartes, the world enjoys the equal certainty of consciousness being reinstated in the cogito and labelled as "thought of" in so far as we experience it. His methodical doubt does not deprive of us anything. According to Merleau-Ponty, the relations between the subject and the world are not strictly bilateral. Otherwise, Descartes would not have started from methodical doubt for the certainty of the world would be immediately given with that of the cogito and Kant would not have talked about his 'Copernican revolution' of the subject constructing the world. Analytical reflection starts from experience of the world but goes back to the subject as distinct even from the experience itself as the condition of its possibility revealing its all-embracing synthesis without which there will not be the world. It is in this sense Husserl accused Kant of adopting a "faculty of psychologism" (Husserl 2002, 93).

It is the absolute mind, though not part of experience, which offers a reconstruction, which was resisted by Husserl, in a Humean spirit, as the negation of an absolute mind as a total alien to the world. Analytical reflection believes in an inner man arrived at following a prior constituting act as a constituting power untouched by being and time. Merleau-Ponty criticizes analytical reflection as losing sight of its own beginning of experience and, indeed, the world of and in which it has got experience. In phenomenology there is no inner man rather consciousness is the project in the world. According to Husserl, I am the absolute source of my experience as it is my existence that moves out towards my physical and social environment and sustains them and my existence does not stem out of those antecedents provided that the world is given pre-reflectively.

One might make a critical point against Husserl in contradiction to Merleau-Ponty's criticism of analytical stand point that the phenomenology too loses its point of beginning as the source of experience though not the experience itself along with the world. But Husserl's negation of the absolute mind is not rejection of subject as such but a subject as a total alien to the world since the subject is always in the phenomenological world even after the phenomenological reduction is carried out. It can be considered that, as far as experience is considered, it is the task of phenomenology of establishing the life-world without falling into the trap of extreme subjectivism and extreme objectivism which are not experienced as themselves though he acclaims the presence of the world as pre-given and in the same manner he acknowledged a pre-given subject but given in the phenomenological world which is of absolute certainty. The subject is not the absolute mind in the sense of "the inner man"[2]. It is not an alien subject on which experience depend one sided and the world depends absolutely that that the latter does not even exist without the former. For Husserl, through consciousness a world forms itself around the subject and begins to exist for the subject from the outset which precedes knowledge and phenomenology aims at returning to both the worlds that precedes knowledge of which knowledge always speaks as a reflected world and the unreflected world as the unified life-world. Even if the absolute origin of phenomenology is consciousness it is not transcendental idealism since consciousness is always what it is conscious of and the world is not some kind immanent entities of consciousness but those of unreflected and reflected givenness. Rather for him, the world is there and the subject is given in the world and the world is given to it by the way it is given to itself.

Life-world has its absolute beginning from consciousness but it does not end up with consciousness not only because it is given in the world or the world is given to it but the world is given to it by the very way consciousness is given to itself that the world is given to it as the life-world. My reflection has to recognize the world given to the subject because the subject is given to itself as it bears upon an unreflective experience that it is an event as it appears to itself in a creative act, a changed consciousness, having the world priority over it. The subject is no longer the subject in itself and the world is not the world in itself but the latter as life-world given to the former as the former is given to itself in both ways of the changed consciousness of the unreflected experience and the creative consciousness of the reflected experience. In the first domain of the unreflected givenness the life-world is the horizon in which it is again given in the form of the relations within it as the givenness of the reflected consciousness.

Impossibility of the Reduction of Time

Even if consciousness by means of transcendental reduction is discovered without a location in objective space-time as transcending the naïve or scientific attitude of objectivity of the world it is still in the phenomenological world. To consider the world as a whole of absolute objective existence is to make oneself a total alien to it which is contradictory to the reality as the subject is in the world to think of it though as objectively and in that sense it is not of absolute objectivity but includes the subject as such within it and it is the very attitude in opposition to the reality, which is to be get rid of by phenomenological reduction.

Mereau-Ponty (1962, xiv) writes, "But even if the cogitatio, which I thus discover, is without location in objective time and space, it is not without place in the phenomenological world. The world, which I distinguished from myself as the totality of things or of processes linked by causal relationships, I rediscover 'in me' as the permanent horizon of all my cogitations and as a dimension in relation to which I am constantly situating myself. The true *Cogito* does not define the subject's existence in terms of the thought he has of existing, and furthermore does not convert the indubitability of the world into the indubitability of thought about the world nor finally does it replace the world itself by the world as meaning. On the contrary it recognizes my thought itself as an inalienable fact, and does away with any kind of idealism in revealing me as 'being-in-the-world'." It is not the things in the causal relationships as existing in total alienation in between as subject and the world but the former is in the very relationship with the world as given in the world as any other thing in relation to the relations among them and it is beyond subject object dualism.

The world re-discovered in me is the directly accessed world though bracketed as pre-given in which the very life-world composed of all intuitive as well as intentional objects as the unified horizon of relations towards which one is constantly oriented being situated within. Even if the cogitatio is without location in objective time and space in the sense that the objective space-time is the domain of causal relations independent of subject, it is not without place in the phenomenological world of totality of interdependent relations between subject and object and among subjects and objects themselves. The objective space and time as taken for granted both by naïve belief as well as by the scientific attitude having the former inherent in the latter often mistakes that cogitatio cannot be in the world.

Once this prejudice about space-time is suspended, the phenomenological place can be accessed as the place where all those objects of naïve attitudes are placed and it can inhabit cogitation as well. Then the world of objective space and time is rediscovered 'in me' as the pre-given permanent horizon of all my cogitations and as a dimension in relation to which I am constantly situating myself. Thought itself is an inalienable fact that reveals me as a 'being-in-the-world'. We are through and through compounded of relationships with the world as thought of, as lived and as existed. Even after the transcendental reduction the transcendental consciousness is still in a world which is phenomenological world and it is the very world distinguished by reduction. Existence in that world is not mere existence thought of and its certainty is not the certainty of thought about it and it is not the world of mere meanings or ideas but it is the world where the thought is a fact as a 'being-in-the world'. The thought which is in the world is not the thought which is in the world as it is taken as mere thoughts of objects which itself is of its objectivity but the phenomenological objects of the unreflected consciousness which are consciousness themselves as unreflected experiences and the objects of the reflected consciousness as the essences or meanings which are consciousness themselves as reflected experiences and of itself as someone having them.

Husserl's notion of transcendental consciousness as essentially is in phenomenological world is related to his notion of consciousness as time-consciousness that it cannot transcend time absolutely though it is not the objective time as such. In science the world is taken for granted without explicitly mentioning it considering my existence is a moment of the world's. In phenomenology, time is taken as the intuitive time of consciousness providing the fundamental elements of experience within the fundamental modes of temporal points making all objects of consciousness temporal objects and making the continuity of experience possible. Husserl's description of consciousness as internal time-consciousness shows that *Cogito* cannot get rid of time and since time is related to space the world bracketed is regained as the permanent horizon of *cogitatio*. The ultimate extremity of reflection possibly allow the reduction of whole place including that of body to internal consciousness. However, reflection itself takes place in time which it cannot get rid of. Accordingly Husserl calls consciousness as internal-time consciousness. Its fundamental phase of flux is constituted of the three elements of impression, retention and protention. They are the tripple moments of now, past and future points within the present of intuitive consciousness (Husserl 1991, 55). According to Albert Einstein time and space are inter related. In this sense, as Husserl could not transcend time even reflectively since reflection itself is in time, it does not transcend space as well. It is the same that Husserl speaks of the life-world of unreflected experiences as changed consciousness and exteriority of the Ego and that of the Alter Ego given in facticity and historicity. In the former case it shows that the world is already there as an inalienable presence and in the latter case it is very presence of oneself and of others.

Time is unreductable since consciousness functions essentially as always consciousness of temporal objects since it is in time as a flux. Husserl's notion that untranscendability of time as regaining the reduced world as the regaining of the world is based on the notion of time as related to space as the space-time of the world. By transcendental reduction Husserl put the subject back into the existence in the world and the essences arrived at by means of eidetic reduction through intentionality back into lived relations in it and the phenomenological objects accessed by intuition into facticity. The basis of Husserl's U-turn as the relation between time and space can be compared to Einstein's notion of relation between space and time, though in a different perspective of objectivity, and it was him who put a hyphen in between them signifying that they are not independent realities but one. When Husserl came to the notion of life-world with reference to pre-given world Einstein's theory of relativity had already got its grip in the intellectual world. Both of them stressed the fact of the same sort that there is no way of transcending the space-time as for Einstein as the impossibility of the trans-local velocity with which a particle can move and for Husserl as the impossibility of trans-local existence of transcendental consciousness though from a non-objective perspective of its being an absolute subject in total alienation to the world. It was Einstein who came with the notion of quantum in his explanation of the nature of light as indivisible discrete unit of energy with the notion of photon for the first time which gave rise to the notion of quantum physics though he disagreed with many of its latter outcomes and standpoints. Husserl's notion of time in this sense also can be considered as intuitive indivisible units of time-consciousness which he called internal time-consciousness and it is not objective time as it is related to the notion of collapse of wave packets to quantum particles only if they are intervened by observation or measurement as signified by the celebrated double slit experiment. This quantum collapse is the very bases of the entire phenomenology enterprise as the unified dimension of singularity of subjectivity and objectivity which does not happen independent of each other and regaining of the world. In case of intuitive elements of time latter Derrida pointed out that it is the eternal return of the same that makes the phenomenological collapse into temporal elements possible and in that case it is more fundamental than what is phenomenologically fundamental. As it is not the moment of the world and its duration is not identifiable with it. Husserl also had recognized this when he mentioned that the real world as mysterious, paradoxical and inexhaustible which is reflected in the life-world itself as mysterious, paradoxical and inexhaustible. However, quantum physics attempts beyond Einstenian notion of local velocity to assure trans-local velocity particles and to establish as its consequence, at least, as one possibility, the extra-dimensions of the universe. For Husserl, the transcendental consciousness is in the phenomenological world and it is not beyond it, at least by reflective meditation, and if non-reflective meditation shows out body experiences it can be the hidden dimensions of the world of the same phenomenological world beyond the space-time that is approached with a naïve attitude.

It is from the essential nature of consciousness as time-consciousness that Husserl regained the world that he bracketed whatever is spatial. As time is related to space it is still in space-time of the world which is the world of existence beyond the naïve attitude of absolute objective existence but as pre-given. It signifies that I am in the world though I am the beginning of my experience since experience is not completely independent of the object rather it is the unified dimension of subjectivity and objectivity of the life-world. Reduction teaches us that there is impossibility of complete reduction. Since our reflections are carried out in the temporal flux on which we are trying to seize there is no thought which embraces all our thought. Radical reflection amounts to a consciousness of its own dependence on an unreflective life which is its initial situation.

"The most important lesson which the reduction teaches us is the impossibility of a complete reduction. ... If we were absolute mind, the reduction would present no problem. But since, on the contrary, we are in the world, since indeed our reflections are carried out in the temporal flux on the which we are trying to seize, there is no thought which embraces all our thought" (Merleau-Ponty 1962, xv). Time is unreductable in the ultimate sense for Husserl. We are not absolute minds that can get rid of the world if not into an ideal transcendence but the real transcendence is impossible as we are in the world which is phenomenological. Radical reflection amounts to a consciousness of its own dependence on an unreflective life which is its initial situation of the unreflected experience. Phenomenological reduction belongs to existential philosophy as subject is a process of transcendence towards the world as a flight of transcendence to the fleeting nature of the world being involved within.

I am my Exteriority and the Other his Exteriority

Existence cannot be reduced to bare awareness of existence but it should take in the awareness that one may have of it. Husserl says that transcendental subjectivity can be intersubjectivity because the cogito must reveal me in a situation. "My existence should never be reduced to my bare awareness of existing, but that it should take in also the awareness that *one* may have of it, and thus include my incarnation in some nature and the possibility, at least, of a historical situation" (Merleau-Ponty 1962, xiv). "The *Cogito* must reveal me in a situation, and it is on this condition alone that transcendental subjectivity can *be* an intersubjectivity" (Husserl 1970, 65). For Husserl existence is not mere awareness of existence and it is more than mere awareness that it can be the awareness of the one who has it.

In this case the reflectively bracketed body and the world comes back to the body of the reflection as its incarnation in the world with a historical situation. For Husserl, there is the problem of the other people, and the alter ego is a paradox. If the other is truly for himself alone, beyond his being for me, and if we are for each other and not both for God, we must necessarily have some appearance for each other. Even if I am truly for myself beyond my being for others since I am also for others I must necessarily have some appearance. The perspectives of For Oneself and For others cannot be juxtaposed. I discover by reflection not only my presence to myself, but also the possibility of an 'outside spectator'. Since I am as the consciousness is nothing more than reflection both in the sense of unreflection and reflection, the former shows me myself and the latter apprehends me as placed in the world and the same reflection can also show that I am there to the unreflective perception as well as reflective apprehension of the other. "I must be the exterior that I present to the others, and the body of the other must be the other himself.

This paradox and the dialectic of the Ego and the Alter Ego are defined by their situation and are not freed from all inherence; that is, provided that philosophy does not culminate in a return to the self, and that I discover by reflection not only my presence to myself, but also the possibility of an 'outside spectator'; that is, again, provided that at the very moment when I experience my existence – at the ultimate extremity of reflection – I fall short of the ultimate density which would place me outside of time, and that I discover within myself a kind of internal weakness standing in the way of my being totally individualized: which exposes me to the gaze of the others as a man among men or at least as a consciousness among consciousness" (Merleau-Ponty 1962, xiii). I am my exteriority as felt by myself as well as by others though they cannot be juxtaposed. There is no other myself beyond these what is immediately accessed by me as well as by others though they cannot be juxtaposed they are not inflexible or unchangeable presences even as felt. The world bracketed along with the body of incarnation is however rediscovered as the dimension of the incarnation as the very phenomenological world.

On the other hand, *cogito* defines me as the thought which I have of myself and I is accessible only to myself. In so far as something has meaning for me I am in no way distinguishable from an 'other' consciousness and world is the unique system in which all truths cohere with which we are immediately in touch with as the immediate access to truth. World is precisely that thing of which we form a representation as participation of all in One unity. World is the unifier of minds and the Alter and the Ego are one and the same in the true world since every consciousness has the theoretically the power of reaching the universal truths. For analytical reflection "There is no difficulty in understanding how I can conceive the other, the I and the Other are conceived not as part of the woven stuff of the phenomena; they have validity rather than existence" (Merleau-Ponty 1962, xiii). They are merely little shadows which owes their very existence to the light. Reduction is not withdrawal from the world to the unity of consciousness as the world's basis but to watch the forms of transcendence fly up like sparks from a fire; it slackens the intentional threads which attach us to the world and thus brings them to our notice; it alone is the consciousness of the world because it reveals that world as strange as paradoxical. Life-world is strange and paradoxical. In order to see the world and grasp it as paradoxical we must break with our familiar acceptance of it and we can learn the unmotivated upsurge of the world. Essences as transparent and accommodative shows that the world is paradoxical. However theses essences are not blind or concealing heavy blocks but transparent and flexible and changing meanings.

Reduction as generally understood as the return to transcendental consciousness gives an impression that phenomenology is transcendental idealism. The problematic of reduction occupies an important place even in his unpublished 6th mediation showing that it was not an issue that Husserl had only in the beginning of his career. Every reduction being transcendental is necessarily eidetic. The apprehension of *hyle* by means of eidetic reduction of phenomenological objects of perception of *hyle* indicates the phenomenon of higher degree as the active meaning-giving operation that define consciousness. Perception of *hyle* and the apperception of *hyle* are the unreflective and reflective experiences respectively and the latter signifies the meaning-giving operation of transcendental consciousness. The meanings are to be reconstituted according to the outcome of unreflective lived experiences and world as meaning of reflective transcendental consciousness is perhaps the way to get rid of the unreflective collapse into the world of its original purity. To define consciousness as active meaning-giving operation as the apprehension of *hyle* makes the world nothing but 'world-as-meaning' making phenomenological reduction idealistic and leads to misinterpretation that phenomenology is transcendental idealism. World as nothing but 'world-as-meaning' is an indivisible unity of transcendental idealism in which perspectives of individuals blend as shared values. Perception of the world by individual consciousness in communication with each other is the doing of pre-personal forms of consciousness. Here communication has no problem and it is demanded by the very definition of consciousness, meaning, and truth. "In so far as I am a consciousness, that is, in so far as something has meaning for me, I am neither here nor there, neither Peter nor Paul; I am not indistinguishable from an 'other' consciousness, since we are immediately in touch with the world and since the world is, by definition, unique, being the system in which all truths cohere" (Merleau-Ponty 1962, xii).

It is the possibility of all the individuals to get into the universal forms of consciousness as an indivisible unity by which values are shared by individuals as the blend of their perspectives. Perception of the world by individual is no more perception of the individual but it is the perception of pre-personal forms of consciousness and it is the definition of consciousness, meaning or truth and there is no problem of communication, the other and the world. "A logically consistent transcendental idealism rids the world of its opacity and its transcendence" (Merleau-Ponty 1987, 59). For Kant, there is no inner perception without outer perception, that the world, as a collection of connected phenomena, is anticipated in the consciousness of my unity, and is the means whereby I come into being as a consciousness. Kant's intentionality is the relation to a possible object and the unity of the world is posited by knowledge in a specific act of identification. World is the correlation to knowledge. For Kant, the subject is not a universal thinker of a system of objects rigorously interrelated. He is not the positing power who subjects the manifold to the law of the understanding. Man discovers and enjoys his own nature as spontaneously in harmony with the law of the understanding. For Husserl the unity of the world is lived as ready-made or already there, not anticipated as the unity of consciousness.

Vienna circle is of the view that we can enter into relations only with meanings. For them, consciousness is not identifiable with what we are. Consciousness is a complex meaning that developed late in time throughout the world's semantic development to the formation of present one have been made explicit. Logical positivism in this sense is antitheses of Husserl's phenomenology which says we enjoy direct access to what it designates as its linguistic acquisition. It is the consciousness which we are. "Whatever the subtle changes of meaning which have ultimately brought us, as a linguistic acquisition, the word and concept of consciousness, we enjoy the direct access to what it designates" (Merleau-Ponty 1962, xv).

The experience of ourselves is the experience of consciousness as what we are. It is based on this experience that all linguistic connotations are assessed, and precisely through it that language comes to have any meaning at all for us. "It is that as yet dumb experience … which we are concerned to lead to the pure expression of its own meaning" (Husserl 1977, 33). Husserl's essences are like fisherman's net bringing back all living relationships of experience. For Merleau-Ponty, it is wrong to say "Husserl separated essences from existences"[3]. The separated essences are those of language which exists actually by the ante-predicative life of consciousness and its separation is only apparent as caused by the office of language. It is merely apparent that the office of language keeps meanings separated from the existence since they actually rest in language through anti-predicative life of consciousness. Wolrd's essence is to look for the fact for us before its thematization. The dumb experience or the silence of primary consciousness is expressed as the meaning of a word and also that of a thing. The acts of naming and expression is centered around the core of primary meaning. Seeking essence is to rediscover my actual presence to myself and it is not to escape into the universe of things. I am the fact of my consciousness as the meaning of the concept of consciousness and of the word as the direct experience of myself.

The essence is not an end but means to understand our effective involvement in the world and made amenable to conceptualization for it is what polarizes all our conceptual particularization. The need to proceed by the way of essences is due to the reason that we are held in the world so tightly in the sense of unreflected experience that we cannot know itself without reflective experience for which the field of ideality is required in order to become acquainted with and to prevail over its facticity. It means philosophy does not take essences as its objects. Reduction is wonder in the face of the world: "Reflection does not withdraw from the world towards the unity of consciousness as the world's basis; it steps back to watch the forms of transcendence fly up like sparks from a fire; it slackens the intentional threads which attach us to the world and thus brings them to our notice; it alone is consciousness of the world because it reveals that world as strange and paradoxical" (Merleau-Ponty 1962, xv). Reduction is not reflective withdrawal from the world to the ideal unity of consciousness as the basis of the world but loosening the intentional threads that is strongly attached to the world in the form of objectivity of the objects in the world held by the subject taking the unreflected consciousness as the objects themselves and the world itself though they are in the world and also in order to see the forms of transcendence of meanings or essences or experiences both reflective and unreflective emerging and vaporizing revealing in the permanent horizon of the world which is mysterious and inexhaustible.

Sensationalism speaks of experience as nothing but states of ourselves and consequently reduces the world to them. Transcendental idealism also reduces the world as immanent in consciousness considering it as the thought or consciousness of the world as the correlative of knowledge. If everything is state of mind then there cannot be a distinction between the perceptions and dreams. The problem of distinction between the real and the imaginary comes because the experience of the real is also like that of imaginary. "The problem then becomes one not of asking how critical thought can provide for itself secondary equivalents of this distinction but of making explicit our primordial knowledge of the real, of describing our perception of the world as that upon which our idea of truth is forever based" (Merleau-Ponty 1962, xviii).

The analysis of distinction between the imaginary and the real and cast doubt upon the real is because this distinction already made before analysis. "We must not, therefore, wonder whether we really perceive a world, we must instead say: the world is what we perceive. In more general terms we must not wonder whether our self-evident truths are real truths, or whether, through some perversity inherent in our minds, that which is self-evident for us might not be illusory in relation to some truth in itself" (Merleau-Ponty 1962, xviii).

Then the problem is making explicit our primordial knowledge of the real. It is to describe the perception of the world as that upon which idea of truth is forever based. We can talk about illusion because we have already identified illusion and it is done solely based on some self-evident perception. We are in the realm of truth and it is 'the experience of truth' which is self-evident (Husserl 2002, 190). To seek the essence of truth is to define perception as access to truth not to presume as truth. The self-evidence of perception is not adequate thought or apodeictic self-evidence (Husserl 1929, 142).

Eidetic reduction is the ambition to make reflection emulate the unreflective life of consciousness. I aim at and perceive a world. Eidetic reduction brings the world to light by means of experience of the essences with the ambition of making reflection emulate the unreflective life of consciousness. It does not reduce the world as state of our mind or immanent in consciousness but access the world by means of unreflective experience that change from moment to moment and by means of reflective experience by making sense of the relations immanent in the world. Essence of the world is not a mere idea as it seems to be once it is reduced to a theme of discourse but it is the fact of experience before thematization.

"The world is not what I think, but what I live through. I am open to the world, I have no doubt that I am in communication with it, but I do not possess it; it is inexhaustible" (Merleau-Ponty 1962, xix). It is the facticity of the world that causes the world to be the world and it is the facticity of my cogito that assures of my existence and it is not its imperfection. "The eidetic method is the method of a

phenomenological positivism which founds the possible on the real"
Merleau-Ponty 1987, 64). Husserl is not speaking of transcendental
other world but the very world deducted of the objective unilateral or
of linear progression of science and naïve attitude transcending such
approaches as world of paradox.

World and Rationality

For Husserl the real has to be described and not to be constructed
or to be formed. It means perceptions cannot be placed into the
same categories as the syntheses represented by judgments, acts or
predications. The real is closely woven fabric. It does not await our
judgments before incorporating the most surprising phenomena or
before rejecting the most plausible figments of our imagination. The
unreflective experiences are not taken as dreamy contents but placed
in the real world. This place is the phenomenological place which is
already there as the place of the world. Though the fleeting sensations
are not related precisely to the context of the perceived world they are
immediately placed in the world without confusing them as daydreams.
The reality of perception is not based on the intrinsic coherence of
representations. Perception is the background from which all acts stand
out and is presupposed by them. The world is the natural setting of
all the perceptions and it is not an object having in the subject the law
of its making. The world is an inalienable presence as we 'live' it. It is
the very nature of essences as changing or flexible and accommodative
of the unreflective life-world into a new reflective forms of life-world.
The life-world is inexhaustible and its essences are amenable as the
world within which it is given is changing, mysterious and paradox
and indeed inexhaustible. For Husserl the world is already there before
any possible analysis of it.

We witness every minute the miracle of related experiences, and
yet nobody knows better than we do how this miracle is worked, for
we are ourselves this network of relationships. "Probably the chief
gain from pheneomenology is to have united extreme subjectivism
and extreme objectivism in its notion of the world or of rationality.

Rationality is precisely proportioned to the experiences in which it is disclosed. To say that there exists rationality is to say that perspectives blend, perceptions confirm each other, a meaning emerges. But it should not be set in a realm apart, transposed into absolute Spirit, or into a world in the realist sense. The phenomenological world is not pure being, but the sense which is revealed where the paths of my various experiences intersect, and also where my own and other people's intersect and engage each other like gears. It is thus inseparable from subjectivity and intersubjectivity, which find their unity when I either take up my past experiences in those of the present, or other people's in my own" (Merleau-Ponty 1962, xxii). Phenomenology, as a disclosure of the world, rests on itself or rather provides its own foundation.

All cognitions are sustained by a ground of postulates and finally by our communication with the world as primary embodiment of rationality. Philosophy, as radical reflection, dispenses in principle with this resource, as, however, it too, in history, exploits the world and constituted reason. For Husserl operative intentionality is that which produces the natural and antepredicative unity of the world and of our life and it is apparent in our desires, evaluations, and in the landscape we see more clearly than in objective knowledge. Our relationship to the world is untiringly enunciated within us. Husserl's intentionality is broadened to become a phenomenology of origins. Intentionality cannot be understood without reduction and it is the intentional consciousness itself as consciousness is the consciousness that is always consciousness of something.

To understand is to take in the total intention. Reflection even on a doctrine will be complete only if it succeeds in linking up with the doctrine's history and the extraneous explanations of it, and in putting back the causes and meaning of the doctrine in an existential structure. There is a 'genesis of meaning' (Husserl 1929, 184) which alone, in the last resort, teaches us what the doctrine means. "Because we are in the world, we are condemned to meaning, and we cannot do or say anything without its acquiring a name in history" (Merleau-Ponty 1962, xxii).

Total intentionality deals with the unique mode of existing expressed in the properties of the pebble or any object; it is also of the unique manner of behaviour towards others, towards nature, time and death. It is a certain way of patterning the world. In this context every human word, gesture even that of the outcome of habit or absent-mindedness has some meaning. "It is a matter, in the case of each civilization, of finding the idea in the Hegelian sense, that is, not a law of physico-mathematical type, discoverable by objective thought, but that formula which sums up some unique manner of behaviour towards others, towards Nature, time and death: a certain way of patterning the world which the historian should be capable of seizing upon the making his own. These are the *dimensions* of history. In this context there is not a human word, not a gesture, even one which is the outcome of habit or absent mindedness, which has not some meanings" (Merleau-Ponty 1962, xx). Even chance happenings offset each other, and facts in their multiplicity coalesce and show up a certain way of taking a stand in relation to human situation, reveal in fact an event.

Teleology of consciousness is not a matter duplicating human consciousness with some absolute thought which from outside is imagined as assigning to it its aims. There is no absolute thought duplicating human consciousness. Consciousness itself is a project of the world perpetually projected in the world but neither embraces nor possesses it and the world as this pre-objective individual's imperious unity that decrees what knowledge shall be taken as its goal. World is the knowledge taken by individual. "For the first time, philosopher's thinking is sufficiently conscious not to anticipate itself and endow its own results with reified from in the world. The philosopher tries to conceive the world, others, and himself and their interrelations. But the meditating Ego, the 'impartial spectator, do not rediscover an already given rationality, they 'establish themselves', and establish it, by an act of initiative which has no guarantee in being, its justification resting entirely on the effective power which it confers on us of taking our own history upon ourselves. The phenomenological world is not bringing to explicit expression of a pre-existing being, but the laying down of being. Philosophy is not a reflection of a pre-existing truth but, like art, the act of bringing, truth into being" (Merleau-Ponty 1962, xxii).

The only pre-existing Logos is the world itself, and that the philosophy which brings it into the visible existence does not begin by visible being possible; it is actual or real like the world of which it is a part, no explanatory hypothesis is clearer than the act whereby we take up the unfinished world in an effort to complete ad conceive it. Merleau-Ponty ends with a note: "The unfinished nature of phenomenology and the inchoative atmosphere which has surrounded it are not to be taken as a failure, they were inevitable because phenomenology's task was to reveal the mystery of the world and of reason" (Merleau-Ponty 1962, xxiii-xxiv).

The phenomenological world includes the two dimensions of life-world which is also real as far as experience is considered. The first dimension is the dimension of that give rise to the unreflected experiences perhaps due to the nature of the senses and the other dimension is the dimension of Logos that give rise to the reflected experiences perhaps due to the nature of intellect as the two spheres of consciousness. In quantum physics it is the attempt of observation or measurement that makes the collapse of the wave, which is otherwise infinite, into a unit of indivisible chunk of matter that mediates energy. Even if it is the case with micro universe, in case of macro universe, it is an issue that how the perceptual collapse takes place in large scale universe, if it is not to invoke God. In phenomenology as well even if it is the case with the micro level of experience that there is perceptual collapse of temporal elements of consciousness constituting temporal objects of consciousness and even if it is regarded that all experiences of objects are constituted of these temporal elements providing the continuity of experience in unrelfected dimension of life-world, in macro-level, it is not simply the unrelfected elements that we eat and drink though the reflected elements as the food of our thought. Husserl avoids the criticism levelled against Hume that Hume eat impressions and drink ideas by considering the real world which is already there as a pre-given inalienable presence. It is where the exteriority of the body is significant as the appearance for the other or of the alter ego in case of even the transcendental consciousness that it is in the world, a dimension with which its existence is constantly oriented.

The place of phenomenology though it is not in objective space, it is not trans space-time or off-world but this world itself and it is in the sense of the place of the life-world as the unified dimension of subjectivity and objectivity and intersections of similarity of experiences of oneself and also with others as the bases of reason. Transcendental reduction is not a meditative reduction for Husserl though he speaks of meditative ego that as supposed to be of capability of out body experience accessing a different dimension of reality. Rather it is the reflective meditation where consciousness finds itself in temporal dimension as time-consciousness functioning in time as its intentionality or intuitive nature in case of both reflective and unrelfected experiences respectively are essentially temporal along with its own exteriority.

In the life-world, I am my exteriority as experienced by myself and experienced by the other beyond For Oneself and the other is his exteriority as appeared to me as well as felt by him though both these aspects felt by both about the one and the same cannot be juxtaposed. Nevertheless, it is not true that it ends up with the appearances of exteriority for others only, but it can transcend even that dimension into a totally out body experience. In this sense transcendence is not merely a kind of logical reflection that I am different from body which can be placed along with other objects in the world and the whole world as such but meditative-trans as the tittle Cartesian Meditation signifies as of total out body experience of transcendental consciousness. Even if the exteriority is perished by death, transcendental consciousness might remain but indeed with its exteriority as "divine double" or as its exteriority of streaming logos in the pre-given phenomenological world of Logos. Towards concluding it can be mentioned that the two aspects of life-world as the unreflective background and the reflective essences are both of immediate experiences.

The latter makes the sense of the former. The former is changing prompting the latter to be re-evaluated and re-constituted as the forms of culture. Essences are relations in manifold dimensions such as a subject as related to itself, related to an object and an object related to itself and also the inter-relations of the objects. It is also the relation of a subject to the inter-relation of the objects. It also deals with the relation of a subject with other subject and also the inter-relation of the subjects. It is also the relation of a subject to the inter-relation of subjects and also in the dimension of being related within that inter-relation. It is also the relation between the inter-relation of the subjects to the inter-relation of the objects and also in the dimension of being inter-related in the totality of the network of relations in the entire historicity.

Where there is relatedness of the experience the miracle of meaning and reason emerge. Past experience blend with present and one's experience confirm with that of other. It is in the intersection of experiences subjectivity is unified with intersubjectivity as the miracle of public meaning and reason. Once there is contrast in the experiences in the place of expected relatedness reason fails and prompts to re-evaluation of essences and their re-constitution in the existential dimension as the task of phenomenology towards the phenomenology as the culture of movement.

Endnotes

[1] Merleau-Ponty mentions this unpublished work edited by Eugen Fink to which G. Berger has referred.

[2] Merleau-Ponty refers here Saint Augustine's notion of inner man.

[3] Merleay-Ponty refers her to the opinion of Jean Wahl to which he expresses his disagreement.

References

Husserl, Edmund. *Formal and Transcendental Logic*, 142,184. Illinois: Springer, 1929.

--------------------. *The Krisis of European Sciences and Transcendental Phenomenology*. Evanston: North Western University Press, 1970.

--------------------. *Cartesian Meditations*. The Hague: Martinus Nijhoff, 1977.

--------------------. *On the Phenomenology of the Consciousness of Internal Time*. The Netherlands: Kluwer Academic Publishers, 1991.

--------------------. *Logical Investigations*. New York: Routledge, 2002.

Merleau-Ponty, Maurice. *Phenomenology of Perception*. London and New York: Routledge, 1962.

——————————. *The Merleau-Ponty Reader*. Ed. Ted Toadvine and Leonard Lawlor. Evanston, Illinois: Northwestern University Press, 1987.

Influence of Culture on Business in Northeast India: A Marketing Perspective of Nagaland

Dr. E. Thangasamy and Dr. C. Periasamy

Universally, the ideas, customs and social behaviour of the people or society do vary from one region to another. Collection, the variations of such behaviour may collectively be knowns as culture. The inner meaning of culture may even vary from one individual to another individual. Under this circumstance, the phenomenon of multi-culture and uniqueness is very common amongst the countries worldwide. Obviously, it is not to be understood as right or wrong, inherited or individual behaviour. Rather, it may be perceived as values and meanings. A successful cross-cultural management, its layers and inter se interaction will assist the entrepreneurs and marketing personnel to set up different large, medium and small enterprises. Accordingly, the entrepreneurs will make attempts to sensitize the diverse needs and wants of the consumers for different products and produce them accordingly at affordable rates to satisfy them. Thus, the cultural variability has a direct relationship with the business ventures and thereby both the manufacturers and consumers are satisfied with their profitability and satisfaction respectively. This cultural phenomenon, therefore, becomes very important for both the domestic and international businesses. Indirectly, these endeavours create adequate avenues not only for generating employment opportunities but also for boosting the economic development through industrial development. India is not an exception on this front. Amongst the States, the Northeast India, including the State of Nagaland, is very rich in terms of its culture, uniqueness, etc. The flora and fauna of the region is an added advantage for attracting the tourists from different parts of the world. This will, in turn, create demand for numerous goods and services and thereby open a wider scope emerges for business activities comprising marketing processes for attaining the broader goals of economic growth and development of the region. Hence, the study on the prevalence of the multi-culture and its inter-relationship with various business activities for promoting the socio-economic growth in the Northeastern Region, especially in the State of Nagaland becomes the need of the hour. This will also be a major contribution to improve the Indian economy in the long run.

In this context, this paper is an attempt to investigate the phenomenon with the objectives of (i) providing the cultural background and economic scenario of the Northeast India, (ii) analysing the socio-economic status of Nagaland, and (iii) to provide valuable remedial measures to improve the socio-economic development of the study area.

Conceptual Background and Relevance of the Study

Generally, variations in ideas, customs and social behaviour constitute 'culture' of a region. From the socio-economic growth point of view, a study is essential for a successful multicultural management. Gradually, the importance of commerce and trade comes to the picture to achieve the socio-economic goals of a nation.

The Northeast India comprises 8 states viz. Arunachal Pradesh, Assam, Manipur, Meghalaya, Mizoram, Nagaland, Sikkim and Tripura. All these states were recognized by the Northeastern Council (NEC) in 1971. Of them, only the State of Sikkim was added in the year 2002. All other states of the region were popularly known as the land of seven sisters.

As far as the State Nagaland concerned, it got its statehood in 1963. It has the rich culture and the social structure of the Nagas that vary from one tribal community to another. The fold songs, dances and musical instruments of Nagas indicate the rich cultural heritage of the people of Nagaland. Each tribe has their unique style of dance form. For instance, Zeliang dance, Cock dance, Fly dance, Cricket dance and bear dance etc., fall under this category. Their traditional crafts include cane and bamboo crafts, traditional hand tools, weapons and textile works, wood carving, pottery, ornaments for traditional attire etc.,

This rich culture and traditions of Nagas is having an enormous scope for attaining the twin objectives through business namely, disseminating the valuable information on their culture in the form of crafts, instruments, dances, songs and also earning profits for their societal wellbeing. It is stimulating an interest amongst the researchers to undertake a study of this kind to identify the areas of development, taking into their cultural influences on business and the related marketing problems.

Literature Review

There have been many researches on the problem in question, being undertaken throughout the world. Some of the literatures reviewed are presented below; *McLean (2010)* talks about the cross-culture management, the impact of culture diversity, cross-culture awareness training, cross cultural communication, and the Lewis Cultural Types 11 Model. Cross-cultural awareness is an opportunity for firms and associated stakeholders to adapt to life in the twenty-first century global village and integrate and communicate effectively with other cultures. Managers must know how best to communicate with individuals, and global business partners, on a cross-cultural basis.

Robert Serpell talked about cultural psychology in his book "Culture's influence on behaviour" in 1976. He addressed that culture has been conceived as affecting motivation at the level of the total personality, of attitudes and of specific motives; it has been conceived as affecting cognition at the level of the broad structure of intellect and of specific processes such as reasoning, communication and perception. That is why culture diversity existing.

Yao Ma & Xi Ran (2011), in their research report entitled, ' How cultural differences influence business' submitted to the University of Prince Edward Island indicated that business students are lacking the sensitivity towards the role that the cultural differences play in the world. They added that the University Education has a large impact on the way the students react when confronted with cross-cultural situations.

Objectives of the Study

The main objectives of the study are as under;

*   To present the cultural background and economic scenario of the Northeast India.

*   To analyse the socio-economic status of Nagaland, and

*   To provide valuable remedial measures to improve the socio-economic development of the study area.

Research Design and Methodology

The research methodology of the current study is as under;

The current study is confined only to one state of the Northeast India, i.e. Nagaland. In the region, the State of Nagaland has 12 administrative districts viz., Dimapur, Kiphire, Kohima, Longleng, Mokokchung, Mon, Peren, Phek, Tuensang, Wokha, Zunheboto and Noklak. It has the population of about 19.57 lakh persons consisting of both males and females. It has increased to 20.53 lakhs. There are about 16 tribes of Nagaland. It includes Angami, Konyak, Zeliang, Kuki, Ao, Phom, Khiamniungam, Yimchungru,Sangtam, Lotha, Sumi, Chang, Pochury, Chekhesang, Kachari, Rengma. Each tribe has its own attire, beaded jewellery and signature hat. They have distinct tribal dialects and identities, though they have a common language called Nagamese.

The current study is based only on secondary data. It is collected from the secondary sources like Government Published Documents, periodicals, newspapers etc. which are relevant to the Nagaland State, the study area. The analysis of data is made through a SWOT analysis for interpretations.

Analysis and Interpretation: A SWOT Analysis

The study has focused on the following key areas;

- Has unique culture amongst the people, having their own distinct dialects, traditions and customs – creates avenues for Tourism and Industrial Development.

- Flora and fauna is also diverse in nature – provides scope for Tourism Development.

- Growth of educational Institutions and rate of Literacy has been showing an inclining trend – provides better quality manpower and creating awareness and sensitivity towards the potential of the state and the need for Economic Growth in the face of competition in business.

Table 1

Cultural Influence on Business and Marketing Perspective in Nagaland: A SWOT Analysis

Strengths	Weaknesses	Opportunities	Threats
Culture - Distinction	No significant efforts are made to capitalize the business opportunities	New enterprises (Micro, Small, Medium or Large) may be set up based on the tastes and preferences of the people based on their cultural diversity.	Financial Constraints Lack of awareness and training for business ventures Lack of guidance and monitoring or follow up at various phases of a business cycle
Flora and fauna - Richness	No significant efforts are made to capitalize the business opportunities	Cultural-based business ventures exhibiting their own customs and traditions may be set up like handicrafts, garments etc.	Financial Constraints Lack of technological exposure Creation of Demand for the products

Education - Good	More avenues are yet to be created for new employment opportunities for educated youth	Demand for various consumer and industrial goods is prevalent for exploitation	Lack of innovation in the face of competition for educational services
Manpower – Good Quality	Needs exploitation	New Employment opportunities will ensure steady income and standard of living of the people	Lack of Finance, awareness, guidance and counselling

Source: Secondary Data

The above table is self-explanatory, highlighting the strengths, weaknesses, opportunities and threats facing the business, highlighting the cultural influences and marketing perspectives in the study area.

Findings of the Study

The major findings of the current study are as follows:

- No significant efforts are made to capitalize the business opportunities.

- More avenues are yet to be created for new employment opportunities for educated youth.

- Threats in the study area include the Financial Constraints, Lack of awareness and training for business ventures.

- Lack of guidance and monitoring or follow up at various phases of a business cycle.

- Lack of technological exposure, creation of Demand for the products.

Suggestions and Recommendations of the Study

Based on the results of the present study, the following suggestions are made:

- New enterprises (Micro, Small, Medium or Large) may be set up based on the tastes and preferences of the people based on their cultural diversity.

- Cultural-based business ventures exhibiting their own customs and traditions may be set up like handicrafts, garments etc.

- Demand for various consumer and industrial goods is prevalent for exploitation.

- New Employment opportunities will ensure steady income and standard of living of the people.

Limitations and Future Directions of the Study

The current study is subject to the following limitations:

- It is based only on secondary data. No primary data is put at use.

- The study is based on general perspective of culture in the State of Nagaland.

- In depth marketing strategies adopted by the business enterprises in the region have not been deeply analysed under this study.

- Except the State of Nagaland, no other states of the Northeast have been investigated in this study.

The above limitations may lead to more researches in future to add additional literature to the existing phenomenon on this front.

Culture influence on business is significant for socio-economic development in the region. Marketing strategies should be formulated to capitalize the business opportunities focusing on the cultural diversity in the State of Nagaland. This will lead to the socio-economic development of the Northeast India in general and the State of Nagaland in particular. Undoubtedly, this will contribute to the faster growth of the nation and the globe as well gradually.

References

Ardalan, K. "Globalization and culture: Four paradigmatic views". In International Journal of Social Economics, 36(5), 513-534, 2009.

BLASCO, M. Cultural pragmatists? Student perspectives on learning culture at a business school. Academy of Management Learning & Education, 8(2), 174-187, 2009.

Gesteland, R. R. *Cross-cultural business behaviour: Marketing, negotiating, and managing across cultures* (2nd Ed.) 1999. Copenhagen: Copenhagen Business School Press. Globalization, 2001.

McLean, J., & Lewis, R. D. *Communicating across cultures.* Manager. British Journal of Administrative Management, (71), 2010, 30-31.

Yao Ma & Xi Ran. 'How cultural differences influence business' in a Research Report submitted to the University of Prince Edward Island, 2011.

Serpell, R. *Culture's influence on behaviour.* London: Methuen, 1976.

Websites

http://files.upei.ca/ss/Ran%20and%20Ma_0.pdf, retrieved on 7th December, 2018.

http://search.ebscohost.com/login.aspx?direct=true&db=buh&AN=52955139&site=bsi-live, retrieved on 07th December, 2018.

Tribal Medicine in Northeast India: Its Practices and Potential

Dr. Hanmanth Rao S. Palep

Wellness and Illness in all the tribes are culturally defined, unlike in modern medicine, where a disease condition is determined by a specific cause. In the tribal cultures, disease is a social recognition, when a person is unable to fulfil his daily obligations being at disharmony with his psyche, soma (body) and his environment. More often age old beliefs, religion and souls of ancestors played great role in causation and management of diseases. Diviners, shamans and herbalists have evolved methods of treatment for various illnesses.

The health care systems of tribes are evolved by following natural laws that affect the universe and man. Earth, water, fire, air and sky are the elements common to both man and the planet they live on. The three prime factors that control universe are air, sun and moon. In a similar way *vata, pitta* and *kapha* exert control in people. Balance of these factors result in health. Disease is when the imbalance occurs due to various environmental factors, lifestyles, diets and lastly the wrath of Gods or the ancestors. Different systems of world medicine, viz., Ayurveda, TCM (Traditional Chinese Medicine) and Greek medicines have their roots in this tribal wisdom. All the tribes have lived in harmony in jungles, where as civilization has created a conflict between a man and animal. Northeastern tribes are no exception. Naga medicine appears to be following these very tenets from Ayurveda and TCM. A book titled Naga Healing by Dr. N. Keizienuo confirms this fact.

Northeast India is a melting pot of different cultures, beliefs and traditions. They speak different dialects and languages. Yet mostly they all live in harmony. Cause of disease was understood from ancient times. This is evident from Charak Samhita compiled by the great Ayurvedic physician, Charaka, almost 4000 years ago. Compared to people living in towns, tribal health status is superior in many ways. This became evident when we conducted medical camps in Nagaland last two to three years, basing on their haemoglobin levels and mean body muscle content despite the fact these people are miles away from the benefit of modern medicine.

Urban class has always undervalued the great contribution of the tribal wisdom. Many powerful modern medicines in fact are the gift of the tribal wisdom. One hundred such medicines are discovered from ninety plants used by different tribes of the world. Quinine from cinchona bark (Peru), Vincristine and Vinblastin from Madgaskar periwinkle flower, Aspirin from willow and poplar bark, Tubocurarine, a powerful muscle relaxant from arrow poison of South Amazon tribes and Datura Stramonium and Rauwolfia serpentine from India are but few examples. Taxol (paclitaxel) a powerful anti-cancer drug is shown to be present in Talisa patra, found in Himalayan regions. Thus the herbs used by various tribes have established so many non- poisonous plants for medicinal purpose through their long and safe usage. Award of Nobel Prize to China's Tu Youyou is a tribute to ancient TCM for rediscovery of an herb Artimesinin as a powerful anti-malarial therapy. Therefore plant wealth of Northeast India should come under the focus of research in quest for new chemical entities.

Nagaland and entire Northeast is blessed by nature with great wealth of flora, fauna and minerals. Nearly 1700 species of plants are found in this religion. Different tribes' posses the knowledge and use different herbs in various clinical conditions.

Ethno medical botanical research is very important from the point of view of discovering new chemical entities in plants. Plants in Himalayas and Northeast are considered to be very potent and are very valuable. Thus the knowledge of the plants transmitted through generations in these tribes become very valuable. Thus it behoves us to study diligently with humility and utmost respect to these tribes, their indigenous beliefs and practices relentlessly.

Current Status of the Tribal Medicine

Herbalists have extensive knowledge of identifying the plants and using them for giving relief in number of disorders. Traditional tribal healer uses herbs, animal products, minerals and divine healing techniques for the purpose of treating their patients. These do not possess any occult powers. They are expected to diagnose illness and treat them. Since they are not institutionally trained and have learnt the art from their elders in the family these people are at great disadvantage. Moreover many of these tribes are located in inaccessible areas.

1. **Diviners:** Through prayers or from messages from souls of ancestors and with witch craft they treat unexplainable diseases.

2. **Traditional Birth Attendants:** Local Dais are only available as the birth attendants. They are ill equipped and poorly trained.

3. Many others treat injuries fractures and know the method of setting the bones.

Indian National Fellowship Centre is inspired by Hon. Governor of Nagaland, Shri. Padmanabhji Acharya, who is working for social and emotional integration of the people of Nagaland with others from the rest of the country. In the last four years our teams apart from educational activities that include developing infrastructure in schools, teaching methodologies and student exchange programs, have also conducted medical camps in different locations in Nagaland. Once we conducted camps in seven district headquarters on behalf of Indian National Fellowship Centre and Rotary Club of Bombay North, a subsidiary of Rotary international. We have treated more than ten thousand people from far flung inaccessible areas. We have found many patients with gastro intestinal problems mostly attributed to high intake of spicy articles in food. HIV infection is highly prevalent. Our study 750 women with Pap's smears has shown high prevalence of HPV infection, which is the forerunner of cancer of uterine cervix. We found 19 cases positive for HPV. Our observation is that most basic modern medical care is not accessible in many remote tribal regions. In Mon district alone, nearly thirty patients are awaiting cataract surgery for quite some years.

My personal interaction with about two dozen Naga herb healers revealed that they were able to identify certain useful herbs for different clinical conditions. Their knowledge is limited and usually based on their experience, but they did not have the detailed information neither of the disease nor of the plant. They possessed this information gathered from their elders in their family or from the local practitioners.

Most of the tribes live in inaccessible places. These herb healers work as physicians and birth attendants. The potential of these healers lies in the fact that they can be trained as barefoot doctors to serve these inaccessible tribal villages.

Identifying useful medicinal plants and extracting the secondary metabolites in the place of their origin will get better value for the products than selling raw plants and also provide new avenue for employment. Providing Intellectual property rights of their knowledge of invaluable plants and empowering these men and women, in my opinion, will go a long way to make sustainable heath care of the tribal population of Northeast India.

References

Medical Botany by Walter H. Lewis & Memory P. P. Elwin Lewis.

Monimugdha Bhuyan. "Comparative study of ethnomedicine among the tribes of North East India." In *International journal of social sciences*, Vol. 4(2), 27-32. Feb. 2015.

Naga Healing by Dr. N. Kezienuo.

Ramashankar S Deb, B. K. Sharmain, "Traditional healing practices in Northeast India." In *Indian journal of history of science*, 50.2 (2015), 324-32.

India's Northeast Culture:
Cosmic Mizo *Tlawmngaihna*

Dr. Laltluangliana Khiangte

*T*lawmngaihna is the term used for the Mizo code of morals and conduct, a highly prized virtue and a wonderful philosophy of life which is so rich in meaning and so wide in scope that it has been found virtually impossible to render it in any single word or phrase of another language. There are writers who, in their effort to get to the nearest core of the concept, suggest words such as "altruism" and "chivalry", only to quickly acknowledge their inadequacies. Putting it contextually, a person who possesses *tlawmngaihna* must be obedient and respectful to the elders; courteous in dealing with the weak and the lowly; generous and hospitable to the poor, the needy and strangers; self-denying and self-sacrificing at the opportune moments in favour of others; ready to help those in distress; compassionate to a companion who falls sick while on a journey or becomes a victim of a wild beast in the hunt by never abandoning him to his fate; heroic and resolute at war and in hunting; stoical in suffering and in facing hardship under trying circumstances; and persevering in any worthwhile undertaking however hard and daunting it might prove to be.

So, *tlawmngaihna* to a Mizo stands for that compelling moral force which finds expression in self-sacrifice for the service of others. In fact, *tlawmngaihna* should be found in every sphere of a genuine Mizo life. It is in fact the essence of 'Mizoness', a concept so vital to the understanding of a culture that all else are eclipsed in importance. In order to fully comprehend its meaning, *tlawmngaihna* may be explained through examples, which will thereby bring to light its global relevance.

Given the lack of an equivalent term in English that can stand as the signifier, a selection of positive words like altruism, dedication, patriotism, sacrifice, selflessness and all kinds of service to humankind may connote to the meaning of *tlawmngaihna* for the community of Mizos across the world.

So, *tlawmngaihna* is the term used for the Mizo code of morals and conduct, a highly prized virtue and a wonderful philosophy of life which is so rich in meaning and so wide in scope that it has been found virtually impossible to render it in any single word or phrase of another language.

There are writers who, in their effort to get to the nearest core of the concept, suggest words such as "altruism" and "chivalry", only to quickly acknowledge their inadequacies. The pioneer missionary to Mizoram Rev. J. H. Lorrain tried to give the meaning of *tlawmngai*, the verbal, adjectival and adverbial form of *tlawmngaihna* in his monumental *Dictionary of the Lushai Language*, parts of which are given below:

1. To be self-sacrificing, unselfish, self-denying, persevering, stoical, stout-hearted, plucky, brave, firm, independent (refusing help); to be loath to lose one's good reputation, prestige; to be too proud or self-respecting to give in.

2. To persevere, to endure patiently, to make light of personal injuries, to dislike making a fuss over anything.

3. To put one's own inclinations on one side and do a thing which one would rather not do, with the object either of keeping up one's prestige, or of helping or pleasing another, etc.

4. To do whatever the occasion demands no matter how distasteful or inconvenient it may be to oneself or to one's inclinations.

5. To refuse to give in, give way, or be conquered.

6. To not like to refuse a request; to do a thing because one does not like to refuse, or because one wishes to please others.

7. To act pluckily or show a brave front (also used as adjective and adverb).

Putting it contextually, a person who possesses tlawmngaihna must be obedient and respectful to the elders; courteous in dealing with the weak and the vulnerable; generous and hospitable to the poor, the needy and strangers; self-denying and self-sacrificing at the opportune moments in favour of others; ready to help those in distress; compassionate to a companion who falls sick while on a journey or becomes a victim of a wild beast in the hunt by never abandoning him to his fate; heroic and resolute at war and in hunting; stoical in suffering and in facing hardship under trying circumstances; and persevering in any worthwhile undertaking however hard and daunting it might prove to be.

A *tlawmngai* person is ever-ready to do whatever the occasion demands, no matter how distasteful or inconvenient it might be to one or to one's own inclinations; vie with others in excelling in sports or any other corporate labour, and try to surpass others in hospitality and in doing his ordinary daily task independently and efficiently. Its dimensions cover both personal and collective levels of activities wherein self-interest is subordinate to the interest of others individually and collectively, and self-sacrifices for the need of others are to come in spontaneously as a natural part of one's life.

To be precise, *tlawmngaihna* to a Mizo stands for that compelling moral force which finds expression in self-sacrifice for the service of others. In fact, *tlawmngaihna* should be found in every branch of a genuine Mizo life. It is a fact that *tlawmngaihna* can only be explained by examples.

Let us examine *tlawmngaihna* in matters of helping the sick. It is the custom in Lushai villages that if a man falls sick, the villagers of every village join efforts to carry him to a hospital or any other nearby health care centre. Supposing someone from a faraway village has to be carried to hospital, he is carried by his fellow villagers to the next village and thence by the inhabitants of that village to the next and so on until the hospital is reached.

When any one has to be carried in this way, two or three young men who are known as *Zualko* are sent on to the next village to inform the villagers that a sick man is on the way. As soon as they get the news, the villagers abandon whatever they are doing and go to receive a sick man. A village that possesses *tlawmngaihna* will go to meet the convoy at the boundary of their lands and offer to carry the sick man from there. If the villagers who are already carrying the man are also keen on *tlawmngaihna,* they will refuse to hand over their burden and will insist on carrying him right up to the village. A village that does this is showing the right spirit of practising *tlawmngaihna.*

Tlawmngaihna can thus be practised by a village as a corporate body as well as by individuals. If a man falls sick in the cultivating season, his fellow villagers are expected to weed his fields for him. The chief will probably call for volunteers for this work and if the rules of *tlawmngaihna* are properly followed in the village there will be numerous volunteers who will vie with each other to get the work done.

In matters of hospitality to travellers, according to Mizo custom, all travellers in the hills are entitled to food and lodging free for a night. Some people churlishly refuse to give the hospitality required by custom. But anyone who follows the rules of tlawmngaihna will never refuse hospitality to strangers.

One of the fields where a man can best exhibit his quality as a *tlawmngai* person is when he is out on hunting expeditions. A traditional hunting expedition offers many opportunities for the exhibition of *tlawmngaihna.*

A man who possesses endurance and is able to go on all day with very little food, who is courageous in following up wounded wild beasts, who thinks of his friends before himself, takes less than his share of the food, is industrious in building the shelter for the night and in collecting wood for the fire is said to possess *tlawmngaihna* and according to the dictates of good form, the young men are supposed to vie with each other in these respects.

If two men go for a hunt, one of whom has a gun and come up to an animal, if he follows *tlawmngaihna,* he will offer his friend the first shot. If a man is hurt by a wild animal, his companions must stay and look after him and must not continue the chase thereby leaving him alone. If a man is caught by a wounded bear or other animal, it would be a fearful disgrace if his companions run away and leave him to his fate, they are bound to stay and help him.

Even in ordinary circumstances, one can exhibit *tlawmngaihna* on the path of a journey towards an interior village. For instance, in a place where vehicle is unavailable, people who are travelling together must help each other. If one member of the party gets ill and falls behind, his companions should wait for him to recover, if they do not, they are lacking in *tlawmngaihna.* Water is scarce in the hills and during the hot weather people suffer severely from thirst, a man who goes a long distance down the hill side and fetches water for his companions is doing his duty and practising *tlawmngaihna.*

Occasions of joyful celebrations such as the feast of *Sechhun* and *Khuangchawi* offer opportunities to exhibit *tlawmngaihna* collectively, particularly by the youths. At the feast, the young men and girls in the village help the giver *(Khuangchawi-pa)* of the feast in many ways by pounding rice, collecting firewood and doing other useful things, re-enforcing the house etc. They are expected to do these things as a matter of *tlawmngaihna.* The giver of the feast for his part is expected to give them food and drink in the *same way.*

Tlawmngaihna could also be exhibited individually and collectively as when calamity strikes a family or a village, as in the case of damage by fire. If a whole village is burnt down, the neighbouring villages contribute food, clothing and household utensils to replace those that have been burnt and also help to rebuild it. This is done due to *tlawmngaihna*. In the same way, if a man's house is burnt down and his property and paddy are destroyed, his fellow villagers help him with contributions of food and clothes and also help him rebuild his house. All able persons come out to work as *hnatlang* (social work).

The practice of *tlawmngaihna* is all the more visible when death occurs in the village. When someone dies in a family, close relatives and friends come with cloth to wrap the dead body; some will bring fresh flowers as a token of their sharing of sorrow. They try to console the family by their presence and conversation, by saying words of comfort and encouraging sermons and by singing songs of mourning.

It was, and still is, the practice of every family in the village to contribute one or two pieces of fire-wood for the bereaved family, and in some towns today a cup of rice is collected for the family. The grave for the deceased person is dug by young men of the village on a voluntary basis. No young man would stay away from this work, because it would be against '*tlawmngaihna*' to do so. It is purely with a willing and altruistic spirit that such help is rendered.

Not only in death, but also in sickness, young men help in attending to the sick especially at night so that members of the family of the sick can get rest and sleep. If death happens in the later part of the day, and it is too late to dig the grave, young people would come together at the residence of the deceased for a wake, and sing for the whole night.

In the past, the only way of sending messages between villages was through voluntary young men. Even a slight mention by members of a family, of their desire to send a message to another village about the sickness or death in their family would get prompt execution.

Whether by day time or at dead of night, a young man would try to be the first to take the message to the other village. To brave the dread of wild beasts and the fatigue of the run of long distances between villages alone at night through thick forests calls for a genuine spirit of *tlawmngaihna.*

How and in what way this high quality of character is ingrained in the Mizo youth through the *Zawlbuk* (Bachelors' Dormitory) system of discipline is clearly brought out in various ways. The practice of early transfer of control of the male child from his family to the *Zawlbuk* discipline leads to easy assimilation of the norms learnt in his family with those prevailing in the society of the grownups; preventing, thus, any cleavage between his own style and that expected of him by the society.

The simple forms of education for life evolved, as a follow up, in the *Zawlbuk* through various activities, code of conduct and mode of living which ensured healthy reciprocity between different age groups and the village elders, as also between the claims of the family as a social unit and the wider society as an organic whole; preventing, once again, any problem of 'generation gap' from raising its ugly head as it always does in more developed societies.

In this task of building the life and character of the youth, the elders and the chief of the village played vital roles. The elders, especially those reputed as *Pasaltha (Knight or Hero)*, through deeds of *tlawmngaihna* would often visit the *Zawlbuk* and recount the heroic past of their lives as young men and of other *pasaltha* with the aim of driving home the message of *tlawmngaihna* to be emulated by the youth.

They thus helped in shaping the personalities and aspirations of the younger ones. The ideals received from the elders usually found practical expressions in the various activities of the *Zawlbuk*, helping the aspirants to demonstrate their worth as *pasaltha*. The chief, in his turn, would uphold the ideals of *tlawmngaihna* by patronizing the *Zawlbuk and* by giving incentives to the proven *pasaltha (a tribal version of undisputed knight).*

While giving due recognition to the qualities of *tlawmngaihna* in the young men, one should not forget to acknowledge the equally high *tlawmngaihna* qualities found in the girls. Due to a different and subtle nature it took in the case of the girls, most writers, particularly non-Mizo writers, fail to see this even while giving generous tribute to them for their quality of hard work. The hard work done in the spirit of *tlawmngaihna* is the result of vigorous training imparted at home. This means that *tlawmngaihna* was taught not only at *Zawlbuk*. As the girls had no access to *Zawlbuk*, their training was confined at home, but in no way was the severity of the training less so, nor its outcome inferior that of the boys.

By the time a girl can carry two bamboo water tubes on her back, that is, about seven or eight years of age, the mother will begin teaching her the ways of *tlawmngaihna* which includes all aspects of household chores and even more. She would teach her how to carry water, collect fire-wood, husking and winnowing of paddy, cooking of the family meal, feeding the pigs and driving in the fowls to the coop. Besides, while the parents work in the *jhum*, she would take care of the baby, if there is one, and thus keep herself occupied the whole day.

When she becomes a young woman she would learn weaving, continue doing all the household work and also start joining her parents in jhum work. She would join *lawmrual*, a party of youngsters engaged in helping one another in turns, known as *inlawm*, especially in field work like *jhum* cultivation. While going to the field, girls would carry the lunch-pack i.e. wrapped packets of rice and other implements of the male members. And even at the time of going back home, they would carry all those important articles. They would also wash their clothes and repair the same whenever required. A girl with *tlawmngaihna* would do all these willingly and happily.

At night, the young men of the village would go around to court girls in their homes. A *tlawmngai* girl would welcome them warmly and would make them sit around the hearth and other convenient places.

She would keep herself busy cooking food for pigs, spinning cotton, rolling the thread into balls or mending torn cloths and all other needful chores while also keeping the young men in good humour. When the young men would get ready to leave, she would extend an appropriate courtesy to make them feel that they are very much welcome to stay on. The courtesies were given so generously that sometimes a young man might be foolish enough not to realize the politeness of the girl and stay on late till the cocks announce the approach of a new day.

Then a girl could nap only for about an hour or two before she gets up again to prepare the day's requirements. She would light a fire (not easily done), fetch water (often from a considerable distance down the stream), and husk paddy (another really difficult job). Soon after the morning meal, which usually was about the time of sunrise, she would be out in the jhum field. Thus girls of the traditional Mizo society practically had no time to rest.

At the same time 'a girl of *tlawmngaihna*' would see to it that she maintained a restraint in food habits, eating as little as possible, especially while eating in places other than her own home. Considering the extent of work they did with the little amount of food they consumed, one wonders how it was possible for the Mizo girls to remain healthy and strong. It is a pity therefore, that traditional Mizo society gave no due recognition of it in the way it is given to the young men.

The practical examples given, both for boys and girls, are by no means exhaustive. As every area of Mizo life was so permeated by the concept of *tlawmngaihna,* it is virtually impossible to recount them all. The thoroughness of the training given in *Zawlbuk* and the splendid result manifested in the character of the Mizo youth in meeting the demands of any situation is well expressed in the following manner. It was in the *Zawlbuk* that all the young boys and lads of the village who slept there at night received their training in matters of obedience, discipline, courage, fortitude, perseverance, self-sacrifice etc.

All other precepts enjoyed by *tlawmngaihna* are also inculcated with such thoroughness that young boys and lads who had been inmates of the *Zawlbuk* know what to do in case of emergency or in the usual course of events. Most of the social work in the village like cleaning paths, repair or construction of houses of widows, were carried out by the members of the *Zawlbuk* under the guidance and control of the older ones, who also inculcated in the young men a sense of social unity and a feeling of responsibility for the village as a whole.

It was in the process of such daily corporate living in the village *Zawlbuk* that a body of unwritten rules or norms grew up in amazing uniformity, and the people, both in groups and as individuals, vied with one another in carrying them out to such an extent that the *Zawlbuk* trained youngsters unhesitatingly lived in accordance with the dictates of *tlawmngaihna* inculcated in them.

However, the Mizos do not claim *tlawmngaihna* to be their exclusive possession. Some of its ideals and practices are to be found in every tribe and nation around the world in varying degrees. And yet, considering the comprehensiveness of its ideal as well as practice, as shown above, one may perhaps be right, at least to a degree, in saying that the concept of *tlawmngaihna* is peculiar to Mizos, so much so that one who is lacking in its qualities is regarded "*Un-Mizo*", a censure which can hardly be met by any other.

On the other hand, '*A complete Mizo*' is one who has *tlawmngaihna* in the fullest measure if that were at all possible. It is of *tlawmngaihna*, the enjoyable life style of the Mizos that Rokunga (1914-69), one of the most celebrated poets, writes:

"Precious tlawmngaihna, oh, life's blossom.

Though many thousand years may pass;

We bid you to dwell ever with us

In our pleasant high land abode...."

So *tlawmngaihna* and Mizo-ness cannot be separated, they are synonymous. All the Mizo ethnic groups across the world are therefore expected to inculcate and nurture it by all means.

References

Lorrain, J.H. *Dictionary of the Lushai Language,* 1940.

Khiangte, Laltluangliana. *Mizos of North East India: Culture, Folklore, Language, Literature.* 216, 2008. First released at Mumbai, Maharashtra, India.

Tribal Languages and Literature (Papers-Edited) p. 202. Aizwal: L.T.L. Publications, 2010.

Unsung Tribal Pastor & Writer (Memorable contribution of a Mizo Pastor). Kolkata: LTL Publications, 2011.

Tribal Culture, Folklore and Literature. New Delhi: Mittal Publications, 2013.

Zairema, Rev. Tlawmngaihna, Aizawl: 2009.

Thanseia, ...Aizawl: 2000.

Representation of Cultural Other: Reflections on Saidian Perspectives

Dr. M. P. Terence Samuel

Edward Said in his magnum opus, *Orientalism*, explains how the unequal relationship between the West and the Orient has established cultural imperialism through the textual exercise of the Orientalists with its supporting institutions. According to Said, the Orientalism represented the people of the Orient in a way as the Other of the Occident. Through the representational theory, Said explains as to how Orientalism Orientalised the Orient which is textual than actual. Though he primarily is concerned with the depictions of the Arabs in the texts of the Oriental scholars of the West, his theory has got a universal appeal to the people of the Third World in general too.

Said takes the oft-quoted remarks of Marx in his *The Eighteenth Brumaire of Louis Bonaparte* that "They (proletariat) cannot represent themselves; they must be represented", to explain the representational character of Orientalism. Further, he uses Foucault's analytics of power, Gramscian notions of civil society and hegemony and many other critical theorists to make a necessary intervention into the texts and the knowledge produced by the Orientalists. His primary concern in the critical elaboration of Orientalism and its structures is that how the dominant self establishes truth about the weak Other through its cultural representations. Having born in Al-Quds (the Arabic name for Jerusalem) and lived in Egypt and USA, he could identify the standardisation and the cultural stereotyping of the Orient, especially the anti-Arab and anti-Islamic prejudices of the West, which he found them to be raucous. His search for the reasons of the origin of the politicised fictional identification of the Arab led him to the critical intervention in the knowledge produced by the Orientalists about the Orient. Out of this critical enquiry is born the critical perspectives on Orientalism.

In such an attempt, he finds the interrelations between society, history and textuality and the role played by ideology, politics and the logic of power in them. Especially, how the Western conceptions and treatment of the Other have been constructed with the role played by the Western culture from its dominant position in the world (EWS 1978: 24-5). Having a clue from Gramsci's *Prison Notebooks* that knowing thyself is a product of the historical process which deposited infinity of traces without leaving an inventory (AG 1992: 324), Said tries to find out the inventory of the traces of the representations of the Orient in the works of Orientalists. This has led Said to analyse the role and the problems of Orientalist representations of the Orient.

Using Saidian perspectives, this paper attempts to extend his theoretical interventions into the understanding of cultural representations of the weak Other by a dominant self in general. The main concern of this paper is to attempt to explore the possibilities of using Saidian perspectives for the general understanding of the cultural representations of the Other, especially keeping in mind the cultural contestations happening along with the rise of hegemonic forces over the parts of the world. With this aim in mind, this paper attempts to explore Saidian perspectives on Orientalism and how it can offer the necessary paradigm for a critical intervention into the issues surrounding cultural representations of the Other by a dominant self. Particularly in the context of this seminar, it would be apt to find certain solutions through phenomenological approach for the problems, issues and challenges posed by Said, if at all possible.

Critique of Orientalism

Said begins his book, *Orientalism*, with an explosive statement that "The Orient was almost a European invention, and had been since antiquity a place of romance, exotic beings, haunting memories and landscapes, remarkable experiences." (EWS 1978: 1) What he means by this statement is that there is no internal consistency between the Orientalist representations/ideas of the Orient and the real Orient. For him, "Orientalism overrode the Orient. As a system of thought about the Orient, it always rose from specifically human detail to the general trans-human one" (EWS 1978: 96). Hence, the correspondence between the reality and the representation is lost in the ontological reification of the Orient validated through the textual traditions and their supporting institutions. Such sweeping generalisations and the non-correspondence between the Oriental textual traditions and the actual Orient became possible, because Orientalism studied the Orient as a 'textual universe'; and the rapport between the Orientalist and the Orient was merely textual till the conquering of the Orient by the West. Even after the geographical extension of Europe into the Oriental lands, "when a learned Orientalist travelled in the country of his specialization, it was always with unshakable abstract maxims about the "civilization" he had studied; rarely were Orientalists interested in anything except proving the validity of these musty "truths" by applying them, without great success, to uncomprehending, hence degenerate, natives." (EWS 1978: 52)

Such distorted representations of the Orient are not due to the problem of the *re-presence* of the reality through language; but Orientalism is itself a complex phenomenon involving various aspects which made possible such representations as truths told about the Orient. For, Orientalism is "a way of coming to terms with the Orient that is based on the Orient's special place in European Western experience. The Orient is not only adjacent to Europe; it is also the place of Europe's greatest and richest and oldest colonies, the source of its civilizations and languages, its cultural contestant, and one of its deepest and most recurring images of the Other. In addition, the Orient has helped to define Europe (or the West) as its contrasting image, idea, personality, experience. Yet none of this Orient is merely imaginative. The Orient is an integral part of European *material* civilization and culture. Orientalism expresses and represents that part culturally and even ideologically as a mode of discourse with supporting institutions, vocabulary, scholarship, imagery, doctrines, even colonial bureaucracies and colonial styles." (EWS 1978: 1-2) It is not that the Orient is considered to be the Other of the Orient, but it is the constituent contributor of the West; it is the geopolitical awareness which created the cultural interest about the Orient, acting along with "brute political, economic and military rationales to make the Orient the varied and complicated place" (EWS 1978: 12).

This is not to say that it is the raw political power which is responsible for such representations of the Orient; rather, the geopolitical awareness is distributed into many learned fields of study through the modern scientific apparatus, such as philology, psychology, sociology, anthropology, history and aesthetics; it is a 'certain will or intention to understand, and in some cases to control, manipulate and incorporate a manifestly different world'; it is a discourse that exists with an uneven exchange of various kinds of power – power political, power intellectual, power cultural and power moral (EWS 1978: 12). Such uneven exchanges of various kinds of power was shaped by the "dynamic exchange between individual authors and the large political concerns shaped by the three great empires – British, French and American – in whose intellectual and imaginary territory the writing was produced" (EWS 1978: 14-15). Hence, at the point of convergence of the national interests of the empires and the individual interests of the Orientalist, such an imaginary representation of the Orient emerged with the other intermittent factors mentioned above. This is further reinforced by the author – reader dialectic "by which the experiences of readers in reality are determined by what they have read, and this in turn influences writers to take up subjects defined in advance by readers' experiences" (EWS 1978: 94), as books written about ferocious lions will continue to reinforce the imaginary ideas about them until the lions talk back. "Such texts *create* not only knowledge but also the very reality they appear to describe. In time such knowledge and reality produce a tradition, or what Michel Foucault calls a discourse, whose material presence or weight, not the originality of a given author, is really responsible for the texts produced out of it" (EWS 1978: 94). Such a complex process explains how the Orientalist imaginary representations came to be considered as truths about Orient through such discursive practices and traditions.

According to Said, Orientalism cannot be misunderstood or be dismissed merely as a structure of lies and myths; it is the sign of European-Atlantic power over the Orient (EWS 1978: 6) which tried to speak for the Orient considering it as a mute object which cannot represent itself. It is not an 'airy European fantasy' about the Orient, but a created body of theory and practice (EWS 1978: 6) where the contributions of Orientalists, travellers, missionaries, readers and colonial administration overlapped through the theory-practice dialectics. It shows the operation of power in the creation of the system of knowledge which reified the identity of the object of study thereby to make it convenient to control, rule and manipulate it. Though the object is not reducible to a particular identity and that such a constructed identity is not verifiable with the object, the power of the West over the Orient enabled it. Such a nexus between the knowledge and power in the Orientalisation of the Orient obliterated the human being from the Orient (EWS 1978: 27) and in a sense objectified him/her.

While explaining the relationship between the knowledge and power in the representation of the Orient, Said makes an important observation that "ideas, cultures, and histories cannot seriously be understood or studied without their force, or more precisely their configurations of power, also being studied... The relationship between Occident and Orient is a relationship of power, of domination, of varying degrees of a complex hegemony... The Orient was Orientalized not only because it was discovered to be "Oriental" in all those ways considered commonplace by an average nineteenth-century European, but also because it *could be*—that is, submitted to being—*made* Oriental." (EWS 1978: 5-6) The considerable material investment of many generations in the creation of a system of theory and practice made Orientalism possible "as a system of knowledge about the Orient, an accepted grid for filtering Orient into Western consciousness" (EWS 1978: 6). In his *Culture and Imperialism*, he explains it further by saying that "The main battle in imperialism is over land, of course: but when it came to who owned the land, who had the right to settle and work on it, who kept it going, who won it back, and who now plans its future – these issues were reflected, contested, and even for a time decided in narrative... The power to narrate, or to block other narratives from forming and emerging, is very important to culture and imperialism, and constitutes one of the main connections between them" (EWS 1994: xii – xiii).

Now the question is how the relation between culture and imperialism became possible in Orientalism through knowledge discourses? There are many interdependent factors which made it possible in the creation of the systematic theory of Orientalism, according to Said. First, the accepted definition of Orientalism is an academic venture. So, it gained strength as an impartial intellectual discourse. Said cites the decision of the Church Council of Vienna for the establishment of chairs in Paris, Oxford, Bologna, Avignon and Salamanca for the study of Arabic, Hebrew, Greek and Syriac which diverged into different field of study of the Orient linguistically, geographically, aesthetically, culturally and ethnically later on (EWS 1978: 49-50). Secondly, such an academic tradition made Orientalism as a style of thought based on the epistemological and ontological distinction between the orient and the Occident. "Thus a very large mass of writers, among whom are poets, novelists, philosophers, political theorists, economists, and imperial administrators, have accepted the basic distinction between East and West as the starting point for elaborate theories, epics, novels, social descriptions, and political accounts concerning the Orient, its people, customs, "mind", destiny, and so on" (EWS 1978: 2). Thirdly, Orientalism functioned as a corporate institution "dealing with it by making statements about it, authorizing views of it, describing it, by teaching it, settling it, ruling over it" (EWS 1978: 3). Fourthly, Orientalism as a discourse of 'enormously systematic discipline', through an interchange between the academic and imaginative meanings, made the European culture to gain strength and identity "by setting itself off against the Orient as a sort of surrogate and even underground self" (EWS 1978: 3). Fifthly, Orient was a career for the Westerners. Citing the statement of Disraeli in his novel *Tancred*, Said says that the bright young Westerners found it to be an all-consuming passion for "the regular constellation of ideas as the pre-eminent thing" (EWS 1978: 5) to be told about the Orient to the interested Western audience and readers. Out of these interdependent factors created the Orientalist representations as truths, by giving validity to them as a systematic, scholarly, intellectual, impartial, academic exercise.

Though the East and the West are adjacent territories geographically, why such epistemological and ontological distinctions have to be made by the Orientalists is another question that confronts us. One of the reasons that Said provides is that "From the end of the seventh century until the battle of Lepanto in 1571, Islam in either its Arab, Ottoman, or North African and Spanish form dominated or effectively threatened European Christianity". Yet India was not an indigenous threat to Europe, but came to be colonised after commercial activities, started by Portugal followed by other European nations, and as the native authority crumbled. After William Jones, who studied Sanskrit and Indian religion and history, Indology acquired the scientific knowledge status; Jones's interest in India too was also due to his prior interest in Islam. Till then, Orient was not synonymous to the whole of Asia (EWS 1978: 74-5).

Though Islam and Christianity lay uneasily close to each other geographically and culturally, the Islamic Orient was a threat to the Christian Europe. For Europe, Islam was a lasting trauma; hence, "European representation of the Muslim, Ottoman or Arab was always a way of controlling the redoubtable Orient". Said continues that "There is nothing especially controversial or reprehensible about such domestications of the exotic; they take place between all cultures, certainly, and between all men. My point, however, is to emphasize the truth that the Orientalist, as much as anyone in the European West who thought about or experienced the Orient, performed this kind of mental operation. But what is more important still is the limited vocabulary and imagery that impose themselves as a consequence… One constraint acting upon Christian thinkers who tried to understand Islam was an analogical one" (EWS 1978: 59-60).

What is problematic in such analogical exercise is the limitations of comparison between the cultural aspects of two different societies. When the Orient as a body of knowledge in the modernised during 19th and 20th centuries, the ambition of the Orientalists was to "formulate their discoveries, experiences and insights suitably in modern terms"; for which they relied heavily on comparative grammar and racial theories, as Renan did. Also, Orientalism was subjected to imperialism, racism, positivism, utopianism, historicism, Darwinism, Freudianism, Marxism, utilitarianism etc. Though such subjections were the accepted grid of knowledge through which the Orient was filtered, it also provided for the hidden problematic of such an exercise – that is the familiarisation of the non-familiar other or knowing the unknown through previously known categories of thought.

In order to prove this point, Said takes a clue from the Levi-Straussian notion of the *Science of the concrete*. "A primitive tribe, for example, assigns a definite place, function, and significance to every leafy species in its immediate environment… This kind of rudimentary classification has a logic to it, but the rules of the logic by which a green fern in one society is a symbol of grace and in another is considered maleficent are neither predictably rational nor universal. There is always a measure of the purely arbitrary in the way the distinctions between things are seen (EWS 1978: 53-4)." However, when subjecting such arbitrariness of cultural symbolism through the theoretical sieve, the differences are levelled. "Something patently foreign and distant acquires, for one reason or another, a status more rather than less familiar. One tends to stop judging things either as completely novel or as completely well known; a new median category emerges, a category that allows one to see new things, things seen for the first time, as versions of a previously known thing. In essence such a category is not so much a way of receiving new information as it is a method of controlling what seems to be a threat to some established view of things... The threat is muted" (EWS 1978: 58-9), as the familiar values impose themselves on the non-familiar ones as 'original' or 'repetitious' or 'fraudulent version of the known' and so on. For example, Islam was termed as 'Mohammadanism' in the fashion of Christianity; Islam was judged to be a fraudulent version of Christianity as in Dante's *Inferno*.

Very interestingly, Said also provides an explanation as to how the critical thinking and the resistance against such constructed knowledge discourses are muted as branding them as 'political and partisan' discourses, claiming that 'true' knowledge is fundamentally 'non-political or impartial'. "No one is helped in understanding this today when the adjective 'political' is used as a label to discredit any work for daring to violate the protocol of pretended suprapolitical objectivity... For if it is true that no production of knowledge in the human sciences can ever ignore or disclaim its author's involvement as a human subject in his own circumstances, then it must also be true that for a European or American studying the Orient there can be no disclaiming the main circumstances of *his* actuality: that he comes up against the Orient as a European or American first, as an individual second. And to be a European or an American in such a situation is by no means an inert fact. It meant and means being aware, however dimly, that one belongs to a power with definite interests in the Orient" (EWS 1978: 10-1).

As discussed above, the question in front of us is that if phenomenology gives importance to the life-world in knowing the object, how far this knowledge is non-partisan or power-neutral when knowing the cultural Other? While commenting on the knowledge produced by the West, Said says that "One can have no quarrel with such an ambition in theory (that the knowledge produced is to be non-political, scholarly, academic, impartial, above partisan or small-minded doctrinal belief), perhaps, but in practice the reality is much more problematic. No one has ever devised a method for detaching the scholar from the circumstances of life, from the fact of his involvement (conscious or unconscious) with a class, a set of beliefs, a social position, or from the mere activity of being a member of a society. These continue to bear on what he does professionally, even though naturally enough his research and its fruits do attempt to reach a level of relative freedom from the inhibitions and the restrictions of brute, everyday reality". This is a challenge thrown by Said in the context of how the self tries to familiarise the cultural aspects of the non-familiar Other.

The problem in front of us is to find alternatives to such cultural representations of the dominant self over the weak Other and "to ask how one can study other cultures and peoples from a libertarian, or a non-repressive and non-manipulative perspective." (EWS 1978: 24) Towards this Said provides two different approaches: one is, elimination of the elements of power through "unlearning of the inherent dominative mode" of knowledge production; another is, to provide autonomy back to the object, rather than privileging the knowing self in the process of knowing and thereby to place the self and the object on a radically democratic paradigm in the process of knowing.

References

Gramsci, Antonio. Quintin Hoare and Geoffrey Nowell Smith (*Eds.* & *Trs.*) *Selections from the Prison Notebooks*. New York: International Publishers, 1992.

Said, Edward W. *Orientalism*, Routledge & Kegan Paul, London and Henley, 1978.

_____. *Culture and Imperialism*. New York: Vintage Books, 1994.

Tribal and Subterranean Culture: Phenomenological Rendering of the Tribal Consciousness

Dr. S. Lourdunathan

Phenomenological Productions of *Differentia* of Meanings

The paper attempts to provision a phenomenological rendering of the consciousness of tribal people[1] (subaltern or indigenous or Adivasi[2]) which in turn calls for (i) a sense of exploration and exposition of the tribal-first-person experience, and the way(s) the tribal make sense of their immediate world, *vis-à-vis* (ii) the non-tribal worldview(s) or the non-sense making of the tribal consciousness that attempts to engage the tribal consciousness/lifeworld/ horizons through their (dominant) geo-political and cultural perspectives and practices. This means that one can possibly situate interrelated multiple phenomenological productions of meanings that shape the phenomenology of tribal consciousness, the layers of which might include (i) the tribal self-consciousness of themselves and their immediate natural and cultural world and (ii) the non-tribal external-other encroaching/engaging of the tribal world. Thus the tribal sense of 'self' and 'the other-self' is the foreground for phenomenological inquiry here. This implies:

1. Clarification of the tribal people's understanding of 'self' and their immediate natural-cultural world namely the tribal sense of being-in-the-world

2. Clarification of the tribal people's phenomenological understanding (the consciousness of the 'other') of the ideological and practical forces of the non-tribal world that continue to encounter and engage the tribal world.

3. Clarification of the non-tribal-other, their construed meanings of the tribal people and their world.

Accordingly, the phenomenological engagement of the tribal world/culture posits serious intriguing concerns, some of which may I outline here: The tribal sense of their world (the tribal self and other consciousness) aims at probing the issues such as *How the world appears to the tribal people or how the tribal people sense-experience the world (subjective experience) and how do they communicate subjective experience by way of living their culture and everydayness? And how could we make sense of the tribal consciousness given to their life-world. To think the very thinking, in the spirit of phenomenology, if it means to render the question of the subjectivity, its essence and existence in terms of authenticity, then - how or in what manner such a phenomenological engagement can be done with reference to the understanding of the subjectivity of the subaltern? How the double positioning³ of the Phenomenology of the Spirit of the subaltern is systematically grounded? To what extent can we establish this phenomenological grounding to reveal and restore the subaltern life-world consciousness? Is the 'science'⁴ of phenomenology potential of the revelation of the subaltern consciousness towards the accomplishment of the subjectivity of the subaltern? What is the scope of such phenomenological engagement? How can we understand the sensibilities of the Subaltern existence? And how the subaltern reveals itself to re-affirm its existence? In other words, how or in what manner can we have an intelligible accessibility or phenomenological listening to be-come conscious of the subaltern life-world consciousness?*

These series of probing concerns, outlined here, though I may not deal it in details (reserve them for a detailed work) , taking into consideration of the scope of the paper, this is meant to elucidate the tribal consciousness in their giveness and the authentic possibility of eliciting it, which can be authentically be done solely by the tribal-first-person lived-experience however this does not preclude the intentional understanding of the insider by the outsider for the "Dasein is essentially for the sake of others,"[5] held Heidegger. The phenomenology of the consciousness of tribal people and their worldview[6] would then mean the fundamental ontology (the Husserlian sense of transcendental phenomenology) that render authentic intelligibility and accessibility of the mode of (Dasein) as there-being-in-the-world because, for Husserl, meaning is essentially linked with (human) experience and it is revealed through a mode of appearance as it is beyond or devoid of any presuppositions. The consciousness and the worldview of the subaltern people of those who are relegated as the 'tribal' is but a living experience, the intentionality of which is directed towards an experience of the being-in-the world by the virtue of its content that represents appropriate conditions of being in harmony with their both the natural and non-natural (cultural) world. Heidegger would say, thought originates, not in some peculiar and special "intuition" of being, but rather in the simple and immediate grasp of being in our own "being-in" the open-ness of place.[7] In this sense the consciousness of the tribal people is foundationally phenomenological, without being non-appropriative, non-dominant, but in continuous consciousness of being relational with the natural/cultural world.

By the non-tribal sensibilities of the tribal world, I mean, the *external* historical-cultural (ideological and practical) forces that 'sight' (engage/encounter/ encumber) the tribal world(s) which can either be enabling or disabling of the phenomenological sensibilities of the tribal consciousness and their lifeworld. The non-tribal worlds/worldviews either the predominant euro-centric and Indian-centric that approach the tribal as *subaltern-other* to thematize or depreciate the native, render indigenous Adivasi people and their consciousness to be interpreted and imperialized by either external or internal conquests. To this the non-tribal sense of tribal world (intends) posits the elucidation of issues such as *how the tribal consciousness and their sense-making of the world is (miss) appropriated by the non-tribal world, the non-sense making of the tribal world or the monopolization of the tribal world? In what sense, the non-tribal perspectives are domineering of the tribal phenomenological experience.*

When speaking about the subaltern, perhaps we/I 'always' assume that we are talking of an *'other'* for the sake of other. We seem to assume a privileged sense of 'I' as the subject, the kind of sense-making-subject who is different from the 'other', namely the subaltern, the object of my perception. Emmanuel Levinas (greatly influenced by Phenomenology) warns us that by way of talking about the other, the otherness is already preconditioned through my phenomenological reduction. This means that we already pre-close our subjectivity and pretend to speak about otherness of the-other in a subjectivised-objectified manner. Such privileged representations, (termed as phenomenological reduction) is strongly resisted by the subaltern collective or intersubjective consciousness as it is a hindrance to reveal the subjectivity of the subaltern self; and it does not wholly represent sensibilities of the subaltern. (The I and the Other in phenomenological consciousness).

The modernist epistemic representation, for instance, when extended and mediated practiced as political representation of the subaltern unfortunately often turned out to be either a politics of misrepresentation or a politics of invisible repression of the tribal world. Thus to speak of the other, in the language of predominant Eurocentric and Indian centric perspectives, as representative of the other, does not any way present the other in his/her lived-experience but turns out to be problematic because by retaining one's privileged subjectivity within his/her self-imposed subjectivity, and to speak of/ for otherness of the other remains to be philosophically problematic in the sense of *not knowing the other minds* or experience in the way the subaltern-tribal knows and speaks for its own subjectivity except as an enchained as objectified category. This is an *infelicitous performative speech act.*[8]

Tribal Consciousness as Multivariate and Consciousness in Flux

The tribal consciousness is in a *continuous flux* identifiable by a process of a *'to and forth'* consciousness trying to consciously and constantly retain and return to its originality, tracing and enacting its rootedness and simultaneously engaging a *'for or against'* (reacting/ resisting/responding) of the 'other' consciousness or 'imperial eyes or colonizing eyes' that is external to it, configured as modes of self-other dichotomies, resulting in cross-cultural reproduction of clan consciousness, new forms of class consciousness, political-party consciousness, subaltern-in gender orientations, combined with promises of cultural identity and transformative cultural identities with a sense of affirming or celebrating diversity. Therefore, speaking of tribal consciousness and the non-tribal consciousness of the tribal world is not necessarily singular but configurations of multiple sensibilities.

The phenomenological productions and the rendering of meanings[9] of the tribal consciousness intersect differentia and way of *differance*[10] of multiple layers of meaning/understanding(s) that either constitute or camouflage the tribal consciousness and their life-world. The eliciting the tribal consciousness to be rendered phenomenologically burdens the excavation of (i) how tribal consciousness is self-conscious of its own world and (ii) how the tribal consciousness is conscious of the other (its own natural world and the non-natural world) (iii) and how the external or the 'non-tribal-other' is conscious of the tribal world which often robs the first-person-experience of the tribal people. As phenomenology itself differs[11] in their meanings/renderings so the phenomenology of the tribal consciousness, does differ. To recast the tribal consciousness would mean clarifying the phenomenological engagement of *differencing and deferring* the multiple sensibilities of the tribal world.

Phenomenological engagement of the tribal world-consciousness posits a sense of *seeing* the tribal-phenomenological (of the insider/ outsider cross fertilized views) within the meaning-context of subjectivity, intentionality, sociality, embodiment, disembodiment, historicity, interpretations, existentiality, phenomenological reduction, bracketing, reduction of the centric meaning to its nothingness, culture, language, phenomenology of subordination and liberation etc. - all intersecting within the phenomenological making and the rendering of the tribal consciousness and its world(s).

Towards Emancipatory Consciousness

The issue ahead for the tribal self-consciousness regarding their 'other-consciousness is to engage the issues namely, *how the subaltern-tribal consciousness/ culture may restore its 'world' by a mediation of phenomenological emancipation? What is the directedness of tribal experience towards and about the things of/ in the world, namely the property of consciousness that the tribal is conscious of/ about its social world? How the social world is intended by the tribal through particular concepts, thoughts, ideas, images etc. that make up the meaning or content of the tribal experience that is distinct from other dominant representations?* Given to the facticity, intentionality, subjectivity, sociality, historicity of the tribal people at the same time thrown (caught) into encountering forms of geo-political colonialism (imperial and alien colonial consciousness of the tribal world), the issue for the tribal consciousness is deep-down -how to let itself away from the non-external-imperial eyes that subordinate, ordinate and dominate the tribal consciousness.

Restoration of the Tribal Self, the Other and the Otherness of the Other: The Tribal Darsana (Consciousness) and its Worldview (Oikos): A Double Reflective Consciousness

Put it differently, the nativity and the navigating of praxis of a *phenomenology* rather correctly a philosophy of liberation of the tribal people (by themselves and in collaboration with friendly-other) as against multiple forms of imperial colonial consciousness or enchainment is direction towards which the tribal consciousness of *self-other and the external-other* intersect. The consciousness of the tribal people to resist or to dispel the encroaching alien consciousness may be termed as the consciousness of the otherness of the other. While in the non-tribal appropriating world(s), the tribal is the-other and for the tribal, in its exteriority and vulnerable proximity, however it tries to encumber the tribal world. In so rendered, the non-tribal's appropriating consciousness, what is deemed exterior calls for/exhibits a political practice exteriorizing that which exteriorizes the tribal-natural world.

The praxis of a *phenomenology* or a *philosophy* of liberation of the tribal people is but rendering the tribal people's sense of being-there-in-their-world authentically (non-appropriately), becoming (being and becoming) conscious of their own presuppositions/ the presupposed enchainment(s) enabled by the non-tribal worlds, simultaneously deconstruct or resist the ideological and practical forms that alienate them; that are extraneous to their rootedness of there-being-in-their-world. It is to practice a philosophy of Heraclitus as against Plato. It is to become conscious of ideological and practical tactics of appropriations of the tribal people (of themselves and their land-world).

Such phenomenological engagement of liberation is already embedded in the history of the tribal people. Given to their social history, the tribal people persistently resisted (bracketed and reduced) those colonizing ontologisms and construed historicism, and technological capitalistic political misrepresentations that are antithetical of the tribal consciousness.

In so doing, the tribal/subaltern asserts its mode of 'being there' through a movement of self-revelation of their affirmative-sensibility of not only as being-there-in-the-world but as being-in-not-becoming into the colonizing worlds. It is to render there-being in the world in a sustaining relationship, resisting forces of appropriation of the tribal land (oikos) with their mother land. in the language of Husserl, such phenomenological engagement (of the tribal people) may be put in this way: "In his *Logical Investigations* (1900-01) Husserl outlined a complex system of philosophy, moving from logic to philosophy of language, to ontology (theory of universals and parts of wholes), to a phenomenological theory of intentionality, and finally to a phenomenological theory of knowledge. Then in *Ideas*-I (1913), he focused squarely on phenomenology itself. Husserl defined phenomenology as "the science of the essence of consciousness", centred on the defining trait of intentionality, and approached explicitly "in the first person".[12]

The sense of *seeing and being* within the tribal world, for the tribal-person is but the philosophical and practical task to restore its first-person-experience by engaging double reflective consciousness or inclusive positioning) which is at the same time a revelatory engagement;

it is a sense of tribal *darsana*, an insight into the reality of the tribal people.

Phenomenologically listened, the double-reflective consciousness (self & other consciousness) or the *darsana* of the tribal people's lived-experience imbibes: (i) A phenomenological philosophical practice of *eidetic bracketing (both Husserlian & Heideggerian sense)* of those onto-logos or presuppositions (capitalistic or cultural) or explanations, antithetical and exterior to the living 'essence-presence' (the transcendental sense of their 'there-being') as inter-subjectively humans of/in the tribal consciousness. It is to practice a specific sense of *"eidetic reduction*, of the so-called capitalistic technocratic sensibilities/practices of objectifying the tribal world, as 'natural objects or resources' to be exploited technologically (under the guise of nationalism and techno-politics of developmentalism by appropriating the land and subordinating the tribal people for cheap labour and reducing them to landless migrations, away from their oikos). This I see, Heidegger would say, "philosophy does not limp along" behind science "as chances to find it" but rather "leaps ahead as it were, into some area of being" and 'discloses it for the first time in the constitution of being."[13]

And for Husserl, this is 'to bracket the (presupposed) being in order to focus on the phenomenon and to consider the entity precisely as it gives itself without committing oneself to the claims that the entity makes for itself. In this way the praxis of *'epoche'* does not 'disregard' being but sets a specific epistemic commitment. It is not denying the reality of the-appropriating-other, but to become aware of the intentionality of conceiving it as 'objects or objective world' and bracketing such epistemic positions demands a phenomenology of elucidation and emancipation. For Husserl, (Heidegger also claims that) the … reduction … is the method of leading phenomenological vision from the natural (scientific) attitude of the human being …back to the transcendental life of consciousness and its noetic-noematic experiences, in which objects are constituted as correlates of consciousness. For Heidegger, 'reduction means leading phenomenological vision back from the apprehension (appropriation of the being of the tribal people) of a being...to the understanding of the being, the being of this being, projecting upon the way it is concealed and unconcealed."[14]

The tribal, as being-in-the-world is unthinkable under the conditions of any exteriorizations, evacuations, and progressive annihilations (through politics of transnational developmental capitalism). The consciousness of the tribal people, their self-consciousness, I hold, cannot be divorced but on the contrary the consciousness of the exteriority depends upon the so-called tribal world. Heidegger would say, 'consciousness depends upon Dasein and it cannot be annihilated under any conditions. Consciousness depends upon the *Dasien* not the other way about. Phenomenologically speaking, the annihilation of being, of the being of the tribal and his/her world can not imply that tribal (Dasein) could be without a world. (ii) A continuous cultivation of intentionality in terms of restoring their phenomenological experience by recapturing authentic inter-subjectivity by the mediation of negations that distantiate and manipulate their own world and that which reduces the tribal as subaltern, the process of which is but a 'revelation' of tribal consciousness.

This revelatory sensibility or the reflexivity of tribal consciousness is but a phenomenology of both a praxis of *from and towards* simultaneously. In practical terms, it is the sense of *going beyond* or from any pre-suppositional or arbitrarily construed legacies towards recapturing tribal consciousness the sense of their being in its naturality or nakedness in relation to the natural world as intersubjective consciousness. This is done and ought to be done by exposing the dominating or appropriating constructs of the tribal culture and simultaneously accomplish the human-tribal subjectivity, rather inter-subjectivity in its everyday life-situations and social relations. There are no pretensions here, that the pretension that dominating ontologies would liberate and restore the life-world of the tribal. No matter the tribal is modernized or patterned into absorbing/alienating categories that appropriate them, the liberative sensibilities of the tribal is a phenomenologically expressed through *political cum ethical discourse*. To explain (domesticating or mystifying) the tribal sense of self/other consciousness through pre-supposed cultural *cum* predominant philosophical and ideological categories is but a pretension and a subtle way(s) of texturizing and thematising the tribal world consciousness for ego-interests. In such paradigmatic practices by the non-tribal world, the tribal people ascribe a phenomenology of double negation, which is but the way of leading away from the forms of mis-leadings or ideological or cultural contaminations; this is the that the tribal people come to grip with their originality, of being-there in the world most authentically.

Put it otherwise, in the Heideggerian sense, it is way of letting the consciousness to the original togetherness of thinking and questioning,'[15] by which the 'thinking itself enters afresh territories. [16] This would mean that a phenomenological engagement on the question of life-world consciousness [of there-being or the sense of being (*Sinn*)] which is not thinking differently or even alternately but thinking new, the thinking phenomenologically.

Motivated by the phenomenological spirit of Heidegger, "we and our activities are always "in the world", our being is being-in-the-world, so we not only study our activities to be there-in-the world profitably and in-authentically but by bracketing the world that consumes us, through interpret (phenomenological hermeneutics) our activities and the meaning, that the things have for us by looking to our contextual relations to things that liberate us to be in the world. Indeed, for Heidegger, such a phenomenological engagement resolves into what he calls, "fundamental ontology". We must distinguish beings from their being, (namely the artificiality of rendering for egoistic ends) and we begin our investigation of the meaning of being in our own case, by examining our own existence in relation to the activity of "Dasein" (that being whose being is in each case my own). This is why, I hold, Phenomenology is perceived as the art or practice of "letting things show themselves". In Heidegger's inimitable linguistic play on the Greek roots, " 'phenomenology' means … to let that which shows itself be seen from itself in the very way in which it shows itself from itself."[17] The tribal self-consciousness if/when rendered in Heideggerian terms, "[It] is a being whose existence posits its essence, and inversely it is consciousness of a being, whose essence implies its existence; that is, in which appearance lays claim to the sensibility of being. As humans, the being of the tribal is in 'being everywhere'. It is a being such that, in its being, its being is in question in so far as this implies a being other than itself.' [18]

Accordingly, the tribal self-consciousness operates as self and other conscious simultaneously but not exclusively. It's primordial sense of being human essentially points towards its existence, whose existence is not merely 'self-conscious' but its self-consciousness is always 'other-conscious' of the natural and inter-cultural worlds in the sense of inter-subjectivity. The self of tribal-person (taking in to consideration, the tribal beliefs in the spirit endowed natural world and the allied ritual social and cultural practices) is not an 'individual' as the euro-centric rational self or self-enveloping ego, but a community-self in the sense of being other that itself in relationship.

The term *tribe (does not mean not-modern)* designate sensibility of community and the communicative performative practices that are communitarian and hence one can infer that the tribal-self is not modernistic in the sense of cultivating a logic self-seeking or master-asserting ego but it is the lived-life and hence foundationally intersubjective and communitarian. By being foundationally communitarian the tribe-self transcends itself (oneself) consciously towards the *being-becoming* intimately of intersubjective consciousness. Its ever-flowing transcending-self, intends meaningful existence in relationship with the natural and its cultural signifying world. According to Husserl, in such intentionality, both the transcendental ego and the world-phenomenon intended by this consciousness, reveal as it were, the very meaning of their relationship, the lifeworld of the tribal people.

The term *life-world* has its roots in phenomenological traditions. I use the term *life-world* not in the sense of a pre-supposed or pre-given ontological world-outlook that afore-supplies preconceived-meaning to the individual; I am not using it in the sense of a central individualistic thought-frame or pre-given ideological sensibilities that provides sensibilities of frame the tribal in a construed cultural patterns, (philosophic-political). By life-world of the tribal, I intend to mean the collective lived-experience (of the tribal-subaltern people) who are denied of their own sense of the world by forces of the politics of either modernity or traditionality in terms of a projected or promised land; I intend to mean the collective lived-experience (of the tribal-subaltern people), the experience of resistance that robs their life world and in so doing the intersubjective-collectivity of the tribal continue to make/re-crated new sense of their world. The subaltern lived-world consciousness is but the collective consciousness, enhanced by collective memory that continuously seeks a sense freedom from the very boundaries of construed consciousness. It is a freedom consciousness, or a free-from consciousness.

Reduction of the tribal community-self, the intersubjective consciousness of the tribe-selves, to modernistic-capitalistic-technocratic interpretation and exploitation renders the tribe-self vulnerable and fragile.[19] Its ontological essence and existence is in question, jeopardized and treated as the 'the subjugated-other' or the subaltern-natural-other. The predominant 'cultural-other' (British colonialism and political colonialism since the Indian independence times) treated the tribal community and its spirit-conscious-world as mundane, as naturalized objects to be colonized for political and economic ends. Due to its naturality and vulnerability the tribal-world has met with the cultural-political practice(s) of appropriation of its essence and existence and hence the tribal people, their selves are forced to form political-selves to combat the forces that subjugates them.

Let me here forth posit the categories that construe a sense of deprivation of the being of the tribal to realize its sense of intersubjective consciousness. Distanciation, vulnerability and subjectivization are perhaps phenomenological categories that inform the problem of the tribal being reduced as the other for reasons appropriation.

Distanciation and Displacement, Deprivation and Destruction

The very identification of a category of people as tribal or *subaltern* (phenomenologically) preconditions the possibility of an exclusive category a category to be excluded as the other by the dominant other. Between the subaltern other and dominant other, there arises the problematic spatial (historical, cultural and political) distance, which is antithetical to the practice of proximity and intersubjectivity. The altern category thus pre-conceives the political possibility of subverting the subaltern[20] given to such categorical distanciation.

Distanciation, displacement, deprivation and destruction are forces that are interlinked and work against the Adivasi people's lives. Displacement meant development and 'induced climatic change' is the scheme where by both the Adivasi people and their lands are deprived of their self-conscious autonomy and dignity, deprived of livelihood and security and once again turned as 'wandering people' in the plains of India. The dominant colonialism in the Independent-India and the deprivation induced developmentalism specifically in the post-independent India politically practice the displacement of the tribes from their forest indwelling lands under the guise of economic interests. The process is named 'migration'. Forced migration is umbilical cut of tribes away from their phenomenological sense of personhood or motherhood, the collective consciousness as inalienable intersubjective tribes. The 'being' of the tribes as people in relation to nature is sadly alienated as subaltern beings to be displaced in fragmentation. A folk song from Santhal illustrates this: 'For just one span of stomach, just to stay alive, I have wandered from country to country. I have travelled twelve countries."[21] "The thorns we have reaped are of the tree we planted; they have torn us and we bleed, we should have known what fruit would spring from such tree."[22]

Within the post-independent period, under the democratic system, governments (non-naturally) are determined and exploited the natural-world-resources of the tribal dwellings, and as a result, many Adivasi communities face evictions and displacements, however perpetuated 'legally'. The high court legitimizes the appropriation of land by employing the 'law of eminent domain' (Colonial land acquisition Act 1894). Hasrat Arjiiumend notes that 57 mining enterprises at the Santhal regions alienated both the people and their dwelling land and crushing all forms tribal resistance to restore their livelihood.[23] N.C. Choudhary observes: 'The Industrialized Hindu State will carry the servitude and degradation to the home territory of the aboriginals".[24]

Thus we may argue that the *subaltern vis-à-vis the altern*, the tribal vis-à-vis the so-called non-tribal world constitute the fore-ground for any phenomenological exploration as to restore and render the communitarian world outlook of the tribal people to its authentic essence/existence. Since the community of tribal people is vulnerable and easily rendered to the practices of ideological, political and economic (philosophical) corruption and fragmentation, the phenomenological intend or project is meant to activate the way(s) of becoming conscious of and restoring of the origin of origins, the true nature, the 'description' of the subaltern by way of philosophically bracketing/delineating the dominant-other as to implore the possibility of the revelation of existence of subjectivity of tribal-self in terms of its intersubjective consciousness with social/natural world around which is but not a construed essence but as existence-in-essence per se.

Tribes' Resistance and Restoration – Phenomenology of Struggle

A series of historical struggle or resistance movements have been registered in Indian tribal history. Phenomenologically rendered their historical struggle and the resistance of tribal communities is but a way dispelling the colonial (extended colonialist projects, be it economic or cultural manipulations) logic/rationale not necessarily 'to antagonize the colonial-other' but to restore themselves and the cultural other-selves to the phenomenal realization that we as humans cannot be divorced from being in the world in consciousness, transcending our pragmatic ends.

The phenomenological engagement with reference to the phenomenology of the subaltern people, the Adivasi communities and their social/political struggle and résistance posits again double-edged process of restorations. Its consciousness operates by negating the negations that are exploitatively construe the tribal people and their world(s).

Phenomenological restoration praxis

The phenomenological engagement, with the subaltern consciousness, hence, has much to do with the *phenomenological restoration of the life-world of the subaltern people*, namely the people whose identity is deemed 'natural and therefore vulnerable' for as they are most often conveniently identified as the people of nature (which implicitly construe fore-ground of a logic of domination/exploitation by so-called developed or modern).

1. The Phenomenological inquiry of those dominant pre-post-colonial ontologisms and its continuity that purport to monopolize/ assimilate/ subordinate the tribal-community for its temporal ends, needs to be analyzed and exposed of its falsely intended and culturally construed meanings (isms) to its illogicality.

2. This process ethically implies (on the part of the philosophical community for instance) to an engagement of a phenomenology of liberation of restoration of the both the oppressor and the oppressed as to provision a mediation of a fraternal human sociality.

Going Beyond Phenomenology

Phenomenological listening of the voice of the tribal people, of their collective lived-experience, ethically implores a proactive listening and accompaniment, which is but a philo-political praxis, towards the proximity of the being of the tribal, not merely by being-in-the-world, as dominant metaphysical presence but it should address those concerns/forces that nullifies the presence of the tribal people as inter-subjective presence. The question of tribal identity, or any identity for that matter, in the phenomenological sense is but *being-with-the-other* that constitutes me - 'my identity is always intrinsically an 'other-identity' (Levinas). It is to think alternatively, the way of not-letting oneself to think through the pre-established noematic consciousness rather it is to seek our own collective selves' consciousness.

Should not phenomenological rendering if it is meant to be the way(s) reflecting/becoming conscious of/restoring the origin of the origin be engaged to restore both the subaltern and the dominant from their pre-conditioned cultural constructs and social practice of deprivation of the tribes from their life world, in order that a sense of intersubjective, face-to-face proximity is achieved/restored? Most dominant philosophical traditions the determinants of essence (of what is defined as pure, esse, essence etc.) is positioned in terms of dominant central essence *vis-à-vis* the existence of the subaltern as secondary or subdued category of understanding. This in turn presupposes an ontological interpretation of being *vis-à-vis* other-than-beings or lesser beings. Heidegger points out: "Every determination of the essence of man that already presupposes an interpretation of being without asking about the truth of Being, whether knowingly or not, is metaphysical (ontological)"[25] such metaphysical construction instantiates and distantiates the logo-centric presence of the dominant essence as against the subordinated and subjugated tribal other. History of philosophy is imbibed such politics of distantiation of the other by specific modes of exclusive or inclusive value hierarchical categories of understanding. Phenomenology properly speaking phenomenology of liberation thus posits an alternate praxis of restoring or letting the sense of being free from the clutches of categorical dispositions.

The Origin and the Site of the Subaltern, Phenomenological Grounding (Cosmo-gonic Narratives)

Most narratives of the origination of the world and the human species are clothed in cultural narratives and metaphors. However, a notable feature of such narrations, for instance, the biblical episode regarding the origination of human is construed in terms of mutual distantiation or exteriority and proceeds to treat human labour as punishment or condemnation, a sense of separation from the creator, and the separation is positioned in infinite regress. Having construed exteriority as mode of distantiation, and posits or projects a sense of restoration (resurrection) of the distanced/condemned human. This is the way the episode of origination is phenomenologically rendered/made-appeared/made-sense of, from biblical worldview. The human is the subaltern (ontologically/culturally construed) whose existence 'demands' liberation or salvation by a non-human, called supreme being. Thus exteriorization or distanciation (also detention) becomes the ontic category of understanding in the *his-story* of the western cultural world. in the same episode, male and female are born differently (non-naturally) but ontologically deduced from an agent of extra-territorial territory. Thus the order of hierarchy (politics of hierarchy) is patterned whereby the Supreme Being, male-being and female-being is systematically sub-alterned. Radical inferiority and subdued subordination and degradation is thus pre-construed through specific narrative(s) and such narrative(s) within the portals of domineering metaphysics is positioned as categorical (oppositional) relations (Aristotle) extended towards colonizing is the colonial history of the Europe. This is how the origin of human is pre-conceived. Perhaps similar narratives may be unearthed from dominant Indian philosophical traditions that pre-suppose and conceive the possibility of exteriorization and systematic subordination of the 'other' as vulnerable determined by a hierarchical servitude.

The subaltern consciousness *if to alter* such subordinating consciousness needs to go beyond the very origin of the system and the system itself. Phenomenologically speaking the practice of a negation of negation or bracketing (phenomenological reduction) is necessary by successive mode of an archaeological excavation of the structures of knowledge that posit sub-alterity of the other. Before the philosophical world-outlooks and we need to be conscious that before we are construed by/of specific ontologies, before we are tamed of/ by ideological narrative moralities, there is and there appears the actual world, the lived-world not of things but of persons both human and natural persons in familial communion. The cosmogenic narratives[26] of the subaltern tribes in tribal culture uphold such filial relations in telling the story of origin of origin. These narratives, mythological in nature, are pregnant of eliciting the fact the consciousness of the tribal people is primordially inter-related consciousness of cosmos devoid of any hierarchical Distanciation. The naming of the different tribes is named after the things or animals of the natural world. This means identify for the tribal consciousness is not ego-logistic (individualistic) but identity is relationally multiple. The 'I' of the tribal is necessarily plural. Myths are mediums the speaking of the story tribal people has been protected and passed on to generation.

The origin of subaltern consciousness is then an anterior to, an origin of many other origins implanted in the ascribed-conscious worlds. When phenomenology speaks of tracing back to the origin of origin as the world of appearance/giveness, there is the need for the possibility of epoch-reductions, which in turn arises this sentient world of beings, as they are in nakedness and neutrality. The tribal cosmogenic narratives stand witness to project feasibility of conceiving the natural world as sacred and beyond any contamination. Before our consciousness though our historical and philosophical and political speculations are thematised and schematized as monistic, monotheistic, dualistic, hierarchical, pluralistic etc. there is the status of tribal consciousness in its presentation or appearance as/of the reality of world.

The Indigenous Worldview is Holistic

As different from the euro-centric, anthropocentric ontologies, the tribal world/consciousness with their own cosmogenic narratives depicted symbolically in myths that pertain to the natural world, genealogy traced and identified with natural objects/animals, natural world treated as endowed with animating spirit, social bonds expressed through specific community rituals, food treated as a shared communion propel the fact the tribal consciousness and world view is holistic in nature. The tribal consciousness operate/regard not in separation from or in any privileged sense differentiated form the natural-animal-cosmic world, but include holistic consciousness of the whole of cosmos and the lifeworld around them. The lands, water, air, trees, animals – all are viewed animated with living spirit enduring and to be endured and not be exploited to egoistic human ends. Forms of life in their immense complexity, interrelated, not fragmented, conceived in continuous movement towards self-other sustenance. Relations with nature, animals, plants etc are familial for the tribal consciousness. The Euro-centric or predominant monolithic ontologies and political practice should phenomenologically listen to this enduring animated conscious spirit of the tribal world view. The tribal indigenous people, ingenious as they are, live in a peaceful solidarity with nature with a perpetual adoration for a return to equilibrium and harmony in their shared community life.[27]

Going Beyond the Ontological Determinations

Anterior and exterior to such thematisation of our consciousness, there is the consciousness of person-to person as human persons. This is what is reflected in the lived collective experience of the tribal world. The Subaltern consciousness by way of standing outside the territory of those ontologically thematised consciousness, strives to open this possibility of human consciousness as humans, not as persons in disposition of caste, class, race, power etc. but as humans in the sense of intra-personhood. Before the activity of social segmentation there is the 'social' without forms segmentation, discrimination, and subjugation and domination. This is the inner subjective consciousness of the people of nature, the tribal, that we have historically missed in our avarice towards colonial development models.

Subaltern Consciousness as Consciousness of the Nearness

Going beyond the ontological determinations is phenomenological in the sense of capturing the realm of nearness of the other, not as other but an inter-subjective-plural-other. This phenomenological consciousness of the personhood of beings within tribal consciousness propels the nearness or proximity of the Other, by way of leaving from the ontological and political imprisonments veiled by politics of modernity and politics of monopolization of the tribal people and natural resources.

To this task, the approach of the subaltern not as the Other, but as sense-making-being(s) has indefinite possibilities. The detour into farness makes future proximity. The status of beings placed in the pre-notioned ontic territories might resist such phenomenological approach of the subaltern, however this is the ethical practical praxis of the birth of a philosophy/phenomenology of liberation – *not only of the liberation of the subaltern but pointedly the liberation of the self-centred being of the system*, as to let the fly out of the fly bottle of the ontic-centre from its self-authored prisms.

The ontological world is different from the metaphysics of the subaltern in the sense that the subaltern, when it speaks of sense-things it does speak about the non-sense things of the self-imposing ontic-thought-worlds. It is not a question of the cosmos as a totality but of real things, real sensibilities of the things/relations of the world. The subaltern speaking phenomenologically progressively unfolds new horizons of meaning, a meaning anterior to the layers of meanings by which it is constituted of. Each dominant ontology and its politics is a totalizing and appropriating totality, as Later Wittgenstein and Kant would put it, every world is not a world of atomic facts[28] but it is a horizon within which all human beings find meanings. Meaning of word for Wittgenstein is multiple not identical but richly differ by its contextual variations. Meaningful identity is then plural.

Dominant Ontology as In-sufficient Sensibility of the Subaltern Consciousness[29]

The Greek, the Medieval and the Euro-centric and Asian dominant ontologies is permeated with the discussion of the status and the nature of Being, placing it as the centre-stage Being. They often exalted Being as pure cognition, different from the beings of nature (physics) because Being as such is pure lumen (the light) the self-revealing lamination, in whose 'sight' the nature, the plurality of existential beings is 'objects' to be seen by the Being as such. The Supreme Being is ontologically construed as the –all seeing seer,' the seer of the Other, the Knower of the Other, and Ruler of the Other, in whose sight the hierarchy of sensual and non-sensual beings let themselves to be seen. Such a predominant ontological *sight* sets aside by specific logic of exclusion an array of beings as hierarchically inferior to each other. Such ontologism conceptually construes a non-proximate relation amongst Being, beings and lesser beings and non-beings. The possibility of a poetic and proximate intersubjective sensibility is thus fore-closed by an Aristotelian logic of oppositional yet relations propositional status. The subaltern Other in most western philosophical thought frames (metaphysics of presence) is located as hierarchically excluded other in mutual oppositional subordination. The nearness to the Being of the Centre is farfetched to the beings of the non-centre, namely that of the subaltern other.

Within and beyond such ontological centrism lies the locus of the subaltern Other in an non-appearance manner; in a subdued or subordinated manner; in an exiled and excluded manner. The approaching of the centre-staged being (the is-being) towards the Subaltern Being (the non or insufficient beings and the non being as is not) is treated as governance (in medievalism this governance is Church) in modern times, this governance is the dominant political state, in the recent times, this governance is the dominance of technological Euro-centered being) whose governance is divinely ordained, self-legitimized on its own authority. The approaching of the Subaltern towards the centre-staged being is either an impossible mission or a possible strategic pilgrim by a mode of successive subordination.

Against Absolving and Appropriating Totalized Consciousness

Consciousness, awareness, nearness, mutual closeness or intersubjective presence is fore-closed in/by the thought-systems of the dominant thought and social practices. The problem then is how the impassable gap between and amongst the hierarchy of beings be at least be shortened if not be completely be traversed. The phenomenological question of the Subaltern-Other, is how to phenomenologically render the shortening the segmentation, categorizations of the categories of understanding as to enable afresh presence in most authentic ways possible? The approach of Subaltern Other (to Philosophy and to Persons) is not approach characterized by the benevolence and gratification but one of a mutual consciousness of each other's subject as inter-subjective presence. To come closer, to the nearness of each other, the subaltern conceives is not a possibility within the ontological territory that constitutes exclusion of beings hierarchically but the origin of the origin of consciousness of the intersubjective presence starts beyond or outside the ontological systems. It is an Outside the racial ontology, outside the hegemonic cultural and ideological underpinnings, outside the 'world' of patriarchy. Such philosophical coming closer begins from beyond the beginnings of the ontological centres.

The subaltern to a major extent remains to be a non-metaphysical exteriority within territory of philosophies in India. The locus of the being of the subaltern does not enjoy or have any 'appearance' to make sense of it. By being kept-away in exteriority, the sense-making of the subaltern, the consciousness of/about the subaltern is either absent or silenced within the classical philosophical discussions. The subaltern as the other is not even an 'appearance' or mere phenomenon or a reality within the philosophical territories to the extent that the being of the subaltern is passed over as unnoticed, if not violently silenced.

The ontological question, namely the question of being of that of the subaltern falls outside the ontological territories of many philosophies in India. As either as non-ontological exterior entity or as a bracketed being, the sight of the subaltern remains outside or the periphery of the centrality of being. The question of being then is either at level of devoid of the world or system-being or relatively reduced to the level of transitory sensibility. The being of the subaltern therefore is both a culturally and ontologically subordinated and surfaced (migrated) entity. In so doing the centre-staged-being epistemologically enclosed to its own consciousness by absolving itself from consciousness of the subaltern/other being. As an absolved consciousness, the ontologically centred-being is curtailed and tied to its self-understanding. Heidegger would say, "What is known through absolving is that knowledge itself is a way of knowing, is aware of itself, and is a self-consciousness."

Thus in self-consciousness we realize two things: (1) that knowledge can be detached and (2) that there is a` new form of knowledge which can be consciousness (whose) ...knowing insists on the I and remains entangled with itself, such that it gets tied to the self and the I. Thus this knowledge is bound and relative in two aspects: (1) this knowledge knows itself as self and (2) it distinguishes this self from existing things (subaltern-being). In this way, self-consciousness remains relative in spite of detachment that has asserted itself. Nevertheless, it is just this self-consciousness, relative in one aspect and not relative in another, that reveals the possibility of a detachment or liberation. This liberation indeed such that it does not discard that from which it liberates itself; but in knowingly absolving itself---knowing it—it takes and binds itself, as that which frees itself. This self–conscious knowledge of consciousness is, so to speak, a relative knowledge which is free; but as relative it is still not absolute, still not genuinely free. " obviously, Heidegger goes on to observe the danger of absolute self-consciousness of itself, that the centred self-conscious being is a 'pure kind of non-relative knowledge that which absolves itself even from self-consciousness."[30] Such absolute knowledge position, Heidegger observes, is conceived and is exclusively aware of itself only as system. Heidegger observes that the western metaphysics is predominantly ontology of the center, (for e.g. Hegel's Absolutism) and there by conceals/constrains self-consciousness as free-from-consciousness.

In other words, the centred positioning of being (system-being) as absolute, absolves the being of the other(s) as belonging outside the system, thereby the system-being is identified with two way mediations – (1) of that of self-enclosure and (2) that of the Other-exclusion. From the sensitivity of the Subaltern-Other, such dialectical meditational process of both self and Other enclosures calls for a sense of a freedom of consciousness of itself. It strives for the (1) freedom of consciousness of the consciousness itself from its systemic (ontological) absolving or absolute positioning and (2) the freedom of the consciousness of the subaltern as the non-conscious entity. Thus, when rendered phenomenologically, the subaltern consciousness operates for/at two intersecting levels – the sense of freedom of consciousness of both *self-conscious-self* (being as pure consciousness) from its systemic ontological boundaries and the freedom of the consciousness of the subaltern from being considered exterior to, as out-caste, as non-centred being. The subaltern consciousness with reference to any absolutism, ontologism, epistemic centralism, operates with a double edged sensitivity – (1) the sensitivity of the slavery of the centered being and the sensitivity of the exclusive enclave of the subaltern being. Liberation sensibility, therefore (consciousness) begins from such phenomenological bracketing of that of the centred-being and the non-centred being(s).

Against this backdrop we may read the Husserlian sense of transcendental phenomenology which asserts the view that meaning is essentially linked with human experience and it is authentically revealed in a mode of appearance that is devoid of any presuppositions. The meaning-making or sensibility of the Subaltern-Other, by departing itself from allowing itself to be treated as exterior entity strives to contest against very system that construes both self and Other estrangement. Thus the phenomenological engagement is the native/starting point of disclosure, a disclosure of the enclosed self and the disclosure of the excluded other-selves.

This is a kind of disembodied consciousness (not in the transcendental/other world sensibility), transcendental of the system that envelops and excludes the sense of authenticity of consciousness. In the terminology of Immanuel Kant, 'we are claimed to have access to phenomena or appearance but not to things in themselves.' The non-accessibility to things-in-themselves, the non-accessibility to authenticity of the sense of being-with is constituted by 'some' ascribed consciousness, from which the subaltern consciousness seeks to disembody itself. The notion of the consciousness as embodied and disembodied takes newer perspective of phenomenological discussion within the phenomenological engagement in relation to the subaltern life-world consciousness.

This seems to be movement from embodiment to disembodiment not in the 'other-than-the-worldly' sense, but in the sense of transcendence from and outside the systems of thought/practice that construe and constrain human consciousness within the specified ontological categories of understanding. All of these views place a great deal of emphasis on the notion of a disembodied consciousness that somehow constructs the world it perceives. The subaltern consciousness thus starts from the existential and of ontological fore-grounds of exteriority and conceives itself as always excluded and therefore partial or non-primary. The (Indian) ontologies that affirm a sense of absolute centrality of being seems to be like a lame person, able to see, but cannot walk, and the subaltern consciousness entranced towards the becoming of the centrality (freedom as movement from exclusion towards inclusive primacy within the system) is like a blind person cannot see but able to walk. What is needed is the able-ness of both the blind and the lame, so that what is phenomenological, what 'appears as' is transcended into what is actual and ethical. Phenomenology from the point of view of the Subaltern is initial force (the starting point) and not the end force towards the sense of freedom-consciousness.

Phenomenology of Liberation

The subaltern life world consciousness is situated from this back-drop (staring point) of what appears and how they appear in the layers of consciousness of those totalizing/absolving/appropriating ontologies. The subaltern is positioned as anterior to and exterior of. If it the entire subaltern can mean anything it can only make sense by non-affirmative attribution. To begin with, from the sight of the ontological center, the life world of the subaltern is not a knowledge by ascription or knowledge by description; it is simply a non-knowledge, a non-entity, a non-appearance because the subaltern as the Other is not a phenomenological (or phenomenal) appearance to make-sense but a disappearance from the sight of the absolute center and therefore it does not make any sense or construed of any sensibility (consciousness) (metaphysical meaning).

The subaltern as the other is not an appearance or mere phenomenon or an object but always held to be in metaphysical and cultural exteriority. From the backdrop of the 'world' and the system-being, the subaltern engagement begins from there but does not end up with that. It seeks for a sense of system-being to intersubjective being. If phenomenology can provide this nativity, capturing its sensibility is important to begin with. Perhaps we can make sense of the subaltern in contrast to the altern. The namelessness of the subaltern, the devoid of subjectivity of the subaltern, the outcasteness of the subaltern, the deprivation of the subaltern, the negations of the subaltern – all are constituted in the sense of non-affirmative categories of understanding, which amounts to the impossibility of cognizing the subaltern within the predominant philosophical territories of India. No wonder, the voice of the women, the voice the subdued, the voice of the out-caste-other is either not heard or kept meditatively silenced in the voice of Indian philosophical boundaries.

The subaltern life world consciousness is not a pre-determined project so that it may be absolutely rendered unconscious to the consciousness of the ontological centre. Consciousness, specifically the subaltern consciousness is constructed by the subaltern themselves and by others, either in for/against the subaltern. The subaltern does not seek its *free-from consciousness* in the hope that it can occupy the authoritarian center or be attracted towards the politics of the center; rather it resists any forms of hierarchical centralities of either of domination or subordination. The subaltern consciousness is not fatalistic and fetish of the system of thought. By mediating against the very mediations that enslave the subaltern consciousness, the subaltern seeks to create afresh its own his/her story. The subaltern creates its own story, along with it its own world-outlook, from the lived experience of this metaphysical exteriorities and denials. The subaltern does not and cannot afford to lament on the pain pathology for long, for it ethically implores upon itself to re-create its/his/her story from the ontological grounds that excluded it. This is a sense of hermeneutical engagement, not exactly a sense of antagonism, but sense altruism. The subaltern consciousness while creating its own histories and with it propels to its life world in time and space by transcending from the live-world enforced upon it. In so doing, the subaltern reveals itself as subjectivity not in isolated sense, but in inter-subjective ways. The excluded extend beyond themselves (go beyond their subjectivities) and do attempt to embrace those subjectivities that are subjectivised by/ into the onto-logos of any totalized systems. The logic of externality axiomatised by the grounding ontologies is progressively transferred to a language of relationalities. The ontological determinations as 'being-is' and the non-being as is-not, is increasingly traversed.

In practical terms, this is to uncover the principles/practices of domination of the system and the practice of subordination towards/ to the system that alienates not only the subaltern-other, but the very being that it claims to enclose. The double alienation, (1) the alienation of the self that is self-imposed in the appropriating system of thought, and (2) the alienation of the Other that is externalized away from the system is alienated by the subaltern for alienation (self-isolation and other isolation) is the veil with which the face of the mutual other is covered (ideologically) as not to be explored, questioned, resisted and doubted. This is the practice of epistemic self-defence, a sense of self-legitimization of truth. Thus 'suffering' is pre-determined (not fatalistic) but phenomenologically of a totalized system of thought. Be it science or philosophy, such body of knowledge/consciousness needs to be practice of a *net...neti* mediations. This process of double negation, the negation of the negations construed by the system, phenomenologically speaking, is but an ethical metaphysics of liberation.

By way of coming closer to sense-making of the totality as non-sense making, the Subaltern-Other is directed towards the every-other-person in proximity. This implies a sense of both metaphysical and physical closeness and nearness in mutual presence, not in the sense of privileged or under privileged sensibilities. Such pre-classificatory discourse is thus resisted by renderings its dubious foundations. Socrates, Marx, Gramsci, Lyotard, Derrida exercises this phenomenological sense of reduction of the Ontic-centre in order that the metaphysical discourse leads physical (political/social) discourse and vice versa.

Husserl, in his work, 'The *Crisis of the European Sciences and Transcendental Phenomenology*,' (1936), argues that it is not the life-world (construed system/ presuppositions) that pre-dispose a sense of meaning to the humans but it is human existential live-world (human lived experience) that gives sense to life. The lived experience of the subaltern human as a deprived-being, his existential conditions of deprivations is the sense-things that urges towards making sense of life. It is the conviction that human beings live in a world not in which life makes sense, but in which humans make sense of life. The subaltern human and for that matter, the human is not a passivity, 'a given-being' but a 'giving-being,' a plural inter-subjectivity that gives meaning from the existential struggle against irrational, insufficiently sensible positions. By way of a practice negation of meaninglessness permeated by these categories, Husserl posits a non-pre-suppositional understanding of life. The subaltern lived-world-consciousness is one such attempt to let itself free from the already-assumed layers of consciousness.

The subaltern consciousness is then a movement from the 'world as appears' to the 'worlds in themselves'. It is to think about thought that subordinates the self and other; it is consciousness as reflective consciousness which is different from merely being in the state of consciousness or experiencing the consciousness of pain, the denial. The phenomenality of consciousness is moving towards reflexivity. It is in this sense; may I call it, a specific movement from phenomenology towards a phenomenology of liberation. This is both and at the same time philosophical and practical, neither of it is an exclusive sophistication or categorization. The social (knowledge) is at once philosophical and the philosophical is at once social, the aesthetic synchronization of both is the way (hopefully) of directional possibility of phenomenology of liberation of dispelling the segmentaization of the subaltern vs. the altern.

In fine, we may infer that the subaltern-live-world consciousness posits a (radical) sense of moving away from, a sense of liberation not purely phenomenologically but practically and in poiesis manner. Beyond any totalitarianism and beyond any relativism there lies the 'revelation,' the liberation of both subjectivised and objectivized selves. Such liberation-consciousness emanates from the ontological system that abnegates both the construed self and the construed subaltern-other. this philosophical engagement is not an inevitable Hegelian dialectics, not a Marxian inevitability of classless society by 'war positioning of classes against each other' but intrasystemic and inter-subjective conscious action that attempts negate or subvert the very negations and subversions constituted by our philosophical ontologies first and simultaneously the social sense of liberation. A freedom that is situated for human is always a 'situated being in the world'. In the practical senses liberation consciousness of the subaltern is both a freedom from and a freedom to; freedom of the subordinated nature and the subjugated people.

This liberative epistemological act calls for specific mediation on the part of the philosophical community from an ethical basis. "Liberation is not a phenomenal, intra-systemic action; liberation is the praxis that subverts the phenomenological and pierces into a metaphysical significance; it is the critical total that provisions, fixed, standardized, crystallized, and dead. Beyond phenomenology way will have the revelation of the other down her face. The release subverts the very phenomenological metaphysical transcendence toward criticizing everything set, being able to speak of an epistemology of liberation ethic, an ability towards voice/pain of the subalterns, rises from the layers of excluded periphery and accept their questing and thinking devoid of any absolutized/culturally standardized discretions. It a sense, this is to go-beyond phenomenology itself. It is a way towards the authentic revelations of the sense-humans to make sense of life. This would be a closure of the system that negates and disclosure of afresh possibilities of beyond the phenomenology of the systems. It opts for a sense of togetherness in conditions of self-other estrangements. When faced with disastrous moments, perhaps, Husserl subjectivity or consciousness of oneself as self-consciousness turns out to be intersubjective. The consciousness of the fragility of the human-subaltern, calls for an intersubjective presence beyond any naming and tagging. The subaltern-other is the other in/for justice. For this what is required of is a phenomenological sense of atheism of the centre-system-being. Perhaps it is the death of the being of the centre and insurrectionary proximity-praxis of the intersubjectivity of beings in simultaneous presence is the way that the tribal consciousness is set its path ahead.

Endnotes

[1] In the Indian context the term *tribal* refers to the people who are also known as *'Adivasi'* meaning the first settlers of the soil, who are constitutionally (Article 342) deemed as scheduled tribes. Refer: Stephen Fuchs, *The Aboriginals Tribes of India,* (New Delhi: Inter India Publications, 1992) 3rd ed.,.11-13. As per 1971 census, six major categories of STs are scheduled – Bhil in M.P, Rajasthan, Gujarat, *Gond* in M.P., Orissa, Bihar, Maharashtra, Santhal in Jharkhand, West Bengal, Orissa and Tripura, Oraon in Bihar Jharkhand, M.P., Chhattisgarh, Orissa, and West Bengal, Meena in Rajasthan, Munda in Bihar, Jharkhand, Orissa, west Bengal, Chhattisgarh, Tripura. However, there are other tribes that are not yet constitutionally scheduled as they remain nomadic.

[2] It is estimated that there are 250 million indigenous people living around the world, and constitute 4% of the global population. Over 7.85% India's population is indigenous (Refer: Amendment Act of 1976).

[3] Refer Heidegger on the notion of double positioning.

[4] Phenomenology as a philosophical engagement is treated 'science' in the sense of providing foundations to all science by letting the science free from its presumptions. op.cit., 10.

[5] Refer Heidegger, *Being and Time,* SZ 123-160.

[6] The concept of worldview (*Weltanschauung*) encompasses human perceptions, attitudes, and experience about time, society, nature, world, relations, causality, self and others, that characterize the social group.

[7] Malpas, J. E. Heidegger's *Heidegger's Topology: Being, Place, World,* © 2006 Massachusetts Institute of Technology.

[8] Expression of J. L. Austin; refer felitious vs infelicitous speech acts.

[9] During the twentieth century, phenomenology made major contributions in most areas of philosophy, including philosophy of mind, social philosophy, philosophical anthropology, aesthetics, ethics, philosophy of science, epistemology, theory of meaning, and formal ontology. It has provided ground-breaking analyses of such topics as intentionality, embodiment, self-awareness, intersubjectivity, temporality, historicity, truth, evidence, perception, and interpretation. It has delivered a targeted criticism of reductionism, objectivism, and scientism, and argued at length for a rehabilitation of the life-world. By presenting a detailed account of human existence, where the subject is understood as an embodied and socially and culturally embedded being-in-the-world, phenomenology has also provided crucial inputs to a whole range of empirical disciplines, including psychiatry, sociology, literary studies, architecture, ethnology, and developmental psychology.

[10] *Différance* (French) term employed by Derrida, known for his *deconstruction,* the view that relationship between text (cultural text for instance) and its meaning needs to be elicited by the method of 'difference and deferral of meanings'.

[11] The Husserlian (transcendental) is different from the Heideggerian and Merleau-Ponty (hermeneutical and existential) and of the rest of the post-Husserlian phenomenologists. (Refer: *Dan Zahav, on* Phenomenology, in Hermeneutics, Existentialism, and Critical Theory, *Routledge Publications p. 662*).

[12] See Husserl, *Ideas* I, 33ff.

[13] See (SZ: 10).

[14] Hubert L. Dreyfus and Mark A. Wrathall, (Eds.). *A companion to Heidegger, Blackwell Companions to Philosophy,* 2005, 60-61. Refer (GA24:29).

[15] Martin Heidegger, *Hegel's Phenomenology of Spirit,* Indiana University Press, 1994, x.

[16] Ibid., xii.

[17] See Heidegger, *Being and Time,* 1927, 7C.

[18] Nythamar de Oliveira, *Between Being and Nothingness: Sartre's Existential Phenomenology of Liberation,* [À la mémoire du Professeur, Dominique Janicaud (1937-2002)] http://www.geocities.ws/nythamar/sartre.html.

[19] Statistics of migration.

[20] Kautilya, the preceptor of Chandra Gupta Maurya (322-184 BC Mauryan empire), grandson of Emperor Asoka, refers to the word 'tribes' several times in *Artha Sastra,* who are to be recruited and set against other tribes to destroy them. The analogy used is, 'the wood apple is broken by another apple'. Refer: Sharma (ed)., Indian Society Historical Probings, (New Delhi: People's Publishing house, 1974), p.68. Also refer Vincen Aind (Ed). Enigma of Indian Tribal Life and Culture, Philosophical Investigation (Bangalore: Asian Trading Corporation 2009), 44.

[21] Mathew Areeparampil, *Struggle for Swaraj: A History of Adivasi Movements* in *Jharkhand* (Chaibasa: Tribal Training and Research Centre, 2002), 24.

[22] A verse from the Munda tribal song that laments the predicament of Tribal life due to displacement. Refer: S.C. Roy. *The Mundas and their Country* (Ranchi: Crown Publications, 2004) 3rd reprint, xi.

[23] Hasrat Arijumend, "Land Alienation: Tribal Accountability in Jharkhand' in *Jharkahand journal of development and Management Studies,* 2-4 Oct-Dec 2004), 1071-1092.

[24] N. C. Choudhary, *The Continent of Circe* (London: Chatto & Windus, 1966), 82.

[25] Ibid (Martin Heidegger, Hegel's Phenomenology of Spirit, Indiana University Press, 1994, x).

[26] The *Santhal* tribe considers that in the beginning there was water everywhere. The supreme spirit having created seven animals, -crabs, crocodile, alligator, eel, prawn, earth worm and tortoise – found the need of solid earth for living species. When most animals could not 'help' the supreme to procure earth, earth worm and tortoise came to help the creator-spirit to produce earth and sustain it. The earthworm dwelt deep into the see and ate the mud at the bottom of the sea for *seven days* and seven nights and excreted it on the back of the tortoise, floating on the surface of water. The piled up earth in the course of time turned land, a

living being that gave birth to other natural and human animals and spirits. The story continues... the supreme spirit created two birds, *Has* and *Hasil*, who flew below the sun and above the earth. They built a nest and laid two eggs, which hatched out *Pilcu Haram* and *Pilcu Budhi*. The *Bugun Khowa* (Arunachala Pradesh) myth informs that animals and other beings are created because of marriage between Earth and Sky. The *Hill Miris* tribe narrates of a big tree that came up out of the sea. The worms ate up the tree; the collection of the tree-dust formed the earth, evolved rocks and hills. The *Minyong* tribe holds that a great *Mithun* dug a pit and dried up the water and enabled the birth of the earth. The *Sherdukpens* tribes believe that there were two brothers who thre lotus on the surface of the ocean. The four winds blew over it, cloud of dust got collected and world appeared. For the *Hrusso Aka* myth, there were two great golden eggs that hatched into earth. In the *Apa Tani* myth the mother earth (Kujum Chantu) 'dies' so the form the parts of her body would emerge different forms of life, from her two eyes evolved sun and moon. The *Bori* myth tells that the first two spirits were in the form of a *mithun* and an elephant. The two fought and died. The world was formed out of the flesh and the bones. (Refer: Subhra Bhattachryya, "Man and Animal Relationship," in Nita Mathur ed., Santhal worldview, New Delhi, Concept Publishing company, 2001,19).

[27] Margot Bremer, Inventing or Discovering Our world's Order: Interpreting a Biblical Text in terms of an Indigenous world view, Carlos Mendoza (ed)., Wisdom and the People's Theology, Concilium, International Journal of Theology, 2018/3, 83-84.

[28] Refer logical symbolism that pattern propositional representation of the world, which is but scientism.

[29] Please refer Enrique Dussell, Ethics and Community, Orbis Books, NY, 1993 for an indepth reading of phenomenology of liberation.

[30] Martin Heidegger, Hegel's Phenomenology of Spirit, (Trans., by Parvis Emand & Kenneth Maly), 15-16.

Vocation of Religions in a Conflictual World: A Philosophcal Narrative of Distancing without Belonging

Prof. Sebastian Velassery

Religions and religious traditions provide their believers with a certain view of the world which may not be always unprejudiced and objective. All religions answer questions regarding the origin and meaning of human existence, the nature of a meaningful life, the significance of suffering, the nature of evil, and the ultimate purpose of human life. Religion also exhorts its believers to live a life according to the values/virtues prescribed in their holy texts and conducts a personal and social life. Many a time, it constitutes a culture, which can mould personal and social identity and can influence behaviour of the people in a concrete sense. Perhaps, such a view point makes Frantz Fanon to make an observation that "she (Church) does not call the native to God's ways but to the ways of the white man, of the master, of the oppressor.[1] It is applicable not only to the white man but also to the black and the Indian. Given such an understanding about religions in general, then, the starting point of any discourse on religious conflicts and prejudiced perception against other religious faith necessarily has its base in religion itself. Although what is sacred differs from religion to religion, yet the sacrality of human soul is appropriated as a reality by all religions. From the earliest times, human beings in their imagination have personified the mysteries they perceive are the outcome of the powers of the spiritual beings, which they have called Gods. In effect, the human beings have created Gods according to their needs and much blood has been shed in the names of each God and the religion such a god represents. I would like to add here that most religious people, regrettably, believe that their violent actions serve a divine cause. This paper is an exercise that the struggle against religious violence and religious conflicts is impossible without a distance from our belongings. I look at the issue from a phenomenological perspective.

Part I

Religious Experience and Human Condition

It is universally accepted that religion is intimately related to man's inner life, so to say, his anxieties, fears, impulses, needs, endowments, propensities, capacities, limitations and so forth. Therefore, one can say that religious experience has something to do with man's inner life. Thus, some identified religion with the apprehension of the absolute, others identified with the sense of the sacred and still others with the feeling of absolute dependance. The experience central to religious consciousness is man's quest for transcendence. As Abraham Maslow puts it, "the experience of transcendence is the dynamic source of all great religions, 'the very beginning, the intrinsic core, the essence, the universal nucleus of every known high religion"[2] Understood Phenomenologically, religious experience, therefore, proceeds from an introspective analysis of man's subjective states. Thus St. Augustine has alluded to it in his *Confessions,* when he referred to the restlessness of the heart that finds fulfillment in God alone. St. Thomas Aquinas too, in his treatment of will and morality takes note of a "native restlessness" or an urge within all creatures and especially in man to "perfect their being by operating". Accordong to Aquinas, all activities of a creature is a striving on its part to imitate as fully as possible its creator who is pure act. These observations imply that phenomenologically religion becomes relevant to human condition and existence and is to be understood in terms of our experience of the consciousness of God as the supreme.

Let me also take note of the referent of the term "God" here. God refers to the 'object' we address in our prayers, supplications and worship. In the words of Tillich, the referent 'God' is that which we are ultimately concerned about. It becomes immediately evident that there is no specific reality in the empirical world that can be identified as the object of our ultimate concern. For, man has conceived as ultimate and worshipped everything on earth including himself. He has also worshipped everything he could think of beneath the earth like minerals, caves, metals, serpents and the underworld ghosts. He has all the more worshipped everythinhg that goes beyond even heavens such as mist, mind, the stars, the moon and even the sky itself. History, then, bears witness to the fact that a variety of objects can be made the objects of man's worship.

In view of the above reflections, we are forced to make a distinction between what is really sought in religion and the concrete form in which it is sought, between the real object of religion and the symbolic constructs of religion. A common mistake is identifying the reality that is actually sought with the concrete form in which it is sought. Martin Buber admirably points to this common fallacy in discussing the individual's relationship to God in relation to Judaism, when he states, "whenever we, both Christian and Jew, care more for God himself than for our images of God, we are united in the feeling that our Father's house is differently constructed than our human models take it to be". ³ Following Buber, we need to acknowledge that God as reality is far greater than our projections of his nature.

Thomas Aquinas claimed a similar truth when he insisted that God as the object of man's faith is infinitely more than the propositional understanding of his nature. Martin Luther gives credence to the same conviction in a hidden God, who is "something more" than our images of him. This is to suggest that there is a sharp distinction between man's symbolic understanding of the ultimate reality and the ultimate reality itself. Therefore, we need to admit that the God of the mythologies is merely a symbol for something else. Even the supposition of God as the necessary being or as the highest being is symbolic. I may also add here that the God of the theologians too is symbolic because they think about him in terms of an object independent of the religious act.

Object of Religion and Religious Consciousness

Phenomenologists are wary of using the term God for the object of religious concern. The term God will not be a proper substitute for such religious objects as the spirits of animistic religion, the manna of the Malanesians, the Brahman of the Vedantins, or the no-self of Buddhism. Their terms 'sacred' and 'holy' have come to serve as generic names for the object of religion. Two classic works in phenomenology of religion –Gearardus Van der Leeuw's *Religion in Essence and Manifestation: A Study in Phenomenology* (1933) and Rudolf Otto's *The Idea of the Holy* (1917)- are primarily devoted to the clarification of the "object" of religion.

Following the above thinkers, one can take cognizance that the object of religion can be classified under three headings. First, there is the God of the philosophical speculation, the first cause of everything that is. This, we must admit, is a theoretical entity, that lacks any personal appeal and leaves the devotee unmoved. He can believe in it and yet ignore it as a reality that has no apparent consequences in his life. This is the God of scientific speculations which has nothing to do within one's life–world and religious experience. Scientific experience transcends that of natural experience and there are scientific facts and natural facts as different facts of consciousness. The scientist goes far beyond the natural objects because his concern is the analysis of "states of affairs". As Frings says "facts of science are "states of affairs" and their substrates are objects meant symbolically. Since their degree of relevancy to human life is less felt than the degree of natural experience, the latter exercises a much stronger effect on a human being, an experience which the scientist has as soon as he leaves his laboratory to find himself back in the world of natural facts, the milieu from which he cannot escape: the *naturliche Weltanschauung, or the Lebenswelt*".[4] On the other hand, religious consciousness is often wary of speculation and based on faith and experience. This is especially the case with mystics. The mystic as a devotee is not moved by speculation but rather ignited by an internal existential dynamism that prompts him to seek the fulfillment of his life and being in an entity which is outside of him. His God is personal, experiential and thus unique.

Third, there is an inner impulse in the human subject to seek for something as an object of his devotion. As Karl Gustav Jung has pointed out, when a reality is so universal as the idea of God and worship, it can come only from an inner dynamism of man's nature. Within his nature, man must have the need to seek something that functions as an object of his devotions. The God of the devotee is something that satisfies such a need in man, not the theoretical ground of all the existents. The God of the devotee is a reality that evokes his feelings of devotion, hope and trust and fills him with the feelinfg of *mysterium tremendum et fascinans*. It is a concrete object like the sun, and other heavenly bodies and also like trees and rocks of the earthly bodies. The underlying idea is that even when man is making these objects as the objects of worship, he is in fact, seeking an intangible reality that goes beyond the tangible objects. Thus, we have two types of entities that can be qualified as the object of religion-those concrete objects that are apparently worshipped and the underlying reality that breaks through the concrete objects and evoking religious responses.

As a matter of fact, most of our knowledge is based on natural everyday experience, ie; *naturliche Weltanschauung*. The objects of everyday experience are not constructed nor abstracted; rather, they are a part of my everyday sensibilities. Let me use an example. In the usual Indian philosophical plane, we employ two terms: Jagt and Samsar which apparently employ the same meaning, so to say, the world. But, a clear analysis of these terms indicate that the meaning of these terms are different. As for example, the meaning of the term Jagat stands for an objective world and the term Samsar points to our subjective worlds wherein most of our anbiguities, anxieties and meaning contents of inner life are derived from and wherein they represent to us as real facts. It is here that I live and experience the totality of my life; it is here that I realize my life as most real and proper. The underlying idea is that there is more in this experience than that is present in the acts of consciousness. It suggests that every human being has a lived world apart from the objective world in which he is situated. This lived world is filled with passion and compassion and devoid of ratiocination. Following Scheler, I am tempted to state that it is neither a feeling, nor a sensation, but an intentional experience. It is prior to all forms of perception. In fact, most of our activities and especially religious activities are not guided and controlled by reason; therefore, the world of religion and religious consciousness cannot be considered as another world alongside the 'real world' of experience. The religious world is the world of events and things as experienced by religious man. As Durkheim insists, the sacred character of objects is not intrinsic to them, but something added by the religious consciousness. According to Durkheim, 'the world of religious things is not one particular aspect of empirical nature; it is imposed upon it'.[5]

As Husserl insists, life-world is much more than the sum total of the physical objects. It is the horizon of meaning without which objects cannot exist; it is in the life-world in which I find food as a means to nutrition, or I find coal as a heating material, a hammer for driving a nail in etc. These objects have meaning as objects of use in the life-world. In the life-world, we speak of water and not H2O, we see colour red and not a particular wave length and we see coal as a heating material and not as combustible and so on. Following Aaron Gurwitsch, we should admit that in order to find access to the life-world, our experience of the world must be stripped of the reference to possible scientific explanation, of the component sense of virtue of which the world is apperceived and apprehended as lending itself to scientific interpretation, whatever that interpretation might be in detail. Another way of expressing it is to say that the reference to an ideal mathematical order must be eliminated from our experience of the world and that the latter must no longer be seen under the perspective of that order.[6]

Lebenswelt and Religious Phenomena

In the preceding pages, I have been examining the meaning and significance of religion by taking recourse to Husserl's concept of Lebenswelt. It is true that one cannot constitute the religious phenomena just like other objects of experiences. What is significant is that the phenomenology of religious consciousness demands a new understanding of subjectivity, so to say, a passive plane of subjectivity. Following Bernard G. Prusak, I would argue that 'in contrast to Husserl's focus on the active, constitutive role played by the ego, this phenomenology probes radically passive levels of subjectivity. The primacy of the ego's intentional activity is challenged in favour of an analysis of passive states, that is, the subject's non-intentional immanence (the auto affectivity of life or the body in Henry) or a reversed intentionality where the ego finds itself subject to, not the subject of, a gaze (the givenness of the saturated phenomena in Marion). The 'I' no longer precedes the phenomena that it constitutes, but is instead called into being or born as the one who receives or suffers this intentionality…Whether or not a new understanding of subjectivity can be developed phenomenologically therefore seems essential to the future elaboration of a phenomenology of religion. And inversely, the consideration of religious phenomena seems to lead to new possibilities for probing the depths of subjectivity."[7] Now the question is: what are these new possibilities of the depths of subjectivity. The locus of this experience, subjectivity, is differently conceived by Husserl, Scheler and Husserl.

As far is Husserl is concerned, this primary experience of consciousness is a doxic-theoretical experience of the real world in its object-being. It is the doxic-theoretical experience of sense data which is the ground for reaching out to beings themselves. As Manfred S. Frings says, 'Beings (das Seinde) are present (vorgegeben) in doxic experience and provide a 'substrate' for cognition, valuations, and actions. ..Being is therefore, object-being and it is this notion of being against which Heidegger's analysis in Sein Und Zeit are directed. While for Husserl, the doxic-theoretical experience is fundamental to all emotional experience (eg ; that of value-feeling)and all willing, in *Der Formalismus in der Ethik und die materiale Wertethik* Scheler asserted the opposite, viz. that all acts of consciousness are grounded in the act of love, as an act of pure-taking-interest-in. Hence, neither simple, perceptive acts nor theoretical acts of thinking are at the bottom of Scheler's subjectivity.[8] Therefore, I would like to argue that 'doxic' experience, 'emotional' experience' and 'practical instrumentality' are the primary types of the constitution of subjectivity for Husserl, Scheler and Heidegger respectively. Following the lines of argument put forward by Frings, we would say that these are the primary types of the constitution of subjectivity in these three thinkers. For Husserl, this is mutatis mutandis his conception of *"Lebeswelt"*, for Scheler it is *"naturliche Weltanschauung"* and for Heidegger it is *"Umwelt"*, "inauthentic existence" or *"Alltaglichkeit".*[9]

Part II

Religions and Violence: The Problematic

So far we have been analysing the concept of religion and religious experience by taking into consideration the phenomenological concept of Lebenswelt. If religious experience demands a new form of subjectivity which I call passive subjectivity and if religion is all that an incidental factor in one's life, why does religious conflicts and violence in so many places? – In Afghanistan, Iraq, Sudan, Sri Lanka, Tibet and China, Israel, India, Nigeria, Lebanon, Northern Ireland etc. Even if religion is used for ulterior and fundamentalist purposes, why, exactly religion repeatedly gets used for fundamentalist and nationalist purposes? To put it differently, why does the assertion of religious identities so frequently involve, as it obviously does, intolerance and bigotry with regard to one's way of life in any country? Why, for example are fundamentalists so readily inclined to favour a repressive ideology demanding strict adherence to the authority of their official embodiments and thereby try to compel and control not only the behaviour of a group of people but also their beliefs?[10] The question that concerns all of us can be put thus: what precisely is the connection between religious belief and religious conflicts? An answer to this question naturally entails to look at the character and role of religion from the perspective of phenomenology of religion. Geertz defines religion as "A system of symbols which acts to establish powerful, pervasive and long lasting moods and motivations in men by formulating conceptions of a general order of existence and clothing these conceptions with such an aura of actuality that the moods and motivations seem uniquely realistic."[11] Religion, in this definition, is seen as a component of the whole culture acquired or created by humans. In the social anthropological approach, religion is a creation of man. This conviction led Geertz to say: "our problem, and it grows worse by the day, is not to define religion, but to find it".[12] And he adds: religion may be a stone thrown in the world, but it must be a palpable stone and someone must throw it."[13] The significance of religion in terms of an anthropology or ethnology lies in its capacity to serve individuals or groups, on the one hand, as a model of general yet distinctive concepts of the world, the self and the relation between the two, and, on the other hand, as a model for rooted 'mental' dispositions, from which cultural functions flow other social and psychological ones. Anthropology thus has two tasks with regard to religion: [14] (1) analysing 'the systems of meaning embodied in the symbols which make up the religions and (2) relating these systems to socio-cultural and psychological processes.

These issues obviate the necessity seek answers to such questions as what is the root of religious bigotry? How, why and when people of religious faiths succumb to the darker side of their lives? Why is it necessary for human subject to embrace fanatically their religious groups to the point of violating the right and dignity of others in the name of a God who is believed to be the creator of all? Why do the human beings affirm at one level of their being the universality of the Divine Revelation and yet hypocritically betray it by dancing joyously at the shrine of their invented Gods? Why do the human beings destroy national monuments, which was suspected to be built by the follower of certain faith and whose identities do not concur with their religious faiths? We reconcile ourselves to the fact that our religious loyalties in themselves are neither enough to guarantee us a stable nor spiritually rewarding life nor sufficient in making the other human being inferior and worthless in the eyes of the creator.

Indeed, there are many of us in this country who still have residual if not substantive hope in the interfaith processes, need to ponder over the frailty of our hopes and aspirations. Let me reflect and begin to explore the how questions on religious conflicts? Let us start with a concrete yet unavoidable question: how can we avoid the repetition of Bosnia, Rwanda and Godhra, three of the most recently enacted examples of man's inhumanity to man? These man-made tragedies which are deeply rooted in man's inhumanity to man and which are daily brought into our living rooms tell us a great deal about the strange and sometimes bizarre psychology which define our identity, our self-image and our self – worth. Watching such gory tragedies unravel before our eyes forces the reflective human beings to ask the longstanding question: Is religion and its message to human kind still relevant? If so, how is its relevance affecting our daily lives? It is indeed to this and other related questions that I now turn.

Coming to the issue of violence, the important question that demands an answer is this: Would I be able to make sense of my existence in a world which is constantly threatened by destruction of sense? This is also to suggest that the more I am aware of the sense of my existence, the more I am becoming aware of the destruction of my senses. In fact, my senses are threatened by destruction of my sense of existence. These issues point to certain serious questions: why does religious violence exists in the world? How is it different from other kinds of violence? What are the modes of its manifestation? Does it affect my senses? Does it have any implication with my sense of existence? Indeed, there is certain violence which is symbolic in character and there is also violence which is more barbarous and meant for the annihilation of masses. The irony is that both these types are fought in the name of religion and claims to be a part of *Dharma*. The arbitrary division and subdivision of the Indian sub-continent has spelled some of the ghastliest human tragedies in human history. As we know, the Hindu-Muslim bloodletting over the creation of Pakistan cost 800,000 lives and uprooted 14 million people.

The thing that strikes me about the psychology of religion is not the differences in dogma (over which so much blood has been spilled) but the commonality of insight; all religions claim that all men and women are brothers and sisters and that we should treat others as we treat ourselves. Thus Christianity: "All things whatsoever ye would that men should do to you, do ye even so unto them" [15] Judaism: What is hurtful to yourself, do not do to your fellow man"[16] Hinduism: Do nought to others which if done to thee would cause thee pain"[17] Buddhism: "Hurt not others with that which pains yourself"[18] The unity of insight encoded in these sayings is all the more remarkable because they seem, for the most part, to have evolved independently, in different parts of the world under the influence of different cultural traditions at different times during history. What these sayings tell us is not merely that we should use a common code of conduct in our dealings with our fellow creatures, but rather that, at the tap-root level, we are our fellow humans that the distinctions which divide us are functions of ego and of differing phases of growth.

Self and the Alterity

The discussion on religious conflicts within the language of phenomenological analysis entails an exploration of the rational and political contexts of scriptural monotheism both historically and contemporarily. The nature of religious conflicts needs to be re-examined in light of its persistence and ongoing relationships of religious and political development. If, indeed the divine is ineffable, what is to make of organised religiosity?

To understand this question, I refer to the Babel story in the old testament of the Holy Bible.[19] The background of the story is Babylonian. Shinar is an ancient name for Babylon. (Babel) The narrative can be divided into three parts: Verses 1-4, Verses 5-8 and verse 9. The first part is a report in which humans are the actors; the second part is a discourse in which Yahweh is the chief actor.

The final verse is an explanatory supplement that includes a popular etymology of the name Babel and concludes the story. The story is this: The people of Babel gathered on the planes of Shinar to build a tower "a tower with its top" in the heavens, to make a name for themselves, else they thought that they shall be scattered all over the world".[20] The Pyramid like tower was purported to reach heaven.

The rabbinic exegesis and textual exploration known as Midrash wondered as to what these human beings wish to do with this tower upon which they intended to enter heaven (as based on the Hebrew idiom which connotes " a tower into the heavens" as opposed to "a tower reaching towards the heavens") One of three possibilities they conclude: (i) to ascend into heavens and wage a war against God; (ii) to take their man-made deities and set them up in the heavens to be worshipped, and (iii) to ascend into the heavens and ruin them into bows and spears. And from this they felt that they would gain a name, an identity, which would be a bulwark against the frightening notion of humanity dispersed across the face of the earth. God intervened to prevent the builders of Babel from partaking of the powers and glory that belongs only to him. The language of the builders was confused; so they could no longer communicate with one another. In their frustration, they abandoned the project.

The incomplete tower of Babel is a symbol of man's sinful pride and rebellion. The tower of Babel was intended to build so that the vanity of the people shall be satisfied. They were trying to approach God on their own self-serving terms and learned that the gates of heaven cannot be stormed. They realized that men and women must approach the Holy in reverence and humility. It points to the tendency of human self to create absolutes which in turn cannot reasonably allow discovering one's self. The implication is clear. As suggested above in the discussion of the tower of Babel, differences in language represent real differences in modes of both perception and expression. Man requires to drop his tendency to form absolutes in order to realize that equal does not have to mean identical. The truth is that makers of absolutes cannot tolerate alternatives. It is precisely when we make God over in our own image as intolerant and discomforted by diversity, that we give false sanctity to the boundaries that divide people, whether by faith, locution, skin colour, facial characteristics, language or whatever. We forget conveniently that the divine response to the making of absolute is to confirm the reality of diversity and alternatives in human experience. These reflections suggest to the idea of keeping a distance in our belonging and yet a belonging in our distancing. It also indicates that one needs to transcend one's belongings of one's religion with a distance. Such a distance in belonging does not distort but dignifies nor does it lead to conflict but to the fulfilment of one's humanity which can live in covenant with Divinity.

Many of the misconceptions and fundamentalist attitudes are erupted from this non-shareability of self with the other. Thus, in many societies, including Indian societies, modernization has accompanied religious revivalism instead of secularization. Today's Islamist movements in several parts of the world, the Hindu revivalist movements in India, Buddhist Revivalism in Sri Lanka, Jewish fundamentalist movements in Israel and Christian fundamentalist movements in U.S are all modern phenomena of the division between the self and the other or to say the product of non-distancing with a belongingness. These "partially eroded group personalities coalesce to form a new national entity".[21] The new national culture replaces the culture of the clerics, priests, Sadhus or ideologues. The price that people pay for this transition from the agrarian – ethnic to industrial-nationalist culture, Gellner points out, is that "they become secularized.[22] That must be reason that religious conflicts have been used inseparably with cultural conflicts. Many times religious conflicts take place between members of the same faith. Hutus and Tutsis are Catholics and butcher each other preferably in Churches. Muhajirs and Sindhis are Muslims and kill each other in Mosques. Religious fundamentalism, again is a factor of conflict for instance between Muslims and Christians in Bosnia and Chechnya, in the Philippines and Nigeria. It is again the major cause of conflict between Hindus and Muslims in India, between Buddhists and Muslims in Myanmar. Surely, the people who ignite the flames of communal hatred and religious conflicts are generally not illiterates. In Serbia, they were mostly University professors. In India, they are people who are highly educated and vested with political powers. But this little crowd of egoistic self-promoters succeed in India only because of a mass of largely illiterate followers whom they can easily instigate. That is why, states like Uttar Pradesh, Rajasthan, Bihar and Madhya Pradesh have significant roles in communal crimes.

The Present Challenge

Now, where should we start from? I recall a beautiful instruction given to Abraham by Lord God in the Book of Genesis of the Old Testament. "Now the Lord had said unto Abraham, get thee out of thy country, and from thy kindred, and from thy father's house unto a land that I will show thee: and I will make of thee a great nation, and I will bless thee, and make thy name great; and thou shall be a blessing and in thee shall all families of the earth be blessed. And Abram was seventy and five years old when he departed out of Haran."[23]

The call of Abraham broke the silence of his inner self as well as the meaning of the universe. The call was meant to transcend and relativize the human grounded ties. It posits universality in human destiny that relativizes all conflict-engendering particularities. In short, the intercession of God was "metaphysical" in nature; Hence, Abraham was told: 'Get you out' – get you out from all that has been, from your old ways and inherited patterns of conflicts and self-indulgence. Get you out from your human assumptions into a new and divine sensitivity. Get you out from the restraints of mental slavery and discover to live beyond yourself; get you out from your apprehensions and lead a life in and toward your ultimate potentials. Get you out from your belongings of mental make-up; Go from where you are to where you can be with a distance. As instructed to Abraham, moving out of the stasis and sharing the divine life of inexorable becoming is the need of the hour. This unfoldment of the divine – human relationship is all about faith and religion. Once we are capable of comprehending the meaning of this unfoldment, there is the starting point towards a non-conflictual world wherein one accepts other religions and their gods. In fact, the call which was given to Abraham to 'get out' is said to be the vocation of all religions in a conflictual world of today.

Such an outlook provides an opportunity in combating religious conflicts by creating an awareness of the reality of our religious practices and even beliefs. The question is: can we afford to desist from emphasizing this relativity in order to safeguard our uniqueness. If we do not come to a new understanding of each religion's uniqueness, the problem of religious conflict will disrupt our society. Our religious leaders and political pundits ought to be more humble and learn to accept that mere adherence to particular religious faith by birth is no special qualification. When prohibition was enforced in Pakistan, tens of thousands of Muslims tried to pass off as members of minority communities, that is, they posed as non-Muslims for the sake of a drink.

The same happened when Zakat was introduced as a kind of Church tax. When Sikhs were brutally killed in this country after the assassination of Mrs. Indira Gandhi, many Sikh gentlemen were compelled to shave of their beards and pretended as Hindus. Similar examples can be adduced from many parts of the world. The issue is this: many of our religious practices are constructed on relative considerations and if that is the case why not our constricted beliefs too? What I would like to suggest is the need to get out from what we have been to what we could be. This mind-set demands a new depth of subjectivity, which I called earlier as the passive plane of subjectivity, wherein one can positively postulate a new meaning of transcendence. In this passive plane of subjectivity, the 'I' do not lead the phenomena it constitutes, but is the one who receives this intentionality. The directionality of consciousness no longer outward in nature but the same consciousness is directed toward itself, so to say, intentional in the sense of coming back to itself. Such a path of inward transcendence is a distancing without belonging and a belonging with a distancing. In the phenomenological tradition of philosophy, distancing without belonging constitutes the initial stage of phenomenological reduction which in turn provides the certainty of the self.

Phenomenologically understood, distancing without belonging has two features that are immediately evident. The first characteristic is that distance presupposes the existence of a consciousness or subjectivity toward which man tries to reach out. The second feature of distancing without belonging demands an otherness within oneself. Human subject needs the presence of an 'other' to realize himself/herself as a concrete and distinct being. All of us need a religious other or a cultural other which enables to realize the certainty of the 'self'. I would like to sum up these reflections by recalling a beautiful verse of the 13th century mystic Muhyuddin Ibn Arabi of Murcia: "There was a time when I used to discriminate against my neighbour because of his ethnicity or religion. That time is long gone. My heart has become a meadow for the grazing deer, a monastery for the monk, Torah Scrolls for the rabbi, a Kaaba for the pilgrim. I profess the religion of love, and wherever its caravan will turn to, I shall follow."

Endnotes

[1] Fanon, Frantz. *The Wretched of the Earth*, translated by Constance Barrington, (New York; Grove Weidenfeld, 1963), 42.

[2] Abraham Maslow, *Religions, Values and Peak Experience*, (New York: The Viking Press, 1964), 19.

[3] As cited by William Horosz, "Religion and Culture in Modern Perspective", in *Religion in Philosophical and Cultural Perspective*, eds; Clayton Feaver and William Horosz, (New Delhi: Affiliated East west Press, 1971), 309.

[4] Manfred S. Frings, Max Scheler: "Focusing on Rarely seen Complexities of Phenomenology", in *Phenomenology in Perspective* ed by F. J. Smith, op. cit., 41.

[5] Durkheim, Emile, *Elementary forms of religious Life* (New York: Collier Books, 1961), 229.

[6] Aron Gurwitsch, *Problems of the Life-world*, op. cit., 49.

[7] Dominique, Janicaud, *Phenomenology and the Theological Turn; The French Debate;* Fordham University Press, Translator's Preface, Jeffrey L. Kosky,116.

[8] Manfred S. Frings, Max Scheler: "Focusing on Rarely seen Complexities of Phenomenology", in *Phenomenology in Perspective* ed. by F. J. Smith, Martinus Nijhoff, The Hague, 1970, 34-35.

[9] Ibid., 36.

[10] Craig Calhoun, "Nationalism and Civil Society: Democracy, Diversity and Self-Determination" International Sociology, 8, 4 (Dec. 1993), 405.

[11] Geertz, Clifford, *The Interpretation of Cultures* (London: Hutchinson, 1973), 98.

[12] Ibid., 3.

[13] Ibid., 3.

[14] George F. McLean, "Ethnicity, Culture and "Primordial' Solidarities" in Paul Peachey, George F. Mclean, John Kromkowski (eds.) *Abrahamic Faiths, Ethnicity and Ethnic Conflicts* (Council for Research in Values and Philosophy, Cardinal Station, Washington D.C. 1997), 169.

[15] Mathew 7:12 (Holy Bible).

[16] Talmud

[17] Mahabharata 5.5.17

[18] Udavavarga 5.18

[19] Genesis 11:1-9 (Holy Bible).

[20] Ibid., 11:4.

[21] Ali A Mazrui, "Pluralism and National Integration" in Leo Kuper and M.G.Smith (Eds) *Pluralism in Africa* (Berkeley, Calif: University of California Press, 1969), 334-35.

[22] Gellner, Ernest, Nations and Nationalism (Ithaca: Cornel University Press, 1983),78.

[23] Book of Genesis, 12:1-4.

Invisible Lives:
Denotified Tribes of Uttar Pradesh

Dr. Archana Singh

Bundelkhand is a hilly region spread in 13 districts of Uttar Pradesh and Madhya Pradesh. There are limited livelihood options of the communities residing there. The marginal castes of this region are engaged in traditional occupations like hunting and catching birds, liquor making agricultural labourers, basket weaving, musicians, snake charming, collecting firewood, manufacturing bamboo furniture, stone cutting etc. They have become more vulnerable due to the arid conditions of the region. Their traditional occupations are not enough for their livelihood support and due to lack of education and technical skills and training. They do not get opportunities for growth either in the government or the private sectors. They are unable to take benefits of state policies of positive discrimination. These highly marginalized de-notified tribes are not even at the minimum economic level of production where they can develop their own politics or their "organic intellectuals" (Gramscian term)[1]. There is a need to identify the factors which lead to the invisibility, deprivation and exclusion of communities and suggest appropriate measures for providing them visibility, voice and democratic space. These communities were considered artists in earlier systems. In the new system of modernism, their 'skills' became worthless. In the new system, arising out of economical liberalism there is no other option left for them, other than to be labourers. They don't want to become labourers. They believe that they are 'skilled community' and have proud of their skills.

Who are the Kabootari Nat

In U.P. Kabootari community is sub caste of Nat and have the status of Scheduled caste. They are mainly distributed in Bundelkhand region of U.P. Generally their girls or women are called Kabutari. Their community name is derived from the word Kabutar, meaning Pigeon. They are settled in the peripheries of Hamirpur, Mahoba and Banda. Most of them are gypsy dancers. They trace their origin from Alwar and Bikaner districts of Rajasthan. The Kabutari Nat is divided into different non-hierarchical clans (Gotra), such as Kalsar, Ajmeri, Dunguwat, etc. the Kabutari Nat are traditionally engaged in performing rope-dances and acrobatic feats. At present Kabutari Nat community scattered in different districts of Bundelkhand Region in Uttar Pradesh. They engaged in making and selling liquor. Community persons live in very vulnerable conditions. They are still suffering the stigma as imposed on them by the British's. They correlate themselves with legend past. Icon for this community is the figure of Rani Padmani of Chittor and Jhalkaribai, a close companion of Rani of Jhansi Laxmibai. Jhalkaribai is believed to have saved Laxmibai while continuing to battle with the British till she died. The Kabutara's preserve Jhalkaribai as a character in the narrative of their own caste history.

Invisiblity

Low numerical strength ("whoever would have the higher number would have the higher share" a slogan given by Kanshiram) is one of the reason of invisiblity. Mayawati said 'a society without history cannot be ruler. Because history gives inspiration, inspiration awakens people, awakening constructs thoughts, thoughts help in acquiring power, and power makes a community ruler. This is true to this community. They have history but unable to disseminate in the community. Kabootari community has its own history, but absence of organic intellectuals, and community leaders, and they are also asserting for a dignified life but their resistance is fragmented and limited to community level. Their resistance is not capable of making headlines in public sphere because of their stigmatized identity. A community needs organic intellectuals, community heroes/icons for visibility of a community.

Identity politics provides democratic empowerment of a few communities or specific sections of communities, while, on the other hand, it produces disempowerment of people within these communities who are not yet able to understand the language of democracy and thus lag behind. The voice of a community is one that can be heard or recognized in a democracy if it acquires the "capacity" to be heard. Communities need to attain a level from where they can aspire, for visibility. The capacity to aspire creates the "capacity to demand". According to A. Sen, *in a democracy, people tend to get what they demand more crucially, they do not get what they do not demand.* Thus, the consciousness of demand and a lack of it in a democracy plays a crucial role in making communities acquire visibility and demanding their rights.

Community and its Life World

During semi-participant observation, my first interaction with Vishnu Panda, priest of the community (a devout worshipper of the deity of Goddess Kali) was surprised when I asked for water. He then asked a child to go hurry up and fetch some water. After which he and other community members felt comfortable around me. He said very innocently "what is the reason to come to our home. Son, how should we serve you?" I asked him to help me initiate conversation with the men, women and children of the community which he readily agreed to do. When I reached my field area, community' members respond to me "Why do you have to come to our poor house, how can we serve you, we are low not even worthy of serving you? Community people inform us that they have no access to any of the welfare schemes launched by the government for the uplift of the downtrodden sections. The benefits of reservation make no sense to them. Most of the people are illiterate and engaged in liquor making. In their hamlets there are no primary schools. Many children or young people work as labourers and supplement the family income by working in rag picking, selling dry fruits, rickshaw pulling etc. The people of these communities still live in small, thatched huts. Their Patti is like a village slum. In the name of development, there are some Pucca houses (walls made from bricks and roof covered from Kush grass or thick plastic sheets), few roads and electricity poles (without electric wires) available in the hamlets. In the name of drinking facility there are only three hands pumps between four hamlets. In every hamlet at most 60-80 people are living. At present only one hand pump is working and other three not. These facilities are provided to them in the period of election by the candidates for votes. They have no Anthodia cards, BPL cards or APL cards. Without any valid id proof, they could not access the benefits of government policy. They always live in fear that any time anybody can displace them from their homes. They are most marginalized in the SCs. They are powerless, resources less, identity less and voiceless persons.

Occupational Displacement: Contestation with Life World

Since long time, they were dependent on natural resources. They were very skilled in their **work** like liquor making, dancing. Their identity and existence was based on this work. With the end of the work, their identity and voice is also becoming weaker. It could be said that it stands on the verge of extinction. Nats are the real gipsy types', in the words of William Crooke, 'with the short stature, black skin, and keen black eyes of the Dravidian. The typical name for such people is Nat, 'dancer', or *bazigar*, 'performer' in northern India. They made 'boxes out of hide, horn combs, little baskets of grass or reed. Women practised the arts of tattooing of girls, 'cupping, dentistry in the form of pretending to extract worms from carious teeth, and palmistry. They wandered through the villages carrying herbs, dried skins of birds and the smaller animals, which were used in 'compounding charms and preparing amulets.' These skill have no place in modern markets. Their main occupation i.e. liquor making is considered as illegal and they especially their women face atrocities.

Claiming their Dignified Identity

In my field survey I found that this community is asserting its dignified identity. But their voices and resistance is fragmented. They have their own caste history, culture, and gods and goddess. And they have powerfully claimed that their ancestors were very brave and kind-hearted. They fought against the British rule for the independence. And they feel pride in being Kabootari. They said that they were Kshatriyas and worked with honesty. They also follow codes of conducts of Hinduism.

With the shrinking of facilities within the SCs, these small castes now desire to crossover to the ST category. Kabootari wants to highlight its tribe identity to shift into ST state category. I met and talked with several people from this community of Bundelkhand region. All of them demand that they get recognition in Bhotia tribe. Their justification for this crossover is that they had originally been forest dwellers who had later moved to plain land and became a part of the SCs but in the process, they had been outcompeted by the bigger, powerful and more dominant SC castes. This is not a problem of a particular caste but a challenge faced by 62 of the 66 castes among Dalits in UP. Their anguish is similar. Castes such as Dusadh, Bansphor, Kanjar, Kharvar, Dom, Nat, Bahelia, Kabutara, Kalabaaz, etc. not only have small population, but the literacy level among them is also very low. Very few youths among them have passed high school exams.

Marginal Life World vs. Mainstream Life World

When asked for how many years have they been living here, Kabootari replied that they were living there from 20 to 25 years. But they left their village because they were facing some problems. When asked, about the problem they responded that they were working for the upper caste, and fighting for them who would beat them up and abuse them: 'The *Almighty has made you [precisely] to serve us*. You who eat the crumbs we leave for you, who eat the grains you pick out of the dung of our cattle, who eat our dead animals, how dare you speak out against us [or, for that matter, even "speak"] in our presence? One day we denied that we will not work and fight for them. Then those people (upper caste) burned our houses and displaced us from our land. A women

Angoori (35) said "if people suppress and cheat you, then one should not live there." There was some problem so we had to leave that place. We are less in numbers, so we could not fight and we left that place for the sake of security of our children. Then we came here and live in congested huts. Sarkar (government) don't do anything for us. We are so weak therefore we can't fight for our identity, self-respect, and dignity. If we plan to do something for ourselves then upper caste people don't allow that. And we always face abuses and humiliation due to our stigmatized identity. A general perception exists about these communities manifested in every day utterances like: *"They are lazy", "They are habitual thieves", "and they cannot save", "They enjoy their idleness", "They lack the ability to handle wealth and liberty". Women are prostitutes.*

They have their own set of problems with upper castes. They are told that "you are uncivilized, illiterate beasts who do not know how to talk in front of officials in tehsil/court. You should do what you are advised to". So everyone wants to rule over them. Upper caste domination, harassment, social control, ridicule and contemporary politics and politicians (who do not support them because they are less in numbers) and modernity and development (which has seized their traditional occupation) are also responsible for muting the community.

Their Interaction with the State

These small semi-nomads groups say that some big and influential castes within the SC category have usurped all the benefits meant for the entire section for their own good. The dominant castes grabbed all the benefits and they were left empty handed due to being small, insignificant and because they lacked powerful voices.

The benefits of government schemes do not reach them because they are not educated and lack political leadership. Thus, they are unable to make their presence felt in the discourses and debates within the SCs and are largely invisible. State government officials, like DMs, SDMs, BDOs, who are responsible for protecting and developing these castes are not even aware about them. When asked if have any caste certificate they responded negatively. Many times we tried for caste certificate and we all went to Tehsil through the *Lekhpal*. We all paid money for this but it was of no use. In 2005, we went to S.D.M court to complaint. We said, Sahib, we have a complaint. We all belong to kabootari community and we are very poor and illiterate. Sahib issue our identity cards please sahib. Then S.D.M said that our caste is not in the records. Your caste is not mentioned in our list. If you want to have voter i-card or caste certificate go to High Court and file a case. If decision came in your favour then I will issue your caste certificate. Go away and don't come here next time. They were surprised that on the one hand, state is not ready to recognize them as Dalits and on the other, they treat them as outcasts. Somehow, they have accepted this status. Due to such unending tortures, they feel better to be mute and anyhow get bread to survive. This shows that their hidden assertion/ resistance is for the betterment of life and identity. Their resistance does not make headlines because of lack of education, icons, heroes, community leaders, their lesser numbers, and so on. These are the major causes of their backwardness. Community resistance is limited only on the grass root level.

Formation of Invisibility

My study areas are different districts of Bundelkhand region. Study concentrates on marginalization of the marginally living kabbootari community of this region. Upper castes, upper Dalit classes, social structure, and contemporary modernity and development are responsible for their marginalization, invisibility, and muteness. Study traces the sense of relative deprivation of most backward small Dalit groups in Bundelkhand region of Uttar Pradesh. In this community culture of silence also exists where people usually do not speak unless spoken to or asked a question, where people respect the views of elders and do not contradict what has been agreed upon. This culture of silence means the views of certain community members are not heard, this culture of not speaking out, raising questions, not questioning decisions made by community, upper caste people, state, elders and leaders, sometimes culminates in conflicts between resource users and resource owners. During my fieldwork, I observed that the presence of state-led democracy in the everyday life of people works in different communities in distinct ways. Firstly, it makes them economically dependent on the state, and secondly, it makes them feel more deprived than other communities.

We may find that communities like Kabootari have not become invisible in a day or in recent times. They have a long history of deprivation, which made them invisible with the process of humiliation and exclusion. It is due to their sharing of Dalit identity. But their mobility has also pushed them further behind and deprived them. Due to lack of community leaders, organic intellectuals, education, they were unable to assert their identities and suffered marginalization and oppression. We have to understand this heterogeneity, only then we would be able to understand the pain and stigma of most marginal Dalits.

Endnotes

[1] Every new class creates alongside itself intellectuals who direct the ideas and aspirations of the class to which they organically belong (Hoare and Smith, 1971),5.

A Phenomenological Study on the Adivasi Culture in West Bengal

Dr. Tapan Kumar De

Today we live in a global village. We feel proud to be a member of this digital village having almost identical cultural and civil lives. It is an open secret today that a cultural chauvinistic attitude appears on earth to wipe out all cultural differences to bring under the umbrella of materialistic culture where everything will be dominated and operated by the criterion of economic development. GDP (Gross Domestic Product) is the sole functional power. Each and every nation runs after this material prosperity leaving its own cultural identity.

In this situation we find that the Advasis in West Bengal have a different attitude towards their own culture. They are trying to keep their cultural identity as it was before though the process of Sanscritization and Hinduization is going on by the present socio-economic conditions and political influence. In this small paper I shall try to find out the common features of their culture besides the differences among the various adivasi groups. We will find that from the birth to death they follow their traditions in the midst of nature. Their culture is nature oriented. The adivasi culture has a deep relation with the nature. Trees, plants, animals, mountain-all have a big role to play to mould the cultural life of the adivasis of west Bengal. The cultural chauvinism of the global age has a little to do with their culture.

The word 'Adlvasi' has a historical existence though it is used as constitutional word later on. We find the birth of the word 'Adivasi' in the first half of the twentieth century. In 1932 there we find a demand placed by the Jharkhandis of Jharkhand for Jharkhand. This demand was placed by the fighters that they need a state for Adivasi. From then a small newsletter was published as 'Adivasi'. In this newsletter the arguments in favour of the state for Adivasi were placed systematically and continuously. This was the first used of the term 'Adivasi'.[1]

It is also true that Joypal Sing one of the leaders of this movement wanted to incorporate the word 'Adivasi' in place of 'Schedule Tribe.' But Dr. B.R. Ambedkar wanted to incorporate the phase 'Scheduled Tribe'. So at that time it was not possible to establish the word 'Adivasi' as official word.

The word 'Tribe' was used for the first time in 1833 by Brian Houghton Hodgson. In 1908 Harbest Risley defined the word Tribe in this way. He says, "… a collection of families or groups of families, bearing a common name which as a rule does not denote any specific occupation, generally claiming descent from a mythical or a historical ancestor. Occasionally the name is derived from an animal but in some parts of the country the tribe is held together only by the obligation of Kinship. Members speak the same language and occupy (or profess to occupy) a definite tract of the country."[2] From the above definition we can infer the basic characteristics of Adivasi culture or tribal culture:

1. They bear a common name.
2. The name does not refer to any specific occupation.
3. The name of group indicates the existence of its mythical or historical ancestor.
4. Sometimes the name is derived from animals.
5. Kinship is the key factor to keep their unity.
6. They speak the same language.
7. They have a definite territory to live.
8. Indirectly here we find an 'others' concept.
9. Others are treated as outsiders.

There is a long debate between the two different groups – Adivasi groups and the outsiders. The outsiders are called Aryans. In India we find the Aryan civilization and Adivasi societies. The debate is regarding the existence of the Aryan race. Some Scholars, like Dr. Bhupendranath Dutta thinks that the so called Aryan race is an imaginary concept of Max Muller. It is also a chauvinistic attitude of the European thinkers, like Max Muller. Max Muller himself rejected his view in the later period. He says, "To me an ethnologist who speaks of an Aryan race, Aryan blood, Aryan eyes and hair, is as great a sinner as a linguistic who speaks of a dolichocephalic dictionary or a brachycephalic grammar. It is worse than a Babylonian confusion of tongues, it is downright theft."[3]

Though Max Muller rejected his idea regarding Aryan society, his followers were fighting in favour of Aryan race till date. Again Max Muller says "Aryan, in scientific language is utterly inapplicable to race. It means language and nothing but language, and if we speak of Aryan race at all, we should know that it means no more than X+Aryan speech."[4]

Let us keep the debate in bracket as my aim is not to throw light on the debate in this small paper. I have, just want to throw light on the Adivasi culture which is unique and self-sufficient, which is dynamic also. In what sense Adivasi culture is unique and dynamic, is the subject of my discussion.

Let us take a look of the existing Adivasi groups in West Bengal. In west Bengal we find 38 groups of aboriginal tribes. They all are divided into four group following the linguistic point of view. Either they are from Austro Asiatic language group or from the Dravidian language group or Tibetan-Chinese language group or Indo-Aryan language group.

There are sixteen aboriginal groups under Austro-Asiatic language group. Five aboriginal groups are there under Dravidian language group, nine under Tibetan-Chinese and eight under Indo-Aryan language group.

Now, if we divide the 38 aboriginal tribes of West Bengal according to language, we get the following list.

a)   Astro-Asiatic language group

1) Asur, 2) Karmali, 3) Kisan, 4) Korwa, 5) Kora, 6) Chero, 7) Nagesia, 8) Birhor, 9) Bhumij, 10) Mahli, 11) Mahali, 12) Munda, 13) Lodha, Kheria or Kharia, 14) Savar, 15) Santal, 16) Ho.

b)   The Dravidian language group

1) Oraon, 2) Khond, 3) Gond, 4) Mal Pahariya, 5) SauriaPahariya.

c)   Tibtean – Chinese language group

1) Garo, 2) Chakma, 3) Magh, 4) Mech, 5) Mru,6) Rabha, 7)Lepcha, 8) Hajong, 9) Bhutia (O Kagate, Toto, Dukpa, Sherpa).

d)   Indo-Aryan language group

1) Kharwar, 2) Gorait, 3) Chik Baraik, 4) Parhaiya, 5) Birjia, 6) Bedia, 7) Baiga, 8) Lohar or Lohra.[5]

The dilemma of the aboriginals was not the same as it is today. They had sufficient wealth and real estate. Even reference of a few kings and zamindars can be found in old chronicles. It is known that, in the 14th century A.D., Syad Ibrahim Ali Alias Malik Baya, who was the commander of Muhanmmad Tughlaq, the Sultan of Delhi, invaded the fort of Champa. The owner of that fort, a Santal king, committed suicide along with his whole family, and malik Baya took possession of it in 1340 A.D.[6]

Let us take alook at the habitat of the Adivasis of West Bengal. The Adivasis or the aboriginals are there in West Bengal from hill to ocean. They live in all the districts.   A few years back West Dinajpur District has been divided into North and South Dinajpur. 24 Pargans was also divided into North and South zones. Midnapur is also divided into Paschim Medinipur, Purba Medinipur and Paschim Medinipur is divided into Paschim Medinipur and Jhargram in recent past. So, it is not possible to offer the exact number of the Adivasis in a particular region. My aim is not also to show the exact location of a particular

Adivasi group or groups. My purpose is to show the phenomenological exposition of the culture of the adivasis or aboriginals in West Bengal. Yet I think that to offer a brief sketch of their habitat will not be irrelevant.

Asure — West Dinajpur distirct.

Oraon — Kolkata, Coochbihar, 24- Parganas, Jalpiguri, Darjeeling, Nadia, West Dinajpur, Purulia, Burdwan, Bankura, Birbhum, Malda, Murshidabad, Medinipur, Howrah and Hooghly districts.

Karmali — West Dinajpur and Purulia dist.

Kisan — Darjeeling and Purulia dist.

Korwa — West Dinajpur and Purulia dist.

Kora — West Dinajpur dist.

Khond — West Dinajpur.

Gorait — West Dinajpur and Purulia dist.

Garo — Kolkata, Coochbihar, 24 Parganas, Jalpiguri, Darjeeling, Nadia, West Dinajpur, Burdwan, Murshibadad, Medinipur, Howrah and Hooghly dist.

Gond — West Dinajpur dist.

Chakma — Kolkata, 24 Parganas, Darjeelign, Nadia, Burdwan, Birbhum, Malda dist.

Chikbaraik — Darjeeling and West Dinajpur dist.

Chero — West Dinajpur dist.

Negesia — Kolkata, 24 Parganas, Jalpauguri, Darjeeling, West Dinajpur, Howrah dist.

Parhaiya — West Dinajpur dist.

Birjia   —   West Dinajpur dist.

Birhor   —   Purulia dist.

Bedia   —   West Dinajpur, Purulia dist.

Baiga   —   West Dinajpur

Bhutia   —   Kolkata, Coochbihar, 24 Parganas, Jalpaiguri, Darjeeling, West Dinajpur, Burdwan, Malda, Murshidabad, Midnapur, Howrah, Hooghly dist.

Bhumij   —   Kolkata, Coohbihar, 24 Parganas, Jalpaiguri, Nadia, West Dinajpur, Purulia, Burdwan, Bankura, Birbhum, Malda, Midnapur, Howrh and Hooghly.

Magh   —   Kolkata, 24 Parganas, Jalpaiguri, Darjeeling, Nadia, West Dinajpur, Burdwan, Birbhum, Murshidabad, Midnapur, Howrah and Hooghly dist.

Mal Paharia   —   Kolkata, 24 Parganas, Jalpaiguri, Darjeeling, Nadia, West Dinajpur, Purulia, Burdwan, Birbhum, Malda, Murshidabad, Midnapur, Howrah dist.

Mahli   —   Purulia dist.

Mahali   —   Kolkata, Coochbihar, 24 Parganas, Jalpaiguri, Darjeeligh, Nadia, West Dinapur, Purulia, Burdwan, Bankura, Birbhum, Malda, Murshidabad, Midnapur, Howrah and Hooghly dist.

Munda   —   Kolkata, Coochbihar, 24 Pargans, Jalpaiguri, Darjeeling, Nadia, West Dinajpur, Purulia, Burdwan, Bankura, Birbhum, Malda, Murshidabad, Midnapur, Howrah, Hooghly dist.

Mech   —   Kolkata, Coochbihar, 24 Parganas, Jalpaiguri, Darjeeling, West Dinajpur, Midnapur, Howrah dist.

Mru   —   24 Parganas, Jalpaiguri, Nadia, West Dinajpur, Bankura, Midnapur, Hooghly dist.

Rabha   —   Kolkata, Coochbihar, 24 Parganas, Jalpaiguri, West Dinajpur, Bankura, Midnapur dist.

Lepcha   —   Kolkata, Coochbihar, 24 Parganas, Jalpaiguri, Darjeeling, Nadia, West Dinajpur, Purulia, Burdwan, Birbhum, Malda, Murshidabad, Midnapur, Howrah and Hooghly dist.

Lodha, Kharia   —   Kolkata, Coochbihar, 24 Parganas, Jalpaiguri, Darjeeling, Nadia, West Dinajpur, Purulia, Burdwan, Birbhum, Malda, Murshidabad, Midnapur, Howrah and Hooghly dist.

Lohar   —   West Dinajpur, Purulia, Bankura dist.

Saver   —   Purulia dist.

Shauria Paharia   —   Purulia dist.

Santal   —   Kolkata, Coochbihar, 24 Parganas, Jalpaiguri, Darjeeling, Nadia, West Dinajpur, Purulia, Burdwan, Birbhum, Malda, Murshidabad, Midnapur, Howrah and Hooghly dist.

Hajong   —   Kolkata, 24 Parganas, Jalpaiguri, Darjeeling, Nadia, West Dinajpur, Burdwan, Howrah and Hooghly dist.

Ho   —   Kolkata, 24 Parganas, Jalpaiguri, West Dinajpur, Purulia, Burdwan, Birbhum, Murshidabad, Midnapur, Howrah and Hooghly dist.[7]

Culture: It is true that each and every Adivasi group has their own culture and if we take a deep look we will find that there are common platform also. Now I am going to focus on the common platform of the culture of Adivasi groups in west Bengal.

The Adivasi culture is constituted with four elements. Songs, dances, literatures and artistic skill are the four pillars of Adivasi culture. It is true that no one can study them separately as the four pillars are interrelated. Songs without dances are incomplete. It is also the real picture of the life style of the Adivasi from their birth to death. There are various songs in the culture of the Adivasi. *Baha, MaaManre, Saharai, Karam, Dasani, Janam, Bapla, Bharan* (Sraddha) etc. are the main songs of the adivasi societies. All the songs are divided into three groups by the experts-1) Religious Songs, 2) Social customs oriented songs and 3) Others.

Some songs are there to be sung at the time of religious festivals. Baha, Maa Manre, Karam and Sahari songs are classified as religious songs to be sung in the time of religious festivals with dance. Dances are also classified like songs. All the songs bear the sense of Animism. In Baha songs we find an attitude to worship the nature in spring time when the nature appears as a beautiful girl with sweet decoration of flowers. The songs are the nature and the natural resources. Maa Manre songs are offered to the local Bongas and also to the ancestors. Karam songs are also important religious songs. All the Karam songs addresses the holy Karam tree and in this way all adivasis show their respect to the nature. Saharai songs, Dansaisongs etc are related to the social customs. Saharai is related with the festival of harvesting. These songs are also sung with dances. They are treated as the sources of joy.

AkaredaJanam Lena-
SaharaiParab.
Akaredabusharlena
VaVakurSaharai dah,
Hihirirejanamlena
Vavakur sari saharai.

(Where is the source of Saharai and where does sweetness appear, the source of the Saharai is Hihiri and the source of the sweetness is pipri. According to the Santali belief Hihiriri is the source of Kettles etc. and Pipri is the place of human beings.)[8]

Dasnai song is devoted to offer respect to Guru. Sometimes we find that *dasnai* songs are sung to worship Hindu deity. Worship of Devi Durga is also there in Dasnai songs. *Longare* songs are also designated as other songs.

Besides these songs there are folk-songs, Jhumur, Tusu, Vadu songs. All these songs are integral part of the Adivasi culture in West Bengal.

Dances: There are various forms of dances in Adivasi societies. Pata dance, Baha dance, Kathi dance, Dan dance, Jawa dance are the main forms of the dances. Dances are performed with the songs and they create a complete cultural environment.

Rituals from Birth to Death: The birth rituals of the Adivasi communities are important. The pregnant lady has to go with some social customs during her pregnancy including prayer to have the bliss of God for safe birth of the coming baby. The role of midwife is also important. In the seventh month after the conception Shadh Bhaksan (Meal with test) ritual is observed to offer good and blended food to the pregnant lady. Ekuse (a special ritual) is also observed after 21 days from the birth of the child. After sixmonths Mukhe-bhator Annaprashan is also observed.

Marriage: Generally a young boy of 18 years old is considered to marry a girl of 12 or 13 years old. Marriage in the same clan or Kinship marriage is prohibited. Inter-cast marriage in Adivasi community is not encouraged.

At the time of marriage, initiation is taken from the end of the girl's house. There is dowry system. Dowry is to be given to the mother of the bride. Colourful ceremonies are observed in various stages and the women have to play crucial role in this connection.

All the aboriginal communities have more or less the same rituals from birth to death. The aim of the rituals is to bring peace and safety to the concerned family. The safe birth without the touch of medical science is the main aim of all kinds of rituals at the time of pregnancy.

The marriage ceremony is also common to all groups. It is regarded that marriage ceremony is attached with love. Sometimes the proposal goes from the end of the bride's house or sometimes goes from the end of the groom's house. Women of the concerned family and the other members of the community play the key role at the time of marriage. Beautiful songs are sung by the ladies. The whole ceremony is nature oriented. The ceremony for exchange oil-turmeric from groom to bride; the preparation of marriage platform (In Bengali, it is called Chhadnatala) with branches of trees, the use of holy water and soil are the signals of the nature orientation.

Widow marriage is also there in all aboriginals or adivasi groups. The unmarried younger brother can marry the sister-in-law after the unnatural death of the elder brother. But elder brother is not allowed the same after the unnatural death of the younger brother. That is if the younger brother dies, the elder brother can never marry the wife of the younger brother. In this case the lady can marry someone else outside the family.

Different kinds of marriage

There are different kinds of marriages in Adivasi societies.

1. Kiring Bahu Bapla: The traditional marriage or the arrange marriage is indicated by the name. After the negotiation made by the *Raibar* (Match Maker) the guardians of the both parties- groom and bride agree for the marriage.

2. Tungki Dipil Bapla: This type of marriage is less costly and generally it is followed by the poor.

3. Or Ader Bapla: This type of marriage is called forced marriage. We can compare it with the concept of the Asurika Marriage in Hindu culture.

4. Nir Bolo Bapla: It is one kind of forced marriage unlike Or Ader Bapla. In Or Ader Bapla the consent of the bride is not necessary, but in Nir Bolo Bapla here we find an affair between the groom and the bride. The guardians of the groom refuse to accept the bride as daughter in law. The bride enters into the house of the groom forcefully to fight against the ill-treatment of the members of the house of the groom and to acquire her position as daughter in law.

5. Itut Sindur Bapla: It is also a kind of forced marriage. The boy forcefully puts vermillion on the forehead of the girl to marry her.

6. Sanga: *Sanga* indicates the second marriage of a lady. *Sanga* (Second marriage) is also natural in adivasi communities. When a bride marries a widow or a divorced woman then it is called *Sanga*. The wife is called *sangali*. Naturally a *sangali* does not receive social status like other bridegrooms.

7. Kiring Jawai Bapla: It is a rare system of marriage. If unmarried girl becomes pregnant and is unable to disclose the name of the responsible person then it is necessary for the girl and for the coming baby to have a husband and a father respectively for social prestige. In this situation this type of marriage takes place and no one takes it as unnatural.

8. Labour Marriage: If the groom is unable to pay the dowry to the bride then he will have to work as a labour in the house of his father- in- laws, to pay the dowry in the form of labour.[9]

Marriage ceremonies are celebrated with beautiful songs, dances and feast. The different types of marriage clearly indicate the economic and social position of the Adivasi families. Those who are poor and socio-economically weak will follow the type suited for them. The others will follow the prestigious traditional marriage system. But after the marriage all are heartily welcomed to the society. The economic condition does not appear as a criterion of social division.

Child marriage: Most of the Adivasi communities avoid child marriage. A few societies, like Sabar have the tradition of child marriage. In this case the bride lives in her father's house until she enters into the circle of menstruation.

Divorce: Divorce is also there in Adivasi societies. If it is proved that the wife is idle or has an illegal relation with other or unable to give birth then the husband has the right to leave the wife.

Death rituals: Death rituals are almost same of all the Adivasi groups. Generally they burn the dead bodies preparing a beautiful platform (Pyre) by dry wood. The people who die naturally are brunt. The dead bodies of unnatural death are buried. The body of the infectious disease victim, children's dead body is also buried. There are some rituals to keep away the evils from the dead body. It is believed that evil soul can enter into the dead body and will harm the concerned family. At the same time, they also believe in ghost. There are some rituals to put the spirit of the dead person far away from the house. All the Adivasi groups / communities observed a brief period as unholy period and offer cooking food to the spirit of the dead person. After the unholy period, the son and the relatives follow a ritual going to a pond or a riverside to offer cooking food for the last time and to shave their heads in the name of the dead person to pay debt to him.

Religious faith: The Adivasis worship many deities. Bonga Burus is worshipped by the Santal. Another important deity of the Santal is Marang Buru. Sing Bonga or the God of the Sun is also worshipped by the Santals. In the same way the other Adivasis also worship Bonga Burus, Sing Bonga, ChanduBonga (The God of Moon), Serdra Bonga (The goddess of hunting), Goshain Bonga (for brothers welfare), Larha Bonga (Riverbank deity), Banlumai (Forest deity), KundriBonga (River deity), Jaher Era etc.

It should be kept in mind that some deities are thought as positive power and are worshipped for good harvesting or good hunting or good health or good rain etc. On the other hand there are some deities having the negative powers. They are worshipped to keep the society from unexpected dangers or diseases. One of them is the highest God having the supreme power. Others are there for the betterment of the socio-economic condition of the members of the society or the society as a whole along with the betterment of the physical and mental health. From the safe birth of a child to death (natural) he/she is there in his/her society under those powers- positive and negative. They always try to gratify the powers to have better life on earth.

Some Bongas are there also as house deity or family diety. Orak Bonga is called house deity. The function of such Bongas is to keep the house safe from any kind of harm coming from the outside. On the other hand family Bonga is there in adivasi society like Aba Bonga to do the same duty for the family.[10]

One important thing is that they do not care for Brahmin priest. The priest culture is consciously ignored by the Adivasi societies. An elderly person of a society will do the role of priest. He is designated as Naeke. They also use their colloquial language at the time of worship. These two factors are important. The priest culture is nothing but the indication of the abolition of class system of a society. Adivasi societies do not believe in class system in their own society. There is no hierarchy in their society. It is the unique characteristic of primitive society. Not only that, they also use their own language to satisfy their deities. It is also an important matter to be noted. It proves that they do not believe any kind of chauvinistic attitude during the use of language. The other use Sanskrit language as Mantras at the time of worship. That means the other give priority to the Sanskrit language and takes it as pure language. But the Adivasi societies do not believe in this way. They use their own language to satisfy their deities as Mantras and establish a cordial relation with them. This attitude comes from the tradition of nature orientation. They think that there is an interdependent relation between the nature and the adivasi society. So they try to satisfy each and every Bongas to show respect to the relation. They also believe that it is their duty to show respect to the Mother Nature as she offers all kinds of necessary things to live.

Festivals: Festivals are the expressions of identity of a society. The Adivasi societies of West Bengal celebrate different festivals in different seasons in different ways.[11] Different festivals are celebrated keeping focus on the cultivation. Erok Sim, Harian Sim are celebrated at the time of sowing seeds in the field. Janthar and Sahari are celebrated at the time of harvesting (Paush, Dec Jan).

Baha Parab (Festival): It is called flower festival. It is held in the month of Falgun (Feb-Mar). This festival starts on the 12th day of the first half of the month Falgun. This festival is dedicated to Sal tree. In Adivasi culture is treated as holy tree. The festival Stars with a chorus:

> "Akaya Mai so birdisama dah?
> Akayamaidahaoiahoatorepaniori?
> Marangburuchiryahobirdisama dah,
> Jaherowaredahaoiahoatorepaniori."

"Who will look for wilderness? Who will set up the village? Marang Buru will do, Jaher Era Will do."[12]

Soharai Parab: It is said that Soharai is celebrated at the time of harvesting. It is held in the month of Poush (Dec-Jan). This is observed for five days. The first two days are spent to satisfy the various deities and the last three days are there for enjoyment. The members, specially the youth enjoy full liberty in those days to enjoy their lives as they want.[13]

Sakrat Festival: It is celebrated in the last days of the month of push. Each and every family follows some rituals and offer sometimes, pies, and other food items to satisfy Marang Buru. The head of the family offers liquor to Marang Buru and the ancestors.

Magh Festival: Magh festival or Magh Sim is observed in the month of Magh (Jan-Feb) to welcome the New Year. They bid good bye to the old year and at the same tire accept the new one with hope.

Mak Monre Festival: It is observed after every five years in the months of ''Vaishak' or Jaistha' (Apr-Mar) for safety from various kinds of epidemics, famine and natural calamities.[14]

Beside these festivals, there are hunting festival, Nabanna, Gunduli (in the month of Sept/Vadra), worship of Marang Buru, worship of

Thakurani Maa, Karma festival, Dhanan Puja (festival), Goroya Puja (at the time of Kali Puja), Goran Puja etc.[15]

These festivals are common in Adivasi societies. The main aim of these festivals is two-fold. One is to offer prayer to different deities for safety in various aspects of lives including agriculture. The other is enjoyment. Besides these there is a unique feature- i.e. the participation of all villagers. There are no customs to divide the people at the time of participation.

Festivals are the mirror of the culture of the society. The Adivasi festivals are nothing but the expression of social identity like Baha Parab, Soharai Parab, Sakrat festival, Magh festival etc. all the festivals indicate that the culture of Adivasis is monitored by the seasons of West Bengal. Baha Parab, the flower festivals indicates the relations between man and environment. The main aim of the festival is to hand over the traditions for nature care from elder to the younger with a religious flavour. Marang Buru, Jaher-Era are worshipped as the source of wilderness. These festivals clearly show that the adivasi culture is purely based on nature. It is a unique characteristic of the adivasi culture. The Soharai Parab is also nature oriented and season based. It is celebrated at the time of harvesting with a satisfaction and enjoyment. Sakrat festival is also season based. It is the festival of celebrating winter with food and liquor. So it can be said that the culture of the Adivasi is constituted keeping focus on the nature.

Literature: We find rich folk literature in west Bengal. The main elements of these folk literatures are the geographical situation, religious beliefs and cultural influence. Animal tales, fairy tales and tale based on riddle will help us to grasp the rich literature as constituting part of the Adivasi culture. The tales are told only for enjoyment but there also some pictures of their life-style. Keeping focus on Mildred Archer's view it can be said that from the circumstances in which Santal tales are told, it will be obvious that whatever other functions they serve, their primary use is to provide entertainment in a manner that is Santal.[16]

Folk tales are not always only for entertainment they also depict the picture of the life of the Adivasi. There is a long and beautiful story the short history of sabaigrass, an economic material came on earth for the first time. Sometimes folk tales are told to indicate the emergence of diseases. In the folklores the common idea of the tradition is handed down generations after generations. These ideas are preserved either in memory or presented through the practices. Written records have a little to do with them. All the folktales are pregnant with various subject matters. Importance of friendship in life, Act of deception, the concept of rebirth, success or failure of life, influence of Taboo, Taboos of eating, drinking, looking, touching, speaking etc. are the subject matters of these folklores.

The existence of separate soul is one of the religious faiths of the Adivasi culture. They believe that the soul can be separated and can be put in trees or animals or birds or any other matters. The concept of separation of soul and the concept of life-token are also the subject matter of Adivasi literature. It is also believed by the Adivasi communities that there is a little difference between man and animal. Animals are able to speak and feel like human beings. The total belief is based on the attitude of anthropomorphism.

Artistic Skill: The artistic skill of the Adivasi is also an important part of their culture. All the Adivasi communities are habituated in handicrafts. Basketry, Rope making from a special kind of grass (Sabai), Masket making etc. are important artistic skills. In the marriage ceremony along with some other occasion different types of basket are necessary. It is said that there are various types of basketry techniques. Primarily it is divided into two forms- hand woven basketry and sewed basketry.[17]

Today the glory of crafts of the Adivasi is in danger. It is said that the Adivasiartisans have lost their past glory because of the advancement of mechanical civilization. New economy is also responsible for the decoy. Now most of the artesian have left their tradition to fight with the tough situation. Yet some of them are still fighting with their traditional craft and hope that they will be able to bring the glorious past again.

Concluding observations

The Adivasi culture in West Bengal is static in the one side and dynamic in the other side. It is static in this sense that they are trying to keep their identity especially cultural identity as it is. Their cultural life is purely environment oriented or nature oriented. It is also local. It is local in that senses the cultural activities are organized locally. It is said that there is one kind of environmental determinism. This concept entails that the Adivasi cultural is mostly determent by the environment. The ecological influence is one of the important factors of Adivasi culture.

In the life of Adivasi, undoubtedly, the environment has a crucial role to play. The core features of their culture are directly related with the environment. The environment is called relevant environment. The trees, rivers and all the other elements of the environment are called relevant environment. The relevant environment has direct influence on the Adivasi culture. The structure of the society and life-style of the adivasis depend on nature.

The culture of the Adivasi is also influenced by the various cultures of non-adivasis or non-tribal culture. We find clearly the influence of Vaisnavism on Adavasi culture. Today we also find that the Durgapuja is also organized by the Adivasis but they don't bother to take the help of the priests' culture for this purpose. Rather the eldest member of the community takes the role of the priest.

In the adivasi culture we find the liberty of women. It is said by the scholars that the adivasi women enjoy more social prestige then the others. Though women oppression is also there, yet it can be said that the Adivasi women have more social prestige than the other classes. Traditionally women are equal partner of the family. They take part in the work-field as well as in family life.

A cultural clash is there between the Adivasi and the other culture from the very beginning. A cultural chauvinism is always there to establish the other cultures instead of the adivasi culture. The culture of the Christian Missionaries is one of them. In 1863 American Free

Baptist Mission was established in Midnapore. In the next year they established a new branch at Binpur. Binpuris twenty kilometres away from Midnapore. Missionaries were interested to spread the Christian Religion among the Santals.[18]

The impact of Vaisnavism is also remarkable. The famous writer Surendranath Sing observed that centuries after centuries the Hindu culture, specially Vaisnav culture influenced the adivasi culture. He says, "Becides centuries of contacts with Hindus there was the more direct impact of Chaitanya Mahaprabhu and subsequent Vaisnav preachers especially in Tammar and BunduParganas. The memory of the exertion made by the Vaisnava preachers to convert the Mundas is still, preserved in the songs of Binanda Das, one of the converted Mundas in Vaisnavism. Those songs elevated the ideas of pap and punya and uselessness of earthly enjoyment. Even among the converted, Vaisnavism has left its mark on songs and religious festivals. Even in the customs of these Mundas who rejected Hinduism there are clear traces of Hindu influenceobservable in manyof their social ceremonies and religious festivals. Birsa drank deep the springs of Vaisnavaism to its depth."[19]

So, the influence of Vaisnava religion is there in adivasi culture. Most of the Adivasis have Tulsi plant in their house and use to lead a Vaisnava life without leaving their own culture.

The process of Sanskritization or Hinduization is there to mould the attitude of the Adivasis in respect of culture yet they are trying to keep their cultural identity as it was before. This attitude indicates that the Adivasis of West Bengal, perhaps the Adivasis of India are struggling for their existence as a whole. To my view the process of Sanskritization is transformed to Aboriginalization as the Adivasis are accepting the other cultures according to their own way.

There are some crucial features of the Adivasi culture that make it special:

1. The Adivasi culture is static as it wants to preserve the tradition.

2. Their culture is not only for enjoyment, but also for life.

3. It is static as there is an invisible boundary of the culture to keep safe distance from the others.

4. It is also dynamic on the other hand.

5. It is dynamic as it incorporates the outside culture with the process of naturalization instead of sanscritization.

6. The Adivasis follow the eco-cultural attitude.

7. The Adivasi culture has a process to assimilate the others culture according to their own traditions. It may be designated as aboriginalization of others culture.

Endnotes

[1] Bandopadhaya Sumahan, *Prasanga Adivasi* (Kolkata: Offbeat publishing, 2014), 20.

[2] Ibid.

[3] Cf. Bhowmic Suhrid Kumar, *Arya Rahasya* (Manfakira, 2013), 16.

[4] Cf. Ibid, 17 (Vedic Age, 120).

[5] BaskeyDhirendranath, *The Tribes of West Bengal* (Kolkata: Subarnarekha,2002), 6.

[6] Ibid.

[7] Ibid.

[8] Roy Pranab and Binod Shankar Das(Ed): *Medinipur, Itihas O sanskritirVibartan*, (Kolkata:Sahityaloke, 2002) , 382.

[9] Baskey Dhirendranath: *The Tribes of West Bengal* (Kolkata: Subarnarekha, 2002), 6.

[10] Ibid., 200-201.

[11] Ibid., 213.

[12] Ibid., 214.

[13] Ibid., 216.

[14] Ibid., 218.

[15] Ibid.

[16] Mildred Archer: *The Folk Tale in Santal Society*, Man in India, Vol.XXIV,35-26.

[17] Roy Pranab and Bino0dshankar Das(Ed): *Medinipur, Itihas O sanskritirVibartan*, Sahityaloke, Kolkata,2002,361.

[18] Ibid, 518.

[19] Singha Surendranath, *Life and Times of Birsa Bhagwan*, 72-74. Cf. JharkhandeMahaprabhu: Suhrid Kumar Bhowmik, *Adivasi Adhyusita Jharikhand Anchale Sri Sri Chaitanyadever Agamaner Itihas O Falashruti*, (Manfakira, 2014), 70-71.

Indigenous Culture of the Zeliangrong Nagas through Orality

Mr. James H. K.

Traditions and cultures have been to any given society. In fact, there is no society without its own unique cultures and traditions. But how do these culture and tradition come about, in the first place? Tracing the origin of it all, it would lead us back to the Indigenous practices, particularly which were handed down over the generations through the 'word of mouth' - the oral tradition. Many of the values, beliefs, behavior, life-styles and material objects which constitute people's way of life were clothed in the oral tradition. And this orality has been with the people since time immemorial. Had this not been the case, I dare say, the indigenous cultures of the people would have been bare and lifeless. Starting from how the ancient tribes chose to sow the seed: the season, the month and the time to which herbal to chew or to mesh and apply on the fresh wounds in the forest while at work, it was all told and instructed to them through this word of mouth. There was no book with them and no prescriptions. They just knew and led their lives harmoniously. It is in this context, this paper is making an attempt to present how the Zeme, Liangmai and Rongmei, conglomerated as Zeliangrong Naga tribes accumulated their presently practicing indigenous cultures from orality. The rich heritage and traditional and cultural values that came to them clothed in the wisdom of the old. It will try to enfold the living and vibrant cultures that these people had obtained through this beautiful orality.

Brief Introspection on the History of Zeliangrong Nagas through Oral tradition

It is widely known among the Zeliangrong that they come from a common ancestors and it has been pointed out that the origin of how the Zeliangrong people came into their present states of dwelling are based on two basic premises: one is essentially mythological, and it describes the supernatural origin of mankind. The other premise describes the Philological, Anthropological and Historical details pointing out of the Zeliangrong people moving to their present inhabitances through the ages. Basing on the first premise, it must be pointed out that the Zeliangrong people believe that they came from a cave called 'Taobhei' which was pushed opened by a bull (Mithun, the Indian bison). This place called was Ramting Kabin, which is somewhere in the region of Makhel (also called Makhiang) in north (Mao area) of present Manipur state. This is also a place of origin shared among many Naga tribes through myths and legends. This was where, they believe, mankind started to take its origin. The first parents from this cave to generate mankind were named as 'Puakrei' and 'Dichalu'. The literal meaning of these names in translation would be 'Puak' means born/emerge and 'Rei' means first. Putting them together would mean 'Firstborn' for the former who was the man; and 'Di' means world/mother earth and 'Cha' means favourable. Putting the two terms would mean 'favourable-world'. The last syllable in the woman's name 'lu' simply means woman/girl which is a traditional practice among the tribes even today to differentiate the name from boy's/man's name. In this regard, 'pou' is usually used as the last syllable in the name of a man/boy. From them, there were three sons. These sons as they grew took different routes for their own settlements: in the river Basins – the Zeme tribe, in the North- the Liangmai tribe in the South, and in the West- the Nruangmei or Rongmei tribe taking the name of the tribe to the geographical locations of their inhabitations. This is how they are inhabited in the three states of India: Assam, Manipur and Nagaland.

It must be pointed out that it is also believed and shared among the Zeliangrong Nagas that from this Makhel, they moved to places such as Ramting Kabin, Chawang Phungning or Guang Phungning before they finally moved to Makuilongdi (also Nkuilongdi), which is the last of the Zeliangrong place as one tribe (Zeliangrong) and also perhaps, the first place where real civilization began for the tribe. It is told through the word of mouth that as many as 7777 (seven thousand seven hundred and seventy seven) households existed here before the final dispersal, as settled in the present day locations.

Basing on the second premise i.e. the Philological, Anthropological and Historical details it is pointed out that the Zeliangrong people moved to their present inhabitance through the ages from South-Western China and the Tibetan Plateau as their possible original home. These geographical origins have been identified based on a number of factors, such as language affiliation, physical features, oral history and mythologies, and also other cultural traditions. This is not only for the Zeliangrong Nagas but also for the whole of the Naga tribes of Northeast India. It has been lately reported that archeological research has provided tools for making a comparative analysis of cultural assemblages from the regions in focus. However, the origin is believed by the people.

Exclusive facets of Oral Tradition among the Zeliangrong Nagas: Historical Dimensions

For almost all the ancient tribal communities, it is the oral tradition that furnishes about their origin. For the Naga tribes, it is the same orality which is the store house of knowledge, particularly for information and knowledge about their origin. Likewise, it is through the orality that the Zeliangrong people come to know of how and wherefrom they believe to have come. The stories shared among the Naga tribes about Khezakeno, Makhel or Chungliyimti about their origins is also akin to the story shared among Zeliangrong people about 'Taobhei' in Ramting Kabin which is just as good as any written record of history about the great World Wars the world has witnessed. From this orality, Zeliangrong people are emancipated from the crudest obscurity about their origin and have come to be as they are proven by the word of mouth and 'wisdom of the old'. Even if it requires that more of Archeological findings and physical excavations are yet to confirm for the concrete establishment of absolute truth, the word of mouth, as believed in by these people is self-evidently sufficient for one reason. The folksongs which are composed and sang from olden time about the origin mentioning this name are a proof for the people of our generation today.

Cycle of the Year told through Orality

January (Rih Ngai Buh) has the occasion of Naptiang Lingmei (symbolic plantation of Rice plant) which is the New Year month of the year. February (Nah Nuc Buh) has Nap Chah Puanmei which is the occasion of baptismal ritual of the children born between the previous year's ritual. March (Lao Kei Buh) has Langcthu (cotton seeds) covered in Siangnui (Wild Leaves) is buried at Raengbang (village gate) to invoke for the good seeds to be sown in the year. April (Lao Phundun Buh) has laophunmei which is seeds sowing in the fields. May (Maliang Buh) has Napkaomei ritual where gudui (ginger juice) and sarou taam (meat chutney) is taken by the whole community. Here weeding starts in the fields. June (Tunh Ngai Buh) comes with pupha dai or Khangchw Kailw (Common Dormitory) has cleansing ceremony and clearance of water sources of the community. July (Naptu Buh) has Maza ngaih (ritual for good harvest) where thungu taam (Bamboo chutney) is served in the community and clearance of the field roads is done. August (Lao Nduang Tai Buh) and observe Napthan Ngai (First harvest ritual) is celebrated and Napkaomei (Ritual of rich harvest) ritual is held and harvest begins. September (Lao Daitai Buh) goes with the heavy harvest and every day of harvest season is celebration. October (Buh Lei) has Duang Zaomei which is 'watch of the barns' of the community by the elders of the village wherein usually three to four families whose harvest are most offer pigs to feed the community to celebrate. November (Lao Namc Buh) comes with the Pumthan Ngai which is cleansing of body and soul. Feast is held and Rih Lamc is performed in the village which means 'victory dance'. Finally the year ends with December (Ngaan Buh) wherein Ngaan Ngaih – Harvest Festival is celebrated by climbing up to particulars hills to have dances and songs competition for the youth of the community.

Religious Outlook through Oral Tradition

Tingwang or Tingkao Ragwang or Heraka is the Indigenous religion of the Zeliangrong Nagas. In the present day, younger people who are not of this Faith lamely call these people as 'Zouzangmei' which simply means 'wine-drinkers'. It is because of the syllabic terms: 'Zou' means 'wine' and 'Zangmei' means 'drinkers'. It is called thus for wine- 'Rice-beer' finds space in every events and episodes in the life of these people of 'Tingkao Ragwang'. However, this faith was practiced, perhaps, by each of these people in the ancient time before the onslaught of Christianity in the region. For any of the religious matters, the belief in the Faith was the supreme. These people believed in the spirits and nature and worshipped them. In fact, many of the natural objects were revered by the practice of this Faith. Unnatural sickness happening to a person or untoward accident of a person would be helped invoking the nature and spirits with sacrifices offered, and administered by an elderly of the Faith of the village. Mention may be made of at least one such instance. If a person suffers from an unknown sickness (unknown to the community), an elder is called who comes to anoint the sick and perform the ritual by killing a cock (usually white in colour) or a piglet. He would sprinkle the blood and would then examine the internals of the said kill to possibly unearth what internals of the sick person could have gone wrong. Then the kill is offered at a spot fixed by the village in the age-old practice as a place of sacrifices by leaving it there for the spirits to come and have their due share of the offering and set the sick free. Such teachings and practices are handed to these people through orality.

Cultural Perspective through Oral Tradition

If the Zeliangrong Nagas are known for the riches of their cultural heritage it is because the orality of these people has been richer. Yes, they have amazing cultural dresses and adorable traditional attires which are often the remarks of the outsiders who come to see for the first time. The orality of Hornbill gifting the girl in the story and also women folk weaving shawls and other clothes taking designs, shapes and colours from the small bird, Nectar-hunter (name not exact in English)- 'Tiangduina' in Rongmei, shared among the people and handed down to the present generation. For sure, Hornbill is revered by all the Naga tribes. Some of the dances these people perform on bigger occasions are 'Raengc lamh' and 'Khuaiguna Lamh' besides numerous other dance forms. These two dances come from emulate 'Raengc'- the Hornbill bird for its grand build and structure; and 'Khuaiguna'- the Honey bee for its uniformity and organization in life, which is also known to the Zeliangrong Nagas as peaceful providers. These stories and observations through orality have made the cultural heritage of the people beautifully rich; and this richness binds them abound for all to see through orality.

Traditional Norms and Oral Tradition

Oral tradition of the Zeliangrong Nagas says that if it is a day of prohibition, with the announcement made by the elders of the village shouting from the village platform or podium, and that no one should go to work, every one shuts off to stay in the village the whole day till the time lapses. They do not cross the gate of the village- 'Raengbangh'. In case of anyone violating the prohibition of the village, nature takes its own course for punitive actions. A story is narrated about a man who was only overly work conscious that he went ahead to harvest his fields on one of such days, he was shown an ear as big as an ear of an elephant. He was also shown a tooth as big as a spade/hoe right in his face. He couldn't take to see such a phenomenon and passed away after instructing his survivors never to violet 'Nuh we, Neih ye'(Nuh means ear and Neih means tooth). So, elders in the villages tell the young to stick to the traditional norms of the community. It is also said of the wisdom shared among these people not to stitch at night (after sun set). No one from the community does this job at this time. Now, there is a scientific reason along with this prohibition. And that is, needle is indeed a small pin with a small head. Using it with precision in the night would require such a strenuous exercise of the eyes; and would spoil the eyes in such fashion. Moreover, the people in the earlier days had no electricity, lamps or lanterns. The only source of light is the hearth in the kitchen. Such orality about the traditional norms and practices are handed down from generation to generation.

Social Ado's and Education Inclinations

For whatever happens in the social milieu of the Zeliagrong Nagas, oral tradition again is the prime source of instruction and means to follow. They have 'Khangchw-Kailw', 'Hangseuki-Leuseuki' or 'Khangchiu-Luchu'- the morung of the village communities. This served them as a social institutions where all the matters regarding the cycle of work, the cultural and traditional practices, the art of making the handicrafts, hunting, weaving, songs and dances are taught through sharing of the knowledge on first hand basis by the senior ones in the dormitory. This played a great role in developing the community. It is not only the learning place where both young and old people are taught the ways of living, their rights, family planning, education, self-employment, health care and civic awareness. This system played a very important role in the socio-cultural life of the Zeliangrong Nagas without which they could not have thought of celebrating any festival to say in the least. The cycle of work, particularly being agrarian based society and without the help of the yearly calendar we have today, these people solely depended upon the lunar signs for the various cycle of cultivation. And the knowledge regarding this was paramountly vital to be taught. This is sorted out by the rich oral tradition the Zeliangrong Nagas have.

Administrative Orientation

As we have pointed out above that 'wisdom of the old' is revered and respected. This wisdom from the older folks in the villages was of supreme command. In order to make up to be the command of the commands, there used to be village council similar to that of the present village development blocks (VDBs) in and around present state of Nagaland. This body would be headed by the chief or chairman known as 'Gwangpuc' who is also by general consensus, the wisest and most respected of them all. He would also be a person of wealth and often times from the clan of the first to arrive in the village for establishment. This head is aided by other people of the older generation and well known in the village as his accomplices. They make up to head and decide the most important affairs of the community. Besides, the dormitory is also divided into youths and children. These dormitories are headed by a leader who is appointed by the chief of the village from the suggestions or nominative voices of the other elders and young alike. The leaders of the dormitories are also people of pride and prestige who are looked up to and respected. They also form an integral part in the administrative functions of life in the rural communities.

Ceremonial and Festive Promulgations

It is in fact the oral tradition that has stored the guides and functionaries for ceremonies and festivities in the rural life. For any social ceremonies, word of the mouth comes up to lead how the celebration should go about. For marriages, festivals like 'Seed-sowing festival', 'harvesting festival', 'victory festival' 'feast of merit' etc. the Zeliangrong people relied on the orality. The songs to be sung, the dances to be performed and what sort of offerings or invocations, orality has it all for further ado. The songs and dances themselves are the product of orality at this time. The rituals too, have their dependence of the word of mouth. The Zeliangrong Nagas have well celebrated their festivals and other social feats due to the store housing power of the orality.

Conclusion

So much endeared and vitally irreplaceable had been the Oral Tradition of the Zeliangrong in the past. It has come to their world though the spirit that people in the ancient time had and the people in the present age have appeared trivially different. It is through orality that life is governed. All the walks of life can be said to have been grounded and supported by this word of mouth. Whether it be for historical accounts, religious matters, social affairs, administrative grips, traditional and cultural norms and their conduct in society, ceremonial and festive proceedings, or even for the other belief systems prevalent in the society, the Zeliangrong people know and feel deep within that

Orality is as important as breathing air for survival. It would almost be impossible to imagine how these people come to the present state of existence had there been no rich oral tradition amongst them. The attempt to showcase the indigenous culture of the Zeme, Liangmai and Rongmei (Zeliangrong) Nagas has been made based on orality.

References

Primary Sources

Ao, Temsula. *The Ao-Naga Oral Traditions:* Baroda: Pasha Publications, 1999.

Bendangnukshi. *Folktales of the Nagas.* Offset Press, 1998.

Choudhury, B. K. Amalendu. *Tribal Songs of Northeast India.* Calcutta: Firma KLM Pvt. Ltd., 1984.

G., Benjamin. *Makuilongdi: The Great Ancestral Home of the Zeliangrongs.* Imphal: Commemoration Publication Committee, 2006.

Jadav, Kishore. *Folklore and its Motifs in Modern Literature.* New Delhi: Mamas Publications, 1998.

Kamei, Gangmumei. *The History of Zeliangrong Nagas: From Makhel to Rani Gaidinliu.* Guwahati: Spectrum Publications, 2004.

Mills, J.P. *The Ao Nagas.* London: n.p., 1922.

Niumei, Akham Gonmei. et. al. Editors. *Zeliangrong Nagas: A Reflective Discourse.* Educare, 2015.

Patton, Nzanmongi Jasmine. *A Girl Swallowed by a Tree: Lotha Naga Tales Retold.* Kolkata: Adivaani, 2017.

Secondary Sources

Abrams, M.H. *A Glossary of Literary Terms.* 7th Ed. Bangalore: Prism Books, 2003.

Aier, Imo Lanutemjen. *Contemporary Naga Formations and Ethnic Identity.* New Delhi: Akansha Publishing House, 2006.

Bhattacharjee, B., Jayanta. *Cachar Under the British Rule in North East India.* New Delhi: Radiant Publishers, 1977.

...........*Proceedings of North East India History Association.* Shillong: Northeast India History Association, 1990.

Dena, Lal. *History of Modern Manipur (1826-1949).* New Delhi: Orbit Publishers & Distributors, 1991.

Elwin, Verrier. *The Nagas in the Nineteenth Century.* Bombay: Oxford University Press, 1969.

Gangmei, Ragoning. *Expanding Zeliangrong and Federalism: A New Challenge before the People.* Imphal: n.p.

Nienu, V. *Naga Cultural Milieu: An Adaptation to Mountain Ecosystem.* San Francisco: Dorylus Publishing Group, 2015.

Pou, KB Veio. *Literary Cultures of India's Northeast: Naga Writing in English.* Dimapur: Heritage, 2015.

Ringthim, R.K. *Odyssey: A Brief Account of the Zeliangrong Struggle for Freedom and Peace.* Shillong: Printmaster, 2009.

Sanyu, Visier. *A History of Nagas and Nagaland: Dynamics of Oral Tradition in Village Formation.* New Delhi: Commonwealth Publishers, 1996.

Sebastian, AJ. *Critical Essays on Naga Poets of Fiction in English.* Kohima: NU Press, 2016.

Shikhu, Inato Yekheto. *A Re-Discovery and Re-Building of Naga Cultural Values: An Analytical approach with Special reference to Maori as a colonized and minority group of people in New Zealand.* New Delhi: Regency Publications, 2007.

Singh, M Kirti. *Folk Culture of Manipur.* Delhi: Mamas Publications, 1993.

Smith, W.C. *The Ao Naga Tribe of Assam.* London: n. p., 1925.

Relooking the Naga Morung Culture: A Stronghold of Tradition

Mr. Mhonthung Yanthan and Mr. Libemo Kithan

The Nagas consist of 47 tribes who are spread over the current states of India i.e. Nagaland, Manipur, Assam and Arunachal Pradesh and Northwest Myanmar.[1] Linguistically, Nagas belong to Tibeto-Burma[2] group and racially Mongoloid (Tibeto-Chinese) stock.[3] The Nagas were the first ethnic communities in Northeast India who started mobilizing culturally related tribal communities along ethnic lines against the Indian State with the avowed objective of protecting their identity and culture from what they viewed as the onslaught of Indian rule and culture. The Nagas claim that they were one homogeneous ethnic community. During the colonial period, the European anthropologists distinguished the Nagas from other communities based on distinguishable features such as head hunting, common sleeping houses for the unmarried men, dwelling houses built on posts or piles, aversion to milk as an articles of diet, tattooing by pricking, the double cylinder vertical gorge, a large quadrangular or hexagonal shield, residence in hilly regions and crude form of agriculture, betel chewing, absence of any centralized powerful political organization, disposal of the dead on raised platforms, sort of trial marriage and simple weaving clothes.[4]

Earlier all the Naga tribes inhabit a particular territory called 'Village' where any individual Naga is identified with that particular village. The idea of Naga village as 'republic', somewhat akin to Greek city states, is an old one, and one endlessly invoked in both scholarly and popular writings on Naga history and life worlds.[5] Conventional descriptions about traditional Naga polities have been about chiefs and democrats,[6] nobles and commoners,[7] bodies of elders,[8] powerful chiefs[9] and the absence of chiefs,[10] sovereign village states and village republics,[11] extreme egalitarianism,[12] clan rivalries,[13] and, on the whole, represented as a continuum with hereditary autocracy, if not near dictatorship, and radical democracy at its opposite ends, with the Konyak Naga usually associated with the former and the Angami Naga as the most obvious example of the latter.[14] Every village was independent of one another and predominantly run on the principles of democracy, either in the form of a republic or in some case monarchy.[15] However, the free homeland of Nagas, comprises of many 'independent village', which was never conquered by outsiders was just divided along the so called Indo-Burma boundary by the Britishers' under the Treaty of Yandabo in 1826 without the knowledge and consent of the Nagas.[16] Nagas in the year 1929 submitted a memorandum to Simon commission stating their desire to remain independent.[17] This process of various Naga tribes coming together for common political aspiration was describe by G. Kamei as "It is a process of absorption of various tribes into a common generic name "Naga" for the different tribes brought under a single administrative roof and law, accompanied by introduction of English education and Christianity spread by the supporters of the colonial rule".[18] However, this Naga case was refused to be address by the British-India administration and Naga homeland was divided and placed them in two different countries on the eve of latter's departure from the sub-continent. On August 14, 1947 Nagas declared independence yet the declaration was out rightly rejected by the newly formed Indian government and suppressed the wishes and decision of the Nagas violently. On the other hand, to legitimize their claim, the Nagas, under newly formed Naga National Council, conducted a voluntary plebiscite throughout the Naga inhabited area on May 16, 1951 whereby 99.9% of the voters voted for a sovereign independent Naga Nation.[19] Thereafter it was officially intimated to the Government of India (GOI) and UNO but GOI rejected the

Naga political mandate and unleashes her military might to suppress the Naga sovereignty. This Naga movement for independence went on to become one of the oldest and longest movements not only in India but in the entire Southeast Asia.

Morung culture: A Stronghold of Tradition

In Nagaland *Morung* Institution is called differently by different tribes. It is known as *'Ban'* in Konyaks, *Kichuki* in Angami, *Arju* in Ao, *Chumpo* in Lotha, *Apuki* in Sema, *Renshe* in Rengma, *Chethiche*in Chakhesang, *Haku* in Chang, *Pang* in Phom, *Awikhuh* in Pochury, *Khiangyam* in Yimchungru, *Pon* in Khiamniungan, *Herangki* in Zeliang and *Singtang* in Sangtam.[20] Simply known as 'youth dormitories', Morung, under many forms and names, existed in a very wide region of the world extending from the Himalayas and the Formosa in the North to the Australia and New Zealand in the South; and from the eastern Pacific and Marquesas to the west coast of Africa. Thus this social institution is found among diverse races, now classed as distinct, such as Dravidians, Indo-Mongols, Malays, Papuans, Polynesians, Australians and Africans.[21] In Myanmar men's houses occur among the Khamtis and the Karen, and further east the institution is found among the Moi tribes of French Indo-China. In Northeast India men's houses are also found among the Abors, Mikirs, Garos, Lalungs and Lynngams, as well as among most Kuki and Lushai tribes.

The *Morung* or the bachelor dormitory system was an essential part of Naga life. Apart from the family, it was the most important educational set up of the people. In Naga tradition, learning was informal: learning by doing and by imitation. Education was a life-long experience aimed at integrating the young Nagas into society and instilling in their mind in learning the social life of the village/community. The primary centre of learning (education) in Naga society was the *morung* (bachelors' dormitory). The *morung* was pre-dominantly an important educational institution for the boys. In Morung, there exists different category of ranks/order which every boy had to pass until they attained adulthood which is an essential criterion for them to be admitted as full member of the village. In each rank or order, a village boy had to perform some distinctive form of service for the man who belongs in the *morung*. Much of Naga cultures, its customs and tradition have been transmitted from generation to generation through the folk music and dance, folk tales and oral historical traditions, carvings of figures on stones and wood, and designs on clothes. Much of this teaching-learning process took place at the boys and girls dormitories. It was also used as a guard-house during times of war when warriors stayed in it. The *morung* was the core of village institution, through which the material culture of the Nagas is derived. This institution is considered as the mother of art and culture. On account of this importance Anand observes, "The *morung* plays vital role in preparing younger generations for post in the village council. The *morung* is the club, the public school, the military training centre, the hostel for boys and meeting place for village elders. It is as well the centre for social, religious and political activities. In short, it is the fulcrum of the village democracies".[22] *Morung* is a vital organisation of the village life, centre of cultural industry and the headquarters of the village military guards.

Like the boys' dormitory, girls' dormitory was also prevalent in most of the Naga villages, where the girls also stay in the dormitory after attaining puberty till they chose their life partners and start family. During her stay in *morung* she would learn spinning, weaving, embroidery works, stitching, sieving, cooking, rice-brewing etc., from her senior friends. Besides, she would also come to know folklore and dances from senior girls. Apart from this learning, she would get moral lessons of life which include good behaviour, manner, character, morality and ethical code of conduct.

Functions of *Naga Morung*

Defence of the Village

The *morung* tradition forms the core of the Naga village institution. The *morung* boys will not permit his villages to insult them and the dormitory in a pejorative way, and when such situation arises it is a bounden duty of every members of the morung to defend it even at the cost of his life. The *morung* acted as the guardian, a father, a police and the court of the village. In traditional Naga society feuds between villages and tribes often turned into a war between villages. Regular raids and conducting human heads hunting by village against another were very common. During such situation, youth in the dormitory act as village guard. Knowing that the youth were on guard even at night, all the villages could spend the night peacefully without fear. The sound of the drum was meant to alert the villagers to know that there was danger in the village and alert them to seek safety. Thus, the duties of the *morung* boys were directly related to the welfare and safety of the whole village community and they were respected and honoured by all the villagers. *Morung* boys acted as the defence force, always alert with their spears, daos, shields and other weapons which were kept in one corner of the morung. At the same time the *morung* boys also venture out for raids against the enemy of their village.

Institution for Learning Folklore and Oral Historical Traditions

Folklore and oral historical traditions have been more or less the primary means of teaching the history of any tribes and villages. Sitting around the fireside at home with elders and telling stories to a group of children constitute the unique and typical setting of the Naga ways of imparting education to the younger generations. It appears that, in the early days, storytelling at the boys' *morung* was more organized. An elder or priest would come prepared; more-involved stories of the past were recited. Folk tales and oral historical traditions are more inclusive than folk music in their content, and thus cover more extensive areas. Folk stories contain fewer romantic episodes; they tell more about customs and traditions of the past. They also tell about animism (nature or spirit worship), the only religion of the Naga prior until establishing contact with Western missionaries in the mid-nineteenth century. In the absence of any written document, folk tales and oral historical traditions remain the sole links between the past and the present.

Training Centre in Cultural Skills, Arts and Crafts

Another important value of the *morung* was the dignity of labour. In the *morung*, boys and girls were equipped with the knowledge of learning different skills and arts that would help them live a productive life. They are required to work with their hands. Girls were taught knitting and weaving, cooking, moral values and good manners from their seniors. On the other hand, *morung* boys were taught in basket making, wood carvings, stone carvings, agriculture related activities like cutting trees, clearing jungles, making footpaths, sowing seeds, constructing bamboo huts etc., from their seniors. Normal activities at the *morung* were never organized; they were spontaneous and members responded naturally.

Military Training Ground

The philosophy of the *morung* was service and sacrifice. The young men of the *morung* were trained to serve the clan and village and the selfless sacrifice was expected from each and every member by the society. *Morung* serves as a military training ground for the village youths. Skills such as head hunting, conducting raids against enemy and other strategic military skills were imparted by the seniors and elders in the village to the *morung* boys. Animal hunting and fishing skills were also taught in the *morung* by the seniors. Pride and shame are often closely associated in this way of life. It was a great shame to carry a small bundle of firewood and a great shame to return to the village with small catch from fishing and hunting expeditions. It was also a great shame to return to the village with no human heads from military expeditions.

Community Service

Community service is the distinctive characteristic in the *Morung* institution. *Morung* boys carried out some manual jobs in the *village/khel*, such as fetching water, cutting firewood and running errands for the elderly man and women in the village. Whenever there are meetings or community works to be done in the village, the *morung* boys are in the forefront taking the responsible of passing information or messages to the members of the village. They also collect rice from each household when guest are to be entertained by the village. They are responsible for hospitality to be accorded to village guest and also supervise the younger grades to carry out such task. In the event of deaths, if death occurs in other places, the *morung* boys would accompany the death to the final resting place. The *morung* boys also entrusted as news gatherers. According to oral source, they travelled to different places and villages and come back to the village with information. It is their duty to inform the village about the happenings and development taking place outside their village.

Promotion of Cleanness and Discipline

The *morung* continue to dominate the social and cultural life of the traditional life of the Naga village institution. This was the institution where the dignity of labour is taught, refine their culture, rectified the personal shortcomings, and together they build strong society. The *morung* boys not only defended their village but they venture out for raids. The *morung* was the core of village institution, through which the material culture of the Nagas is derived. This institution is considered as the mother of art and culture. On account of this importance Anand observes, "The *morung* plays vital role in preparing younger generations for taking leadership and responsibility in the village's higher institution like village council. The *morung* is the club, the public school, the military training centre, the hostel for boys and meeting place for village elders. It is as well the centre for social, religious and political activities. In short, it is the fulcrum of the village democracies".[23] *Morung* is a vital organisation of the village life, centre of cultural industry and the headquarters of the village military guards.

Decline of Naga *Morung* Culture

However, in spite of such a healthy institution, its influence on the Nagas witnesses a considerable weakening with the advent of Christianity in the land. Critics point out that this new western phenomena came as a sort of invasion at the very core of the Naga social institutions. The extinction of the *morung* institution began with the spread of Christianity in the hills. The Christian missionaries directly attacked the institution by forbidding the Baptist boys to sleep in the *morung,* and they further advocated that the *morung* is a 'heathen institution'.[24] The cultural disconnection caused by conversion to Christianity created an identity crises and cultural alienation among the Nagas. As Abraham Lotha stated, in their attempt to rapidly convert and transform the Nagas "the missionary instilled in the converts a negative attitude towards the Naga culture".[25] The Christian missionary alone were not held responsible for the disintegration of the *morung* but the introduction of modern education in the soil of the Nagas and its impact let to the fall of *morung* in the non-Christian villages. Squeezed between the church with its various programmes and the daily school routine and studies, socialization at the *morung* began to decline. Today, the *morung* as an institution preparing youth for full membership in the village community is almost non-existent in any Naga village. J. P. Mills writes about the fall of the *morung, "Decaying Morung"* means decaying a village and well-kept *"morung"* a vagarious community.

It is in the *morung* that the old men tell of the great deeds of the past, and the coming generation is thought to carry on the old traditions in the future. When the past is no longer glorified in and the future seems dark and uncertain, the *"morung* fall into decay".[26] Again in 1930s J.P. Mills observed:

> 'Of the mistakes made by the mission, the gravest, in my opinion and the one most fraught with danger for the future is their policy of strenuously imposing an alien western culture on their converts. I think I am right in saying that no member of the mission has ever studied the Naga customs deeply, but nearly all have been eager to uproot what they neither understand nor sympathise with and to substitute it for a superficial civilization'.[27]

Morung is in fact the life line of every Naga village. It is equivalent to that of the modern educational institution. However, for the Nagas, *morung* was more than an educational institution, it was a social institution. It was in the *morung* that Nagas not only learnt the cultures, values, norms and warfare tactics of their village but it also provided the structure for the working principles of the village council. Basically, *morung* was instituted in a hierarchical fashion. The eldest group took the responsibility of teaching the younger groups as well as making important decisions. In this way, *morung* provided a system for the best possible governance to the villages, which need to be cherish, and in a way need to revamp and practice by the modern Naga society, if modernity cannot offer any better alternative to the modern Nagas.

Although from where we stand today, it is understandable that we have been convinced that our traditional ways were incongruous with the so called modern ways, introduced by British imperialism, reinforced by American missionary, reinvented by post-independent Indian aspiration and now turned topsy-turvy by the winds of globalisation and liberalisation blowing over us. True, our history, culture, political, economics and our very ways of life were hijacked by irresistible forces of modern history but should we remain prisoners of history forever? We will, if we do not reclaim the entirety of our lives as it was in the past and as it is today and work on it to make it better for future generation of Nagas.

Endnotes

[1] R. Vashum, *Nagas' Right to Self-Determination: An Anthropological Perspective*, (New Delhi: Mittal Publications, 2005).

[2] R. Vashum, *Nagas Right to Self-Determination* (New Delhi: Mittal Publications, 2000), 11.

[3] Chandrika Singh, *Political Evolution of Nagaland*, (New Delhi: Lancers Publishers, 1981), 1.

[4] M. Horam, *Naga Polity* (Delhi: Low Price Publications,1975), 35-41.

[5] Sing Chandrika, *Nagaland Politics: A Critical Account* (New Delhi; Mittal Publications, 2004), 14.

[6] Jacobs, J., A. Macfarlane, S. Harrison, and A. Herle, *The Nagas: Hill Peoples in Northeast India* (London: Thames and Hudson), 1990.

[7] Fürer-Haimendorf, C. Von: "Social and Cultural Change among the Konyak Naga", *Highlander*, 1973, 3-12.

[8] Mills, J.P. *The Ao Nagas* (London: Macmillan, 1926).

[9] Fürer-Haimendorf, C. Von, *The Naked Nagas* (London: Methuen & Co. Ltd, 1939).

[10] Hutton, J.H. *The Sema Nagas* (London: Macmillan, 1921a).

[11] Venuh, N. *British Colonization and Restructuring of Naga Polity* (New Delhi: Mittal Publications), 2005.

[12] Woodthorpe, R.G., "Notes on the Wild Tribes Inhabiting the So-Called Naga Hills on our Northeast Frontier in India" in Elwin, V. (ed.) (1969): *The Nagas in the Nineteenth Century.* (Bombay: Oxford University Press, 1881), 46-82.

[13] Hutton, J.H., *The Angami Nagas: With Some Notes on Neighbouring Tribes* (London: Macmillan, 1921b).

[14] Jelle JP Wouters, "Performing Democracy in Nagaland: Past polities and present Politics", *Economic and Political Weekly*, 2014, 16.

[15] R. Vashum, *Nagas' Right of Self-Determination: An Anthropological-Historical Perspective* (New Delhi: Mittal Publications, 2000).

[16] Raile Rocky, "Tribes and Tribal Studies in North East: Deconstructing the Philosophy of Colonial Methodology", *Journal of Tribal Intellectual Collective India*, Vol.1 Issue 2 No. 2, 2013, 25-37.

[17] V.K. Nhu, *The Naga Chronicle*, Shillong ICSSR, NERC, 2002.

[18] Kamei, G., *Ethnicity and Social Change: An Anthology of Essays* (New Delhi: Akansha, 2008), 72.

[19] V.K.Nhu, *op. cit., 2002.*

[20] A. Nshoga, *Traditional Naga Village System and its Transformation*, Anshah (Publishing House, Delhi, 2009), 78.

[21] N.L. Dongre, *Institution of youth dormitories among tribes of India.* Access on 17/06/2013 from www.nldongre.com/Magzin/72.pdf. 2.

[22] V. K., Anand, *Nagaland in Transition* (New Delhi, 1967), 91-92.

[23] _____*op. cit.*, 1967, 91-92.

[24] J.P.Mills, *The Rengma Nagas* (Guwhati, Spectrum Publication, 1980),49.

[25] Abraham Lotha, *History of Naga Anthropology (1832-1947)*, (Dimapur: Chumpo Museum 2007), 46.

[26] J.P.Mills, *The Rengma Nagas, op. cit.*, p. 49.

[27] _____ *The Ao Nagas* (London: OUP, 1973).

Te-L khukhu, A Festival of Felicity: A Case Study with Special Reference to Viswema Village

Mr. Kelengol Neikha and Mr. Vizapo Kikhi

The Angami tribe is one of the major tribes in Nagaland. John Butler, an early British political agent, described the Angamis as "the most powerful and warlike, also the most enterprising, intelligent, and civilised of all the Naga tribes" (Pieter Steyn, *Zapuphizo: Voice of the Nagas* (Abingdon: Routledge, 2010), 8). The Angami traditional religion is primarily called *"Krünä"* or simply called the indigenous religion. They (Angamis) believe in *"Ukepenuopfü"* which is believed to be the Supreme Being. They also believe in the existence of other spirits but not in terms of worshipping. For the Angamis, all festivals revolve around the cycle of paddy cultivation. Therefore, many festivals are celebrated all year round to express accomplishment and rejuvenate themselves from the whole year agricultural activities. One such festival is *Te-l khukhu* which is especially celebrated by the Viswema village. Viswema is the third biggest village in Asia which is situated in the Southern part of the Angami region and is about 22 km away from the capital city of Nagaland. *Te-l khukhu* is a festival of sharing food and exchanging food which acts as a strong element of social contract in the olden days enjoyed by old and young alike.

The study focuses on three core objectives: 1) To unveil the festival, 2) To bring into light the essence of the festival, 3) To examine the continuity of *tel-khukhu* in the present society. This paper is an attempt to unveil the age old festival with the intention to expose the essence and the rich social composite values to the modern society.

Tel-khukhu: A Festival of Felicity

Te-l khukhu is an important festival for the Angamis and is colourfully celebrated in modern Viswema village. This festival is a festival of the damsels. It falls somewhere in the month of July or August, at the end of sowing the paddy fields. The festival is named as '*te-l*' which means toad and '*khukhu*', to share. Therefore, '*te-l khukhu*' means "toad's share." The origin of *te-l khukhu* cannot be ascertained. However, there are two legends which are orally circulated among the Angami community. The first one suggest that at the beginning of time, a man, a mouse and a toad who were bosom friends found rice which they distributed among themselves. But the mouse finding it difficult to transport his share, requested the man that she may be allowed to eat in the corner of his field. The toad refused to take any rice but prayed to the man that some rice be offered in its name once a year, hence the festival of giving the toad its rice. In another legend it is said that, one day a lady saw fully ripped *Othsü bo* (millet plant) in the middle of a pond. Seeing the plant, the lady asked a squirrel to pluck an ear for her but the squirrel did not return. Then the lady sent a parrot but the bird instead started eating the millet and never returned. Finally, the lady sent the toad for the same favor. The toad felt greatly honoured and brought her an ear of millet. The lady gratefully received the ear and told the toad that she would give a portion of her millet harvest. Thus, *te-l khukhu* is celebrated every year in Viswema during *chünyi* (end of July or the first part of August) season.

Prior to the festival, men folk would go for hunting, fishing and collect carpenter's worm particularly from oak trees whereas the women grind millet and catch snails from the paddy fields for the festival. *Te-l khukhu* is observed with strict rituals and the girls are not allowed to do any household chores apart from taking bath. The food to be distributed to the damsels on *te-l khukhu* morning is cooked the night before or early in the morning. To this day, millet is a very important component in the preparation for this feast. The food is distributed preferably in a big papal leaf, sycamore leaf or banana leaf which will be rolled into cone shape and pinned with small bamboo pieces. The serving includes a handful of millet and rice, meat, snail and other delicacies depending on the availability.

Traditionally, the food that is cooked for the rituals is not allowed to be served before the first damsel performs the rituals in the household. During this festival, the mother of the household performs a special rice giving ceremony by offering a little rice wrapped in the plantain leaf saying; "take your share, toad" and places it somewhere underneath the bed. It is also said that the first damsel invited to perform the rituals on arrival, receives a serving and drops a morsel of rice along with some meat twice near the hearth and taste the food. Then she leaves the household heading for the other houses where she is invited to collect her *khukhu* (food distributed from the leaf). Once the ritual is performed the damsels gather at the decorated *chokrwu* (eaves at the entrance of a house) wearing brand new dresses and have their *"khukhu"* together. The *chokrwu* is decorated with some wild flowers like *khwüso pü* (ginger lily flower), *phakü pü* (rock butterfly lily flower), wild orchids and tender maize. The flowers are orderly arranged on the eaves and the roof openings including the *"ki kä"* (house horn). A single wooden ladder (better known as *osozho* in Viswema) with a V-shape at the base is used to climb the *chokrwu*. Usually, the damsels eat their meals together in *chokrwu,* sing and make merry. During the day, they also visit their friend's *chokrwu* and also visit prominent places. In the evening, the *chokrwus* are flooded with songs and laughter.

The festival is believed to be for girls only. Therefore, boys are not permitted to take the ritual food so they are given the *kobjo khukhu.* *Kobjo khukhu* means frogs' share. This is just to make an excuse to let the men folk eat the ritual food prepared for the girls so that the boys can also enjoy the special food prepared in their household. The boys are neither allowed to climb nor go near the *chokrwu* on the day of *te-l khukhu.* It is believed that on the day of *te-l khukhu,* if the damsels throw snail cones on them or accidentally fall on them, they will permanently remain a failure in hunting and also will never be able to compete with their contemporaries in future for any task.

Unlike other festivals of the Angamis, this festival holds a special emphasis on the women folk as most of the activities are performed and involves them. This festival gives higher platform to the women to break through the walls of conservative lifestyle. On this special event the women folk are given special privilege to wear brand new cloths and enjoy special delicacies with their peer mates. It also ignites the creativity of the women folk by way of decorating *chokrwu* with wild flowers and decorative items available locally. As far as the women folk are concerned, the beauty of celebrating this festival is that it gives the women folk full privilege to celebrate the day and make merry giving them a higher platform to cherish and celebrate their womanhood.

Since this festival is a festival of felicity, every household brings the best delicacies and distribute to their near and dear ones, thereby ushering love, peace and joy in the community. Further, exchanging food during the festival bridges the gap of unfavourable contingencies arising among the individuals and families.

Nevertheless, with the coming of modernisation, the closely knitted fabric of the community is fading away. Therefore, rejuvenating this festival would enhance the calibre of the festival bringing out the best possible results to fill the gap in the community. Some years back, the magnitude of this festival has been dropped down, but realising the importance and the benefits of the festival, the civic bodies have taken up its course of action to revive this festival. The civic bodies have also organised *tel-khukhu* as a part of their annual activity and distribute food to the girl child and conduct competition on the best *chokrwu* based on decorum and creativity. Thereby, the village community can take up the initiatives to organise the festival in a more grandeur and honed this festival to a greater height.

While enriching the community life by celebrating this festival, the village community also invites guests to uplift the spirit of this festival. In the past years many distinguished personalities were also invited to grace the celebration of *tel-khukhu*. Thus the festival of *tel-khukhu* was celebrated colourfully adding more flavour and meaning to the ethos of the festival even by the others.

Though the rituals of *tel-khukhu* have shrunk down in the present day, everyone in the village celebrates this festival colourfully and cheerfully, thus preserving the rich values and the essence of the festival. However, with the intervention of modern technologies and gadgets we are driven towards the fallacies of this world. Thereby the authenticity of the values and customs are been diluted making the younger generation perplex with their own culture leading to cultural crisis. The festival itself is vibrant and robust in its nature contributing richly towards the social bonding of the community. Therefore, uplifting the festival in this present society is a source of power-packed to the individual and society at large.

In the process of this research, it has been found that the impact of this festival is an emerging element for unifying the community. Although, special emphasis has been given to the women folk on this festival, the male counterpart too plays a dynamic role in making this event joyful and memorable. It is also found that, this festival gives more weightage to the women folk to break through the walls of conservative lifestyle and showcasing their innate abilities and creativity thereby emulating the traits of the festival to the younger siblings. Similarly, it enriches the women folk to cherish and celebrate their womanhood. Sharing food to their near and dear ones illuminates the social fabric and eliminates several misunderstanding that divides the families and the neighbourhood.

The status of women is raised through celebrating *tel-khukhu*. It teaches boys and men to respect and honor girls and women. It also showcases the beauty and grace of the fairer sex. It is a great source of socialisation of girls among their peers. On the whole; celebration of *tel-khukhu* and its talent functions enriches the community life.

References

Changkiri, Atola L. *The Angami Nagas and the British*. Guwahati: Delhi Spectrum Publications, 1999.

Epao, Vepari. *From Animism to Christianity*. Dimapur: Hindustan Print O- Print, 1998. 2nd edition.

Hutton, John. H. *The Angami Nagas*. London: Oxford University Press, 1969.

Kharütso, Nokhwenu. "The Angami at the Crossroads." In *Family and Clan in North East India: Reflections by Christian Scholars*. Edited by Alphonsus D'Souza, Lalnghakthuami and Pangernungba Kichu. (Guwahati: North Eastern Social Research Centre, 2015), 34-50.

Linyü, Keviyiekelie. *The Angami Church since 1950*. Kohima: Khedi Printing Press, 1983.

Nagi, Khrieno. "Traditional Values and Practices: Their Relevance in the Naga Culture Today." In *Perspectives*. Edited by Sanyü Iralu, Rümatho Nyusou and Shürhisieü Meyase. Kohima: Shalom Publication, 2014.

Steyn, Pieter. *Zapuphizo: Voice of the Nagas*. Abingdon: Routledge, 2010.

Suri, Rinu. *The Angami Nagas*. New Delhi: Mittal Publication, 2006.

Viswema Students' Union, Golden Jubilee, *Souvenir* (December, 2013).

Valedictory Address
From Cultures of Peace
to a Culture of Peace

Dr. Fr. C. P. Anto

It is said that people without the knowledge of their past history, origin and culture is like a tree without roots. So, the same way I personally congratulate and appreciate seminar coordinators for choosing the apt topic for the national seminar. The main objective of this paper is to visualize critically how can the sub cultures of peace can contribute in creating a new inclusive culture called a global culture of peace. Since you have taken a phenomenological approach (a subjective experience) in understanding the celebration of cultures in Northeast India, I would like to start with my own story, which took place around twenty-eight years ago.

In 1990, one of my best friends Bro. James Sangtam, took me to his home village Philingeru village under Kiphire district. The day we reached, it was already getting dark and had a community meal together with all denominations and community members of the village. I personally expected we will have dinner in the Naga traditional wooden stand plate, in Sema they call it *Asuku*, in Ao *Sungphu, youyunpou*, in Phom *Lakoh nungshung*, in Lotha *Chokung*, etc., but we ate in the bigger plate than the expected. We eat in a biggest plate possible, it was five meters long and one-meter breadth, a bamboo table. Thus, the first meal was served with lots of local delicacy the *Akhuni, Bastanga*, worms and even a few pieces of dog meat. We also noticed the village houses were built very close to each other, what is spoken in the one house could easily heard in the other house. These houses were never locked during the day time.

We learned a new culture of honesty, simplicity and hardworking mentality of elders. We also observed their sincerity, hospitality, sociability, contentment as individuals and communities, a strong sense of obedience to the elders and community feeling also was a commendable value. Having stayed with the village community more than ten days, personally I felt that they have a lot to teach and we have lots learn from each other's culture. From that day onwards, my mental programming of culture has been changed and my brain has been rewired. My brain started rewiring and rewriting new script to locate myself in the Naga social matrix. In Nagaland we sixteen major tribes and around twenty-four different dialects people speak in the state. We also observe here the subcultures (different tribal cultures) of Nagaland is brought together under an umbrella culture called Hornbill Peace Festival or HORNBILL CULTURAL FESTIVAL, celebrated in the first week of December every year.

Then coming to the cultures of Northeast India, the festivals are very dear to all the communities and tribes in the region. For Ahomias is *Bihu*, Mizos *Chapchar kut*, Arunachalis *Monpa,* Manipuri's Yaoshang, for Nagas its still different: Aos *Moatsu*, Angamis *Sekrenyi,* Konyak *Aoleang*, Lothas *Tokhu Emong*, Phoms *Monyu* etc., In this region there are around two hundred tribes, spoken two hundred twenty different dialects and the people belong to mainly three races. My many years of experience in the region prompts me to say it is a paradise on Earth. I don't see such a variety of cultures and traditions in any part of the country or doubt in the world. Many subcultures can form in to the culture of peace. As Hornbill festival is the festival of festivals in Nagaland. Can we not dream to have a new culture or festival which can bring all the cultures in to one umbrella? I would like to call it a RAINBOW CULTURAL FESTIVAL. It can be the festival of festivals of the region or the Rainbow Festival of Peace in Northeast India.

Then India is a cradle of many religions, spirituality, civilizations, cultures and traditions. Thus, Mark Twain calls India the mother of history, grandmother of legends and great grandmother of traditions and cultures. India has twenty-two major languages and seven hundred twenty dialects, six hundred twenty-five tribes and has six main types of races. Therefore, my question here is diversity or the incredible differences among the communities in Northeast India or in India asset or liability? For, me these diversities, is an asset rather than a liability.

A few months back, I had travelled to Ireland to study its tradition and culture. One day while on a sightseeing city tour, a lady initiated a conversation with me. Having introduced to each other, she started to speak about education system in her country. She said, that she is coming from a country where all our children learn in a happy environment. Then, immediately I asked her, are you from Denmark or Finland? Because these countries have the best education system in the world. She said, that she is from Denmark. What makes the Danish system a happy environment is that they have developed a new culture of questioning and constant training? A culture of questioning develops the subculture and then to develop in to a new culture.

Continuing the conversation, she then turned to ask me about the Indian education system. I made it very simple. Our children learn different methods mainly most of the things are taught in traditional method and they often struggle to learn. At times I think, "In Indian educational system, I am afraid whether we teach the elephant to fly." Indian cultures have lots of positive and negative aspects. We have too much of respect, reverence for our teachers and elders thus our students don't ask questions. If then, what is the possibility of creating 'happy environment and questioning culture' in the state, region and the country as a new culture? I think we need to build our educational institutions, organizations and communities which should be built on the scientific and universal human rights principles, values and practices.

Let me also share my experiences of having travelling another country in Africa. A couple of years back I visited Rwanda, after the genocide in 1994. As many as 800000 to 1000000 peoples were killed within a matter of 80 days in a war between Tutsis and Hutus. After the genocide the Church initiated empowering and educating women. As a result of reconstructing that war-torn country, Rwanda topped among the countries in the world for electing the highest number of women parliamentarians. The elected women comprised 67% which declined to 53.2%, recently. The second is Cuba with 52% women parliamentarians. A new subculture is borne by the rise of empowered women from the ruins of war devastated country. This has relevance to Naga society, here, also. I said this because in our Naga traditional cultures the women bear the maximum impacts of 60 years old violent conflicts. Unfortunately, they still continue to struggle for their active participations in decision making bodies that directly affect their lives and wellbeing. We don't have even a woman member in the Nagaland assembly. The time has come to move from subculture to develop a new of empowering culture for women.

Today, universities and organisations abroad have changed their approaches. Being an Advisory Board member at the International Institute of Peace Education (IIPE) in New York, USI observe that having women in the board help taking better decisions, some studies show that Governing board or advisory boards comprising of both genders perform 15% better than the boards' mainly one gender. Studies also show that boards comprising of different cultures perform 35% better than the boards of same culture. Study also shows that cultural diversity increases problem solving ability and it increases creativity and innovations. The real challenge here is to make people being able to communicate, well. We do it through cultural differences rather than commonalities. What I would like to ask you, therefore, what is culture, after all? Culture is a notoriously difficult term to define. It's a fuzzy concept. There are a lot of difficulties in defining culture. An American Anthropologist, Kroeber critically reviewed concepts and definitions of culture, and compiled together and brought out in gist form. Culture, according to Kroeber, is the collective programming of the minds which distinguishes the members of one group or category of people from another.' Another author, Hofstede, looks at culture as the traditions and customs that govern behaviour and beliefs that are transmitted through generations by ways of social interactions and learning. Julien Bourrelle, defines culture as mental programming and it tells us the good behaviour and bad behaviours or wanted or unwanted behaviours, what we should do and what we should not do.

There are three ways to connect or relate with people in culture. **Confront:** When you confront you believe that your behaviours are the right behaviour. **Complain:** When you complain you isolate yourself from others and society will segregate you. **Conform:** when you adapt your way to behave to conform to whole society: then you can truly benefit from diversity. It means you are observing and learning and adapting yourself to the situation. Thus, if we are able to stand ourselves into other's shoes, I believe, we can understand values beyond cultures and we can understand them better and we can accept them and respect what they stand for and where they come from and where they are heading to...

Antonio Gramsci, an Italian writer, politician and political theorist, who is a founding member and onetime leader of the Communist Party of Italy said that the *old is dying and the new cannot be born*. Why the new cannot be born? The dilemma and crisis we are faced with today are so intense and thus it's so difficult to bring a new culture. What is the biggest problem that people face in the world? Its lack of love. And what do the people long to have it but very difficult to get it? Its peace. Here we speak about the culture of values and it is so difficult to be born. In this context Antonio said, that old is dying and the new cannot be born. Here, what I think a culture based on the universal principles, values and traditions very difficult.

On the other hand, everyday a new culture is being born. We experienced in the early 18th century the industrial revolution and the discovery of steam engine brought a new culture of workmanship. Then after 100 years came the second revolution, the invention of bulb and electricity brought another culture to work over night and increased the production. Then after 50 years came the revolution of computers brought another culture a culture of perfection and speed. Then after a decade came the fourth revolution, a new culture also was born with it, namely digitalization. The whole life has been digitalized and now we have a new culture called digital culture. Undoubtedly we can say that these were the result of a questioning culture. As a result, we have today, artificial intelligence, Machine learning, cloud computing, and 3D printing recently someone was speaking about 4D printing. There will be reduced demand of skilled labourers in the days to come. In the process of setting the new trend in building a culture we need speed, efficiency and commitment.

Thus, there is a dilemma today, whether we need our culture and education system should be technology induced or driven method or we need to go back to education system with values and principle based. In this context, is it possible to build a new world order, a global culture, a new transcended life of culture?   Dr. Martin Luther King Jr. said, "If we are to have peace on earth, our loyalties must transcend our race, our tribe, our class, and our nation; this means we must develop a world perspective." A new world order, where we all love, respect and uphold the dignity of life of all, this culture can be called the culture of *"vasudhaiva kutumbakam"* the whole world is a family. A common culture where we all be belonged, cared, connected and reared without any discrimination and judgemental.

To achieve this culture we need to be transcend and transformed persons, we need to move from the present culture of violence in to a new culture of peace. Transforming the culture of violence and conflicts in to culture of peace and harmony. This transition is possible when we move from the culture of authoritarianism to democratic participation, control of information to transparency, competition to cooperation, misunderstanding to mutual understanding, tolerance or solidarity, exploitation to respect human rights and dignity, control of resources to sustainable development, domination to equality and lastly, education to education of culture of peace, nonviolent communication and inner peace.

Let me conclude here, by quoting the United Nations understanding of creating this new global culture called "culture of peace", it is a "set of values, attitudes, modes of behaviour and ways of life that reject violence and prevent violent conflicts by tackling their root causes to solve problems through dialogue and negotiation among individuals, groups and nations." Thus UN encourages us to take a pledge to promote this culture of peace that "in my daily life, in my family, my work, my community, my country and my region: Respect the life and dignity of each human being without discrimination or prejudice; Practise active nonviolence, rejecting violence in all its forms: physical, sexual, psychological, economic and social, in particular towards the most deprived and vulnerable such as children and adolescents; Share my time and material resources in a spirit of generosity to put an end to exclusion, injustice and political and economic oppression; Defend freedom of expression and cultural diversity, giving preference always to dialogue and listening without engaging in fanaticism, defamation and the rejection of others; Promote consumer behaviour that is responsible and development practices that respect all forms of life and preserve the balance of nature on the planet; Contribute to the development of my community, with the full participation of women and respect for democratic principles, in order to create together new forms of solidarity."

The peace channel a youth peace movement of third millennium is striving to build this new global culture of peace by transforming the culture of violence in to culture of peace by peace education in the communities and educational institutions. We are working towards making Nagaland and Northeast India a model state and a region for the culture of peace by 2030. Let me wind up by quoting, Alvin Tofler, "The illiterate of the 21st century will not be those who cannot read and write, but those who cannot learn, unlearn and relearn".

References

Ao, A. L. "Traditonal Self Governing Institutions Among the Hill Tribal Population Groups of Nagaland." In A. Goswami, *Traditonal Self Governing Institutions Among The Hill Tribes Of North-East India* (Guwahati: OKDISCD, 2002), 102-114.

Dobashis, K. C. *Traditonal Method Conflict Resoltuion among the Angami.* (B. D. Killinger, Interviewer) Kohima, Nagaland, India. (2013, November).

FGD, K. v. *Traditonal Method of Conflict resoltion among the Angamis.* (B. D. killnger, Interviewer) Kohima, Nagaland, India. (2013, November).

FGD, Z. *Traditonal Method of Conflict Resoltuion among the Angami.* (B. D. Killinger, Interviewer) Zakhama, Nagaland, India. (2013, May).

Imkongmeren. "Indigenous Models for Peace Building in The Naga Polity." In Y. V. James, *Peacemaking in North East India: Social and Theological Exploration*, 1st ed., Vols. Triba Study Series, No. 21, pp. 125-149, (Jorhat: Tribal Study Centre, 2012).

Manchanda, R. (2011, March). *No Women No Democratic Peace.* Retrieved May 16, 2014, from WOMEN AND PEACE: a symposium on role of women in post conflict sitauation: http://www.india-seminar.com/2011/619/619_rita_manchanda.htm

Village Headman, K. Traditonal Method of Conflict resoltion among the nagamis. (B. D. Killinger, Interviewer) Kohima, Nagalnd, India. (2013, November).

Contributors

Prof. Prasenjit Biswas is Associate Professor of Philosophy, North Eastern Hill University, Shillong. E-mail: gpbiswas69@gmail.com

Sri Dipok Kumar Barthakur is the Vice-Chairman, Office of the State Innovation and Transformation Aayog (SITA), Assam. E-mail: dkbarthakur@gmail.com

Sri. Lipokmar Tzudir has an MA Ethnomusicology. He is the former Director of NEZCC, Government of India. E-mail: tzudirl@yahoo.com

Fr. Peter Haokip worked as a professor at Orients College, Shillong and now he is attached to the Archbishop's House at Imphal in Manipur. E-mail: tphaokip@gmail.com

Professor Sivasish Biswas BA(Hons) & MA (Visva-Bharati), M.Phil, Ph.D (NEHU), PGDTE (CIEFL), Fulbright Fellow (2013-14), Pro-Vice Chancellor, Assam University, Diphu Campus(A Central University by Act of Parliament). E-mail: sivasishbiswas@gmail.com

Prof. V. C. Thomas is the Director of the Centre for Phenomenological Studies, Pondicherry. He was the former Dean of Pondicherry University. E-mail: ashishantony@yahoo.com

Dr. K. Jose SVD belongs to the Society of the Divine Word. He is a socio-cultural anthropologist and Founder/ Director of Sanskriti-NEICR (North-eastern Institute of Cultural Research), Guwahati in Assam. E-mail: kjosesvd@gmail.com

Dr. Paramananda Rajbongshi is an acclaimed short story writer, novelist, playwright, and a folk culture scholar. He teaches Assamese literature as a senior Professor in Pragjyotish College, Guwahati. A noted theatre, film and television producer-director, Dr Rajbongshi is the winner of the Assam State Film Awards for his film 'ANAL' and also is an empanelled director of Doodarchan Kendra, Guwahati. He had served Assam Sahitya Sabha as its General Secretary for six years since 2011 before being elected as the President of this century-old organization of the greater Assamese nationality.

Dr. Kaba Daniel is the Assistant Professor in the Department of Political Science at St. Joseph's College (Autonomous), Jakhama in Nagaland. E-mail: kabadanpou@gmail.com

Dr. Babu Joseph Karakombil belongs to the Society of the Divine Word. He is the Ex-member, Executive Council, Central University of Kerala, Indore, M. P. E-mail: bkjoss@gmail.com

Dr. C. V. Babu is the Assistant Professor of Zakir Husain Delhi College, Delhi University, New Delhi. E-mail: babukarun@rediffmail.com

Dr. E. Thangasamy is the Assistant Professor at PG & Research Department of Commerce, Poompuhar College (Autonomous), Melaiyur, TN. E-mail: nu.thangasamy@gmail.com

Dr. C. Periasamy is the Associate Professor at the Department of Economics, Government College Zunheboto, Nagaland. E-mail: periasamy1963@gmail.com

Dr. Hanmanth Rao S. Palep, Ayurveda Nishnat, Formerly Hon. Professor, Ob. & Gyn. Dept. Grant Medical College, & R. A. Podar Medical College, (Ayurvedic) National professor & Visiting Scientist, Haffkine Institute, Mumbai.

Dr. Laltluangliana Khiangte is Professor and Head of Mizo Department at Mizoram University and is the President of the Mizo Academy of Letters in Mizoram. E-mail: profkhiangte@gmail.com

Dr. M. P. Terence Samuel is the Assistant Professor in the Department of Philosophy and Comparative Religion, Visva-Bharati, Santiniketan, West Bengal. E-mail: mptsamuel@gmail.com

Dr. S. Lourdunathan was the Professor of Philosophy at Arul Anandar College, Karumathur in Madurai. Presently he is the Head of the Department of Research and Development at the Indian Social Institute in Bangalore. E-mail: nathanlourdu1960@gmail.com

Prof. Sebastian Velassery is UGC National Emeritus, and currently at the Centre for Philosophy, JNU in New Delhi. E-mail: velassery1953@gmail.com

Dr. Archana Singh teaches at G. B. Pant Social Science Institute at Jhansi in Allahabad. E-mail: archanaparihar@gmail.com

Dr. Tapan Kumar De is the Associate Professor, Department of Philosophy and the Life-world, Vidyasagar University, Midnapore, West Bengal. E-mail: tapande4@gmail.com

Mr. James H. K. is a Ph. D. Scholar and is the Head of the Department of English in St. Joseph's College (Autonomous) at Jakhama in Nagaland. E-mail: jameshkkamei@gmail.com

Mr. Mhonthung Yanthan is the Asst. Professor in the Department of Political Science at St. Joseph's College (Autonomous), Jakhama in Nagaland and Mr. Libemo Kithan is the Asst. Professor in the Department of History at Mount Tiyi Govt. College, Wokha in Nagaland. E-mail: mhonthung10@gmail.com, libemo18tid@gmail.com

Mr. Kelengol Neikha is the Asst. Professor in the Department of Economics at St. Joseph's College (Autonomous), Jakhama in Nagaland. E-mail: kelengolneikha12@gmail.com and Mr. Vizapo Kikhi is the Resident Officer at Japfü Christian College, Kigwema in Nagaland. E-mail: leenaga@gmail.com

Dr. Fr. C. P. Anto serves as a Principal of Master's Degree College in Social Work, Northeast Institute of Social Science and Research (NEISSR). His Specialization is in Peace and Conflict Transformation Studies. He is the Founder-Director of Peace Channel, a youth Peace Movement of third millennium and Secretary to the Commissions of Interfaith and Ecumenism and Peace and Justice, Diocese of Kohima, Nagaland, India. E-mail: cpanto@gmail.com